THE HUNT BEGINS

There it was, a call from the Navy Radar controller on UHF frequency 497.2. "Range Cat Flight Three Five, this is Big Eye."

"This is Three Five. Go ahead."

"Three Five, turn to course three four zero and descend to seven thousand. Intercept and escort back to base or destroy an F-15 at your two o'clock position, altitude six thousand feet, and forty miles."

"Big Eye, this is Three Five. Please repeat last transmission." The lead F-14 pilot wanted to make sure that he had heard that word "destroy" correctly.

"Flight Three Five, turn to course three four zero and descend to seven thousand. Intercept and escort back to base or destroy an F-15 at your two o'clock position, altitude six thousand feet, and forty miles. I repeat, either escort back to base or destroy."

KNIGHT HAWK

PAT O'CONNELL

LEISURE BOOKS **NEW YORK CITY**

To God for His blessings,
to my family for their love and support,
to my friends for their enduring encouragement,
and to my friends at Dorchester Publishing Company
who believed in me and made this dream come true.

The characters in this book are fictional. Any similarities to
actual persons, living or dead, are purely coincidental.

A LEISURE BOOK®
May 1997
Published by

Dorchester Publishing Co., Inc.
276 Fifth Avenue
New York, NY 10001

Printed in the United States of America.

INTRODUCTION

Throughout recorded history there has been a glorifying awe and respect for the mounted warrior, whether he be a knight in shining armor, a Spanish Conquistador, or a cavalry officer leading a charge. That same sense is still alive today and awe is given to every fighter pilot that flings his winged steed through the air to answer the call of combat.

Today's fighter pilot is much like the warrior of the past, but in many ways he is drastically different. He is a fighter pilot because he loves to fly, not because he likes to kill. The modern fighter pilot rarely sees the face of death. He doesn't see death in the eyes of the man he just killed. He doesn't see the lifeblood flowing from a mortal wound. He doesn't hear the dying screams of pain. When he kills, it's clean. When he fights, his opponent is not human, it's a machine. Either the pilot kills the machine or the machine kills him.

The fighter pilot's world is a mix of roller coaster ride and video game. It's a place where a man can be a boy, and death (preferably the opponent's) is just part of the game. It's a place of speed, power, and unbelievable excitement.

The fighter pilot's world has long been a man's domain. Until fairly recently, women pilots were rare oddities and were never fighter pilots. Over the past few years women have earned the right to wear wings and be called fighter pilots. They've worked hard and have proven that they can be just as deadly as men, and some even deadlier.

Chapter One

The blue stepvan drove onto the eighty acres of rain-soaked flight line, the nighttime roost of over a hundred fighter aircraft. The driver, a young technical sergeant named Steve Myers, looked left then right through the rain-covered windows. He looked for automotive traffic, but his greater concern was the taxiing F-15C jet fighters. The storm gray F-15s were called Eagles, but on the ground they seemed more like giant sharks on wheels prowling the asphalt sea for a meal. Myers knew an encounter with one of these fifteen-ton denizens would take a fatal bite out of his career as well as cause a bad day.

Even though it was dark and the weather was miserable, the flying day for the First Tactical Fighter Wing was not over. The stepvan crossed the flight line and stopped short of the taxiway that ran parallel to the east-west runways. To his right Myers could see a pair of F-15 Eagles rolling toward him in single file. He knew they were returning to roost in the parking area to his left. Their landing lights made the wet asphalt taxiway ahead of them sparkle like a river of diamonds. Even though both jets were running their engines at idle as they taxied by, they were still loud enough to drown out the radio in the van.

The jets passed and Myers waited till the second jet was fifty yards away before pulling in behind it. The stepvan rocked in the buffeting wind from the engines' thrust until the jets ahead of him turned left into the parking area. Myers continued down the taxiway. After five hundred yards, they were away from the F-15 area and were now approaching the area that bordered the EC-135 tanker aircraft. The EC-135s were the military version of a Boeing 707. Not only were they equipped with special electronics, but the entire lower cargo area in the fuselage was fitted with fuel tanks to turn the aircraft into a flying gas station.

The passengers in the back of the stepvan were the change-out crew for the Alert Hangar Facility. The four security police (SP) assigned for the shift were Sgts. Steve Michaels, Kathy Dickerson, Karen Lysiak and Sr. Airman Dave Johnson. They were dressed in their camouflage battle dress uniforms, commonly called BDUs. Their ensemble was completed with lightweight Kevlar body armor vests and helmets. All four were armed with M-16s. Sergeant Lysiak and Airman Johnson each carried the additional firepower of an M203 grenade launcher mounted on their rifles and each wore an ammo vest sporting eighteen 40mm grenades. The reason for the heavy armament wasn't public knowledge but was obvious to base personnel. The alert area was one of the few places on base where the use of deadly force was authorized, and for good reason.

Dickerson was a compassionate and gentle human being, but if the need arose to defend the armed aircraft and nuclear weapons under her protection, she knew that she'd have no problem following the "shoot-to-kill" directive. She often wished she had the opportunity to challenge her marksmanship with the grenade launcher against a speeding vehicle.

Myers could barely hear the conversation of the foursome behind him, which was just as well. He was keeping a mother's ear to the radio and trying to monitor all of the calls. He was always leery of driving on the taxiway behind the EC-135s. A year earlier one unfortunate step van driver had tried to cross behind a running EC-135. When the van was hit by the engine exhaust it was blown over like an empty shoe box in a hurricane.

Seeing that none of the big jets was running its engines, Myers continued to the west end of the parallel taxiway and stopped a hundred yards short of the active runways. His destination was dead ahead, the Alert Hangar Facility on the other side of the runways. Myers tuned in the tower frequency and picked up the radio microphone. He remembered that the ends of the runways were labeled by the first two digits of the compass headings a plane used when it was ready to take off. Since this was the west end of the runway, a plane taking off would have to face east, compass heading 090. Therefore this was the 09 end. He keyed the mike and said, "Tower, Guardian Three."

After a short pause, the tower responded, "Go ahead, Guardian Three."

"Tower, this is Guardian Three. Request permission to cross the zero nine end of the active runways."

"Guardian Three, tower, you are cleared to cross the active runways at the zero nine end. Expedite crossing and notify tower when you are clear."

After looking left and right, Myers pushed the gas pedal to the floor. He liked crossing the runways; this was the only place on the base he was allowed to speed, or at least try to. Step vans weren't known for their rapid acceleration. On the other side of the runways, Myers keyed the mike button again and said, "Tower, Guardian Three is clear."

"Tower copies, Guardian."

A moment later the stepvan stopped at the closest guard shack in the alert area. Michaels, Dickerson, Lysiak and Johnson stepped out of the van's relative warmth into the cold, wet drizzle.

Airman Johnson was the first to complain. "Oh, man. I hate this kinda weather."

Sergeant Michaels, the eternal optimist, responded, "Johnson, you don't know how good you've got it. Why, in Thule, Greenland, this would be a balmy summer night."

Sergeant Dickerson leaned over and whispered into Lysiak's ear, "Don't get him started or we'll be hearing stories about Greenland for the rest of the shift."

Lysiak whispered back, "Oh, I know. I've heard his stories before."

The four SPs on duty had seen the stepvan coming and were eagerly waiting. They climbed in and Myers drove away.

The alert area was surrounded on three sides by a double row of ten-foot-high chain-link fence that was topped with coils of barbed concertina wire, the kind of wire that grabbed clothing and skin and didn't let go. There were two guard shacks on each side of the hundred-foot opening in the fence. The fenced-in facility and the aircraft inside belonged to the 48th Fighter Intercepter Group. The two alert hangars in the area were built on the NASA side of the runway so the alert jets would have the shortest and quickest access to the west end of the runway.

It was the SPs' job to stand out in the weather and guard the area and the jets. It was a boring, thankless job, consisting of little other than watching jets when they weren't flying. A common pastime for these aluminum bird watchers was to count rivets on the wings as they walked around. On this night, besides being bored, the foursome also had the weather to look forward to, periods of cold mist punctuated with bouts of drizzling rain.

Inside the alert hangar, a pair of F-15C Eagles, the most formidable fighters in the air force inventory, were poised for combat. Each Eagle carried a deadly array of weapons. In the leading edge of the right wing root was a titanium-lined football-shaped hole that exposed the business end of a six-barreled 20mm Gatling cannon capable of firing two thousand rounds a minute. Under each wing was a pair of radar-guided Advanced Medium-Range Air-to-Air Missiles, AMRAAM-120s. Nestled snugly against the conformal fuel tanks on each side of the fuselage was a Knight Hawk nuclear-tipped missile. The Knight Hawks were the most lethal weapon carried by any aircraft in the world, and each of these jets was armed with two. The Eagles were ready for immediate takeoff at the first sign of an impending attack. Minutes after the stepvan drove away from the alert area, a blaring warning horn sounded from one of the alert hangars. The blast of the horn was joined by the sound of electrical motors groaning under strain and the movement of the heavy metal hangar doors. As the thirty-foot-tall doors divided, the brilliant golden glow from the argon gas-lights spilled from the hangar onto the wet asphalt ramp. The SPs watched the doors open and could see the F-15C Eagles within. These Eagles were the reason they were there.

The hangar doors stopped in the full-open position. The warning horn stopped and the night was again silent. A tall, slender feminine figure emerged from around the door on the left side of the hangar and was silhouetted by the intense hangar lights. The glare from behind the figure kept the SPs from seeing who the individual was, but from the person's stride and the gleam of light reflected off the metallic cylinder in the left hand they knew it had to be none other then Captain K. They were right: it was Capt. Kim Kenada. Captain Kenada, a statuesque and shapely dark-haired woman, walked up to the four newly arrived security police guards outside the alert hangars. She was a pleasant and familiar sight to the guards who stood this watch.

Most maintenance personnel and pilots on the base rarely associated, let alone talked, with the guards on duty. Guard duty on any base was usually a thankless job that nobody noticed or cared about. That is, until something went wrong. Langley was no different. As far as the guards were concerned, Kenada was a pleasant surprise. She was among the few people who took the time to come over and talk to them. Tonight, as on numerous other cold nights, she carried a thermos of coffee. This wasn't the first time they had accepted and appreciated a hot cup of coffee from her.

Often, when there was to be movement of aircraft off or onto the alert area, Captain Kenada would, out of courtesy, inform the guards what was about to happen. This was not required of her, but it helped eliminate problems caused by miscommunication. Captain Kenada also had her own ulterior motive for being so friendly: it was to gain their trust. In fact, she was one of the few people outside the security police squadron whom all of the SPs trusted.

As Kenada approached the four guards, she could hear the two men talking to each other. The two female guards were about to walk over to the guard shack on the opposite side of the taxiway opening when they saw Kenada coming. They knew why she was approaching them and decided to wait just a few more minutes.

The loud voices of the men carried across the distance, and Kim heard Sgt. Steve Michaels first. "Hey, how about those Redskins? Cowboys didn't stand a chance." Michaels wasn't really interested in talking football; he was more interested in inciting a riot with his coworker. Since Johnson's football team had lost over the weekend, it was easy to push his emotional buttons.

Sr. Airman Dave Johnson, a Texan by birth, resisted the urge to punch his partner and just said, "The 'Skins were lucky this time; wait till they go to Dallas."

Captain Kenada, not being a football fan, smiled and changed the subject. "How's it going? Ready for another action-packed evening out on the flight line?"

"Ha! Right," Johnson said. "I've watched late-night TV test patterns that were more exciting than this place. You know, Captain, I sometimes wish something would happen. I'm getting bored to tears out here."

Michaels looked at Johnson and said, "Hey, you should be careful what you wish for; you might get it."

Sergeant Dickerson said under her breath to Sergeant Lysiak, "I'm just glad I'm not teamed up with either one of these two."

Sergeant Lysiak gave a smile of agreement and said,

"Ditto, but you know, Johnson is kinda cute."

Lysiak asked Kenada, "What's on for tonight, Captain?"

As Kim spoke she started pouring coffee into Styrofoam cups she pulled out of her fatigue jacket pocket. "Well, we have an alert swap-out tonight. Later on we'll be bringing in jets zero seven six and four five zero to swap out the birds on alert. The two on alert now will be downloaded after the new birds are uploaded in the Baker hangar. After zero seven one and zero zero eight come off alert they're scheduled for a night sortie at twenty-one thirty hours. All in all it looks like it's going to be a slow night."

Sergeant Michaels gulped down the first cup. Kenada had purposely let the coffee cool slightly so it would be drunk quickly. If it was too hot it would only be sipped, and last too long. Kenada had plans for the evening, and having the guards drink all of their coffee quickly was part of them.

Kenada stayed and chatted with the SPs just to make sure they each drank their coffee. After pouring seconds to Michaels and Johnson, she handed them the thermos. She looked at her watch, smiled and said, "Well, guys, I've got to fly and I've got lots to do before I leave for the night. Go ahead and finish the coffee. I'll pick up the thermos when I come by to see you later."

The four guards, their coffee cups in their left hands, snapped to attention and saluted sharply with their right. Captain Kenada smiled, returned their salute and turned to walk back into the alert hangar. They all raised their coffee cups as if to say thanks.

Sergeants Lysiak and Dickerson started walking to their post. They both wanted to get into the warmth of the shack on the other side of the taxiway.

"Bye, Captain. Thanks for the coffee," Michaels said.

He thought, *If only she weren't an officer, she'd be lots of fun to be with.*

Johnson smiled and echoed, "See ya." He too was lusting in his heart and was amazed at how good Kenada looked, even in fatigues. Both Michaels and Johnson watched in silence as the captain walked back into the alert hangar. As she disappeared from view they both snapped out of their trances. Michaels spoke first. "Now, where were we? Oh, yeah, how about them Redskins?"

Capt. Kimberly Kenada was the aircraft maintenance officer for the 48th Fighter Interceptor Group. She was truly a gifted woman. She was physically strong, beautiful and intelligent. On duty her long, dark auburn hair was usually pulled back away from her face and up in a bun to conform to the dress code standards found in air force regulation 35-10.

Kenada had the face of a model and the body of a movie star. Her olive complexion even in the dead of winter gave the illusion of a healthy tan. Her sharp features and dark brown eyes could easily have graced the cover of a fashion magazine. Being just an inch and a half short of six feet tall, she was a stunning sight. Even the baggy, uncomplimentary and drab fatigue uniform couldn't hide her Barbie-doll figure. Years of swimming had only enlarged her shoulders and chest, while running track kept her hips and waist trim.

Kenada was very competitive, athletically and scholastically. She had often competed in triathlons with men . . . and won. Even as a cadet at the Air Force Academy, she was almost unbeatable in any race over two hundred meters.

Scholastically she was the top cadet in her class at the academy. In fact, she was one of the few who had kept a 4.0 average all four years.

All in all, Kenada was a complex and dynamic individual, intelligent, cunning, charming and beautiful. However, since the death of her husband, she had been disturbingly mysterious and very distant to men. At work Kenada was always very professional, and with her height and no-nonsense attitude she also projected a formidable but attractive presence. She was not a woman easily intimidated, but she could easily intimidate others.

In her younger years her beauty and inexperience had been taken advantage of, professionally and personally. She had had more heartache than she cared to admit and now she was always on guard. She kept her emotions in check and protected by a wall of mystery. And she did her job well.

To put it in the simplest terms, Kenada's job as an aircraft maintenance officer was to make sure that all of the pilots had safe jets that were ready to fly and fight. She was very possessive of the aircraft under her control. They were her jets and she pampered them as if they were a stable full of fine Arabian horses.

19:08

Captain Kenada bent over and walked under the right side of aircraft 071. She half knelt under the fuselage just aft of the wings. From her vantage point she had a clear view of the guards' activity. They were still standing and drinking the last of their coffee.

Captain Kenada looked around the hangar and the area outside to make sure she was still alone. With her thumb she pushed two buttons on the right engine bay panel door. The spring-loaded latches released with a metallic pop. The twelve-by-eighteen-inch inspection door swung down, exposing the main fuel control and

16

the dozen stainless-steel one-inch pipes converging into it. Kenada pulled a small flashlight and pair of wire cutters from her right field jacket pocket and wiggled the cutters into the hole up above some of the pipes. She snipped the safety wire on the locking clasp of the throttle control linkage, lifted the locking arm on the clasp and slid the linkage off the splined shaft of the fuel control.

To make sure the engine would start, Kenada turned the fuel control shaft so it would already be in the start position, and said to herself, "This ought to give somebody a thrill." She replaced the wire cutters and flashlight in her pocket, then closed and latched the access panel door. With another quick glance at her watch she stood up and walked out from under 071 and over to aircraft 008.

On the other side of the base an unattended car in the base exchange parking lot caught on fire. Later investigations would find the remains of an alarm clock, batteries and a road flare that had ignited a plastic gallon milk jug full of gas in the pile of melted metal.

"Oh my God, look! Look at that! Fire! Fire! That car's on fire!" A customer in the cashier's line first noticed the blaze through the window; then when the gas tank exploded with a window-shattering boom, everybody noticed. The cashier made the 911 call. Seconds later the klaxons in the firehouse blasted out the alarm, and a loudspeaker announced the position and description of the fire.

Three huge fluorescent yellow Oshkosh fire trucks lumbered out of the firehouse with flashing lights, blaring horns and racing engines. One by one the three trucks weaved their way off the flight line onto side roads toward the base exchange.

Johnson and Michaels heard the distant explosion

and watched the commotion at the firehouse on the other side of the runway. They could see the tops of the flames flickering above the surrounding buildings and the billowing black smoke rising out of the BX parking lot. With a little envy in his voice and stifling a yawn, Johnson said, "Well, at least somebody will have a little excitement tonight." Johnson turned to Michaels for a response but Michaels didn't hear. He was out. His boots sticking out of the guard shack showed that he had fallen fast asleep. With a glance across the taxiway to the other guard post, Johnson could see another pair of petite feet.

Even in a daze, Senior Airman Johnson finally realized that something was very wrong and he needed help. His hands fumbled, pulling his radio from his utility belt, and the radio fell to the ground. Johnson dropped to his knees in a drugged stupor and picked up his radio. Before he could key the radio and call for help, he forgot why he wanted to make the call. He looked at his empty coffee cup, then collapsed into slumbering oblivion.

As the SPs slept, Captain Kenada was busy kicking the chocks out from in front of the main landing gear tires and pulling the gear-locking pins. She went to the leading edge of the right wing root and opened a small panel. She reached in elbow-deep and pulled out the gun safing pin, then closed the panel and pulled the two pins from the Knight Hawk missiles.

She did a quick cursory preflight walk-around of aircraft 008, occasionally glancing at the sleeping guards outside. She almost giggled to herself when she thought about the coffee. Not only was it laced heavily with Halcion left over from her doctor's prescription, but it was even decaffeinated.

Knight Hawk

The hangar-side exits of the alert barracks were already blocked. The maintenance crew that was to prepare the jets for launch had been sent to the other side of the runway to bring the two replacement jets over. It wouldn't be long now, she thought.

For the moment Kenada was alone, and for the next few minutes, she would be the only one in the hangar. She knew time was running out, maybe four more minutes, tops. Kenada could see that the maintenance crew had crossed the runway from the other side and was returning with 076 in tow behind a big yellow Oshkosh tractor.

It was now or never. Her actions now would change the course of her life. If she was successful, her actions would change the lives of millions, maybe the world. She and others had planned this for months.

Kenada climbed the ladder on the left side of the fuselage and stepped into the cockpit. Then she lifted the ladder hooks off of the canopy rails and dropped the ladder to the ground. It landed with a metallic clang that echoed in the hangar. Kenada wondered if when this was over she would need a ladder to get down from this cockpit or if she would die in her seat.

She started positioning the dials and switches so that as soon as the engines started and the electricity came on-line, all of the systems she needed would be activated. She recited the checklist to herself while flipping the switches. "Communications, on . . . inertial navigation, on . . . global positioning system, on . . . radar . . . and armament, standby . . ."

Except for the gentle and systematic clicking of the switches and dials, the cockpit was deathly quiet. The din of fire trucks across the field was just a distant howl.

The only noise she could hear after she lowered the canopy was the pounding of her heart. Some occasional chatter came over her maintenance radio, and over the frequency scanner she routinely carried in her breast pocket.

Kenada strapped herself into the ACES II ejection seat (Advanced Concept Escape System) and plugged in the air hoses for the helmet and the G suit that was underneath her baggy fatigue pants. She pulled the barrette out of her hair and shook her head to let her hair fall down. She donned the helmet and plugged in the communications cord. Now she was ready to go, with the exception of her oxygen mask, which was hanging loosely from the left side of the helmet.

With a last look around and a deep breath, she committed herself to fate. A quick peek at her watch, "Nineteen seventeen. Good, right on schedule." She flipped the guarded Jet-Fueled Starter (JFS) switch and held it for ten seconds in the start position until it accelerated up to operating speed.

The screaming howl of the JFS engine cut into the sounds of the night. After an eternal fifteen seconds, with her feet pressing heavily on the brakes, Captain Kenada engaged the left engine and it started with a deep-throated roar. While the engine accelerated up to its idle speed of 67 percent, the electrical system came on-line. Simultaneously the lights from dials and gauges lit up the once black panel. Kenada reached over to the light rheostat and dimmed the blinding lights.

Maintenance troops and security people on the flight line heard the engine start. They had no idea that the roar and the telltale hiss from thousands of cubic feet of air being sucked down the intake of the Pratt and Whitney F100 engine came from a bird on alert. Even if they did, so what? Jets on the flight line started all the time. As long as it wasn't one of their jets, who cared?

Maintenance Operations Center (MOC)

Master Sergeant Davis, the flight line maintenance controller in maintenance control (MOC), heard the JFS kick in over the radio net. Since no one had called in to inform MOC and request permission to run an engine, he was curious. He pressed his radio mike button and checked with each of the aircraft maintenance unit supervisors. "Red One, Gold One and Blue One, this is MOC One."

The flight line supervisors echoed their call signs over the radio. They were listening.

"OK, you guys, I just heard a JFS crank up. Who's running engines out there? You know you're supposed to clear it with us before you run."

Red One responded with, "MOC, it's not a Red jet."

"It's not Blue either."

Gold responded, "MOC, this is Gold One. I heard it coming from the alert pad."

"Eagle Perch, MOC . . . Eagle Perch, MOC." After a few seconds without a response, Davis mumbled, "I don't like this."

Just then the radio crackled as Captain Kenada keyed the mike. "MOC One, this is Perch One. Go ahead."

"Perch One, are you guys running anything?"

"Yes, MOC, were running zero zero eight to check a fuel leak on the number-one engine Bendix fuel control. I'm sorry, but didn't Perch six contact you on the engine run?"

Davis, now a little indignant, responded, "No, Perch One. We've not been contacted about an engine run, and in the future tell your troops to follow the notification procedures." Davis, more relaxed now that he had given his lecture, sat back in his chair to resume the doldrums of duty. Davis had no affection for Kenada or any of her primadonna maintenance technicians. Little did Davis know that while his brief lecture of maintenance etiquette was going over the airwaves, Kenada was quickly finishing her preflight checklist.

The two pilots scheduled for the 2130 hours flight were inside the alert barracks facility behind the alert hangars. They were finishing up their flight plan for their dissimilar aircraft combat training (DACT) night mission on the range off of Cherry Point, North Carolina. At first, they were too involved discussing the strategies they were going to use against a pair of Navy F-18 Hornets and two F-14 Tomcats out of Norfolk Naval Air Station. They heard the JFS engine start but didn't think anything of it. On an operational air base, it was no big deal to hear a plane start. That happened all the time. Maj. Rick Platt, a tall, blond, ex–college football jock, was busy flying his hands through the air, his left hand chasing his right, and telling Capt. Dave Reed, an egotistical hotshot jet jock, how to finesse a maneuver that would put him on a Tomcat's tail. Platt also commented on how the navy jets at the range had a tactical advantage because of "Big Eye," their radar ground-controller that gave them vectors to best intercept their target. However once they were engaged eyeball-to-eyeball with the other jets, Big Eye couldn't help them.

The volume and pitch of the JFS dropped as it engaged the left engine. Platt was getting a little annoyed trying to speak over the now idling engine. In the back of his mind the question popped up as to why the jet on alert was being started. The question was answered when he overheard Captain Kenada's voice on the maintenance radio net mention something about running the engine to check a leak in the fuel control. Besides, Platt was too busy to stop and give the running engine much thought.

When Platt heard the engine run up and the volume drop as it taxied out of the hangar, he mumbled to himself, "Wait a minute, that jet's taxiing. What's going on out there?" Thinking that one of the other pilots was taking their jet on a sortie by mistake, Platt and Reed jogged down the hall to the alert hangar. Without slowing down they both hit the push bars to shove open the doors, only to be rudely slammed on their butts by the resistance of the unmoving doors.

"Hey, what gives?" Captain Reed said. "These doors aren't supposed to be locked." The doors weren't locked, but a two-by-four board through the outside handles was just as effective.

Platt, being a quick study in mathematics, quickly put two and two together. "Somebody's taking our jet! We've got to stop 'em!" That was wishful thinking on Platt's part. They couldn't even get out of the building. Platt was at least smart enough to run back to the operations desk and phone the security police.

With the inertial navigation ring laser gyros powered and aligned, Kenada was ready to roll. She dropped her feet off of the brake/rudder pedals, and with her left hand pushed the left throttle, advancing the engine up to 70 percent. She started rolling with only one of the two engines running. This would reduce the time needed to make good her escape. Kenada would start the right engine while taxiing to the runway. As the Eagle started to roll out of the hangar, she moved her right ring finger down to the base of the joystick grip, and squeezed the button that activated the nose-wheel steering. Now she was steering with her feet by using the rudder pedals. Her left hand came up and latched her oxygen mask snugly over her mouth and nose.

She was now fifty yards out of the alpha hangar, with another hundred yards before she hit the taxiway, and another three hundred yards to the runway. Kenada looked left and right. No one was coming. She finished punching her coordinates into the inertial navigation computer and hit the enter button. Then she switched the GPS (global positioning system) link switch from STANDBY to ON.

Kenada had never flown an F-15 before, but she was no stranger to them. And she had had close to a thousand hours as an undergraduate pilot training instructor flying the supersonic T-38s before she had been so unjustly grounded.

As the maintenance officer in charge of the F-15 aircraft flight simulator, she had become proficient on all of the Eagle's systems, especially the armament. Over the past few months, she had spent several hundred hours flying the simulator, and had also practiced and timed this event numerous times, but being an expert on a multibillion-dollar computer game was nothing like the thrill of the real thing.

As for computer games, Kenada had always kept honing her flying skills by using her IBM personal computer in her apartment. One of her bedrooms was as close to a flight simulator as a civilian could get. Her computer was loaded with a complex flight simulator program, and she had also loaded it with the New York Scenery program. Rather then using a traditional thirteen-inch color monitor, she used an entire wall. She spared no expense and had bought a multimedia theater projector to get the added effect.

Months of planning and practice were about to yield either success or deadly failure.

Knight Hawk

Maintenance Operations Center (MOC)

The MOC officer in charge, First Lieutenant Jarvis, knew Kenada and was jealous of her because she had a better job then he. He commented to Davis that Captain Kenada was not as competent a leader as she was good-looking. "If I was running that outfit—" he said, but he never finished his statement.

The radio blared with a loud cry: "MOC, this is Gold One. You've got a jet rolling off the alert pad and it looks like it's still armed."

Davis keyed the mike button again and radioed, "Perch One, MOC . . . Perch One, MOC." This time there was no answer from Kenada.

"Damn. What the hell's going on with that captain?" Davis went into a cold sweat, finally realizing that someone was trying to steal a jet, one armed with nukes. He keyed the mike and said, "Attention all personnel, this is MOC. We have a Stop Alert in progress. This is not a drill!"

Davis repeated the statement, then yelled to the Gold net controller, "Call the fire department and tell them we have a Stop Alert in progress and to block both ends of the runway with the fire trucks."

The Gold controller, remembering the car fire, yelled back, "That won't work. The fire trucks are at the BX; they'll be too late."

After the initial shock passed, Davis called to the AMU controllers in MOC, "OK, you guys, we've got to block the runway. Gold, block the twenty-seven end, Red, the zero nine end, and Blue, midfield. Lieutenant Jarvis, notify the command post and the SPs."

Kenada was just reaching the 09 end of the parallel taxiway when she saw the maintenance vehicles approaching their assigned positions on the runway. Behind her she could see the flashing red lights of the speeding security police trucks in hot pursuit. It would take another twenty seconds to get on the runway and push the throttles to military power, and by then the SPs would be on her.

The taxiway was her only alternative. With a quick kick on the left rudder pedal, she pointed the plane's nose down the dark blue–lighted taxiway. There wasn't enough time to start the right engine. She would have to air start it. She pushed both throttles to the military power detente, raised the finger lifts and advanced both engines into max burner. With her left hand she reached to the dash and flipped on the emergency igniter switch for the right engine. The autoigniters would automatically kick in and start the engine once the air ramming into the intakes raised the rpm of the engine high enough. That would be somewhere around ninety knots. As part of her takeoff habit she glanced at her watch to check the time: 19:25, right on schedule. Even with just one engine running on the takeoff roll, the twenty-five thousand pounds of thrust was still a kick in the pants.

Six hundred yards down the runway, 008 was accelerating through 90 knots. The right engine air-started with another explosive kick. Behind her the thrust and heat from the afterburner was kicking up a steam cloud off of the wet taxiway. The ten-foot blue-white flame from afterburners lit the steam and made it look like a rolling wall of fire behind the jet.

The drivers of two of the pickup trucks tried to block the runway at midfield. They could hear the thundering roar of the engine. Because it was dark, wet and cloudy, only the dark silhouette of the F-15 could be seen against the glowing steam cloud behind it. Like automotive kamikazes, they raced to block the taxiway. Little did the two drivers realize that their behavior was potentially suicidal.

The two trucks reached the midpoint of the taxiway and turned their trucks just in time to see fifteen tons of rolling death a hundred yards away. Like wild deer caught in the headlights of an oncoming car, they froze. One driver, Sergeant Jamison, seeing his imminent death, had the presence of mind to flee. The other driver, Sergeant Emmery, just screamed. Jamison dove out of his truck and rolled onto the wet taxiway seconds before impact.

Kenada's level of excitement was about to peak. Her body was flooded with adrenaline; her heart was racing as fast as the Eagle's engine. She had almost forgotten how good it felt to sit in an accelerating jet, her innermost parts vibrating with fifty thousand pounds of thrust. Kenada kept alternating her focus between the trucks and the rising airspeed shining at her in the heads-up display (HUD). To herself she read off the airspeed. "ninety-eight . . . one hundred three . . . come on . . . one hundred eight . . . one hundred seventeen." With only seconds before she hit the trucks blocking the middle of the taxiway, she thought, "Now or never," and then, grunting out a throaty scream, pulled the stick hard toward her crotch with both hands.

The landing gear made a loud bump as the weight came off the plane's wheels and the struts extended to their full length. To Kenada it appeared that she cleared the trucks with feet to spare. Sergeant Emmery knew different. His last conscious sight before fainting was the underbelly of the Eagle and the left main landing-gear wheel hitting the top of his windshield. The glass shattered, and the wheel left a two-inch dent on the top of his truck cab.

Both drivers were relieved to be alive instead of beheaded by this aluminum guillotine. Fortunately for them, other than the one wheel, the only thing that touched their trucks was the afterburner flames that torched the water off the hoods, and the three hundred decibels of engine roar that were still ringing in their ears.

Sergeant Jamison, the driver who dove from his truck, rolled over faceup on the wet tarmac, watching the fireball disappear into the clouds. As he lay there in a puddle of water, he uttered a sigh of relief. When he stood up and turned to get into his truck, it was gone. In his haste to get out he had failed to take the transmission out of drive. In addition to the Eagle leaving him on the tarmac, so had his truck.

19:27

Captain Kenada kept a firm grip on the joystick and kept her nose pointed up in a near vertical seventy-five-degree angle of climb. In a moment she would be into the cloud deck only two thousand feet above her. As her G suit deflated after the three-G pull, she shot a quick glance over her shoulder. For a moment she felt a wave of relief flow over her as she saw the runway behind her disappear.

Deep within her she could still feel the tingle of excitement. Just as her view of the outside world disappeared in the clouds, so did her thoughts. In that moment Kenada realized that life for her would never be the same. The deed had begun. The rest of her life depended on what she would do in the next few hours. That is, if she could survive that long. Great power, wealth, death or destruction were all possible outcomes of the situation at hand. Now that the plan was started, it had to be finished. She had committed herself to the plan . . . with her life.

Back on the ramp, still incredulous that someone could or would steal a jet, Gold One radioed, "MOC, Gold One. She's gone, Davis; the dog's in the fog."

Lieutenant Jarvis, a ring-knocking Air Force Academy graduate with chief of staff aspirations, just realized that his career was being flushed down the toilet before his very eyes. He picked up the radio, keyed the mike and responded to Gold One's radio call with a simple "Roger." He did not relish the fact that he was to be the bearer of really bad news. He picked up the phone as if it were a loaded .357 Magnum, held it to his head and said, "I think I'd better tell the colonel."

Chapter Two

The roar of the engines from Captain Kenada's Eagle hadn't totally faded away into the clouds before the panic-filled phone calls were being made.

Within minutes all of the top brass on base were informed of the theft. Brig. Gen. James Thompson, the wing commander, was at home when he was notified. He left a half-eaten New York sirloin at the table and rushed to the car for the five-minute drive to the base command post. After collecting as much information as he could about the theft, he had the dubious honor of calling on the hot line to the Pentagon. He hated using the hot line, because in the past the hot line had invariably been used to pass on bad news. This call was definitely going to be on the top of the bad news list.

Deep within the bowels of the Pentagon, basement

level two, corridor A, ring C, there was a large dark room called the National Military Command Center (NMCC). The working locals who labored within it just called it "the Tank." On the walls were numerous huge video displays showing maps, status screens of all of the services, charts, and computer terminals. The sixteen men in the room who monitored and updated these screens were from all of the services, and were busy assuming their duties from the previous shift. Air Force Col. John Miller was the officer in charge of the evening shift. He was often referred to as the Tank Commander by the crew slaving away at the terminals, phones and radios.

In the Tank, Major Dorchester answered the phone and said, "Colonel Miller, you'd better pick up the phone and speak with General Thompson from Langley. You're not going to believe this one."

The general had to repeat his story twice to Colonel Miller, before he would believe that a jet with nukes had just been stolen. Miller, still in disbelief, put General Thompson on hold. Is this guy for real? he thought. But he had to be; he was calling over the Tempest secured phone line, using a scrambler.

Miller was at a total loss. There was nothing in the book of checklists to cover this situation. There were checklists for bad weather, checklists for nuclear attack, chemical attack, and even conventional missile attack, attack by foreign ships, and for various types of attacks by terrorists, but there was nothing at the Pentagon level for a stolen jet, let alone one with nukes. Never in his wildest dreams had he ever thought that this nightmare could happen. Since there was no checklist to cover this situation, obviously neither had anyone else. Colonel Miller made a mental note to write another checklist when all this was over.

Colonel Miller paused and with a stoic air turned to

Lt. Col. Don D'Auria, the second-ranking officer in the control center. Since he couldn't think of anything better to do, he said, "Initiate Defcon Two, alpha alert, and initiate the battle staff emergency recall."

D'Auria sat down at a computer terminal and typed out the message: DEFCON TWO, ALPHA ALERT, STAND BY FOR DETAILS. The colonel moved the cursor over the TRANSMIT icon on the screen and then hit the left mouse button. The computer prompted D'Auria for his name and personal password. D'Auria typed in the information and hit the ENTER button. At the bottom of the computer screen came the reply: MESSAGE SENT.

D'Auria knew that his simple action was the snowball that was about to start an avalanche of activity all over the United States. Within minutes all of the navy and air force bases with combat aircraft east of the Mississippi would be responding to this message, as well as everybody in the Pentagon and, of course, the White House.

Colonel Miller knew that Defcon Two was the war-alert posture that caused all nonnuclear forces to prepare for attack. The alpha suffix limited the alert to flying forces of the air force and navy. The order to scramble the jets would come from the battle staff after they determined the proper action.

Colonel Miller motioned Lieutenant Colonel D'Auria and Major Dorchester over to his desk to listen in on the conversation. Miller reached for the phone and pressed the button labeled SPEAKER. "General, I have you on the speakerphone so Colonel D'Auria and Major Dorchester can hear. Now if you would, sir, please give us the details."

A hundred thoughts a second were still racing through General Thompson's mind. He was wondering what was going to become of him, his job, as well as other ramifications. He was brought back to reality by Colonel Miller's voice on the phone. He had been on hold for just a few seconds, but they had been some of the longest seconds of his life.

Thompson gathered his thoughts and responded, "At the moment, all we know is that at nineteen twenty-five hours, an F-15C aircraft loaded with two Knight Hawk missiles armed with nuclear warheads made an unauthorized takeoff from the alert pad here at Langley. The aircraft was last seen climbing into the clouds, and our radar controllers on base last had it on a southern course heading one nine five degrees. We don't know for sure who, but we believe that it was taken by one of our maintenance officers, a Captain Kim Kenada. Why, I don't know yet."

"Is that it? Is that all you can tell me? What else do you know?" Miller, furious and frustrated by this lack of information, couldn't believe how uninformed this general was. How could he be so ignorant of something that happened in his own backyard? Miller remembered that this was a superior officer he was talking to, and resisted the urge to address him with degrading four-letter words.

After a very pregnant pause to collect his thoughts, Miller said, "General, I need more information, like who, how, what and why. And as long as I have you, I am informing you to go to full alert. I have initiated a Defcon Two alpha alert. Your message center should be giving the coded message to your base command post any moment now."

The general responded with the proper checklist phrase: "I acknowledge Defcon Two alpha alert." As an afterthought the general suggested, "We don't have any jets in the air, but we do have another jet on the alert pad that's ready to go, and we have eight more that are scheduled to fly within the hour. We could launch those jets to chase zero zero eight."

"General, are they all armed for air-to-air, and if they're not, how long will it take to load and get them airborne?"

"Just the alert bird is armed and ready right now, and it'll take five minutes before we can launch it. We have to finish downloading the two Knight Hawks."

"Well, General, stand by please. I'll be right back." Miller pushed the hold button and paused to think about what to do. He turned to Major Dorchester, who was still standing quietly beside him in the dark. "Major Dorchester, call the air-traffic control at Richmond; notify them that an aircraft took off from Langley at nineteen twenty-five hours, and tell them to find it and tell us where it is and where it's going. Tell them it's extremely urgent . . . and nothing more." Miller pushed the button on the phone again. "General, don't wait to download the Knight Hawks. Go ahead and launch the alert and pursue that F-15. Let me know when your alert bird is airborne."

General Thompson responded, "Will do," and they both hung up.

At that moment the command center door flew open, and in charged the first member of the battle staff to arrive, a three-star air force general, Lt. Gen. Dick "Buster" Price. He looked around the room for somebody in charge. Not seeing any other generals or members of the Joint Chiefs, he focused his gaze on Colonel Miller. With a take-no-prisoners tone of voice, he boomed, "John, what the hell is going on here?"

Miller turned to Price and replied, "Sir, we've lost an F-15 that was loaded with two Knight Hawk missiles."

"Where did we lose it?" Price asked. "Did it crash in a populated area?"

Knight Hawk

"No, sir, it didn't crash. It was stolen."

"What!" General Price was momentarily dumb-founded. "When did this happen? How could this happen? Where is it now? Where is it going? Who took it?"

Before Miller could begin to answer the barrage of questions the phone rang again. Miller answered it, scribbled a few notes on a piece of paper and said, "Keep tracking that jet, and stay on the line." Miller turned to the general to give him a quick brief of the jet's location. "Sir, the jet is currently just south of Norfolk, flying at six thousand feet at a speed of four hundred fifty knots. It's still heading south on a course of one nine five. It's not answering any radio calls and it's not squawking a code on its IFF transponder."

"Excuse me, General," Major Dorchester said as he approached Price and Miller, "but all of the Joint Chiefs of Staff have departed for the day and they are en route back here from their quarters. They probably won't be here for another thirty minutes at least. Since the chief of staff of the air force is not available at the moment, you are the next in command. What are your orders?"

Coincidentally, General Price was the ideal battle staff leader for this particular emergency. Not only was he an accomplished and decorated fighter pilot, he was also a brilliant aviation strategist. His most noticeable accomplishments to date were during the air war against Iraq. During Operation Desert Storm, Price planned and orchestrated all air operations of the U.S. Air Force, the U.S. Navy and all of the allied NATO air forces.

A cold, steely calm had come over Price's face. With the facts that he had, he could only guess what the motive would be. "Well, considering the course she's heading, south, she must be going to Cuba. Miller, scramble all alert jets in Maryland, Virginia and the Carolinas.

Also have the wings in Georgia and Florida stand by for launch just in case she gets past the Carolinas." With a penetrating stare he said, "Pass on the coordinates to all of the units."

Miller nodded and said, "Yes, sir."

"Miller, one more thing," Price said. "Have them either bring her back or shoot her down."

Miller nodded.

"Oh, by the way, does the president know yet?"

"We sent the message over the comm line but we haven't received a reply yet."

"Well, if he doesn't reply to us in a few minutes, we'll call him."

General Price spoke his thoughts aloud. "She's not too bright. Flying at that speed, straight and level at that altitude, she'll be an easy target to find. If she was smart, she'd be at treetop level so radar couldn't see her, and flying like a bat out of hell."

Three more battle staff members came into the control center, an army general and two admirals. They were quickly briefed on the situation by Price.

One of the reasons Price was such a brilliant strategist was because he was always thinking of alternatives and playing the what-if game. "What if she's not going to Cuba? Where would she go? What if she goes below radar coverage?" Price turned to Miller. "We need to scramble all available KC-135 and KC-10 tankers. If the fighters don't find her right away, we'll need tankers to keep those jets airborne until we do. Also launch three AWACs aircraft and have them orbit over Norfolk, Myrtle Beach and Jacksonville. If she drops down on the deck, we'll need airborne radar to find and track her."

Miller responded with a quick, "Yes sir," and turned to carry out the orders.

Then Price turned to Lieutenant Colonel D'Auria.

"Don, get the wing commander from Langley on the video comm line and run it into the battle staff war room. I want that captain's boss there too. Contact Personnel and pull her personnel records. I want to know everything there is to know about this woman. Oh, yes, while you're at it, have a couple of psychiatrists look at her files so they can give me a profile of her. Oh, wait a minute, there are those two women doctors working on that congressional study. Something about women in combat. They gave the Joint Chiefs a briefing last week and they're here in the building doing research down in the personnel area. One of the doctors is an air force colonel and the other is a civilian. Get them on it; tell them I want to know all about our thief, her background, who and what kind of person she is, and why she's doing this. You have five minutes. While you're at it, find out what kind of name Kenada is, what nationality."

Miller immediately began delegating the different tasks to the officers sitting in the room.

Miller turned to Major Dorchester and the three captains sitting near him and said, "Tom, bring up the placement map screen for the East Coast and reduce it in size to include Maryland through Georgia. When the different bases call in with their scramble status, update their positions into the computer. Put it on the main computer screen."

"We're already on it, and we'll have a visual display in about a minute," Major Dorchester responded.

"Good."

Major Dorchester had continued his conversation with the air traffic controller out of Richmond, but since the stolen F-15 was heading south, he needed to link up with a controller in North Carolina to pick up tracking before the Eagle was out of range of Richmond.

Captain Keeslar watched Major Dorchester in his dilemma, and suggested, "Major, since this F-15 is heading south, we should be able to pick it up through a tie-in with the radar system there at Cherry Point Naval Air Station. I know we normally use this tie-in as a K-band weather radar system, but we could have them hook into their air traffic controller's X-band radar system. That way we could see where it's going in real time."

"OK, that'll work; do it."

After a few minutes, one of the large display screens went blank for a few seconds. The crisp picture on the screen was interrupted by static and snowy flashes, as if someone were changing TV channels. Suddenly a distinct circular image came on the screen. Price recognized the mapped area. It was the bottom half of the Chesapeake Bay and all of the Outer Banks of North Carolina. Brilliant green lights appeared on a black background, with a bright green line quickly traveling around like a very fast second hand on a clock. The image was from the radar scope from navy radar scanning the area a hundred miles around Norfolk.

The war room was starting to fill up with more generals and admirals, not that more were needed. It was standard procedure for them to report, just in case they were needed. It was a fairly large room dominated by a large horseshoe-shaped, polished oak table surrounded by twenty chairs and rows of twenty more chairs along the two side walls. At the open end of the horseshoe was a wall covered by six display screens and two large rear-projection screens. Behind the chairs at the top of the horseshoe was a wall of windows with a view into the Tank.

Time was of the essence, so General Price did not stand on protocol. He looked about the room, saw no one there better qualified in this aerial arena than himself, and he took charge. While the battle staff members came into the room, General Price gave them a quick briefing. Adm. Dave Watson, the chief of naval operations, came in on the tail end of the brief and asked one of the admirals who had arrived before him, "Is Buster glossing over the facts?"

Admiral Watson was the naval equivalent to General Price, and in many ways just as brilliant. Watson, however, was a legend in his own mind, and at no time would he be second to any air force general. Rather then waiting and deducing what was happening by the unfolding events, he insisted, "General Price, could you brief again from the beginning? I'd like to get the whole story."

General Price knew that this was no time for a power struggle and was about to politely tell Watson to shut up when the video comm line to Langley activated. On the screen was General Thompson, the wing commander; Colonel Proctor, the director of air operations; Lieutenant Colonel Prator, the 48th Squadron Commander; and Colonel Byrd, the deputy commander for Maintenance.

When the video comm line first activated, General Thompson was a little taken aback by the constellations of stars on his screen. He was not used to addressing so many superior officers at one time, especially with such bad news. Thompson introduced himself, along with the other officers with him. General Price introduced only himself. Time was short, and the boys at Langley should already know who the battle staff members were.

Admiral Watson, not to be left behind, quickly

blurted out, "General, tell us what you know."

"Well, Admiral, at nineteen twenty-five hours, we believe an aircraft maintenance officer here in the 48th stole an alert F-15 that was loaded with two Knight Hawk missiles. She was detected taxiing out of the alert barn and going to the runway. We blocked the runway but she took off using the parallel taxiway instead."

Watson jumped up and said, "Knight Hawks! She's got Knight Hawks? Can she arm the warheads?"

Slowly Thompson replied, "Well, I don't know for sure, sir, but it is possible. Normally I'd say no because the maintenance officers don't have access to the arming codes, but since she is also our squadron security manager, she does."

"Colonel Prator, why do you think she did this?" Price asked.

"I'm sorry, sir, I have no idea why. Captain Kenada has always been an excellent officer. She's highly dedicated and hardworking. In fact, she's usually at work twelve to fourteen hours a day. She's even at work on Saturdays and Sundays. This is totally out of her character."

Watson interrupted with another question. "What can you tell me about her personality? Who and what kind of people does she associate with? Do you think she had help?"

"Well, outside of work, she's quiet, not very sociable. Her job is very demanding and stressful, and I know she's had a few personal problems in the past, but it's never interfered with her work."

"What kind of problems?" Watson asked.

After a moment of thought Prator answered, "Well, sir, recently she was passed over for promotion to major and she was selected to be separated from the air force because of the presidential reduction-in-force policy."

That's a bit odd, Price thought. *Why would somebody who's going to be fired be so dedicated?*

"Is that all?" Watson asked. "Is she married?"

"No, she's not married; she's widowed. If I remember correctly, her husband died a few years ago, while they were both deployed to Saudi Arabia during Desert Storm."

Price was not interested in Captain Kenada's personal life; he wanted more pertinent information. "Colonel Prator, how is it that a maintenance officer knows how to fly an F-15?"

"Well, sir, as the maintenance officer, she knows how jets work. As for flying them well, she does have the responsibility to make sure our flight simulator is operational. I would imagine that she could have learned the systems and how to fly an F-15 there.

"Also a few years ago she was on flight status at her previous base, but for some reason or other she was permanently grounded."

Price was becoming intrigued by the combination of seemingly insignificant details about Kenada's life. "Colonel Prator, you mentioned that this Captain Kenada was grounded from flying. What kind of flying did she do?"

"She was an undergraduate pilot training instructor at Williams, and she has about a thousand hours in T-38s. I don't know exactly why she was grounded, but scuttlebutt among the pilots here has it that it might have been a repercussion caused by sexual assault charges she made against her squadron commander there."

"Oh, really." Price was taken aback by this tidbit of ominous information. He realized that he might have underestimated this captain's flying abilities. "Well, Prator, what you've told me is very enlightening. I hope I'm wrong, but I think that the light I see at the end of the tunnel is actually from an oncoming locomotive. Gentlemen, this is going to be harder than I thought, and I think we'd all better start praying that we can pull this one off."

There was a knock on the door, and through the glass Price could see that it was Colonel Miller. Price motioned with his hand and Miller came in.

"Sir, the radar controller for the navy down at Cherry Point has the F-15 on radar and has vectored a flight of four F-14s to intercept and destroy. We've also been able to patch into the Cherry Point radar system through our weather radar hookup, and now we've got the Eagle on the screen. If you wish, we could activate the image on one of the monitors in here."

"Do it. Put it on the main screen."

Chapter Three

Major Platt and Captain Reed had found an open door on the other side of the building. They had run around the barracks to the open doors of the alert hangar just in time to see their F-15, 008, make its takeoff roll and disappear into the clouds. While there was still a thundering rumble, Major Platt turned and ran into the hangar, pulled out the two-by-four that Captain Kenada had run through the door handles and threw it aside. He yanked the door open and raced down the tunnel toward the operations desk. To the surprise of the sergeant at the desk, Platt jumped up onto the chest-high counter, reached over and grabbed the hot line phone to the command post. The duty officer answered, and Platt said in an excited voice, "Major Mangus, this is Major Platt of the 48th. There has been a theft of one of the armed alert aircraft, zero zero eight. I am going to take zero seven one and go in pursuit. I'll need clearance. Get it for me."

Before the duty officer could ask any questions, Platt said, "You've got three minutes to get with the wing commander, Base Ops, and the SPs and get me my clearance." Without waiting for an answer Platt threw the phone to Captain Reed and said, "Answer his questions; I'm outta here." Major Platt reached over the counter, found the button labeled SCRAMBLE and pushed it. With the klaxon blaring, Platt jumped off the counter and ran back to the alert hangar. Once inside he climbed into the cockpit of 071 and immediately started strapping himself into his parachute harness and ejection seat. While he was putting his helmet on, the maintenance crew chiefs for the two alert birds heard the klaxon and raced in from the alert lounge area where they were having dinner. One of the two crew chiefs, Sgt. Don Adams, was surprised to see that his jet was missing. Sgt. Matthew Miles was just as surprised to see someone rushing to take his jet.

Platt yelled, "Sergeant Miles, Adams, start pulling my pins. I've got to launch."

Miles and Adams couldn't hear what Platt had yelled over the klaxon, but they did know their jobs. When the klaxon sounded, their job was to launch the jet. They both automatically started pulling safety pins and unplugging the power cables and grounding cords.

The Oshkosh towing 076 stopped on the apron just outside the alert area. The driver of the tow vehicle had heard the klaxon and, not wanting to interfere with the launch, towed 076 off the taxiway area and out of the way of the maintenance crew. He hopped out and disconnected the towbar from the nose landing gear, then climbed back in and drove the Oshkosh into the alert area to the baker hangar, where he waited to pull out a jet.

In the alpha alert hangar, 071 was almost ready to launch. Major Platt had started the JFS and was ready to crank up his engines. Looking to his left at Sergeant Miles, Major Platt raised his left hand, pointed straight up and started moving his finger in a tight circular motion. Sergeant Miles recognized the hand signal to start the left engine. He responded with the affirmative thumbs-up, a nod of his head, and raised a twirling left index finger.

Major Platt nodded and flipped the switch to engage the JFS and start the left engine. He advanced the left throttle, and out of reflex applied more pressure to the brakes. He watched the engine instruments level off at the proper idle settings. Again Miles responded with the affirmative thumbs-up to tell Platt that everything looked normal, then ran around well in front of 071 over to the right side.

When the left engine stabilized at idle, Platt raised his right hand, this time with two fingers up and moving in a tight circle. Sergeant Miles again nodded, repeating the gesture, and gave the thumbs-up signal. Captain Platt flipped the JFS switch for the right engine and advanced the right throttle. He felt a noticeable difference in resistance between the two throttles, but it didn't register as a problem. He just thought the lower resistance was due to better lubrication.

Major Platt watched the white tape rising on the engine instruments, and waited for the right engine to stabilize. He looked to his right at Sergeant Miles to see if he had pulled all of the pins and was ready to go.

In the belly of the Eagle, the Bendix fuel control was functioning as designed. Whenever the fuel control linkage was disconnected for whatever reason, the fuel control was spring-loaded to automatically go into full throttle. The reason for this was to protect the pilot in combat. If, for example, the aircraft took a hit and the throttle linkage was somehow disconnected, the engine would go into full afterburner to give the pilot all of the power he might need to escape.

As the right engine went into full afterburner, Platt felt his Eagle lunge forward. He instinctively stepped harder on the brakes. His efforts were in vain. When the Pratt and Whitney TF-100 jet engine was pushing out twenty-five thousand pounds of thrust, short of using a logger's chain, there were no brakes that would hold it back. The Eagle jumped over the chocks and started accelerating. Platt knew something was definitely wrong. As Platt stood on the brakes, his jet just kept moving faster. He took a quick glance at his engine instruments and saw his right engine was pegged at maximum power.

Platt saw that he was heading directly toward the right guard shack. He eased up on the right rudder pedal brake to turn left to miss the shack, then chopped both throttles to the off position. The nose of the jet veered to the left, missing the shack, but it continued to accelerate. He looked down at his instruments for some kind of clue to his problem. As a last-ditch effort he reached up to the top of the dash with both hands and pulled both of the fire-control handles. He knew that this would cut off all fuel going to the engines.

Confident that he had avoided death and saved a multimillion-dollar jet, Platt started to breathe a sigh of relief but was still a little nervous. On the dark ramp, he didn't notice Eagle 076 directly ahead in the shadows. Platt waited for the fuel to burn out of the lines and for his engines to stop. As he coasted he looked up in horror just in time to see where he was going. He heard his engine winding down, but he could see that the jet's inertia was going to carry him into the parked jet right in front of him, 076. In an instant he knew he was going to die. Platt's sigh was cut short as he saw the nose of his jet plunge underneath the left wing of 076. He watched the leading edge slide up almost in slow motion and shatter his fiberglass radome. The edge continued sliding toward him. The noise screaming at him sounded like a Greyhound bus going through an alley full of garbage cans. Platt thought about ducking down, but he couldn't move. The inertial reels on his seat belt and straps had locked, and he didn't have the precious two seconds needed to release them.

Suddenly the two-inch-thick Plexiglas canopy in front of him shattered under the weight and force of the oncoming wing. Platt's next thought was an instantaneous prayer: Oh, Jesus, save me!

Ask and you shall receive. Platt's prayer was answered.

Miraculously, the leading edge of 076's left wing changed direction. Instead of coming straight at him it rose up above the canopy and over Platt's head. For what seemed like an eternity, he watched in amazement as the tennis court–size wing cast a dark gray ceiling over his head. Directly ahead of him, Platt could see what lifted the wing. The pointed front of the missile pylon hanging down from the left wing of 076 had jabbed into the radar bulkhead of his jet's nose. The front mounting point of the pylon broke away from the wing, and the pylon pivoted on the its rear titanium mount. It lifted the wing of 076 just like the long, thin fiberglass shaft of a pole-vaulting Olympian.

No sooner did the flaps on the trailing edge of the wing pass over Platt's head than the missile pylon broke loose from the bulkhead, and the wing of 076 dropped on and shattered the canopy behind him.

After another few seconds of movement, everything stopped. In that moment of quiet and disbelief, Platt remembered an old war adage: "There are no atheists in foxholes," and he added to himself "or cockpits of crashing jets." With that Platt said, "Thank you, Jesus! Thank you, thank you, thank you!"

Platt's prayer of gratitude was suddenly stopped when he pushed the canopy lever to the open position and nothing happened. Now he was concerned about becoming a crispy critter. Thinking that he was about to die by fire, he decided that being beheaded would have been better.

Sergeant Miles ran past the drugged guards at the gate and couldn't believe what he had just seen. In less then ten seconds he saw a perfectly good airplane, aircraft 071, go into full burner, travel just over one hundred yards, collide with aircraft 076 with enough force to push it back fifty yards from the point of impact, and then turn both of them into an eighty million–dollar pile of junk metal destined for the recycling bin. Miles's only concern at the moment was to get Platt out before the two planes flamed up into a funeral pyre.

As he approached the two mated jets, he still couldn't believe his eyes. The nose of 076 was twenty feet up in the air, poised as if it were ready to bolt into the sky like a missile. The only parts of 076 still touching the ground were the right wing tip, the right main landing gear and the right horizontal stabilizer. The nose landing gear strut of 076 had caught and cut halfway through the left wing of Platt's aircraft. Several hundred gallons of JP4 jet fuel were still cascading out of the ruptured wing fuel tanks.

Miles got closer and splashed through some of the

puddles of fuel on the asphalt. He could see Platt's damaged jet nestled under the left wing of 076, and in horror he saw the shattered remains of 071's canopy. A wave of nausea came over him. He didn't know if it was from smelling all of the fumes of the fuel or from imagining that the top half of Major Platt had just been ripped off and was probably imbedded in the damaged leading edge of aircraft 076's left wing.

Awed by the level of destruction, Sergeant Miles slowed down and started to walk around the two aircraft, giving them both a wide berth just in case they ignited. He had no intention of being fried. There was no hurry now. Miles knew that Platt had to be dead.

Sergeant Adams, being fatter and obviously not as fast a sprinter as Miles, finally caught up. As he caught his breath he gasped. "Holy moly. Look at that!"

When Miles and Adams rounded the wing tip, they were amazed again when they heard Platt's voice yelling verbal abuse at them.

Major Platt, unable to raise the canopy, hollered at the pair, "Hey, Adams, Miles, quit your gawking and come over here and get me out of this mess. I'm up to my butt in gas and this bird's gonna blow!"

"Major, is that you?"

Almost in disbelief, the two sergeants turned to each other and said in unison, "He's alive!" Adams and Miles were thrilled to see that their friend was among the living and not a headless pile of body parts. The two of them ran around to the tail end of 076 like two playful dogs glad to see their master returning home. They jumped up on the narrow, flat fuselage section between the two engines, climbed up the backbone of the jet between the twin fifteen-foot rudders and then maneuvered over on the wing to help Platt.

Platt had tried in vain to free himself from the cockpit. The trailing edge of 076's left wing was resting on the back half of Platt's canopy, which kept it from raising. Miles and Adams stood on the wing, pondering Platt's predicament. There was too much clutter in front of and behind Platt for him to crawl out the holes in the canopy. The only way out for Platt now was through the canopy's unbroken section of half-inch Plexiglas. Miles, with his wits about him, shouted, "Oh, I know!" Then he went back the way he had come. He slid back down the jet and disappeared around the front. Thirty seconds later he scampered back up to Adams with one of the wooden wheel chocks under his arm. It was a shoe box–sized block of yellow-painted wood with a six-foot piece of rope attached.

Miles looked at Platt as he started to swing the wheel chock by the rope over his head and said, "If you don't want a hell of a headache, I suggest you duck."

Platt, realizing what Miles was about to do, quickly took his advice and buried his head between his knees, helmet and all. A second later the twenty-pound block of wood smashed through one side of the canopy and out the other. The cold plastic of the canopy shattered into hundreds of pieces. Platt popped his head up to see his gateway to freedom and wasted no time in making good his escape. When Adams and Miles saw Platt scurry out of the cockpit and hit the ground running, they looked at each other and followed his example.

They finally caught up with Major Platt and stopped a safe distance from the two jets. Platt was looking back to survey the damage. After a few minutes of staring in disbelief, Sergeant Miles was the first to speak. "No offense, Major, but when you screw up, you do a damn good job of it. There's nothing half-assed about you."

Platt just looked at the two jets and then at Miles and said, "The colonel is going to have my butt big-time."

"Well, Major," Adams replied, "just think, two more flights like that one and you'll be an ace."

Chapter Four

The President of the United States, Richard Pethers, was in the Oval Office with the vice president, Yolanda Borda, his cabinet members, and the rest of the White House staff. President Pethers was practicing his State of the Union address using TelePrompTers. His address was to be televised live in less than two hours. The speechwriters and the president were busy making the final changes to suit everybody at the table.

The phone rang and a woman smartly dressed in a gray wool suit answered it. Susan L. Wilson, White House chief of staff, identified herself and asked, "Can it wait? He's in a meeting at the moment. . . . OK . . . Oh, yes, I understand." She handed off the phone like a hot potato and said, "Mr. Howard, it's for you. It's Alex

McKenna, and she's with General Price at the Pentagon war room."

Jeff Howard, the secretary of defense, looked curiously at Wilson, took the phone and walked to the far corner of the room to give himself some privacy as well as to avoid disturbing the president's rehearsal. Howard wondered why he was getting a call from the secretary of the air force at this time of day.

"This is Howard; go ahead, Alex."

"Mr. Howard, I am calling to notify you and the president that we are currently on Defcon Two alpha alert. We have a very dangerous situation that has developed in the last half hour, and is still unfolding. General Price had briefed me that an air force officer, a Captain K-something, has stolen an F-15 aircraft from Langley Air Force Base in Hampton, Virginia. What makes the situation worse is that the jet is loaded with two nuclear weapons. They haven't made radio contact with her yet, but they do know she's heading south."

"What! I hope you're kidding."

"I wish I were, sir, but this is nothing to joke about. This is for real."

"Have we scrambled anything up there to shoot her down?"

"At the moment none of the jets that have been scrambled has taken off yet; however, we have vectored jets over to her to intercept her and bring her down, one way or another. We expect to have the other scrambled jets in the air within fifteen minutes."

"Alex, do you think she's capable of arming the weapons?"

McKenna, confident in her knowledge of the system, said, "There's no way that she can. General Price has told me that it would be impossible for one person to arm and detonate a nuclear weapon because of all the built-in safeguards, and because certain parameters have to be met before there can be a detonation. There are security codes the pilot has, codes the unit security manager has, and codes that the maintenance personnel have. The weapon can't detonate unless all of these codes are programmed into its computer and the weapon is loaded onto an operational jet.

"We know that this officer has direct access to one set of the security codes, but that isn't enough to disable the rest of the safeties so she can set them off."

Howard thought for a moment and said, "I don't think we should take any chances. Flying a fighter is a pretty damn complicated thing to do, and if she can do that we should assume that she's fully capable of launching a missile. Where is she right now, Alex?"

"I'm going to let General Price answer that, since he's just gotten the latest briefing from the control center."

General Price said, "Mr. Howard, we have her about forty miles south of Norfolk, Virginia, heading southwest."

"OK, General, let me inform the president and we'll talk to both of you in just a minute on the monitor."

Howard turned to the president, who was asking Wilson to have the barber come up in a few minutes to give him a quick trim. He was still unaware of the impending peril.

"Mr. President, there is a development that needs your immediate attention. We are currently on a Defcon Two alpha alert status. General Price is on the monitor to brief you."

"Damn. Of all of the times . . . Well, I hope this doesn't take too long; I still have a speech to give. Stay here, everybody; we'll be right back." Pethers, Borda, Howard and Wilson got up and walked into the monitor room, a small room adjoining the Oval Office. Pethers took the center seat, while Howard activated the video camera and turned on the monitor. Borda and Howard sat in the chairs on either side of Pethers. Wilson stood by the door. After a few seconds of static, General Price's face came into sharp focus on the six-foot-square wall video screen. Behind him the president could see the score of video monitors of the Pentagon control center. Even before Price spoke, Pethers noticed the ominous level of activity.

The foursome sat in complete silence as General Price briefed them on what had happened. Just like everyone else who had been given this news, they sat stupefied.

"General, let me get this straight," the president said. "We have a renegade pilot who has stolen a jet loaded with two Knight Hawk nuclear missiles. Is that correct?"

"Yes, sir, that is correct."

The president stood up, slammed his fist on the table in front of him and yelled his favorite word for times of crisis. "Damn! Price, what are you doing to stop her?"

General Price knew that he was under the gun, and that whether he liked it or not his career was on the line. In a calm voice he said, "Mr. President, at the moment we have a flight of four F-14s on an intercept course with her. They will be within combat range in approximately three and a half minutes. Their orders are to bring her back or shoot her down."

The president stopped for a moment and faced General Price's image on the monitor. With his left arm folded across his chest and his right hand stroking his chin, he thought of all of the ramifications. Questions raced through his mind. How was he going to get out of this mess? How was he going to explain this? Should he let the country know, and if so, when? How could this situation be averted? Where would the first bomb be dropped?

Pethers asked, "General, can we shoot her down without setting off a nuclear explosion?"

General Price stared matter-of-factly into the camera and said, "If we find her and catch her by surprise, yes. The key is that we destroy the missiles while they are still on the jet. If she arms them, and then launches one or both of them, then it would be almost impossible to stop a nuclear detonation."

"That doesn't sound too good, Price." Pethers paced back and forth behind the desk for a few seconds; then without hesitation he leaned over his chair and menacingly pointed at the monitor and said, "General, you have five minutes to shoot her down. And whatever you do, don't let this leak out to the press, especially anything about Knight Hawks. If anybody asks, tell them that this was an accident during a normal training flight or something. Understand?"

Price, unflinching, responded, "Yes, sir, I understand."

"OK, Price, keep this line open. Wilson is going to stay on the line here and monitor your progress. I've got other business to attend to."

Pethers, Borda and Howard walked out of the room back to the Oval Office. During the stroll back Pethers was trying to comprehend what was happening and how he was going to explain this to the American public, or even if he should. In a way, this current predicament was partially his fault.

Although the Knight Hawk missile defense system was not his own personal brainchild, he was responsible for its existence. There were several congressmen who had lobbied for the acceptance of President Reagan's Star Wars defense program, but it was President

Pethers who had promoted the less expensive Knight Hawk program. It was President Pethers who had pushed the Knight Hawk program through Congress, and it was President Pethers who had pushed the Department of Defense for a quick procurement of the system and for an even quicker activation into operational status.

Even though the old Soviet threat no longer existed, there was still a need to have jets armed with nukes and ready for immediate takeoff at the first sign of an impending threat.

Prior to the "Fall of the Wall" in Berlin, these F-15 aircraft were kept on alert to fly into the face of oncoming Soviet Bear Bombers and simultaneously set off several nuclear weapons in a row. This would set up a nuclear curtain, a huge wall of fusion fire, to prevent entry into American airspace and to destroy aggressors. Now that the old "silver bullets," the nuclear B-61 bombs with the polished aluminum exteriors, had been replaced by the Knight Hawk missiles, the alert mission had been expanded. These aircraft-launched missiles were capable of carrying a nuclear warhead hundreds of miles away via a suborbital trajectory, or they could use their sophisticated guidance system to intercept high-speed objects hundreds of miles in space, much like the Patriot missiles did during Desert Storm.

Once they were back in the Oval Office, Pethers turned immediately to Dave Edison, the head man on the crew that had been helping him with the speech. "Dave, I think it's time to wrap up my practice. Go ahead to the hill and make sure everything is set up."

Dave was glad to hear this news. Not that he didn't want to help Pethers with the practice, but this would give him just a little more time to prepare. "Yes, sir, Mr. President, everything will be ready when you are." Dave motioned to the crew by dragging his fingers across his throat. Seconds later electrical cords were popped out of wall sockets and the equipment was being rolled out the door to the vans outside the side doors.

When the door closed behind the departing crew and the room was empty except for the three, Pethers said, "Howard, refresh my memory about these Knight Hawks."

"Well, sir, the primary mission for these aircraft on alert was to launch the nuclear-tipped Knight Hawk missiles at inbound intercontinental ballistic missiles, possibly originating from Iraq, Iran, China or even what's left of the USSR. The Knight Hawks would detonate in the upper atmosphere and destroy the inbound warheads with a nuclear umbrella. This is the less expensive version of Reagan's Star Wars program.

"A secondary mission would be against any surface-launched missile from a ship at sea. We knew for a fact that over a hundred Russian short-range missiles with nuclear warheads had made their way into the hands of black-market arms dealers. It would be an easy task to launch one of those missiles from the cargo hold of an old freighter.

"CIA intelligence reports indicated that several of the Soviet-made long-range cruise missiles, the AS-15 Kents, had even made their way into Cuba. What made this threat worse was the fact that they were exporting their revolutionary ideals across the Caribbean and into Central America and Mexico. The CIA also believed that Cuban advisers were supporting the revolution in the southern states of Mexico."

With a little impatience in his voice, Pethers interrupted him. "Yes, I know all that; get on with Knight Hawk."

"Sorry, sir. In the event of a long-range cruise-missile

attack, a nuclear curtain could also be initiated farther out to sea."

"Well, this definitely changes things," Pethers said. "What do you think I should do?"

Borda and Howard looked at each other to see who would field Pethers's question. Then Borda looked at Pethers and said, "Before we answer that, let's consider our options first. This is an internal emergency, so we don't need to notify any foreign countries. . . ."

"Yes, and since this is purely a military affair so far, I feel that we should let the battle staff handle it," Howard said.

"I agree with you both on those points," Pethers said, "but what about tonight's address? Do I go on with it, postpone it or cancel out?"

"Well, I would postpone it because of this pending emergency," Borda suggested.

"Yes," Howard interjected, "but if you do postpone your address, you'll have to give a reason why. Do you really want to announce to the country that a crazy woman is loose up there in the wild blue with a pair of nukes that can blow away a couple million people? That would cause a coast-to-coast panic. On the other hand, it's possible that this crisis could be resolved successfully without the public knowing anything about it until much later."

Borda responded with a "Yes, but" of her own. "I agree with you, Howard, but if this Kenada woman is successful in setting off a nuke, we'll have to explain our cover-up, and why we didn't tell anybody."

"OK, let's look at it this way," Howard answered. "Whether we go on with or postpone the address, will that affect the outcome of what's happening with this K woman? No. And how do you think it's going to make you look if you announce to the public that this woman has the country by the balls?"

Pethers nodded at Howard and said, "Not good."

Howard continued. "Personally, sir, I think that you should press on with the address and pray to God that the battle staff generals know what they're doing. Besides, if they don't and, heaven forbid, a nuke is set off, we'll all be too busy trying to recover. Who knows, we may all be dust in a few hours."

Pethers stood up, walked to the window and looked outside as if for the answer. After a moment he turned to Borda and Howard and said, "We will continue with the address and press on as if nothing is happening. We will say nothing. If anybody asks the question, it's 'no comment' time. Yolanda, you and I will go to the Hill on schedule. Howard, I want you to go back with Wilson and see what's going on. Let me know when anything important happens."

Chapter Five

USS Eisenhower

Four hundred fifty miles east of New York, the world was dark, wet, cold and windy. The USS *Eisenhower*, a nuclear-powered aircraft carrier, was plying the Atlantic toward Norfolk for a well-deserved rest at its home port. Carrier life was rarely heaven, but for most it was often hell. It took special people to crew on a carrier. They voluntarily did a job in a place sometimes described as an iron prison with a thousand-mile moat. They gladly made this sacrifice for duty, honor and country.

The *Eisenhower* and her crew were returning from a torturous ten-month tour in the eastern Mediterranean. Med cruises had always been considered prize trips, but not this one. They had been performing a containment police action and supporting actions against

60

the Serbs in Bosnia. They had flown flights along the Saudi-Iraq border to maintain pressure on Saddam as well as to deter any Iraqi attempts to acquire Kuwaiti or Saudi real estate. They had also been on constant alert for Libyan fighters that kept playing cat-and-mouse games. The Libyans were more of a nuisance than a threat, but they could still be dangerous. The fighters kept trying to get as close as possible to the carrier group before they were chased away.

While the Pentagon was issuing the Defcon Two alpha alert, the *Eisenhower*'s crew of 5,800 were eagerly preparing to come home and be with their friends, families and loved ones. The crew's morale meter was pegged to the fun side, just under winning the lottery. Some of the crew were more fortunate than the others; they were already with their loved ones. To be more accurate, they were with their loved *one*. Now that women were stationed on U.S. Navy warships, such was the case with two F-18 pilots, Lt. Dawn Rutherford and Lt. Comdr. Dan Haley.

While most of the crew were busy doing their jobs or eating or joining into any of the festive "going home" parties, Rutherford and Haley were enjoying their own private party in Rutherford's quarters. Rutherford's roommate was still on watch till midnight in the ship's hospital, so the two of them knew that they would have some privacy. They were lying together in her stateroom bed, basking in the afterglow of a little premarital passion. Dawn, lying on top of Dan, was gently fingering his chest hairs while he ran his fingers through strands of her blond hair. Dawn was talking about the wedding plans she had arranged through her mother, and Dan smiled as he half listened. He was completely enamored of the beautiful woman in his arms.

Dan, like many men, didn't really care about getting

Pat O'Connell

involved in the plans. He would help when and where he was needed, but so far Dawn was happy doing it herself. He still couldn't believe how fortunate he was. His ex-wife, from whom he was recently divorced, had hated the navy life, and she particularly disliked his first love, flying. Why she felt this way, Dan didn't know. He thought perhaps she was jealous that he could enjoy something more than he enjoyed her. Maybe it was because it took him away from her, or maybe it was both. Whatever the reason, he didn't care. That part of his life was over. Now he was with a woman who not only loved him, but also shared the same love of life, adventure and, of course, flying.

As far as Dan was concerned, he had found the perfect mate. The two of them had thought about getting married while they were on this tour, but hadn't. They knew the old man on the bridge, Captain Shephard, frowned on shipboard romances. At the start of the cruise Shephard had declared, "I am not Captain Stubing, and this is not the Love Boat."

Dan and Dawn both knew that if Shephard ever found out they were having an affair, he would do his best to split them up by transferring one of them out.

While Dawn talked, Dan was lost in her eyes. Besides Dawn's other physical charms, Dan had always been enticed by her eyes. It was like looking at a total eclipse: rare, fascinating and dangerous. Her eyes were a bright sky blue with thin rims of gold surrounding her pupils, like the fiery golden ring of the sun's corona shining around the dark disc of the moon. Dan knew that he'd get burned if he stared too long at an eclipse, but it was too late for that. He was already a victim of the heat. It was the sparkle in Dawn's eyes that had earned her the nickname of Twinkle. Those close to her, like Dan, called her Twink.

Knight Hawk

Rutherford was a remarkable woman. She was intelligent, beautiful and uniquely talented when it came to flying jets. She was in the top ten percent of her class at the Naval Academy and the top of her class at the Naval Flight School in Pensacola, Florida. Her grades, along with other qualifications, had earned her the right to be among the first women in the U.S. Navy selected to fly fighters and to see combat duty off a carrier.

At five feet, six inches tall, Rutherford just barely met the height requirement for flying jets. Nonetheless, she was a great pilot. Her skill with the F-18 was exceptional.

For Dawn, Dan was the man of her dreams. Besides his good looks and fit body, he was a man she could look up to without having to compete against. And she thought of him as a good listener.

Dan had always considered himself one of the top guns of the squadron, but after flying with Dawn, he was beginning to wonder. When Dan first met Dawn, he cringed at the thought of having a woman as his wingman, but after a few flights together, he had changed his mind. He was duly impressed; in fact he was amazed. He fondly referred to her now as his wingwoman.

Over time Dan was amazed that they had so much in common. In some ways, Dawn was a female version of himself.

In the command room behind the bridge on the USS *Eisenhower*, the coded message came through the descrambler and showed up on the screen.

... CONDITION RED ... CONDITION RED ... CONDITION RED ... DEFCON TWO ALPHA ALERT ... DEFCON

TWO ALPHA ALERT. ONE F-15 HAS BEEN STOLEN FROM
LANGLEY AFB, VIRGINIA. IT IS ARMED WITH TWO
KNIGHT HAWK MISSILES. LOCATION UNKNOWN. PRE-
PARE ALL AVAILABLE AIRCRAFT FOR IMMEDIATE AIR-
TO-AIR COMBAT. STAND BY FOR FURTHER DIRECTIVES.
PREPARE TO LAUNCH ON OUR COMMAND.
THIS IS NOT A DRILL. . . . THIS IS NOT A DRILL.

Comdr. Kenneth Wayne, the ranking officer on duty
in the command room, quickly read the message and
immediately hit the print button on the terminal key-
board. While the message was printing, Wayne keyed
the mike for the ship's intercom. "Captain Shephard,
please report to the command room immediately. Captain Shephard, please report to the command room immediately."

One of the officers in the mess said, "Uh-oh, I don't
like the sound of that. I know the captain's not going to
like this one."

Capt. Joseph "Ship Hard" Shephard was having dinner, his last supper on board, in the officers mess with
most of the other officers when he heard Wayne's page.
Without a word he quickly stepped out of the mess and
made the fifty-five-second trip to the command room.
Shephard had an ominous feeling about this page. In
the past, whenever he had been summoned to the command room it was usually not for something good.

When the captain came in, Commander Wayne
handed him the printout of the message. He read the
message and said under his breath, "Damn, I was afraid
of this. What a hell of a way to end a cruise. Wayne,
sound the alarm for general quarters."

Dan started to nibble on Dawn's ear, hoping to distract her from discussing plans and start another pas-

sionate interlude. They were rudely interrupted.

The relative quiet of the stateroom was broken by the blare of the klaxon, followed immediately by the command, "Attention all hands, Attention all hands. Battle stations, Battle stations. This is not a drill. . . ."

Both naked bodies flew off the bunk as a conditioned reflex to the klaxon. Dan grabbed his shorts and was hopping on one foot, hurrying to put his underwear on. He lost his balance and fell back on the bed. All the while he was uttering something similar to what was being said all over the ship: "Great, this is just friggin' great. What the hell's going on?" He was definitely disturbed by the timing.

Dawn too was having difficulty finding all of her clothes amid the pile of blankets and clothing on the floor. Since it was January, Dawn ripped out a fresh pair of Nomex long underwear from a cabinet drawer and put them on under her flight suit. Dan saw Dawn's long underwear and realized that his were in his quarters. He grabbed his boots and socks and ran barefoot down the maze of halls to his stateroom to get it.

On this ship of more than five thousand men, everybody was affected when the klaxon went off. What puzzled the crew was why, especially when they were so close to home. After all, who was there to fight?

The parties and get-togethers throughout the ship came to an immediate halt. The euphoric bubble of happiness had burst. The beat of music and drums was replaced by the beat of thousands of feet. The most common expression uttered was, "Oh, man, now what?" The greatest fear was, *Oh no, we're going back*.

Nonetheless, everybody on board knew their duties and went about their business. Each knew they would soon learn the reason for the alarm.

Chapter Six

A young woman's soft voice came out of the earphones in Captain Datz's helmet. "Hoots, warning, warning, multiple launches detected, two o'clock low and six o'clock high. Impact in twenty-eight and forty-seven seconds. Hostile aircraft at two, six and nine o'clock."

Along with the verbal warning, Datz, the pilot, felt two different electrical shocks, one on her forehead above the outside corner of her right eye, and the other directly in the back of her head. The shocks weren't painful, but they did get her attention. This electrical stimulation of the scalp was designed to be another means of alerting the pilot to where threats were coming from. As Datz turned her head, the location of the shocks changed in relation to the position of her helmet, not her aircraft. When she looked in the two o'clock position, one pulsing shock moved to the center of her forehead, and the other moved behind her right ear.

Datz took a deep breath before responding to the computer's voice recognition system, "Peggy, Auto Defense. Engage." She prepared herself for a wild ride and thought, *Here goes.*

To most fighter pilots, this deadly situation would be extremely alarming, but not to Captain Diane "Hoots" Datz. Captain Datz was concerned but calm. Her confidence came not from her above-average flying skills but from her aircraft. Datz was snugly strapped into the ejection seat of the Lockheed F-22A Advanced-Technology Fighter (ATF), the most advanced fighter aircraft ever to take to the sky. The F-22A, which she had nicknamed Pegasus, was the result of extensive research and innovation. Its state-of-the-art features were the last word in agility, speed, stealth, sight and artificial computer intelligence.

Captain Datz was just as remarkable as her aircraft. The only thing average about her was her height. She was as attractive as she was intelligent, and when it came to computers and airplanes, she was a genius. She rarely wore makeup, didn't really need to, and personally thought it was a waste of time and effort. Her blond hair was cut collar-length in a pageboy cut to complement her favorite fashion ensemble, which consisted of a crash helmet, Nomex flight suit, and combat boots.

Datz worked hard and loved her job. She was given her nickname, "Hoots," for her sense of humor and fun-loving personality—but also for her physical attributes. Once at a happy hour at the Columbus Air Force Base officers club in Mississippi, one pilot had said, "She's a real hoot." The other pilot replied, "Yes, and nice hoots too." Hence her name.

The missile warning was all that Captain Datz needed. She had spent the last fifty minutes in hostile airspace and had worked up a sweat. The only thing that momentarily broke her concentration was the occasional drop of perspiration that trickled down her chest. She hated that. Datz tugged on the center strap of her bra and pushed her T-shirt around to sponge up the moisture.

Peg was the name that Datz gave to the jet's computer mainframe. The voice-recognition system in the computer recognized the command and obeyed. At that instant the aircraft battle computer (BC) went from partial to total control of the aircraft, and until the autodefense mode was disengaged, Datz would remain a passenger, electronically relegated to being a backseat driver. As Datz expected, she suddenly felt the retaining straps retract and hold her shoulder, waist, arms and legs close to her seat. Both of her wrists were brought tightly against the flat computer touch plate on her lap. The only real free movement she had now was in her fingertips, but she had the utmost confidence in the computer-controlled autodefense mode of her aircraft.

The battle computer was linked to every sensory system on the aircraft as well as all weapons systems, engines and flight controls. The BC turned the aircraft into a thinking, almost living creature. It was the latest in artificial intelligence. It would receive information through all of its senses—radar, infrared cameras and sensors, radar detectors—and then respond. The BC even used "fuzzy logic." It had the ability to make an educated guess. When the information it received was incomplete, it would assign values for uncertainties and then guess. That was why Datz called it Peg. The BC was a Programmed Educated Guesser.

In the active mode the BC was programmed to do everything a pilot could do and more. Even without the manual flight controls, the pilot could still control the jet through several means: by voice, by the lap touch pad, and in some modes by eye movement. The BC system was the most advanced computer system ever to wear wings. Just as different parts of the human brain performed different functions, the BC system itself was a community of computers all joined collectively into one brain: inertial navigation, autopilot, radar, target detection, defense, attack, flight, weapons, and even a medical diagnostic of the pilot. The BC was also equipped with a boomerang function that would return to base and land if the pilot was unable to.

In the night sky over Iraq, Datz could barely see the missiles' plumes approaching from two o'clock with the naked eye. Fortunately for her, she had help. A wealth of information was being projected onto her visor, allowing her to see things her eyes alone couldn't. To Datz the world outside could have passed for a complex virtual-reality game that was being projected onto the helmet visor. In many ways, it was. This jet was equipped with the best set of eyes money could buy, Multi-Vision (MV). MV was the combination of several eyes that enhanced the pilot's sight. Besides normal vision it enabled the pilot to see with infrared, low-level light, and radar. Using MV took a little time to get used to, but once pilots realized what they were seeing, they loved it.

Datz could see a floating red transparent bubble to her right. The bubble was a radar-detected threat area several miles across. At the center of the bubble, the approaching missiles were framed in a targeting square.

Datz wanted a better view of the targeting square, so she said, "Peg, magnify target, fifty, project left." Instantly the view from Datz's left eye changed, while the right eye's view remained the same. In the split-vision magnification mode, Datz could quickly acquire a target with normal vision in her right eye, then see the magnified image with her left. The trick of this was to let her brain sort out the two different scenes. It was much like taking a picture with both eyes open: while one eye looked through the magnifying viewfinder of the camera, the other eye saw the subject normally.

Datz's right eye saw a tiny square, while her left eye saw the square magnified fifty times. Inside it were three flashing circles with *R*'s in the center of each, indicating that the missiles were radar guided. There were also four triangles that framed the hostile aircraft.

The F-22 fighter quickly rolled forty-five degrees hard to the right. Datz felt her G suit tighten on her legs and abdomen just before the jet started the turn. The accelerometer, the device that measured the gravity strain on the aircraft, measured the force of the turn at six Gs. Out of habit she tensed her abdominal muscles to restrict blood flow to the lower parts of her body. In an instant Datz saw four lasers point to the center of each of the three circles, and one point at an aircraft in the triangle. As soon as the bubble was directly ahead, Datz heard three tones followed by a quick series of loud pops and swishes. The laser-guided hypervelocity missiles were launched out of the carrier pod. Simultaneously the launch message flashed in red on the bottom of her visor, "8 HYPERS AWAY," and the female computer voice confirmed, "Eight hypers away."

The Pegasus continued the turn. The missiles that had been at two o'clock were now at ten, and the missiles at six o'clock were now coming from two. The tiny electronic jolts pricked both of her temples.

To the left, Datz could see that the infrared lasers were still locked on the incoming missiles. With a quick look to the right, Datz saw another bubble with a targeting square framing a similar set of circles and triangles. In this targeting square the circles had *H*'s in the center, for heat-seeking missiles.

Another message flashed on the bottom of her visor—FLARES AWAY—while Peg voiced the message.

Datz looked back to her left at the radar bogeys homing in on her just in time to see three flashes. The three target-designating lasers flickered and became four beams of light. The only difference this time was that now all of the lasers were pointing at the triangles. A few seconds later there were two more flashes and two of the target triangles disappeared, as well as two of the lasers.

Three seconds later the remaining two lasers cut off, and Datz's jet cranked in ninety degrees of right roll and turned directly into the approaching heat seekers. As it turned Peg spoke again. "Three missiles and two aircraft destroyed. Two aircraft not destroyed are turning away. Engaging next threat."

In the bubble and targeting square ahead, Datz had no sooner counted two circles and four triangles than she saw and heard the four radar-guided AIM-120 missiles launch in sequence, about two seconds apart. The familiar voice announced, "Four AIM-120 away" as the same message flashed on her visor.

Datz watched her four missiles rocket toward their targets. They looked as if they were on a collision course with the two heat seekers coming at her. At first she wondered why Peg had turned the jet directly into the oncoming missiles and why it wasn't firing flares to decoy the missiles. Datz guessed that Peg had turned into the missiles to hide the heat of her jet's exhaust from the heat-seeking missiles. But she also thought it should have fired flares to further distract the missiles, and made a mental note to ask Peg why later. To Datz's surprise there were two brilliant flashes a mile ahead. The heat-seeking missiles coming at her had detonated prematurely. Evidently the plumes of the passing missiles caused them to change their lock and go after the AIM-120 missiles Peg had launched. When Datz's missiles passed, the heat seekers lost their lock-on and their own proximity fuse initiated detonation.

Datz thought, *Now that was a neat trick. I'm impressed. Peg, did Meridith teach you that or were you just lucky?*

On the other side of the flashes came three more flashes.

As the F-22 turned hard right to engage the last group of approaching fighters, Peg announced, "Two missiles destroyed, three fighters destroyed. One fighter still approaching. Engaging third group, forty-five seconds to guns."

"Peg, Engage ETM and go EMIS." Datz didn't want to leave any loose ends, at least not just yet. Not to mention she wanted to have a little fun. As long as I've got the best toys, I might as well play with them, she thought. "Go EMIS" (emission limit) was the command that put the F-22's electronic transmissions, such as radar, radio and electronic countermeasures, into a standby mode, in effect going to electronic silent running. This would make it more difficult for the enemy fighters to find their target.

To use the ETM (eye-targeting mode), Diane held her left index finger against the touch pad on her left thigh, which activated the laser eye-movement trackers in her helmet. Now wherever Diane looked, the F-22 would follow. Diane looked left at the lone fighter that was still approaching. "Peg, target lock."

As the F-22 snapped back quickly to the left, following the movement of Diane's eyes, Peg responded, "Hoots, target locked. Select weapon."

"Peg, select hypers, four. Engage Touch Fly."

"Hoots, hypers selected, Touch Fly engaged." Datz kept her eyes fixed on the bogey as she lifted her left index finger off the left touch pad and put her right middle finger on the right thigh touch pad. Datz had disengaged the eye-targeting mode and was now flying the F-22 by touch with just one finger. Using her right eye in the magnified view, Diane could see a single laser locked onto the approaching bogey. She lowered her right index finger to the pad and four laser-guided hypervelocity missiles launched into the darkness. Three seconds later Diane saw multiple flashes, followed by one large flash two miles away.

With a slight movement of her right middle finger to the right on the touch pad, the F-22 rolled hard right, turning back to the next threat.

Ahead Datz could see another bubble in the sky, and within it four triangles. Directly behind the four hostiles she could see the lights of a city close to her target: Baghdad.

"Peg, resume autodefense and state intentions." Datz wanted to know just what her jet was about to do next. So far Peg had performed flawlessly.

"Hoots, I am approaching for head-on gunshot on the lead jet. I will continue through the formation and proceed to primary target for weapons delivery. OK?"

Datz responded, "OK, proceed. State intentions after each event."

"OK."

Suddenly the sky around her turned red and Datz heard growling and chirping over the headphones and felt electric shocks in all parts of her helmet. She knew she was in big trouble. All of the noises Datz was hearing were coming from her radar detectors. Several ground radars were now tracking her and trying to lock on to fire. Huge red bubbles were forming in all directions as far as Datz could see. The red wall around her went from just above the ground to ten miles high.

Seeing the danger, Datz yelled, "Peg, it's a trap; evade and continue, evade and continue."

"Hoots, I comply. Evading." As Peg spoke, the F-22 rolled, inverted and went into a six-G pull toward the ground. As she dove and spiraled down from ten thousand feet, the aircraft rolled back upright and executed another high-G pull to level out at two hundred feet. With the wings level, Datz could feel a sudden lurch as the afterburners ignited. Peg spoke up again. "ECM and TFR engaged, proceeding to target, accelerating to mach 1.5 for toss maneuver." The ECM, electronic countermeasures, would confuse any missile-guided radars, and the TFR, terrain-following radar, would keep her at just above treetop level.

The sky was no longer red. Above her she could see the bottoms of the red bubbles and the cone-shaped bottoms where they were anchored to ground radars. Above and to the left and right Datz saw several rocket plumes of SAMs, surface-to-air missiles, vainly pursuing a vanished target. In seconds the SAMs would run out of fuel and fall back to earth. Under her breath Datz mused, "Oh, well. What goes up must come down."

Peg heard Datz and asked, "Hoots, what goes up?"

Datz realized that Peg's hearing was better than she expected and reminded herself to be more careful when she spoke. "Peg, disregard 'what goes up.' Proceed to primary target."

"OK, Hoots."

Ten miles directly ahead the lights of Baghdad were blurring toward her. Twenty miles past that was the primary target, a chemical processing plant that was believed to be producing chemical nerve-agent weapons. The target was not and would not be visible to Datz on this mission. When her F-22 was within five miles of the target it would pitch up at forty-five degrees, and at six hundred feet above ground level it would release the thousand pounds of computer-guided explosives. The camera and computer in the nose of the bomb would guide the bomb to its target while Datz made good her escape.

Datz had lost sight of Baghdad under her nose. Seconds later she felt her F-22 pitch up and release the ordnance. Peg announced, "Ordnance away, returning to base."

"Proceed," Datz replied.

Just as quickly the F-22 rolled hard right and dove back down on the deck under the enemy radars. "Boomerang engaged," Peg said.

Datz watched as Peg guided the F-22 to a northwestern heading toward safe haven in Turkish airspace. Datz started to relax now that her mission was almost over. Suddenly she heard a loud bang. Her plane shook and she felt as if she were in a small car rear-ended by a Mack truck. The fire "T" handle for the left engine was flashing red, and her engine instruments showed it was on fire. Datz instinctively reached up and pulled the red-lit handle. Since there was no warning of a missile coming at them, she asked, "What the hell was that?"

To Datz it was a rhetorical question, but to Peg it was a pilot-initiated request for information.

Peg responded, "Compressor failure, left engine, possible bird strike."

Before the left engine started spooling down, Peg said, "Warning, missile launch six oh—" The computer's voice was silenced by another sudden violent shudder of the F-22. Datz didn't even have time to reach for the ejection handles on her seat. It was too late; her vision went black and her world was suddenly and silently dead. Datz's flight was over. The ultramodern F-22 Pegasus was now just another multimillion-dollar smoking hole on Iraqi real estate.

"Meridith Henson! That was not fair. Since when do birds fly at night, and how did that SAM get me without radar?"

Meridith giggled at the sweat-drenched Captain Datz as she climbed out of the simulator cockpit. "Hey, Diane, haven't you ever heard of an owl? How about a nighthawk? As for the missile you took in the tail, that wasn't a SAM. Do you remember the two fighters in the first set of bogeys that turned away? Well, one of them shoved a heat seeker up your tail from two hundred meters away."

"No way, Meri. Neither of those jets could've closed that quickly."

"Oh, yes, Diane. I flew the Mig-29 myself. The bird strike was just a distraction. Besides, you have a hot phone call from Col. Terry Lee at Base Ops. He told me to bring you down, ASAP."

"Well, this had better be good. We've still got to load the flight-profile program for tomorrow's test flight on the range against that F-4 drone."

Meridith Henson was the simulator programmer and operator for the electronic flight test center at Eglin Air Force Base in Fort Walton Beach, Florida. She was attractive and petite. Her dark brown hair was turned under on her neck. Her disarmingly innocent smile and cute appearance were often misleading to the macho fighter jocks who would come in to show off their aeronautical talents to impress her and win her favor. She would routinely bring them down to their electronic knees in the simulator. For most hotshot pilots a flight against Meridith in the simulator was a humbling experience. Henson had acquired quite a reputation in the fighter squadrons. Now whenever a pilot was scheduled for a simulator ride, instead of writing "SIM"—for a simulator ride—by the pilot's name, the scheduler in the squadron would write "MDM," for Merry Death by Meridith.

Meridith was a frustrated fighter jock if ever there was one. She stood five feet, four inches in heels, so she didn't meet the air force's height requirements for flying, but when she operated the simulator controls she became a ruthless giant.

Diane picked up the phone and quickly rolled her head to toss her hair away from her ear. "This is Captain Datz."

"Captain, I'm Colonel Lee at Base Ops. I have a priority-one message for you."

"Go ahead, Colonel."

"I'm sorry, Captain, I can't give this to you over the phone. Report to the briefing room in hangar seven immediately, and be prepared to fly."

"What? Fly? Now?"

"Hangar Seven, *now*, Captain."

"Yes, sir."

There was no response, just the click of a phone hanging up.

Datz, puzzled, hung up the phone, then turned to Meridith and said, "I've got to go to hangar seven. The colonel wants me to fly. Now."

Datz and Henson both knew what was in hangar seven. It was the F-22A.

"Well you can't go without me. You'll need some help

loading all of the new program parameters I've written for Peg." As she spoke, Meridith was busy shutting down the simulator and turning off the power. Before all of the electronic whirring coming out of the simulator cockpit had stopped, Meridith was in it, yanking out the core of stacked hard drives from the battle computer. "I just thought I'd bring Peg along too." Meridith gently placed the hard drives in a padded carrying case, latched it shut and said, "OK, I'm ready; let's go. I'll drive. I've got a flight line pass."

Datz collected all of her gear and stuffed her helmet into its carrying case, grabbed her Nomex flight jacket and ran to the door. Henson was right behind with her drives in one hand and her car keys in the other.

Datz continued running toward the parking lot, and just as she was about to ask which car, the engine and lights of a red '97 Camaro Z28 came on and the rear hatch popped open. Meridith placed the drive case in the back, and Diane put her helmet case beside it and closed the hatch.

Diane looked at Meridith as she climbed into the passenger seat. "Meri, the engine, the lights, the hatch, that was neat. How'd you do that?"

"Easy, Diane, remotes. Now buckle up; it's time to rock and roll."

Chapter Seven

On entering the cloud deck, Captain Kenada immediately started cross-checking her instruments. Attitude indicator, to airspeed, to attitude, to altimeter, and back to attitude. She relaxed her pull on the joystick and let the nose drop to a forty-degree angle of climb and held it. She gently pulled the throttles back to mil power.

After a half minute in the gray emptiness of the clouds, her jet burst out into the clear, deep blue sky above the clouds, like a dolphin jumping out of a foamy sea. The remaining droplets of water on her canopy rolled backward and glistened from the light. A three-quarter-full moon was already high in the southeastern sky. She pushed the stick forward and to the right, and watched the moon move from the right side of her canopy to the left. She continued turning to the right till she had a southern compass heading of 195 degrees. Kenada leveled off at an altitude of 5,930 feet and let her Eagle settle so she was flying through the very tops of the clouds, and occasionally through the open air in between.

The gain on her radar had been turned up to the maximum setting so it would get the greatest range. There were two things Kenada was trying to do: First, set up a decoy trail and let everybody know—or at least think—that she was heading south. Second, to look for a big jet, a commercial liner, flying north.

Kenada had been airborne for twenty minutes. She had gone from a cold, dark, wet world below the clouds to a pristine and serenely alien world above. A sea of blue-tinted white clouds lay below, and the dim star-laden sky above was still lit by the twilight glow of the setting sun.

Several thousand feet above her and to the west, Kenada could see the last glints of the day's sunlight reflecting off the aluminum bellies and wings of airliners heading west. It was a strange contrast, this peaceful and beautiful world meeting her eyes, and the intensity and harsh volume of all the radio communication invading her ears. Ironically much of the radio chatter flooding the airwaves was because of her. The presence of an unidentified aircraft in a major air-traffic corridor always got air-traffic controllers excited, especially if it was flying against the traffic.

Kenada could hear the Richmond air-traffic controller calling to the unidentified military aircraft, asking for identification. *Here's one controller who's been paying attention,* she thought. *He must have picked me up on his screen not long after takeoff and assumed I was military because I was so close to Langley. Of course,*

*there's not too many Cessnas with a rate of climb of ten
thousand feet per minute.*

Kenada could hear other air-traffic controllers trying
to contact her for some form of identification. Her frequency scanner was also abuzz with chatter. She had
taken it out of her breast pocket and clipped it to the
knee board strapped to her right thigh. Now she could
see what frequency the scanner was tuning in on. At
the moment it was searching through a range of UHF
frequencies. After all, those would be the channels her
attackers would be communicating on. Commercial
liners were always tuned to FM frequencies.

There it was, a call from the navy radar controller on
UHF frequency 497.2. "Range Cat Flight Three Five,
this is Big Eye."

"This is Three Five. Go ahead."

"Three Five, this is Big Eye. Turn to course three four
zero and descend to seven thousand. Intercept and escort back to base or destroy an F-15 at your two o'clock
position, altitude six thousand feet and forty miles."

Before he could respond, the lead pilot heard the
voice of his radar intercept officer (RIO) on the intercom say, "Hey Packman, what the hell do you make of
that?"

The pilot responded, "Beats me; let's check."

"Big Eye, this is Range Cat Three Five. Please repeat
last transmission." The lead F-14 pilot wanted to make
sure that he had heard that word *destroy* correctly.

The lead pilot looked at his radio to verify that the
discreet frequency switch was in the on position. It was.
That meant that no local ham radio operator could be
giving him a false command.

"Flight Three Five, turn to course three four zero and
descend to seven thousand. Intercept and escort back
to base or destroy an F-15 at your two o'clock position,

altitude six thousand feet and forty miles. I repeat, either escort back to base or destroy."

"Range Cat Three Five, copy RTB F-15 or destroy."

There it was, the call that Kenada was waiting for. She knew from watching all the heads-up display videos that Big Eye was the call sign of the navy's radar controller, which vectored aircraft to intercept targets over the combat training range. Kenada now knew the word of her theft was out, but they still wanted her to return to base. Otherwise they would have said *splash* or *shoot on sight*. Kenada said to herself, "Maybe they think a show of force is enough to make me give up. Well, it's time for a little surprise."

From the vectors that Big Eye gave to intercept and the Range Cat call sign, Kenada knew that these jets were coming from the dissimilar aircraft combat training (DACT) range off the North Carolina coast by Cherry Point. She also knew that they must be on a training flight. More than likely they were unarmed, or at least minimally armed. They might be armed with bullets, but would not be loaded with live Phoenix air-to-air missiles or live heat-seeking Sidewinder missiles. She also knew that since this was a night flight for these jets, they probably wouldn't be armed. Air force and navy jets rarely fired during night training flights unless it was scheduled.

At her altitude Kenada could not be seen from below because of the cloud deck; however she could easily see any jets above her level without being seen. Of course she knew that she couldn't use those clouds to hide from the electric eyes of radar, and for the moment, that was the way she wanted it. It was not time to hide . . . yet.

On her radar display screen she was able to pick up several aircraft ahead of her. There appeared to be a tight group of four blips, forty miles ahead in the ten-o'clock position, traveling west at about ten thousand feet. Kenada said to herself, "Aha. Tallyho, Range Cat."

On Kenada's radar the four ships' IFF squawked back just one four-digit number: 1035. She knew it had to be the Range Cat formation of jet fighters coming back from the range. If she picked them up on her radar she knew they could see her on theirs. Her belief was confirmed when the TEWS (tactical early warning system) screen lit up, showing that a radar threat was coming from her ten-o'clock position. There were a few other blips on her radar scope, but the only other one she was interested in was about seventy-five miles away at thirty thousand feet, and heading her way, north.

Kenada was prepared for this confrontation. It was time for a little confusion. With her IFF still in the standby mode, she punched in the same squawk number as the flight of jets, 1035. She thought, When the time comes, this will mess with any Big Eye controllers' minds.

On the radio Kenada heard the fighters call, "Big Eye, this is Range Cat. We have a radar tallyho on target but no visual."

"Big Eye copies."

With a little smile, Captain Kenada said, "Well, boys, that's just what I've been waiting to hear. It's time to even the odds." Kenada flipped the switch and activated the electronics countermeasures (ECM) pod. At twenty miles she could barely see their red and green anticollision wing lights against the darkening sky. Since her lights were off, they didn't see her. A gray jet in gray clouds was tough to see even in bright daylight, but in the dark it was impossible. Covered by the cloak of clouds, Kenada was invisible. She immediately pushed the joystick to the left, turned the Eagle into ninety degrees of bank, then pulled back into a turn. A thirty-second pause and a hard roll to the right were followed by a complete change of course. This circling maneuver would bring her below and almost behind the formation of Tomcats.

"Big Eye, this is Range Cat; we lost her. Our radar is jammed; can you give us a vector?" There was no answer, just a jamming static, and a high-pitched whine on the UHF radio. The lead pilot said over his intercom to his backseater, "Damn, he must have ECM. Keep looking for the Eagle; we should be seeing it anytime now."

Kenada was keeping a close watch on the flight of jets coming her way. As she came closer she dipped a little deeper into the clouds. On the armament panel, she flipped the arming switch for the 20mm six-barreled Gatling cannon. When she was almost underneath them, she could see how vulnerable and unprepared for battle they were. They were still in a tight formation, not the spread-out combat formation, and with their lights on. *This is too easy*, she thought. *I see you guys don't remember Pearl Harbor.* She was now in their blind spot, right under their tails.

Kenada prepared for battle and ran through her checklist out loud. "Armament panel to guns, throttles, military power, ECM—off, IFF—on." She pulled hard on the stick and instantly went into a six-G climb at the Tomcats above. With nothing but four F-14 bellies in the sight of her HUD, she unloaded the pull on her stick and let loose a raking 20mm strafe on the undersides of the lead jet and the right wingman. The three-second burst of 20mm combat mix from the six-barreled Gatling cannon in the right wing root sounded like a two hundred–decibel air horn from a diesel truck. A total of eighty-six rounds flew from the Eagle at speeds of over a thousand feet per second, and almost instantly they found their mark.

Like lasers against the dark of the night, the tracer incendiary rounds, the armor-piercing rounds and the high-explosive rounds ripped through the metal and instantly crippled two jets. The right wingman, wingman 3, felt the hits through the control stick. He saw the streaks of tracers cut through the air between him and the lead plane and slice into the lead's right wing and engine bays.

The right wingman took hits in the right engine afterburner, the fuselage fuel cell behind the canopy and the left engine compressor section. While pulling hard right on the stick he instinctively reached up and pulled the left red-glowing fire "T" handle on top of the dash. He didn't even verify against the other engine instruments to see if he had a fire in his left engine. He knew he did. For the moment, he could still barely fly, but only on half power on one engine.

With horror the right wingman saw the tracers erupting through the top skin of lead's airplane, and in a slow-motion instant saw the skin peeling backward from the aerodynamic forces of the wind, revealing the ruptured fuselage fuel cell and the flaming engines. A moment later there was a catastrophic failure of the lead's right engine turbine. Fragments of the turbine ripped through the air and the midsection of the jet like a rocket on the Fourth of July. The combustion section of the left engine was pummeled by the shrapnel, and repeated the same scene with a similar engine failure. The explosion engulfed the jet in flames from the engine bays back to the tail. In another instant, the back half of the lead's jet was reduced to a skeletal framework and a ball of flames.

With a quick snap on the stick and a hard left kick

on the rudder, Kenada went into a climbing vertical barrel roll fifty yards behind the flight of jets.

The lead pilot and the right wingman were stunned with disbelief. The lead pilot, Packman, screamed into the radio, "We've been hit! We've been hit!" The backseater in the lead's jet heard the thunderous roar of air whistling past the shattered canopy behind him. He could feel the heat of the flames on the exposed skin on the back of his neck. A quick glance confirmed his worst fears. He didn't have to be told; he knew it was time to get out of Dodge. He yelled out the key warning words over the intercom: "Eject, eject, eject!" To himself he recited the emergency procedures for ejecting: "Arming handles raised, triggers squeezed." The ejection sequence had been initiated, but the canopy didn't move. The canopy ejection mechanism was damaged by one of the 20mm rounds that had ripped through the floor behind the backseater and out the back part of the canopy. Even though the canopy stayed down, the rest of the ejection mechanism functioned as designed. A flash of light came from the backseat of the lead jet's cockpit, followed 2.5 seconds later by a duplicate flash in the front of the cockpit. The Aces II ejection seats worked as advertised. They catapulted the two crewmen through the canopy, first the backseater, then the pilot.

The crewless lead jet fell out of formation with an uncontrolled nose-low pitch, dropped down to the cloud deck a thousand feet below and disappeared. The right wingman pulled his stick hard back and to the right with flames trailing off his right wing. After another explosion in the operating engine, another pair of ejection seats launched its crew into the cold night air.

Wingmen 2 and 4, the two jets on the left side of the

lead, were also stunned. They saw the tracers explode through the top wing skin of the lead jet and the right wingman's plane. They even saw the gray blur of the Eagle roaring and climbing above them from behind. "Hey, he's using real bullets! What the hell's going on?"

The lead wingman, 2, had changed his focus. Instead of watching his lead jet, he whipped and turned his head to see where his attacker was. First right—nothing—then left—nothing—then up. There it was. He yelled a desperate radio call to warn his wingman: "Break, break, break."

Wingman 2 found the Eagle and saw that after passing behind them it had now pulled a hard Immulman maneuver and was nosing down to start another strafing pass, this time from above. To counter the threat wingman 2 rolled right in a hard turn.

Wingman 4 on the left heard the break command and immediately cranked in ninety degrees of bank to the left and did a four-G turn to escape. After starting his turn he pitched his head around, looking for the attacker.

Kenada, after slicing behind the formation, slid the speed brake button forward, idled the left engine with the right one still in burner, and kicked the right rudder pedal to induce a lateral yaw with a turning effect, then pulled the stick straight back. As the nose was dropping down and turning on the two jets, she retracted the speed brake and hit full throttles again. She heard the break command and saw the two Tomcats split apart.

Wingman 2 broke away to the right, while wingman 4 broke left. Wingman 2 was making an effective maneuver to evade—he was cutting away from under her nose. Wingman 4 was just breaking away. He hadn't made visual contact with the Eagle yet. Otherwise he

Pat O'Connell

would have known that he was turning into her gun-
sight.

A quick four-second burst ripped into and exploded
the right engine bay of wingman 4. By the time he could
see where the tracers were coming from, it was too late.
His jet was hit. The right vertical and horizontal sta-
bilizers peeled off and separated from the tail of the
Tomcat, along with half of a flaming fuselage fuel cell.
The explosion from the engine flipped the Tomcat over
and sent it spiraling into the clouds below.

Kenada watched the trail of her bullets rip into the
Tomcat. She saw the detonation and watched it plunge
into the clouds. For an instant, even the clouds were on
fire, with a light like the sun shining through the morning fog.

Wingman 2 saw the Eagle closing in on the tail of
wingman 4. He rolled and pulled to come about and
position himself for a gunshot at the Eagle. He could
see the line of tracer fire rip gaping holes into wingman
4's engine bay and cut off half of his tail. And he saw
the Eagle was still in pursuit of 4.

Kenada knew that since she didn't get wingman 2, he
would quickly go from a defensive status to the attack
mode, so she continued her chase of number 4 into the
clouds. She saw that number 2 was turning to follow
her. That was just what she wanted.

Both of them had now disappeared into the cloud
deck below. On his radar scope and his HUD, wingman
2 still had a target pipper on both jets. "I can't see them,
but at least I can track and shoot using radar. But
which is which?" Wingman 2 had just finished saying
this over the intercom to his RIO (radio intercept officer) in the backseat, when he rolled over and entered
the clouds in hot pursuit. As soon as he was enveloped
by the dark grayness of the cloud, his radar screen went

blank. "Damn! ECM! He's jamming us again."

On entering the clouds, Kenada activated the ECM, turned the IFF back to standby, and went into a four-G turn, pulling hard on the stick. With full burner she held her joystick back until she went into an immediate ninety degree climb. This maneuver worked out perfectly. Kenada wanted to fool the remaining Tomcat pilot into thinking that she had broken off the engagement and was making her escape at low level well below the clouds, under the cover of darkness and rain.

Wingman 2 continued his pursuit into the clouds. After a few seconds, he broke out of the bottom of the clouds. He did a quick scan while turning hard right, looking for the Eagle and checking his own tail. He saw nothing but the lights and flames of the three smoking Tomcats, one already a hole in the ground, the other two still spinning crewlessly in flames.

Alone above the clouds, Kenada could see the faint trace of contrails above her. Well, I see that Air Florida Flight 305 is right on time, she thought. She pulled her throttle back out of burner and climbed into the contrail behind the 747 from Miami en route to New York. After positioning herself directly underneath the belly of that whale of a jet, she flipped the IFF back to standby and deactivated the ECM. Now Kenada was visible on radar again, but her radar image blended into the radar reflection of the 747. She looked around and below for the Tomcat that got away but saw nothing but clouds. Except for the aluminum ceiling above her, she was again alone.

Inside the 747 above the Eagle, the chief pilot was Capt. Mark Richmond. For the past few minutes he had been feeling a little worried. He couldn't figure out why several of his avionic systems had mysteriously quit working. He was equally puzzled when the same systems came right back on-line.

The flight engineer and navigator, Nancy Walck, was still concerned. Although all of the systems were back on-line, the Doppler radar was still giving strange readings. Walck hit her intercom button to pass the info on to the pilot. "Mark, all of my nav systems seem OK, but the Doppler radar is giving screwy readings. It keeps jumping between readings of fifty feet and thirty-two thousand."

Richmond keyed the intercom button to respond. "Nancy, go ahead and turn it off. That could be the reason why all the systems went out. I'll call maintenance at JFK to have one ready to swap out when we land."

Captain Richmond's tension eased when everything returned to normal. Little did he know how far from normal his day was about to become.

Chapter Eight

19:40
Pentagon—National Military Command Center

General Price, Admiral Watson and the other battle staff members watched the large screen with its radar display. One of the controllers in the command center had tuned in the UHF radio to the Big Eye controller's frequency. Since they were watching the same screen as Big Eye, it was easy to understand what was happening. The radar screen displayed close to eighty aircraft within a two-hundred miles radius. The radar controller monitoring Big Eye's screen had placed his cursor on the formation of F-14s and the F-15 and clicked them both. This caused the selected blips to start flashing. They could hear Big Eye vector the four-ship formation of Tomcats to intercept the Eagle. On the radar scope the IFF number flashed alongside the radar blip for the Tomcats. The blip for the Eagle was also flashing, but was conspicuously without any IFF numbers.

Price looked over at Colonel Miller. "John, call Big Eye and have the controller isolate and magnify the area with the Eagle and Tomcats."

Miller nodded and made the call. Seconds later Price saw a red square appear around the five jets, and then the area in the square expanded to fill the screen.

In the war room they could see that there was about a forty-mile separation between the Tomcats and the Eagle, and that it was closing fast. The Eagle was cruising with an airspeed of 450 knots; the Tomcats were closing in at five hundred. With a closure speed close to a thousand knots, the forty miles would be covered in less than three minutes. Admiral Watson was arrogantly confident that the navy F-14 pilots would make quick work of the F-15. He said to Price, "Well, Buster, it looks like you're about to lose a jet. Even if that was a real pilot, the Eagle is no match for one Tomcat, let alone four of them."

"Watson, excuse me for correcting you, but we are not about to lose a jet. We already did. As for real pilots, I hope yours are."

Just as it seemed that Price and Watson were about to place bets on who would be the victor, the radar screen went white with snow.

Watson stood up and yelled, "Damn, she's jamming us."

A wave of cursing flooded the room when the images on the viewing screen faded out. After two minutes the images on the screen reappeared. The Big Eye radar controller reselected the flight of Tomcats to get them flashing again, but now instead of four flashing blips on the screen there were five. All five were close together but at different altitudes and heading in different directions. Two of the jets were squawking the same IFF code.

"What the hell is going on? Who's who," Watson yelled, "and where's that damn F-15?"

Price looked at the screen and said, "One of the two jets squawking the same IFF code is the F-15. She must have turned her IFF on to confuse us." Before Price could say more, the IFF numbers beside one of the blips disappeared.

Admiral Watson watched the blip that had just lost the IFF number. The data display beside it showed a conspicuously rapid decrease of altitude. Seconds later it disappeared off the radar screen. "All right!" he yelled. "We got her!" He just knew that his Tomcats would make short work of the Eagle.

A quick cheer and applause filled the war room. The tension level dropped considerably. The country had been saved, and it took navy pilots to do it.

With an arrogant haughtiness in his voice, Watson said, "Well, Buster, that's that. Sorry about your jet. I guess we can come off alert now."

Watson hadn't even taken another breath when suddenly a panic-filled male voice came from the UHF speaker. "We've been hit! We've been hit!" A few seconds later another equally frantic voice shouted, "Break, break, break."

As they watched the screen in stunned silence, a smaller sixth blip appeared momentarily. The data displayed by the smaller blip showed no direction of travel, just a rapidly falling altitude.

"What was that?" one of the generals asked.

The battle staff studied the screen, but before they could answer, the screen went blank with snow again. Another volley of disapproving groans swept across the room.

Over the speakers came the shocking news. In a tense voice the remaining Tomcat pilot announced, "Mayday, Mayday, Big Eye, this is Range Cat Three Five flight. Mark my position. We've lost three jets: lead, and two wingmen. We're returning to base. We lost the Eagle. I saw it dive into the clouds and followed it, but we lost it in the soup. It's probably on the deck below radar. You'd better scramble some helos to this location to locate and pick up survivors."

From the tone of the pilot's voice, they knew he was shaken. They could tell by the swiftness and efficiency of the attack that the probability of survivors was minimal.

Big Eye responded calmly, "Roger, Range Cat, we're scrambling helos now. Is it possible for you to continue searching for the Eagle?"

"Yes, I can, Big Eye, but I'm at bingo level for fuel right now, and in twenty-five minutes you can send choppers for me too. Besides, Big Eye, I've been looking for the past few minutes, and even with radar I can't find it. It must be on the deck somewhere."

Big Eye hesitated before giving the Tomcat pilot the command to continue searching. Price and Watson both knew the reason for the delay. The flight operations officer for the range was trying to decide whether to bet the lives of the two crewmen and a multimillion-dollar aircraft on a shot in the dark.

After the pause, they heard the response. "Range Cat Three Five, this is Big Eye. Return to base."

Price turned to Watson, and with a touch of smugness in his voice, said, "What was that you were saying about real pilots?"

Watson didn't respond. He was still too stunned to be embarrassed. In his mind he wondered, *How can battle-seasoned, experienced pilots be beaten by someone who isn't even a fighter pilot? And a woman at that.*

The radar screen had stayed blank for five minutes; then suddenly it cleared up. The jamming had stopped. Over the UHF radio came a distinctly female voice. "Big Eye, this is the Eagle and I'm in the F-15."

"Go ahead, Eagle. Where are you; what do you want?"

"Big Eye, I want you to deliver a message to the president of the United States. I want ten thousand pounds of gold bullion loaded onto a KC-135 and airborne in seventy minutes or I will destroy a major metropolitan area. Do you understand, Big Eye?"

"Eagle, this is Big Eye; could you repeat the last transmission?"

"Negative, Big Eye, you heard me the first time. Also, I will rendezvous with that tanker and refuel over Lexington, Kentucky, in seventy minutes. Pass it on. I'll be listening on Guard. Don't call me; I'll call you. Eagle out."

"Eagle, Big Eye . . . Eagle, Big Eye, respond please."

There was no answer. They suspected Kenada knew that Big Eye was stalling. If they kept her talking long enough, they could triangulate her position and send jets to intercept her.

Admiral Watson's shock and confusion had now turned to rage. Now that the navy had lost three jets, he felt that the navy should be in charge. Its honor was at stake, and he was the one to get it back. He turned to Price and the rest of the staff, and in an authoritative voice said, "OK, it's time to set up a trap. This Eagle is heading toward Lexington, and since we can't seem to find her on the radar, then she must be flying at low level. We need to combine our forces and set up a gauntlet to trap her. This is how I think it should be done. . . ."

Admiral Watson went into great detail describing how to set up the gauntlet and how to spring the trap. He described where intercepting jets needed to be positioned, how many, the type of armament they should use, and how and where to scramble tankers and AWACS aircraft.

Price, too, had been surprised by the short but deadly encounter between the Eagle and the Tomcats. In less than five minutes she had downed three of the four jets. What he found most amazing was that the Tomcats had gone down by guns and not missiles. This Captain Kenada must be an exceptional pilot, he thought. Admittedly, he was horrified by the turn of events, but in a small way he was pleased. To Price it just proved that the best air force jet was better than the best navy jet. After all, if a novice nonfighter pilot could best four experienced fighter jocks and their weapons officers in the navy's best jets, well, it stood to reason that the F-15 was a better jet. Unfortunately for Price, he did not realize that the real decisive factor for this engagement was Kenada's advantage in having the element of surprise, not the quality of the flying machines or the experience of the crew in them.

Watson continued detailing his plan as to how to weave a net to entrap the Eagle. But General Price didn't hear a word. He said nothing. He was mad at himself for so quickly underestimating this pilot's flying abilities. Price remembered something he had heard Gen. Chuck Yeager say years ago: "The ability to be a great pilot doesn't depend upon the shape of one's genitals." To himself Price said, "Well, Chuck, your words were never more true. This Captain's damn good. I seriously misjudged her. I won't let that happen again."

Chapter Nine

19:50

For the moment things were quiet. If Kenada's tactic was successful she would not be detected until she was on a fifty-mile final for JFK International Airport in New York. The weather and the darkness were to her advantage. Since she had given her ransom demands and requested a tanker over Lexington, she knew they would not be expecting her to be heading for New York. In addition to giving her the element of surprise, this would also give her close to an hour without being disturbed by any intercepting jets.

Kenada settled her Eagle into the slot, a position directly underneath the tail section of the huge 747. The only thing she had to do now was follow the jumbo jet to New York. In comparison to her fighter, the 747 was big and slow, but flying at this altitude and speed would save fuel that she would need later.

In the relative calm under the jumbo jet Kenada started to prepare for the rest of her mission. It was time to program the detonation coordinates for both of the Knight Hawks.

With her left hand she reached up to the armament control panel and switched the select switch from GUNS to MISSILE 1. Under the armament control panel a six-inch video monitor lit up. Flashing on the top of the screen were the words SECURITY CODE. Kenada touched out the code on the number pad, then touched the word ENTER. Even while she wore Nomex gloves, the screen was still sensitive to Kenada's touch. The screen went blank for a second, then displayed SECURITY CODE APPROVED, ARMING MODE ENABLED. The screen blanked out again, and then two words appeared, RADAR and COORDINATES, each in a square. Kenada touched the word COORDINATES and the screen changed. It prompted her with the word LATITUDE. Kenada touched the number pad on the screen below the prompt and typed out N40.00'00" ENTER. The display changed again and now flashed LONGITUDE. Kim touched out W72.00'00" ENTER. The monitor changed again and prompted the word ALTITUDE. Kenada touched 50.00 and the word MILES, and then ENTER. A map of the New York area appeared with a flashing circled X off the eastern end of Long Island. On the bottom of the screen was displayed MISSILE ONE and the coordinates that Kenada had entered. She touched the words CONFIRM and SET on the screen. The screen now said MISSILE TWO. Kenada repeated the procedure and touched in the coordinates N38.53'45", W77.02'50", and 800 FEET. This time a map of Washington, D.C., appeared, with the flashing circled X directly over the Washington Monument.

After she touched in CONFIRM and SET, the display

screen prompted her with two more words, LAUNCH MODE and STANDBY. She touched STANDBY. She reached back to the armament control panel and turned the SELECT switch back to GUNS.

Now that both missiles were in the standby mode, their navigation systems would be continually updated by the Eagle's inertial navigation computer and the satellite global positioning system (GPS). This computer link between the Eagle and the Knight Hawk missiles was what gave the Knight Hawks their deadly accuracy. Not that pinpoint accuracy was that important—with that warhead it could miss by a mile and still destroy its target. As the saying went, "Being close is only good in horseshoes, hand grenades and nuclear weapons."

Now that both missiles were programmed, all Kenada needed to do to launch one was to turn the SELECT switch to MISSILE ONE or TWO, flip up the cover on the guarded switch on the stick and then squeeze the trigger. It would be so easy to do that, but it was important to continue the ruse of a ransom. Otherwise, world opinion would be swayed if the truth ever came out.

As Kenada settled in for the hour-long flight and held her position under the 747, she thought back on all of the things that had brought her to where she was now. Things were so much simpler when she was younger.

She remembered her cadet days at the Air Force Academy in Colorado Springs. They were long, hard days, full of sunup-to-sundown classes and studies late into the night. They were fulfilling and happy days. Academically they were the most challenging and demanding days of her life, as well as the most satisfying. Socially, though, it was a time of romantic doldrums. Even though she was surrounded by a few thousand men, the cream of the American crop, the academy lifestyle was not conducive to romance. In fact, her studies and schedule kept her too busy even to think about dating. Because of her shyness, Kim wouldn't ask any of the male cadets at the academy out on a date even when the opportunity presented itself.

Another paradox that had diminished Kim's social life was "pretty-girl" syndrome. The male cadets wouldn't ask her out because they were either afraid of being rejected, afraid they were not good enough or, worst of all, they assumed that because she was so beautiful somebody else had already asked her out. The real irony of her situation was that if they had asked, she would have gladly gone out with them. Oddly enough, most of the male cadets would've given anything just to be stranded on a deserted isle with her. Unfortunately most of them were too intimidated by her beauty even to ask her out.

After four long years of study, newly commissioned 2d Lt. Kim Kenada showed great promise for her military career. She graduated number one in her class. She was also the first woman to receive the top athlete award at the academy. Many of Kim's professors predicted that if she continued performing the way she did, she would be the first woman chief of staff of the air force. She had everything to live for. Life was good.

After graduating from the academy she went into undergraduate pilot training (UPT) at Williams Air Force Base, Arizona. It was one of the high points of her life. During the yearlong course in UPT, her ability to fly changed from that of a ham-fisted novice to that of a golden-handed wizard of the wind. She wore her airplane well.

Second Lieutenant Kenada graduated at the top of her UPT class. Because of her flying skills she was selected to remain at Williams as a flight instructor in the T-38s, the air force's supersonic jet trainer, a position she gladly accepted. Kenada knew that if she played her cards right, she would more than likely continue flying high-performance jets, even possibly transition into a fighter aircraft in four years on her next assignment—maybe a next-generation fighter like the F-22. The only alternatives were the heavy cargo jets, no fighters.

Under her oxygen mask Kenada started to smile while reminiscing about those days. She remembered the thrill of flying and couldn't believe she was paid to have so much fun. As quickly as it came, though, the smile faded into an angry frown when she felt that familiar searing pain within.

Kenada remembered the incident that had started it all and was the source of all of the hate and anger she felt pent up inside.

It started at a promotion party for several officers in the squadron who had been selected for their next rank: the squadron commander, Lt. Col. Sam Dickman, who was selected for colonel, Maj. Stephen Levesque, who was selected for lieutenant colonel, and three first lieutenants, Kim Kenada, Brad Smith, and Mike Teboe, who were promoted to captain.

In addition to the promotion, Kenada had another reason to celebrate. Along with her new rank she was given her new assignment. She had been one of the first women in the air force selected to be a fighter pilot. She was to have that honor as an F-15 pilot at Tyndall AFB in Florida. In three months she would be at fighter lead in school, flying in the jet of her dreams.

The promotion party was at Colonel Dickman's home. He was a handsome man and he knew it. He stood six-two with a full head of dark blond hair, and deep, sky blue eyes. His winning smile was even brighter against his dark tan.

Basically Dickman was a fun guy and was well liked

by the other officers in the squadron, and even by some of their wives. His prowess with the opposite sex had been well known in his younger, single days. Marriage kept him monogamous for several years until boredom eventually set in. Then Dickman resumed his feminine conquests, however more discreetly. Like so many other fighter jocks, Dickman had a big ego, and was used to getting his way, even with other officer's wives.

Kenada went to the party with Capt. Skip Pruitt, who was also an instructor pilot in the squadron. He stopped by her apartment off base to pick her up. When Kenada came to the door wearing a low-cut black velvet dress, Skip was speechless.

The dress was sleeveless, tight and hemmed at mid-thigh. Skip couldn't help himself. His gaze alternated between Kenada's ample cleavage and her mile-long legs. He was in heaven. He never realized how much beauty had been hidden by her baggy flight suit.

Kenada brought Skip's hormones back in check and broke his trance by saying, "Well, are we going?"

Skip blushed a little when he realized that he had gone stupid in a hormonal brain lock. He looked at her face and said, "Oh, yes."

Kenada grabbed the matching short black velvet jacket and put it on. She picked up her purse and closed the door behind them.

She went with Skip, not as a date, but more as a convenient escort. She knew of Dickson's reputation as a womanizer. She had been on the receiving end of his advances on numerous occasions, but had ignored him. Since she would be with someone, Kim thought that Dickman would curb his advances, especially while his wife was around.

But Skip had an agenda of his own. He had offered his chauffeur services with the slight hope of falling into Kenada's favor. He was sure Kim knew of his amorous feelings toward her, but she still only considered him a friend. He hated that. He wanted more.

At the party Kim had been nursing her second beer for at least an hour and was enjoying the festivities along with everyone else. Skip had stayed close to her during the evening, telling jokes and swapping stories about the antics of their students. Each of the IPs were telling "can-you-top-this" stories to see which had the worst student.

Kenada remembered how Skip had brought her a beer and then instigated a little chugging contest with her and the other two captain selectees. She didn't see any harm in it; she wasn't driving, and this would have been only her third beer. She couldn't smell any harm either. She didn't know that Skip had mixed her beer with vodka. She downed the beer, hardly tasting it, let alone tasting anything in it.

After the chugging challenge, Skip could see his plan falling into place. Kim would get drunk, her resistance would be down and tonight when he took her home, he would score.

It was getting late and the party was thinning out. The music was still loud, and Kenada was starting to feel faint from the vodka.

She went upstairs to get her jacket from the master bedroom and sat on the bed for a moment to put it on and to regain her bearings. Feeling a little dizzy, she knew that in the morning she was going to regret drinking that third beer. She lay back on the bed, giggling, and fell asleep.

The next thing she remembered was feeling a great weight on her body. She couldn't move. Her hands were held tightly together above her head and she could feel strong fingers interlocked with hers, keeping her arms from moving. Her knees had been bent and were split wide apart, but something was holding her ankles together.

In horror she could feel . . . it. The repeated thrusting of him into her. Realizing that she was being raped shocked her into sobriety. Kenada started to fight. The rapist covered her mouth with his to muffle her screams and forced his tongue into her mouth.

Kenada was not totally defenseless. With a deep anger, she knew she had to fight back, but how? Just then she remembered Felix, her childhood pet that she had found in a Maryland pond. She also remembered the lesson that Felix had taught her. At that moment she thought, I know what Felix would do.

After she caught her breath, Kenada relaxed her body and stopped struggling to give her rapist a false confidence. The rapist sensed the change and probed his tongue deeper into her mouth. Kenada then bit as hard as she could. She clamped down on the intruding tongue and part of his lower lip till she could taste blood. She clenched her jaws on his tongue and lip as tight as she could. She could feel her front teeth cut deep into the flesh of his tongue. It was as if she had ripped a big bite from a raw steak. From that moment on Kim would have a new appreciation for her childhood pet Felix, a snapping turtle.

It worked. Her hands were released and the rapist pulled himself off of her. Now it was his turn to scream, and he did, but it was muffled. Kenada still clenched her teeth together on the hunk of partially severed flesh in her mouth. She could feel his hands pulling on her face, desperately trying to force her mouth open. She finally let go when she began to choke from the blood flooding her mouth.

Nausea overcame Kenada and she lost the contents

of her mouth and stomach. Vomit mixed with the rapist's blood splashed onto him, the bedspread and the remaining coats. It was not a pretty sight.

She kicked the rapist off of her and with a loud thud he fell off the bed, screaming in pain. He started to run to the bathroom, only to trip on his pants, which were down at his ankles.

Now that this rapist was away from her, Kim was shocked by who it was. It was Colonel Dickman. Dickman stood up and was desperately holding his tongue with one blood-covered hand and trying to pull up his pants with the other. The bedroom door opened. There in the open doorway stood the colonel's wife in shock and disbelief. Behind her and equally shocked was Skip.

The following day Kenada was supposed to be on an out-and-back flight with one of her students. Instead she was at the security police headquarters pressing rape charges against Colonel Dickman. Colonel Dickman spent the night in the base hospital's emergency room having his tongue and lip reattached.

As soon as he was released from surgery he too went to security police headquarters, not under arrest but to press charges against Kenada for assault.

The next few months were extremely painful. There were two different military court cases, one against Colonel Dickman for rape and the other against Kenada for malicious assault. Colonel Dickman was acquitted of the rape charges. He claimed that she followed him into the bedroom and locked the door behind her, and that she was trying to seduce him. No other witnesses testified, and it was his word against hers. In such situations where it was a colonel's word against a captain's, the colonel usually won.

Mrs. Dickman could have testified against her husband, but she wouldn't for fear of losing her meal ticket. If Dickman was convicted of the rape, he would do time; he would lose his promotion as well as his commission. Mrs. Dickman was most concerned about her husband losing all of his retirement benefits. If the colonel lost his benefits, so would his wife. Mrs. Dickman knew that even if they got a divorce, she would still be entitled to half of her husband's retirement check.

Captain Pruitt wouldn't testify against the colonel for fear of reprisals. After all, the colonel was his boss and his friend.

Colonel Dickman kept his promotion, but the incident cost him his marriage. Kenada was branded as a troublemaker, a tease and a homewrecker. She was cleared of any malicious assault charges, but Dickman's influence with other officers at Williams destroyed Kenada's future career plans.

The real kick in the face came from the psychiatric doctors on base, some more of Dickman's friends. They had called for a psychological profile test to determine the status of Kenada's mental health. Of course, they determined that her mental health was not stable enough for her to continue flying at this time. Kenada was grounded, and the letters that every pilot fears, DNIF, were boldly stamped onto her personnel folder: duties not including flying. Her long-sought assignment to be an "Eagle Driver" at Tyndall was canceled and forever lost. She was exiled from doing the only thing she truly loved doing, flying.

Two weeks after the court case ended, Kenada had her new assignment. She was kicked out of the cockpit and off the base. She was sent to Langley AFB in Hampton, Virginia, as an aircraft maintenance officer for the 48th Fighter Interceptor Group. She was pleased to get away from Dickman, his influence and the whole ugly mess, but she was crushed and very bitter to be leaving her job flying. What added more insult to the injury was being sent to take care of aircraft that she had would have been flying, the F-15 Eagle. Whenever she watched others fly she felt the pain of extreme jealousy. Water, water everywhere, but not a drop to drink.

At Langley, her life eventually started to return to normal. The following years didn't heal her deep emotional scars—they were still there. The wounds weren't bleeding anymore, but the hate and anger were festering. At least she could sleep through the night without waking up in tears. Her fiancé, Captain Gordon, was sympathetic to her feelings and helped with her recovery. Although they had been dating over a year, Kenada found it difficult to open up to him completely. He was a tender, loving person, but he was still a jet jock. Even though she loved him, there were times when she felt almost consumed with envy when he would talk about what a great time he had had flying a recent mission.

Gordon, on the other hand, was frustrated by his lack of sexual intimacy with her, but he respected Kenada's wishes. He finally proposed marriage to her, and she felt more comfortable and trusting with him. When she said yes to Gordon, she had decided to put her pain behind her and get on with her life.

They had set the date for their marriage, but Desert Storm forced them to move it up. Instead of having a large church wedding, Kenada and Gordon were married five months earlier than planned at the base chapel. After her three-day honeymoon, she and her unit were deployed to Riyadh in Saudi Arabia for the support of Desert Storm and the air war over Iraq. Gordon was part of a different squadron, the 71st Tactical Fighter Squadron, in the 1st Tactical Fighter Wing. His squadron was deployed to Dhahran, about two hundred miles to the east of the Arabian coast.

They wrote to each other almost daily, and called each other at least once a week. The months went by and the war progressed. After the Iraqi forces were crushed and the "hundred-hour" ground war was over, Kenada had earned a well-deserved rest. Her unit was being replaced by a reserve unit coming in, which gave her a few free days. She was able to catch a hop in a C-130 shuttling cargo between the bases.

Once on Dhahran Air Base, it was easy for Kenada to find her husband's quarters, which were only a quarter of a mile from the flight line. Following the directions in his letters, she came to the complex of the bachelor officer quarters, and saw the 71st Squadron emblem, the flying fist. It was a medieval knight's metal glove shaped into a fist with wings on it. She immediately recognized the emblem, and despite the hundred-degree heat of the Saudi sun, she ran up the stairs to the second floor, eager to be with the man she loved.

This war with all of its close calls, with scud missiles, air raids and alarms, gave Kenada a new appreciation for her own mortality. Life was too short. She had enjoyed consummating her marriage those three days of the honeymoon. They had made love till they were both totally contended and drained. Now that they were to be together again, it was time to resume where they left off.

Kenada walked down the hall, checking the room numbers and the names on the doors. There it was, room 211, Captain Gordon. There was music coming from beyond the door. Kenada turned the knob. It was unlocked. With her heart racing she opened the door and started to squeal with joy, but stopped when she saw a pile of clothes on the floor. She stared in utter disbelief. There on the floor was a green Nomex flight suit and boots, along with the white skirt and blouse of a nurse's uniform. She stepped into the room and gently closed the door behind her. Leaving her overnight bag by the door, she walked to the pile of discarded clothing and picked up the Nomex flight suit. The name tag read *Capt. Gordon*. She followed a trail of lingerie that led toward her husband's bedroom, and heard the orgasmic groans of a woman. Peering through the crack of the door she saw her naked husband suckling on the groaning woman's breasts while he lay between her nude legs.

In the few moments she had been in Gordon's apartment Kenada's emotions had gone from joyful anticipation, to surprise, to the pain of hurt from betrayal, and finally to intense hatred and anger. Almost without thinking she walked back over to Gordon's flight suit lying on the floor, picked it up, reached into the thin pocket on the left-leg inseam and pulled out the fluorescent orange-handled switchblade knife that was issued to all aviators.

Clenching the unopened knife in her right hand, Kenada walked softly back toward the bedroom door. She walked over to the side of the bed and stood there unnoticed. Finally the nurse opened her eyes with smiling contentment on her face. When she saw the tall woman looming over them she screamed and clutched Gordon closer to her chest. Gordon had finished and was resting his full weight on the nurse beneath him when he heard her scream and felt her dig her nails deep into his back.

Gordon looked first into his partner's face to see the cause. He turned quickly in the direction of her frightened stare and saw Kenada. Impulsively he pushed himself up and away from the embrace of the naked woman. He brought himself up to rest on his knees on the bed and said, "Kim, uh, honey . . ."

The nurse sat up, backed over to the headboard away from Gordon and pulled a pillow over her to cover her nakedness. With both anger and fear in her voice, the nurse said, "Who are you?"

Kenada, now consumed with rage, just looked at the naked woman and answered her question with a vicious backhand to her chin. The weight of the closed knife in her right hand, combined with the unbridled force of her anger, was as effective as a set of brass knuckles on a street fighter's fist. The nurse's head jolted backward into the headboard; then she slumped forward into unconsciousness.

Gordon, still reeling from shock, said sheepishly, "Honey, it's not what you think. I love you . . ."

Gordon's words only fanned the fire of rage that burned in her heart. Kenada looked deep into Gordon's eyes and with sadness in her voice she said, "You promised to be faithful to me till death do us part, you cheating bastard."

"Kim, I meant it when I said it. Honey, I'm sorry. Please—"

Kim cut his pleading short. "Well, honey, it's time to part." With a flick of her thumb she slid back the safety lock on the knife and pushed the button on the side. The four-inch blade flicked out and locked into position with a metallic click. Kim plunged the stainless-steel blade deep into Gordon's chest, mortally piercing the left ventricle of his heart. He looked down in disbelief, then back up into Kenada's face. Before he slipped into eternal unconsciousness, Gordon coughed and said, "Honey, I'm sorry."

"So am I," Kenada replied.

Gordon fell back onto the edge of the bed, dead.

Kenada turned to the unconscious nurse, put both of her hands around her throat and squeezed. She could feel the throbbing pulse of the carotid artery under her thumb. She held her grip until the breathing and the pulse stopped forever.

Kenada pulled the limp body of the nurse back down on the bed and positioned her the way she had first seen her, flat on her back with her legs spread. She lifted Gordon's body, with the knife still imbedded in his chest, and laid him back on top of the nurse. She took the nurse's hands and wrapped both of them around the handle of the knife. Then she took Gordon's hands and positioned them in a death grip on the nurse's neck.

Satisfied that this morbid scene would look like an attempted rape at knifepoint that had gone bad, Kenada looked around the room for any clues that would indicate her presence there. Seeing none, she walked into the kitchen and rinsed her husband's blood off her hands, then wiped her fingerprints off of the faucet handles with a washcloth. She pulled a tissue from a box on the counter as she walked quietly to the front door and listened. She heard footsteps walking down the hall and heard a door open and close. With the tissue in her hand she quietly opened the front door, poked her head out and looked up and down the hall. It was empty. She quickly turned the lock on the knob, picked up her bag, stepped through the door and gently pulled it shut.

Kenada took a deep breath and then, acting as if she had just arrived, knocked on Gordon's door. Obviously there was no answer. She knocked again, this time louder, and when there was still no answer Kenada called out, "James . . . James, honey, it's me, Kim. James, are you in there?"

Kim wanted to make sure that if anybody was around

they would hear her and know that she knocked on the door but never went into Gordon's apartment.

Inside the apartment across the hall Capt. Steve "Rhino" Jefferson heard Kenada calling. Steve knew that Gordon and Capt. Beverly Jones were in there together. He had walked back from the officers club with them. Steve quickly thought up a plan to save a brother pilot from the scandal of being caught in the arms of another woman. The situation Gordon was in reminded him of the time he had been in a similar predicament. Fortunately for him one of his fellow pilots had had the presence of mind to come to his rescue. It was time to repay the favor. After all, the unspoken code said that what happened while you were away, stayed away.

Steve called Capt. Dave "Dodger" Padgette, another pilot, at his apartment down the hall. "Dave, this is Steve. Gordy is in trouble big-time. He's in his room with a woman, and his wife is at his door."

"No way. Boy, is Gordy going to get it."

"Well, hopefully he won't. I'm going to tell her that I saw him heading to the O club, and then I'll take her there. After we leave, you get Gordy out and have him meet us there."

"Gotcha. That'll work."

The door behind Kenada opened and Steve walked out. "Kim, what a pleasant surprise. I haven't seen you since the wedding."

"Hi, Rhino, it's good to see you too. Do you know where James is? I hear music from his place, but he doesn't answer, and the door's locked."

"You know, he's always leaving his radio on, even when he's not in. Anyway, you just missed him. Not too long ago he said he was going to the club. If you want I'll take you there."

"No, I'd hate for him to come back and then I'd miss him. I'll just wait down in the common area in case he comes back soon."

"Well, Kim, I don't know. He's not on the schedule for flying tomorrow, so he'll probably make a long night of it. Come on; I'll buy you a drink."

"Well, OK, I guess that would be all right. I could really do with something cold to drink right about now. I just got off a C-130, and with this heat, it was an oven."

"Great, let's go. You can leave your overnight bag in my room until we come back." With that Steve took Kim's bag and laid it inside his room and shut the door. The two of them walked down the hall, down the stairs, out the front door and into the heat.

A door down the hall opened and out came Dodger. He ran down the hall and started pounding on Gordon's door. Receiving no answer, he yelled, "Yo, Gordy, it's Dodger; come on out. Your wife was just here looking for you." After a while with still no answer he knocked some more.

At the officers club Kim and Steve both waited impatiently for Gordon to arrive. Kim was cool and stayed calm, but inside the strain of waiting and maintaining the charade was unnerving. *Why is it taking so long to discover the bodies?* she thought. *Surely they would have found them by now and reported the deaths to the security police.*

Steve, on the other hand, was becoming more impatient and angry about Gordy's delay. He thought, *The balls of that guy, screwing Beverly while his wife's here waiting for him.* Steve was beginning to wish he had let Gordy get caught with his pants down. Maybe then he could get Kim on the rebound.

As they sat there and chatted, Kenada knew that the longer it took to be contacted about the deaths, the better chance she had of not being suspected, and her chances of getting away with murder increased.

She knew that Steve was lying to cover up Gordon's infidelity. She knew he was clueless to the morbid circumstances, but was lying to protect a fellow pilot. Just to keep him off guard, Kenada would occasionally suggest that they go back to Gordon's quarters to see if he had returned. Steve would immediately come up with a convincing reason to stay.

Three hours later, Col. Larry Moore, the commander of the 71st, along with two security police sergeants, walked up to the table where Kenada and Steve were sitting. Kenada recognized Colonel Moore as he approached, and both of them stood up to greet him.

Kenada quickly scanned the colonel's face, trying to find an insight into his thoughts, his emotions, but more specifically to see if he had any idea about what she had done.

He doesn't know, or does he? she thought. *If he did suspect me, I'd see anger in his eyes. But he must know; why else would he have brought the SPs.*

Colonel Moore had a very troubled look on his face. Notifying the next of kin was never a pleasant thing to do, and neither was having to arrest someone who was a good friend. "Kim, Steve, I have bad news for both of you. Kim, I'm sorry that I have to tell you this, but your husband is dead."

On hearing the colonel's words Kenada let her face go blank, and she fell to the floor in a dead faint. Steve stood there in total shock. Finally coming to, Kenada found herself being lifted and cradled in Colonel Moore's arms. "Are you all right?" he asked her.

Kenada, convincingly enough, spoke in loud sobs. "No! No! I don't believe you. It isn't true."

"I'm sorry, Kim, but it is."

Kenada sat back down in the chair and, with her face buried in her hands, continued to cry. After a moment she regained her composure, looked into the colonel's face and asked, "Where is he? Was he shot down? I want to see him."

"You can't see him just yet. His body is at the clinic, and the doctors are examining him. If you want, I'll take you there and you can talk to the doctors. Maybe they'll let you see him."

Kim, with a puzzled, forlorn expression on her face, looked into Colonel Moore's eyes and said, "Colonel, I don't understand. Why are the doctors looking at him at the clinic? Did he die in a crash? How did he die?"

"I'm sorry, Kim, I don't know the details yet. When I do, I'll let you know. Would you excuse us for a moment? I need to talk to Captain Jefferson for a moment. I'll be right back."

"Sure."

Colonel Moore, Captain Jefferson and the two SPs walked outside. In a nonthreatening tone the colonel said, "Steve, there's a Major Nelson who wants to talk to you in your quarters. I told him you'd be right over. These two sergeants will go with you."

"Ah, excuse me, Colonel, but what's going on here?" Steve asked.

"Steve, I have bad news for you too," the colonel said.

At that, one of the sergeants held up a little card and started to read it to him. "Captain Jefferson, you are now under arrest for murder. You have the right to remain silent, and you have the right—"

"What? What the hell are you talking about?" Steve was shocked beyond belief. "What, you think that I killed Gordy? I wouldn't do that; he was like a brother to me. In fact, I walked back from here at lunch with him and Captain Davis."

Colonel Moore looked at Steve and said, "Steve, did you ever spend much time with Captain Jones?"

"Well, yes, sir, she's a good friend of mine. Lots of us in our squadron know her. Why?"

Colonel Moore didn't answer. He just looked at Jefferson and said coldly, "Steve, I suggest you don't say anything else until you're in the presence of a lawyer."

The colonel nodded to the two SPs. They stepped forward, grabbed Captain Jefferson by the upper arms and led him away.

Through the glass double doors Kenada could see the two SPs escorting Captain Jefferson away while the colonel came back in. *Boy, this is a twist*, she thought. *They suspect Steve and not me. Talk about irony.*

The official news report for that day included two accidental deaths. One was the accidental death of Capt. James "Gordy" Gordon, who apparently died in his barrack apartment when he tripped on a rug and was impaled by a knife that he was carrying. The other was the death of Capt. Beverly Jones, who apparently died from a broken neck after falling down a flight of stairs while she was leaving her quarters.

Kenada was surprised by the creativity of the people involved with the report, and by how far from the truth it actually was.

To her, the reason for the lie was obvious. When the bodies were found, the investigators for the security police were called in. From the clues in the apartment, the investigators had determined that Captain Gordon was using his knife to force Captain Jones to have sex with him. Sometime while they were having intercourse, Captain Jones got the knife away from Captain Gordon and stabbed him in the chest, killing him. Captain Gordon, as he died, choked Captain Jones to death. This kind of scandalous situation would blemish the names and records of both victims and embarrass their families, not to mention cause a tidal wave of unfavorable publicity. The powers that be decided to cover it up.

Captain Jefferson was not charged with the murders and was released because of a lack of evidence to implicate him. But for a while he was sweating bullets.

Kenada was never told the truth about how her husband died. She did talk to Major Nelson, though. It seemed that he didn't want her to know that he was investigating a murder, and the questions he asked her were couched within normal small talk. After he was satisfied that she knew nothing about Gordon's death, he excused himself and said he had a dinner engagement to go to with Colonel Moore.

There was a short memorial for the two fallen servicemen there at Dhahran. The following day, after the service, Kenada accompanied her husband's body back to the States. The funeral service and burial were held in a little town outside of Dayton, Ohio. Kenada spent a few days visiting with his parents. After all, she had to at least give the impression she was heartbroken. A week after the service, Kenada was back in Riyadh with her unit.

During the transition period, when her unit was being replaced by the guard unit, she found a comforting shoulder and a sympathetic ear in her friendship with a Saudi officer, Maj. Ahneese Ahkmed.

Kenada first met Major Ahkmed under unusual circumstances. It was her third day in Saudi Arabia. She and the other maintenance personnel in her unit were at one of the mobility processing areas, moving newly arrived technicians and their equipment to the different hangar work areas. Normally he never would have met her had it not been for a minor disturbance that he was summoned to resolve.

Major Ahkmed's specific duties were to manage the large group of translators who were serving as intermediators between the American and Saudi forces. During their stay in Saudi Arabia, the Americans were to be treated as welcome guests. Their needs would be provided for by the Saudis.

The translator who was originally assigned to Kenada's unit was finding it difficult to take orders from and deal with a woman, especially one who was a superior officer. In his culture, men did not take orders from women. Kenada could have lived with this translator's cultural bias, but she could not tolerate it's interfering with her duties.

On his first day with Kenada's unit the translator made a major mistake. When he saw that he was to work for a woman, he turned to one of his Saudi comrades and made a particularly nasty remark about Kenada in Arabic. Since Americans rarely spoke Arabic he felt it was safe to say anything he wanted in his own tongue.

This young Saudi translator said in Arabic, "Look at these stupid American men. How can they take orders from a woman? They are following this woman like castrated eunuchs. If she were not American I would take this woman to my house, beat her to show her who is boss, make babies with her, and if she didn't obey me then I would sell her to the whoremongers in the bazaar."

This insult would have gone unnoticed except for two things. One was that he made the statement in Kenada's presence. His second mistake was that he didn't know that Kenada spoke Arabic.

Kenada was furious. She turned to two of the armed

sergeants near her and said, "Come with me. There is someone I want you to arrest."

One of the sergeants, a little puzzled, said, "Yes, Captain, but who?"

"You'll know," was all that Kenada said.

Kenada walked up to the Saudi translator, who was still laughing about his comment. He had his back to Kenada, so he didn't see her coming. The other young Saudi laughed until he saw the American woman marching toward them with two armed guards in tow. He could see the fire in her eyes. In a moment of brilliance he knew that his friend was no longer funny. He motioned with his eyes for his friend to turn around, and said to him, "Be quiet, Amir."

Amir turned around to find the tall American woman standing inches away from his face and looking down into his eyes. He stood silent, and the smile fell from his face when he saw the look in her eyes.

Without breaking the stare, Kenada said to the two sergeants in English, "Arrest this man." And then in Arabic she said distinctly, but only loud enough for Amir to hear, "You are not even fit to have sex with pigs."

Amir was furious. He knew who this woman was, but he didn't care. He was not going to be insulted by a woman. Without thinking he brought his right hand up and slapped Kenada across the face.

Kenada said nothing. She just raised her right knee quickly and forcibly into his crotch. He doubled over, clutching his masculinity in pain. Kenada grabbed him by the hair on his head with her left hand and jerked him up until he stood erect. Without hesitation she drove her right fist into his chin. The force of the blow was strong enough to lift him off his feet and put him on his back.

Satisfied, Kenada looked at the man groaning on the

asphalt, then turned to the sergeants. For the benefit of the man on the ground she said in Arabic, "If he moves, shoot him." Then in English she said, "Watch him. Keep him here until his supervisor arrives."

The two sergeants glanced at Kim and then at the man on the ground, and sharply responded, "Yes, ma'am."

Kenada then turned to the other Saudi translator, who was standing in awe of what had just happened. With her face inches from his she said in Arabic, "You. Go to his superior and bring him here to me now. Understand?"

The young Saudi nodded his head vigorously several times, saying, "Yes, yes, yes."

Kenada yelled at him again in Arabic, "Go! Run!"

The young Saudi did as he was told. He ran.

Fifty yards away from Kenada and the two Saudis were two C-141 pilots waiting for their airplane to be unloaded. Kenada's attractive figure had caught their attention. With time on their hands and nothing better to do, they resorted to a favorite American male pastime, girl watching. They had observed the whole incident, and when they saw Kenada swiftly incapacitate the young Saudi, one pilot said to the other, "Oh, man, that's gotta hurt."

With a chuckle the other pilot said, "Oh, yeah. Must be a case of PMS. Speaking of which, I understand that General Schwarzkopf wants to have women with PMS on the front lines in the desert."

"Is that so?"

"Oh, yeah. Not only are they mean as hell, they retain water."

Both pilots laughed, and one said to the other, "Well, I don't care how good she looks, just remind me not to talk to her at the club."

Knight Hawk

Within minutes, Major Ahkmed arrived with several armed Saudi soldiers, not knowing what to expect. He saw the young man on the ground with several Americans standing by him, their weapons drawn and pointed at him.

As Major Ahkmed approached the group, he recognized Captain Kenada as the ranking officer. "Captain," he said to her, "I am Major Ahkmed. Is there a problem here?"

Kenada looked at the Saudi officer and said, "Yes, Major, there is. I would tell you myself, but I think it would be better if you found out from the source." She turned to the man squatting on the floor and said in Arabic, "Repeat the words you said to your comrade. Be honest or I will tell your supervisor exactly what you said, and then I will ask him to punish you severely."

With fear in his voice the young translator repeated his statement word for word.

Major Ahkmed was shocked, embarrassed and momentarily speechless. Honor was at stake. To insult and degrade an invited guest was extremely bad manners, to say the least, and this man's statement was more than just an insult. He realized a potentially volatile situation had dropped in his lap. He knew he had to apologize for this soldier's insulting remarks. He looked humbly at Kenada and said in English, "Captain Kenada, I am deeply sorry for what this boy has said. He will be punished for his insubordination. Please forgive us."

Kenada turned from the man on the ground to Major Ahkmed and said in Arabic, "He is young and ignorant of other cultures. But he has spoken his words with honesty and with remorse. I forgive him and ask for no other punishment. His embarrassment at being humiliated by a foreign woman should be sufficient. If you agree, no more will be said of this."

Relieved that a major incident had been averted, Ahkmed said with a smile, "Agreed." He then dismissed the Saudi soldiers, and to the young man on the ground he said sternly, "Stand up and go to my office. I will talk to you soon."

Kenada nodded to the two sergeants with her, and they shouldered their M-16 rifles and walked back to the others in their group. Then she said to the Saudi major, "I am sorry for the inconvenience, Major, but I will not tolerate disrespect. It destroys my ability to perform my duties effectively."

Major Ahkmed smiled. He was quite taken with this mysterious Western woman. She was beautiful, powerful, intelligent and even fluent in his native tongue. He had known many European and American women before, but had never met a woman like her.

Still smiling at Kim, he said, "Captain Kenada, please do not apologize for your actions. I understand completely why you did as you did. I admire your ability to show such mercy for his . . . his . . . slanderous disrespect. My punishment would have been much more severe. He is an Omani who was living in Kuwait before the invasion."

Kenada satisfied that the incident was over, said good-bye to the major and turned to leave.

The major started to watch her walk away, but he was intrigued. He wanted to know more about this woman. "Oh, Captain," he said, "please forgive my poor manners. I failed to introduce myself to you. I am Maj. Ahneese Ahkmed. I am the military liaison officer assigned to the American air forces. While you are here, I am to make your stay as pleasant as possible under the current conditions."

Knight Hawk

Kenada smiled at him and said in Arabic, "Major Ahkmed, I am pleased to meet you. I am Capt. Kimberly Kenada. I am the aircraft maintenance officer for the 48th Fighter Interceptor Group, in the 1st Tactical Fighter Wing."

"Captain, please call me Ahneese," the major responded. "I am amazed that your Arabic is so good. How is it that you know my tongue? You must be from here in the Middle East."

"My father is Iranian and my mother Iraqi. My mother didn't speak Farsi, only Arabic and English, so that's what was spoken in our house. My father was assigned to the Iranian embassy in the USA before the fall of the Shah. When the Ayatollah took over, my parents sought political asylum in America. Of course, since I was born and grew up in the States, English is my mother tongue. Major, how is it that your English is so . . . so British?"

"Well, Captain . . . May I call you Kim?"

She nodded.

"My father was a diplomat assigned to the Saudi embassy in London, and my mother was born and bred in the little coastal village of Orford, about ninety miles northeast of London, in Suffolk County of East Anglia. I lived in England most of my life, and I was educated at Cambridge University. I am multilingual, thanks to my mother, who spoke English with a proper London accent."

Both Kenada and Ahneese were surprised by the similarities between their lives. "Kim, there is much we have in common. I would be honored if you would have dinner with me this evening at the officers club," Major Ahkmed said.

"Yes, I would enjoy that too," Kenada responded graciously. "But I must tell you that I am a happily married woman."

"I am envious of your husband. He is a lucky man. But nonetheless I would still enjoy the conversation and your company. I will meet you at the club at eight, if that is acceptable to you."

"Eight will be fine."

Since that meeting the two of them had become good friends, but after the death of Kenada's husband they became even closer.

After Desert Storm, Kenada and her unit returned to the hustle-bustle routine at Langley AFB. Ironically Captain Gordon was the only one in the 71st Fighter Squadron to come home in a box.

Major Ahkmed was promoted to lieutenant colonel and transferred to the Saudi Arabian embassy in Washington, D.C., as the military attache. He had kept in touch with Kenada through letters and phone calls.

Now, two years later, back in the States, it was Ahkmed that Kenada loved. It was his life and his causes that she wanted to share. Ahkmed was destined for greatness, and with him, so was she. If it were not for him, she would not be here doing what she was doing.

"Damn!" An obnoxious beeping brought Kenada's attention back to the here and now. The warning lights on the TEWS scope showed that things were about to become interesting.

Chapter Ten

The door to the Oval Office flew open, and Susan Wilson, the White House chief of staff, raced in. "Mr. President, the situation with this K woman has just gotten worse."

Pethers and Borda both knew that this was not good. They had imagined what this situation could lead to, and their worst fears were about to come true.

Pethers was almost afraid to ask the question. "How?"

"She's just shot down three of the jets that were sent to intercept her, and she's made ransom demands."

"What kind?"

"She wants ten thousand pounds of gold loaded onto a cargo jet or she's going to nuke a major metropolitan area."

Pethers didn't wait to hear any more. He stood up behind his desk and headed straight to the monitor room. Torn between disbelief and anger, he mumbled under his breath as he walked, "Damn, if it isn't one damn thing, it's another. It's not like things aren't bad enough already. We're almost involved in another war in the Middle East. We're in an economic war with Japan. The economy is shot to hell, and we're having double-digit inflation. And now to top it all off, I've got some crazy woman loose with a pair of nukes. Just great!"

Pethers, Borda and Wilson walked back into the monitor room, where McKenna and Price were briefing Howard. Pethers sat down on the table in front of the monitor and said, "Mrs. McKenna, General Price, what the hell is going on? I thought you said not to worry, that you'd have her brought down in just a few minutes. And what's this I hear about a ransom?"

"Sorry, Mr. President," McKenna said, "it appears that we have underestimated Captain Kenada's abilities. Just a few minutes ago she shot down three fighters and has gotten away. Not long after she disappeared, she contacted a military air-traffic controller and gave us her ransom demands. She wants five tons of gold bullion loaded onto a KC-135 aircraft, and she wants to rendezvous with it in seventy minutes over Lexington, Kentucky."

"What! I don't believe this. OK, Howard, what does this mean? How is this going to change things?"

"Well, sir, we've got big trouble now," Howard said. "This woman has already proven herself to be very capable. She has taken on a formation of four F-14 Tomcats manned with war-seasoned pilots all at once, and shot down three of them and eluded the fourth. I don't think we should take any chances. We should assume that she is fully capable of living up to her threat."

Pethers looked at the monitor and asked, "Where is she right now, Alex?"

"Sir, I'm going to let General Price answer that, since he's just gotten the latest briefing from the control center."

"Mr. President, we don't know the exact location of the jet. However, there is a good possibility that she is at a low altitude somewhere between Norfolk, Virginia, and Lexington, Kentucky. She said that she wanted to rendezvous with an airborne KC-135 at 20:45 hours over Lexington."

Coldly and analytically, the president said, "General, can she be shot down without setting off a nuclear explosion?"

General Price stared matter-of-factly into the camera. "If we find her, and catch her by surprise, yes. The key is that we destroy the missiles while they are still on the jet. If she arms them, and launches one or both of them, then it would be almost impossible to stop a nuclear detonation."

"General, what do you suggest?"

"Well, sir, that depends on whether or not you plan to meet the ransom demands."

"Hell no!" the president answered. "There's no way we're going to make that payment! If we did, every terrorist organization east of Egypt would try to extort money from us. Now, General, what would you do?"

General Price knew this question was coming. The trick now was how to answer it. The most difficult part about offering a suggestion to the president was phrasing it in a way that would not alienate him. If the president decided to take command and not listen to the advice, he could blow the whole situation into a nuclear disaster.

Price had already prepared a few alternatives for the president. He knew that neither the president nor the secretary of defense had any military experience or background, and both of them had a history of distrust and dislike for the military.

The president was personally in favor of reducing the size of the military so he could divert more funds to his pet social programs. Needless to say, he had not made friends in any of the services. Price also knew that neither of them had faced any predicament at all like this before.

General Price took a deep breath and moved closer to the camera. His face filled the monitor, which almost gave him an omnipotent presence in the room.

"Mr. President, before I give you my suggestion, let me inform you what has been done so far. Although we don't have her on radar, we believe that she is somewhere east of Roanoke, Virginia, and that she is heading toward Lexington, Kentucky. We believe this because she said she wants to rendezvous with a tanker there. She also wants five tons of gold bullion. Since there is only one source for that amount of gold, Fort Knox, which is not that far from Lexington, we are sure that she is heading in that direction. We don't know her motives, but we here on the battle staff think that she wants to take the gold and the two nukes to the Caribbean, most likely Cuba. Anyway, sir, with that in mind, this is what we've done so far.

"We've scrambled armed fighters all up and down the East Coast. We've also scrambled three AWACS aircraft to enhance our radar capabilities. The AWACS radar has the look-down capability that will help us find her, and also has a computer deciphering system to negate the electronic countermeasures pod used for jamming radar and radio."

General Price backed up from the camera and sat on the desk behind him. He had positioned himself so that his image would appear on the right-hand side of the president's monitor, leaving the president a good view of the main monitor screen in the control center. The screen now showed a narrow map of the eastern sea-board. In the center of the screen was a red-highlighted corridor that extended from Norfolk, Virginia, to Lexington, Kentucky. In the center of that there was a large yellow circle.

General Price motioned the screen and said, "Mr. President, the main screen behind me displays the probable path that the stolen jet is on and will follow . . . that is, if in fact she's going to Lexington. The yellow circle, which has a radius of three-hundred miles, shows all of the areas within the range of the Knight Hawk missiles. The numerous blue dots on the screen represent the locations of the airborne fighters. The larger blue circles indicate the location of the AWACS aircraft. The green dots are the locations of fighters on alert on the ground that are ready to be launched.

"What I would recommend, sir, is that we say that we agree to meet her demands to pay the ransom, and arrange for a tanker to rendezvous with her near Lexington. We then allow her to pass into this corridor, intercept her somewhere over West Virginia and shoot her down long before she ever gets to Lexington.

"There's one AWACS aircraft that is starting a sweep of this area from the western end and working east. Once we find her position, we will vector the closest fighters along the corridor to intercept and engage her in combat. Shooting her down over West Virginia will pose the least amount of danger of radiation contamination because it's sparsely populated."

The president mulled over Price's suggested strategy

and looked for possible weaknesses. It seemed logical, and for the moment, he couldn't think of anything better to do. "Howard, what do you think about that?"

Howard squirmed a little bit in his chair. He too was clueless as to just what to do. Reluctantly, he agreed with Price's plan of action. "Sir, it sounds like a good plan to me."

"OK, General, go for it. Mrs. Wilson is going to stay on-line here, so keep her posted." Pethers looked at Wilson and said, "I want an update every five minutes, or whenever something new happens, understand?"

"Understood." With that the general walked off-screen, leaving Wilson with a clear view of the main viewing screen in the control center.

Pethers hopped off the table, walked around it and sat in the center chair. He looked up at the ceiling as if for the answer. After a moment of pondering, he turned to Borda and Howard and said, "We will continue with the address and press on as if nothing is happening. Howard, I want you to go over to the Pentagon now and monitor the situation. Let me know when anything important happens."

Howard stood up and said, "I'm on my way. I'll report back to you when I'm in the battle staff room."

"Well, Yolanda, we'd better get ready to go, ourselves. I'm on in less than an hour. Wilson, you got it, so watch the fort."

As Pethers and Borda left, Wilson replied, "Will do, sir."

Chapter Eleven

Col. Ed Rupert knocked on the door to the war room and was waved in by Price. Under Rupert's arm was a thick manila folder containing a freshly printed computer document. Behind him were two women, one an attractive blonde, five feet six inches tall with short curly hair. She was dressed in the uniform of an air force colonel. The other woman was two inches taller, equally attractive with brunette hair, and dressed in a gray plaid business suit.

"Sir, I have that information you requested on Capt. Kim Kenada. We've brought in two experts to help us get a quick analysis. They're working together on that congressional study about women in combat. This is Dr. JoAnne Laut, a psychiatrist from Malcom Grow at Andrews, and Dr. Debra Hollidge, a civilian psychiatrist from Johns Hopkins in Baltimore. Dr. Laut's specialty is the behavioral study of women in combat situations and hostile environments. Dr. Hollidge's work has been on women's behavior under stress. She has also been involved with studies of criminal behavior of women."

Colonel Rupert handed the thick folder to Price. He quickly flipped through it, and as he handed it to Dr. Laut he said, "Doctors, come with me."

The three of them walked into the battle staff room, where General Price motioned Drs. Laut and Hollidge to the front in the center of the horseshoe-shaped table. At first Dr. Laut was a little overwhelmed by all of the rank in the room. She had never addressed so many generals at one time, let alone all of the Joint Chiefs of Staff. She overcame her uneasiness by concentrating on her briefing. She refrained from the old speech class trick of imagining them in their underwear. Somehow that would have been inappropriate. Dr. Hollidge was unfazed by the brass—as a civilian, she was unimpressed by rank.

General Price addressed the members of the battle staff and introduced the two newcomers. Both doctors waited for the din of murmurs in the room to silence before starting. Everyone there wanted to hear about this mystery woman.

Admiral Watson was the first to speak. "Well, Doctors, what have you got?"

The two doctors looked at each other to see who would start; then Dr. Laut turned to the head of the table and said, "Admirals, Generals, does the phrase, 'Hell hath no fury like a woman scorned' mean anything to you?"

By the hushed silence in the room, Dr. Laut knew that she had everybody's undivided attention. "We've had a few minutes to go through the personnel folder of Capt. Kim Kenada, and from the few details we've uncovered, we believe this Captain Kenada is the proverbial loose cannon. She is a woman with a score to settle, and it appears that she is going to do it in a big way. She feels that life has treated her unfairly, and now she is taking revenge. We don't know all of the details of this current situation, but we know that in a mental context, she is obviously a very dangerous woman, and we are on the verge of a serious incident.

"Captain Kenada is a perfectionist, an overachiever, and from her academy grades and her SAT scores we can tell that her IQ level is in the top five percent. From her high school transcripts we've seen that she's also artistic. This would indicate a high degree of creativity as well as intelligence. With that combination, I would say that this woman can be very unpredictable.

"We've examined her recent history for any motives that would cause a change in behavior from positive to negative. It appears that Kenada has always thrived in a stressful and demanding environment. However, in the last few years it appears that she has experienced several significant emotional events that have triggered a behavioral change. The causes for her behavior seem to be the unsubstantiated rape by her squadron commander, losing the case, getting transferred from her job as a flight instructor, the death of her husband, and last but not least, the fact that she has been selected for separation by the presidential reduction in force program.

"Basically, her world has crumbled before her eyes. The same service that she planned to be a leader in is now kicking her out the door. I would say that now she's hurt, mad, and is striking back."

Dr. Laut paused to let her words sink in, and also to

answer any questions her audience might ask.

The first was from Admiral Watson. "Doctors, do you think we can negotiate a deal with her?"

"That is a possibility I would not count on," Laut responded. "She is the one dealing from strength. In addition to that, she probably knows that there is little that we could offer. I'm sure she would not believe an offer of amnesty, especially since she has engaged in combat and killed. I would also say that she is prone to kill again. To her at this moment it will make no difference whether she kills one more person or a million people."

Dr. Hollidge stepped forward and said, "Although we believe that revenge may be the primary motive for Captain Kenada's behavior, we also believe that there must be more to it. There are a few more missing pieces to this puzzle that we haven't figured out yet."

Admiral Watson was a little puzzled. "What do you mean by that, Doctor?" he asked.

"Well, Admiral, in most situations where revenge is the motivation, all of the behavior is usually directed at a specific person or a group of people that the individual feels is responsible. For example, disgruntled postal workers don't walk into their workplace and start shooting everybody; they usually target their specific supervisors or other coworkers who have caused conflict with them."

Admiral Watson was still trying to figure out the significance of Dr. Hollidge's statement. "I'm sorry, Doctor, but I seem to have missed something. Could you explain once more what you're saying?"

"Yes, Admiral, we feel that revenge may be part of Captain Kenada's motives, but we do not believe it is her main motive."

Dr. Laut again spoke up. "The reason why we believe

there is more than revenge at work in this instance is because, up to this moment, Captain Kenada's behavior has been very rational and calculated. She is performing tasks that because of their complexity are best done by a calm, rational and logical mind, not a mind clouded by hate or other intense emotions."

"Doctors, can you give us a little more history about this woman," General Price asked. "Specifically, her cultural and family background."

Colonel Rupert answered the general's question. "Sir, it appears that Kenada is a first-generation American. On the EEO form in her folder she lists her ethnic background as Persian. Persia is the old name for Iran. Her parents both immigrated to the U.S. from Iran back in the early seventies after the fall of the Shah. Her parents were part of the Iranian embassy staff in Washington, and when the Shah was deposed, they asked for political asylum. There is no religious preference listed in her personnel folder; however, we assume that Captain Kenada was raised under a Moslem, Middle East influence. In her personnel folder we've found that she is also multilingual. In addition to English, she also speaks French and Arabic fluently."

General Price was surprised by the last tidbits of information. They didn't quite provoke more questions, but he found Kenada's Middle East background disturbing, as well as something to think about. He looked around the table and asked, "Does anybody else have questions?"

Admiral Watson spoke up. "That's a fine report, Doctors, but how in the hell does this woman know how to fly that jet? Is she some kind of trained spy or something?"

Both doctors stammered for a moment. They were unprepared for this question. In their preparations they hadn't had time to look at everything in Kenada's records.

Colonel Rupert, the chief of personnel records in the Pentagon, was standing off to the side. "I can answer that question, sir," he said.

As he walked to the center of the room, he looked at Price and Watson and said, "I've done a quick review of Captain Kenada's personnel folder, concentrating on her officer effectiveness reports, and over her six-year career she has held the positions of an undergraduate pilot training flight instructor and an aircraft maintenance officer. One of her duties as a maintenance officer was the maintenance of the F-15 simulator. Being an instructor pilot would mean that she was an accomplished pilot, and being in charge of the simulator would mean that she had the means to learn how to fly the Eagle and use all of its systems.

"All of her ratings have been straight ones. As for her flying abilities, she's either very good or very lucky. It seems that she is one of the few people who have ever gotten a T-38 out of a flat spin. She has a commendation medal from Williams, which she received for not only saving the life of a student pilot, but also saving the T-38 jet trainer the two of them were in. The write-up in the award says that the student put the jet in a flat spin and flamed out both engines. The emergency procedure when this happens is to eject, but the student blacked out from the G forces of the spin and was unable to. Kenada was able to recover from the spin and restart the engines, which saved the student and the airplane. There's more kudos in here from other things, but basically that's it. Questions?"

Price looked around the room, then said, "No questions? Good. Dr. Laut, I want you to go up front and get the details from Dorchester and D'Auria and then come back to me. I may need your insight when we deal with Kenada. Colonel Rupert, I would like you and Dr. Hollidge to continue reviewing Kenada's file for more clues. You can use that adjoining room behind you."

Colonel Rupert took the folder and motioned to Hollidge to join him in an adjoining room. Together the two of them would finish dissecting the life history and psyche of Kim Keneda.

McKenna, still a little bothered by the course of attack they were following, turned to Price. "General, I think she's lying," she said.

"Who's lying, one of the doctors?" Price replied.

"Oh, no, it's Kenada. I don't think she has any intention of going to Lexington. I think she told us that just to distract us, so we would divert our attention from where she's really headed."

"What makes you say that?"

"Well, first, let's presume that she doesn't want to get caught. If you didn't want to get caught, would you tell everybody where you were going?"

"Of course not," Price responded.

"She said she would bomb a major metropolitan area. Well, to me, the largest metropolitan area would be New York City. Besides having the greatest population density, it's the economic heart of the country. It's the place where one bomb would do the most damage.

"I don't think that her ransom demand is for real either. The file on this woman says that she is an aircraft maintenance officer, correct?"

"Yes."

"Well, if I'm right, the supply line that keeps the spare parts coming is very important to maintaining equipment in an operational condition."

"Mrs. McKenna, get to the point. I can't see how what you're saying has any relevance."

"Stay with me, General, I'm almost there. Aircraft maintenance lives or dies by getting the parts on time to fix things. This woman knows logistics; she's not stupid. She knows what it takes to get something from point A to point B, and I'm sure she knows how long it takes too. Here is my point. Her demand for loading five tons of gold on a tanker in seventy minutes is totally unrealistic. Not because it's an enormous amount of money and we won't pay it, but because it's logistically impossible. Here's why. First, there's only one place in the world where you can find that much gold together in one spot: Fort Knox. It would take almost an hour just to get it out of a vault and load it all on a truck, and another hour to load it onto an airplane. Second, where's the nearest runway to Fort Knox? I'd be willing to bet that it's close to an hour away too. And third, how long would it take us to get a tanker to that airport? If we already had one in the air or ready to take off, it would be at least an hour, right?"

Price nodded. "You're right. Even if all the manpower and vehicles were ready and in place, I'd say that we'd be talking at least three hours."

"Anyway, General, since this woman knows logistics, she must have considered how much time it would take to fill her demands. She has to know that her demands are impossible, but to her that doesn't matter because she doesn't think that we can or will meet them. That's why I think she's lying."

Suddenly the proverbial lightbulb lit above General Price's head. He turned to the other members of the team and was about to give a command when McKenna's words tickled his subconscious. *What if she isn't going to Lexington?* he thought. *If I were going to nuke a major metropolitan area for the greatest effect, which city would I choose? New York, Washington, Phil-*

adelphia, Pittsburgh, Richmond, Atlanta or maybe Chicago. If I were going to ransom a major metropolitan area, it sure as hell wouldn't be Lexington. Price frowned and said, "McKenna, I agree; my first choice would be New York, with Washington as a close second. As for the ransom, I think you're right; she has no intention of going to Lexington."

Price took a quick scan of the radar terminal monitor, and picked up the phone to one of the controllers in the control center. "Colonel Miller, play back the recording of the Cherry Point radar screen just before it was jammed and the F-15 disappeared. We need to find out what other aircraft were in a fifty-mile radius at that time, where they were going and where they are now. After that we need to scramble armed fighters out to intercept them and make a visual confirmation that she isn't hiding in the radar shadow of another jet. Start out with any of those jets that were heading north toward New York."

"I copy," Colonel Miller responded.

"Oh, John, if they find her, the use of deadly force is authorized."

To clarify Price's direction, Miller repeated, "Shoot on sight, shoot to kill?"

Price considered the finality of his words, then said, "Yes, but only after they have a positive target confirmation. We can't have Rambo pilots shooting down everything they get their sights on."

Chapter Twelve

Suddenly there was a green flashing light from the tactical early warning sensor (TEWS) screen, accompanied by a corresponding warning beep coming through Kenada's earphones. The light was flashing in the seven-o'clock position on the three-inch circular screen. Kenada knew that she was found. Her TEWS, a fighter pilot's version of a radar detector, had sensed somebody's radar trying to lock onto her for tracking. She was still eighty miles out of New York City, and dropping down in altitude to twenty thousand feet. *Well, it seems they finally got around to checking the possibilities,* she thought. *I was wondering how long it would take for them to send a jet to look for me here.*

She cranked in eighty degrees of left bank and pulled back hard on the stick. This gave her a three-G quick-descending left-hand turn to the west. *It's time to see who I have for company.* She continued her turn until she had completely reversed her course. Then she scanned the skies with her eyes and radar to find her hunter.

The stars above were now bright in the clear, dark winter sky. Beneath her was the broken cloud deck. Through the gaps in the clouds Kenada could see the lights of some coastal New Jersey cities. Visibility was excellent, in fact too good. She could see the running lights of over fifty big commercial jets going into the Jersey airports within fifty miles of her. *Which one is it? Let's see if radar will help. Ha! Bingo, that's got to be him.* Kenada found a bright blip on her radar display. It was thirty miles directly ahead, twenty degrees above the horizon, heading right for her, and closing fast.

She gripped the small joystick on the bottom of the radar control panel and used it to move the cursor on the radar screen directly over the blip, then tapped the track button. Now the radar tracking information would be shown in the heads-up display. As she looked through the HUD she began to chuckle. She could clearly see that the square radar-targeting window was around what appeared to be one of four stars in a row. How ironic, she thought, that I should find my hunter in the constellation named after a hunter. The targeting square had framed an extra star in the belt of Orion.

Kenada had no sooner identified her threat than the flashing light on the TEWS turned to a steady light, and the warning beep became a steady tone. *Would you look at that*, she thought. *He's got a lock on, and at this range.* Kenada checked the range again. Her hunter was now at twenty miles, and there was another blip at eighteen. She looked back at the square in the HUD and could now see the rocket flame and plume of an incoming air-to-air missile. Talking out loud to herself, she said, "You stupid jerk, who do you think you are, Captain

Kirk? You didn't even get close enough for a visual to make sure I'm your target."

Kenada assumed a defensive posture. She turned the Eagle so the missile would be coming at her from the ten-o'clock position. Nine miles. She flipped the ECM switch back from STANDBY to ON. She reached over to the countermeasures panel and punched the chaff button. On the underside of the Eagle's tail section, nestled in the fuselage, a cigarette pack–sized box was explosively ejected out of the chaff carrier and into the airstream. A second later, the small box exploded, scattering thousands of thin strips of aluminum foil. The cloud of aluminum strips would reflect more radar energy back to a tracking radar than an aircraft. If the strategy worked properly, the radar-guided missile would lock onto the stronger radar image and go for the chaff instead of her airplane.

Seven miles. Keeping the flaming missile plume at the ten-o'clock position, Kenada pulled back and to the left on the stick and held it. The Eagle went into a three-G barrel roll at the oncoming missile. Five miles. Another touch of the chaff button.

The light on the TEWS and the tone in the headphones were still steady. Two and a half miles. Kenada continued the barrel roll and punched the chaff button again. "Come on, damn it, get off my butt. Go for it." She pushed the throttle into full burner, and pulled three more Gs. The G suit inflated completely, constricting the blood flow to her legs and lower abdomen.

The steady tone was still screaming in her ears, and at a mile away, the rocket plume looked like a flaming telephone pole coming at her. Half a mile. Kenada punched the chaff button twice and kept pulling on the stick.

Now inverted and at the top of the roll, Kenada saw

the plume pass within five hundred feet underneath her and continue on. The ECM blinded the missile enough so that even the proximity switch didn't activate a detonation. Kenada stopped the roll, flipped the ECM back to STANDBY, and checked the radar screen and HUD. "Where is that guy?" she muttered aloud. "There he is. Five miles, ten-o'clock high. Three miles. Two miles." She initiated another three-G barrel roll to bring her into head-on climb at her aggressor, and turned the ECM back on. "Now is not the time for him to get a good lock on."

There was a tiny flash in her rearview mirrors. The AIM-7 radar-guided missile that had been fired at her finally detonated. One mile. *What a dummy, he's still got his anticollision lights on. Doesn't he know you're supposed to turn your lights off when you're in combat? It will be a piece of cake to get on his tail.* Kim pushed her stick forward to drop under the oncoming jet. *I'll use the same maneuver on this guy that I used on those Tomcats. I'll just slide underneath and sneak up on him from behind. He'll never know what hit him.* As she passed underneath, she looked up to see the passing blur of an inverted gray navy F-4 no more than two hundred feet above her.

"Oops." Realizing that the bright light coming from the other jet's canopy was a reflection of her own afterburner flame, Kenada said, "Damn, he's seen me."

The F-4 Phantom immediately rolled over and dove into a split *S* maneuver. Still inverted, the F-4 pulled down in a vertical circular turn to get on the Eagle's tail. Kenada pulled the stick hard and straight back to counter the F-4's move. As she turned she moved the ECM switch back to STANDBY. As she came over the top of the loop, she could pick up the lights of the Phantom almost directly underneath her.

There was an excited voice over her radio making a Mayday call. Kenada didn't catch all of it, but she did hear "Air Florida" and "engine fire."

"It's time to fly the egg," Kenada said to herself under her breath. She remembered sitting in the pilots' debriefing room, listening to pilots talking about how to use the shape of a vertically placed egg to advantage. Starting from the equator of the egg, the jet that circled down under the egg traded off altitude to gain the energy of speed, but it also made a larger turn. The jet that went over the top of the egg traded off speed energy for altitude, but more important, it could turn more quickly to face its opponent, which meant the upper jet would be able to get off the first shot because it was turning inside the other jet.

Coming over the top of the egg, Kenada was able to bring her nose down on the F-4 and line up for a head-on shot. As soon as the targeting pipper in the HUD covered the aircraft cursor, she squeezed off a four-second burst. Three of the 20mm rounds found their mark. Two passed through the left-wing fuel tank, and one hit the left aileron. Other than leaking fuel through the gaping holes in the left wing, the F-4 was relatively undamaged. The burst of tracers did, however, upset the pilots' concentration. The pilot of the Phantom shoved the stick forward to get out of the tracking window of the Eagle. The holes in the left wing also induced additional drag, causing a slower rate of turn.

Kenada rolled 180 degrees so that she could keep sight of the phantom that was about to pass under her belly. *Throttles to idle, speed brake out. It's time to turn the egg upside down.* She brought her Eagle around and again outturned the Phantom. As her nose started to track in on the Phantom's tail, she retracted the speed brake and went to full burner. With the bright lights of the F-4's afterburners tracking into the center of her HUD, Kenada squeezed off another three-second burst. This time her shots were deadly effective. The two J79 engines of the F-4 exploded into flames. Both crewmen in the F-4 ejected into the dark. Kenada throttled back to military power and started a level turn toward New York City. As she watched the flaming spiral of the F-4 disappear into the clouds below, she whispered, "Happy landings, guys."

A few miles ahead she could see the lights of the 747 she had been shadowing earlier. In another two minutes she would be safely cloaked under its radar shadow again.

As she came within a hundred yards behind and below the jumbo jet, she saw the damage. She pulled in a little closer under the left wing to survey the extent of the damage to the 747. Fuel was cascading out of the gaping holes in the bottom of the left wing. Burn marks were all over the engine cowling on the outermost engine and the trailing edge of the left wing. "Well, it looks like you guys didn't take a direct hit, but it was damn close," she said aloud. *"Judging from the shrapnel holes, I'd say that missile went off within a hundred feet. If I had turned off the ECM pod sooner, that missile would have gotten a good lock and you would have been goners. You're lucky."*

Kim stayed with the 747 as it began its emergency descent into JFK International. When the jumbo jet had first depressurized from the shrapnel into its fuselage, it had dropped down to ten thousand feet and leveled off above the clouds.

Kenada tuned in the radio frequency for JFK and checked the radio compass. The DME (distance-measuring equipment) indicator showed sixty-two miles to JFK. The tactical early warning sensor was lighting up again. This time it was in three different areas on the TEWS screen, the eleven-, the ten-, and seven-o'clock positions. *Well, what have we here? I guess they know where I am.*

She dropped down another fifty feet below the 747 to give her radar an unobstructed view ahead while still masking her radar image with the jumbo jet's. A quick check on her radar screen warned her to expect company. On the screen she could pick out five big jets. The HUD marked the jets with pippers, but they were below the cloud deck, so Kenada couldn't see them. Needless to say, they were big blips, and they were neatly aligned at ten-mile intervals for a straight-in approach for the JFK runway.

Off slightly to the left were four more blips, fifty miles and closing. From the tightness of the group Kenada knew they had to be fighters. *Those guys must have scrambled from the New York Naval Air Station on Jamaica Bay. If that's true, they must be F-18s.* She pulled gently back on the stick and tucked her Eagle close below and behind the 747.

Well, let's see what these guys are up to. Kenada turned the radio frequency select switch to GUARD and keyed the mike button. "This is the Eagle transmitting on guard, to the flight of jets departing Jamaica Bay. Return to base. I repeat, the formation of jets departing from the New York City area, return to base immediately, or I will launch my missiles."

Other than the thundering roar of the engines behind her and the whistling wind outside, the world had become deathly quiet. All military jets monitored the emergency guard frequency. There was no response from the formation of jets, and their course remained unchanged. *I know they heard me. The whole military world must have heard me. That's why all of the radio chatter stopped. I guess everybody's waiting to hear what happens next.*

Kim keyed the mike button again. "This is Eagle transmitting on guard. I am flying an F-15 and I am carrying two Knight Hawk nuclear-tipped missiles. I want all military jets to stay outside a fifty-mile radius of New York City or I will launch my missiles. I repeat, all military aircraft stay outside a fifty-mile radius from New York City." The radio remained silent, and the F-18s continued their steady approach.

Well, I guess none of you guys believe me. OK, it looks like it's time to get down to business and prove myself.

Kenada checked her radar screen. Off to the ten- and nine-o'clock positions were three more groupings of blips, between sixty and eighty miles out. *I don't know who you guys are, but I'm not going to stick around to find out.*

Things were about to get busy quickly. Kenada knew that if she turned to the east and ran, that would expose her flanks and leave her easy prey for the F-18 Hornets, not because they were better jets, but because she would be outnumbered and outpositioned. Kenada considered her alternatives. *I could turn to the west and engage the oncoming jets,* she thought. *That would be unexpected. A bit risky, but fun. That would confuse the hell out of everybody. I'd enjoy the challenge, but that would not be sticking to the plan. I need to show them that I mean business. It's about time to launch one, but first I need to get on the backside of these jokers.*

Kenada climbed her Eagle back under the belly of the 747. *I'll wait here until the Hornets pass; then I'll launch,* she decided. *This jumbo jet will at least keep them from launching a missile at me, at least until they can get a clean shot. If I'm lucky, they don't know I'm here.*

Let's see, where are they? Twenty miles. Oh, yeah, they know."

The target-tracking box on the HUD had a lock on the approaching fighters, but Kenada couldn't see the planes in the dark. *No lights. These guys are ready for combat.*

The DME on the radio compass showed twenty-five miles from JFK, and the jumbo jet continued its descent from ten thousand feet. In another two minutes the 747 would be entering the cloud deck below. *Damn, they're closing too fast.* The targeting box in the HUD framed the now very distinct four blips.

One mile.

Suddenly the targeting box split into two as the formation of four divided. Then the two targeting boxes dropped off the bottom of the HUD. Kenada quickly rolled her Eagle to the right. She could see the glowing neon green formation lights of two F-18s streak by a few hundred yards below her. Over her shoulder she could see the twin afterburners of the two jets pulling up to get behind her.

"Well, boys and girls, I can't stay here any longer," she said as she pushed her throttles forward past the detente and went into full burner. She could feel the rapid acceleration from the additional thrust. She dropped her nose down slightly to give herself clearance from the 747 as she passed one hundred feet underneath.

With her radar she picked out the next jet liner on the approach to JFK. She maintained her course, but dropped down into the clouds.

Inside the 747, fear was the emotion of the day. All that the crew and passengers knew was that there was an explosion by their left wing and that it was on fire.

They knew that pieces of metal peppered the left side of the fuselage, and now air was screaming through the small holes. The danger of a rapid decompression had passed, and the oxygen masks still hung from the ceiling above the passengers, adding to the level of tension.

The 747 pilot, Capt. Mark Richmond, thought his number-one engine had blown up sending shrapnel into the fuselage and the wing. He pulled that engine's fire handle to cut the fuel flow. The fire on the number-one engine went out.

As the F-15 passed underneath, everybody on board the 747 was shocked again by another loud explosion. This time they were lucky; it was only a sonic boom. Unfortunately the passenger in seat 32D didn't know it was a passing jet. He went into cardiac arrest.

Kenada reached over to the arming control panel and switched the number-one Knight Hawk missile from STANDBY to ARM.

On the monitor came the message, REALIGNMENT OF INERTIAL NAV COMPUTER IN PROGRESS. Underneath the message, a TIME TO ALIGNMENT clock was counting down: 02.00, 01.59, 01.58, 01.57 . . . "Damn, that wasn't in the manual. This isn't supposed to happen. The ECM must have dropped the comm link from my inertial nav to the missile's navigation computer. I know those guys will be on my six in a minute. I need to look for cover." 01.53, 01.52, 01.51 . . .

The little TEWS screen was starting to light up again, this time from the five- to seven-o'clock positions as well as from the nine- through twelve-o'clock positions. "Trying to get a lock on, I see. Well, I'll just have to stay in the crowd. They'll have to get close enough for guns. With all of these jets around, missiles will hit the wrong targets. That will buy some time."

The alignment clock continued its countdown: 01.47, 01.46 . . .

On the HUD there were two target-framing squares pointing out the two jets on final approach to JFK, and about fifteen to twenty other pippers marking distant inbound jets. The closest liner was three miles ahead, and the other about twelve. The DME showed Kenada about eighteen miles out of JFK. She steered toward the closest blip with a five-hundred-knot closure rate. "Let's see, at this speed I'll be by that jet in about twenty-five seconds and at JFK in about ninety seconds."

01.41, 01.40, 01.39 . . .

Seven thousand feet. Still in the cloud deck, Kenada nervously kept a close watch on her HUD. Her instrument cross-check was becoming intense. She centered the target-framing square in the HUD and kept an eye on the distance. Slamming into the ass-end of a jet liner was not how she wanted to end this flight.

01.35, 01.34, 01.33 . . .

Airspeed at 750 knots, two miles to the first jet.

01.30, 01.29 . . .

One mile. Kenada pushed the joystick forward slightly; the altimeter reading on the HUD fell more quickly. Six thousand feet, still in the clouds . . . Half a mile, 5,500 feet, still in the clouds. As Kenada approached the liner, the image of a big bug smashing into a windshield popped into her head. With a little grin she thought, I don't think I could scrape a bug that big off my windshield.

01.25, 01.24, 01.23 . . .

Suddenly, like fireworks beneath her, the lights of Newark, New Jersey, came into view. Beneath the canopy of clouds the drizzle had stopped, and visibility was good. Even at twelve miles away the dazzling lights of the Big Apple dead ahead were easily seen.

Although the anticollision lights of the jet ahead of her were almost lost in the city lights, Kenada could tell by the large, dark silhouette against the lights that she was coming up to a DC-10.

Over the headphones she could hear intermittent tones beeping. *What idiots. They're trying to get lock for a radar shot. I'll have to use this jet for cover.*

01.05, 01.04, 01.03 . . .

Airspeed 950 knots. I'm sure those 18s are not far behind. Where's that other liner? There it is. The target-framing box had captured the blip of the other liner dead-ahead about nine miles. Kenada could see the runway lights directly ahead of the liner. *He's about two miles from landing and looks like he's on the glide slope dropping out of 2,000 feet. I should be there in about twenty-five seconds.*

00.59, 00.58 . . .

The tones in the headphones stopped for a moment. *They must still be behind that DC-10. Now I can concentrate on the traffic and launching this sucker.*

00.57, 00.56, 00.55 . . .

Kenada pushed the joystick slightly forward, and the nose of her Eagle pointed straight at JFK's landing lights and the Lockheed L-1011 on final approach. Airspeed 975, eight miles to JFK, seven and a half to the jet. Kenada glanced at all of the glowing blips on the TEWS radar screen. The threats that had been off in the distance in the nine- through eleven-o'clock positions were now just over twenty miles away and closing fast. In less than a minute, they would be within striking distance.

00.54, 00.53, 00.52 . . .

Suddenly the beeping lock-on tone drowned out all

of the other noises on Kenada's headphones. Six miles to the jet and seven to JFK.

Kenada started jinking random movements of the stick to try to keep the pursuing F-18s from getting a radar lock. For a few seconds it worked.

00.51, 00.50 . . .

The beeping tone on the headphones turned steady. *Damn! Somebody's got a lock on me.* The TEWS showed the threat coming from directly behind him. Kenada whipped her head around to the left and right to look for a missile. None. She reached over and punched the chaff button just in case they fired. The tone remained steady. Four miles to the jet ahead. In the rearview mirror on the bow of the canopy, Kenada could see the faint light of the approaching missile coming closer. *Damn! They've launched.*

Kenada fired off two more salvos of chaff, and this time included flares. She chopped the throttle back to the idle power setting, slipped the speed brake button to the out position, and pulled hard back and to the left on the stick to try to outturn the missile. She grunted and tightened her abdominal muscles to fight the eight Gs. Her G suit inflated snugly against her legs and lower torso to constrict the blood flow going to her lower extremities, but it wasn't enough. Her sight turned into tunnel-vision before it totally blacked out. Fortunately for Kenada, the G suit did make a difference. She could still hear, feel and think, but with these G forces, not for long.

The AIM-9L exploded one hundred feet below and behind the Eagle. Kenada heard and felt the missile detonate. It was close enough to give the Eagle a good shake, like hitting a speed bump at ninety miles an hour. She unloaded her pull on the stick and her vision came back. A quick glance at the gauges and at the wings showed that everything was OK. Her evasive maneuver had put her in a barrel roll, but with a slight dive. She retracted the speed brake, advanced the throttle back into full burner and continued the roll till her wings were level.

00.32, 00.31, 00.30 . . .

Kenada had dropped down to a thousand feet and was now a mile from the jet ahead. The lights of JFK a mile and a half dead-ahead were a beautiful sight. From her angle the runway lights looked like a giant Christmas tree outline. The sequential strobe lights, along with the brilliant white approach lights pointing to the runway, added to the image.

The beeping tone was back. This time the RTS on the TEWS radar screen showed the threats were coming from behind and to her left. The liner ahead was on the glide slope, coming down quickly, making a faster-than-textbook approach. The air-traffic controllers there at New York Central were going berserk, and had advised the Continental 727 out of Atlanta to expedite its landing on runway four, right.

In the New York Central Air-Traffic Control Center, panic was rampant. Overtaxed controllers were already busy directing the normally heavy evening traffic. With the sudden addition of twenty plus military jet fighters flying five times the normal speed of the liners and all converging at JFK from different directions and altitudes, the controllers were overwhelmed. They had never faced a situation like this before. Thirty-plus commercial liners on approach or in holding patterns, an in-flight emergency, air combat between fighters, radar-fouling chaff, air-to-air missiles, and now supersonic fighters chasing each other against the normal flow of traffic. Things were not going to be easy.

Finally the lead controller had a sudden insight as to

what was about to happen. He could see the mixup was turning into a controller's worst nightmare, and it wasn't getting any better. He made a judgment call and directed all of the controllers to divert traffic to Philadelphia, Washington and Boston. He also had them shut down JFK and LaGuardia.

For the pilots of the attacking fighters, it was a different story. They were like a school of blood-crazed sharks in a feeding frenzy in the middle of a school of whales. Each of these hotshot jet jocks saw Kenada as fresh meat, and since they were briefed that she was not a fighter pilot, they assumed that she would be an easy kill. Or so they thought.

She had become a prized target, and a chance for them to become national heroes. Whoever shot down this Eagle could make his claim to fame as the savior of America. Well, maybe of New York City. No American pilot had ever fought against an F-15 in actual combat, let alone shot one down. Sure, many of the pilots had gone one-on-one with an Eagle at various times and places, but only under controlled situations, and even then it was against brother pilots who had gone through similar training in aerial combat.

Little did these pilots know that Kenada, because of her lack of conventional training, posed a deadly threat. She was intelligent, unpredictable, elusive, fearless and had a take-no-prisoners attitude. She was a wildcat being chased by a pack of hunting dogs, and she had nothing to lose.

The air-traffic controllers watched in awe and disbelief as the drama on their scopes unfolded. All they could do was watch. A wall of fighters was converging on the JFK aerodrome, and the blips on their radar scopes were moving so quickly, it was next to impossible to track each individual jet. Before their radar had time to scan the skies in an area, the jets would be gone. 00.10, 00.09, 00.08 . . .

Kenada cleared the backbone of the Continental 727 by a hundred feet as it touched down on the numbers on runway four, right. Slightly off to her left she could see the bright landing lights of another liner at a thousand feet making its approach to runway twenty-two, right. It was a Lufthansa Airbus out of Frankfurt. Her radar showed two groups of fighters coming directly at her from around the Airbus on approach. She knew the F-18s behind her were closing in fast, and if she wasn't careful they'd squeeze off a gunshot right up the proverbial tail feathers. *It's time for a little more confusion*, she thought. *Let's play chicken.*

Kenada reached over to the lighting control panel and turned on her external running lights. She cranked in a quick, hard left and then a hard right. This put her on a head-on course with the approaching Lufthansa jet. The fighters countered her move and were now directly behind the Airbus and coming fast. The two groups were at different altitudes and in loose combat spread. *Looks like they're going to try to get a head-on shot after I clear this jet. This'll mess up their plans.* With that thought Kenada fired off a short burst from her 20mm gun. The tracers streaked directly under the nose of the Airbus.

The Lufthansa pilot saw the approaching lights of the Eagle and the line of tracer fire, and given the choice of dying in a ball of flame or going around, he chose the latter. He went into full throttle, pulled back on the yoke to avoid the collision and started to execute his missed-approach procedures. He had no intention of dying today.

Kenada saw the Airbus pulling up and flew her Eagle directly underneath.

00.03, 00.02, 00.01, 00.00 . . . The arming panel screen flashed REALIGNMENT COMPLETE, then flashed off, and then lit up #1 ARMED.

The copilot of the Lufthansa Airbus, realizing how close they had all come to being a burned spot on the tarmac, looked at the pilot and echoed an appropriate line from the on-board movie they had shown on that flight. "You have chosen wisely, my son."

The sudden climb of the Lufthansa flight was unexpected. The two groups approaching it from behind, with a five-hundred-knot closure speed, had merged into one large group of eight. When the Airbus pulled up, at least six of the eight now had a new obstacle to avoid. Immediately four fighter pilots pulled back on their sticks. Two F-16 pilots pushed their sticks forward to try to drop underneath.

Kenada anticipated that some of the fighters might try to go underneath to avoid the liner. To make sure that her way was clear, she squeezed off a three-second burst. One of the two jets took an incendiary round through the leading edge of its right wing and directly into the right-wing main fuel tank. In the six-hundred-knot wind, the leading edge mushroomed open and pulled the fighter into a hard right yawing turn that progressed into a flat spin. The spinning and aerodynamic forces were too much for the fighter, and it disintegrated in flight. Debris from the explosion flew everywhere. A large portion of the fuselage slammed into the other F-16 that had maneuvered under the Airbus. The thousand-pound piece of flying debris crashed into the cockpit area, bisecting the pilot, then tore deep into the main fuel tank in the fuselage. The results were flamingly explosive. The pilot never knew what hit him.

Kenada pulled her Eagle up and over to avoid a collision.

Knight Hawk

The F-18s on her tail had another sudden predicament. They had initially stayed low, following the Eagle to get off a shot. Unfortunately there was now a huge fireball directly in their flight path. Instinctively, all four F-18s broke formation. The outside two turned left and right away from their group and the fireball. The inside two pulled hard back to climb above the flames and the Airbus directly ahead. For the lead Hornet, this was not a good maneuver. The lead F-18 had no sooner cleared the climbing Airbus then it pierced the underbelly of one of the passing F-15s that flared above the Lufthansa liner. It happened so quickly, neither pilot knew what hit him.

After passing over JFK, Kenada made a hard, banking right. With a quick glance over her right shoulder, she could see three distinct, flaming balls of fire. "Does this make me an ace?" she asked no one in particular.

She reached back over to her light panel and turned off her outside lights. A hundred feet below her and stretching off into the eastern horizon was the line of red taillights of the evening rush-hour traffic on the Long Island Expressway. She kept this line close to her left and used it as a guide away from JFK. *It'll take them a few seconds to figure out where I went, and that should give me all the time I need to launch this sucker.*

On the ground the chaos had just begun. JFK had turned into a war zone. There were three flaming piles of metallic rubble on or near the field. Fortunately, none was an airliner. The crippled 747 that Kim had shadowed had made its landing at JFK amid the rubble of the four jets burning on the ground.

Out of all of the controllers on the ground, the six men in the tower had the best view of the fifteen seconds of aerial carnage. They saw the afterburners of the speeding fighters and heard the roar of their engines a hundred decibels louder than the engines of the airliners. They saw the tracer fire that nearly hit the Lufthansa Airbus. They saw one F-16 jet get hit with tracer fire and go into a flat spin, and then saw it crash into another F-16 aircraft that was following close behind it. That midair collision at low altitude was followed by another at higher altitude, when one F-18 slammed into the belly of an F-15.

As quickly as they came, the fighters were gone. Only the distant roar of their afterburners could be heard above the clouds. Now, seconds after the brief blitz, the only thing left was three flaming bonfires: One large one, where the two jets collided under the airbus, was two hundred yards away from the north end of runway twenty-two, right. The other two smaller fires were the remnants of the F-15 and the F-18 that had collided above the Airbus. After the two jets collided with a closing speed of over a thousand miles per hour, they were both ripped violently apart and ignited. The flaming debris first rose high in the air following the flight path of the two jets, and then arced down to earth and landed in the fields beside the runways. One little child inside the terminal witnessed the fireworks display from the side and saw the two flaming arches hanging in the sky from the ignited JP-4 jet fuel. He turned to his mother and said, "Look, Mommy, McDonald's."

There was chaos on the radio net. Emergencies were being called in by some of the liners that had just witnessed the explosions. Air-traffic controllers were calling the various liners, trying to warn jets away from the combat zone at JFK. Over the guard radio net, Kenada heard somebody calling out to the other fighters, "The Eagle's running east."

Kenada took a quick glance over her shoulder, but

couldn't pick out any of the fighters she had just evaded. She knew they were there, but with all of the lights of the city, the airport, and the fireballs and smoke, it was too visually confusing to see any of the swiftly moving jets. She continued east in full burner. Time to get a little clearance from these guys, she thought.

The radio crackled again on the guard net. "All fighters turn to heading zero eight five and pursue. Target is heading same at deck level, approx. five miles." Whoever it is, Kenada thought, he'll have the fighters on my tail in no time.

Somebody was trying to organize this gaggle of warriors. Without organization they were more dangerous to themselves than to Kenada. The flaming debris midfield at JFK would testify to that.

Since all of the jets had come into the area using different radio frequencies, the only way to communicate with all of them at once would be on the emergency guard radio net. Fortunately for Kenada, she could hear them too.

The TEWS radar screen was lighting up and beeping again. This time the threats were all behind her. The screen showed them coming from the four- through the eight-o'clock positions. From the last radio transmission, Kenada guessed they must be at least four to five miles back. Being so close to all of that Detroit steel on the expressway below probably kept those fighters behind her from getting a radar lock.

Kenada reached up to the guarded switch on the armament control panel, broke the wire seal and lifted the cover. With her thumb holding the cover up, she pushed up the toggle switch underneath it with the side of her index finger and held it in the active position. The screen below the panel lit boldly with the words, #1 LAUNCH READY.

Kenada hesitated before squeezing the firing trigger on the joystick, not from guilt or remorse, but from uncertainty of being in the proper launch window. As she remembered the technical data launch tables on the Knight Hawk missile, she faintly recalled that to best achieve the desired detonation altitude, the missile should be launched from ten thousand feet or above, and with the launching aircraft in a near vertical climb.

Kenada looked back over her shoulder for any signs of the pursuing fighters. It was a futile gesture. All she could see were the lights of Manhattan framed by the twin rudders of her Eagle. The jets were back there; she knew it. She knew that at the moment at least one or two actually knew where she was. The others would be following loosely in a wide, searching spread. She also knew that as soon as she pitched up to launch, all of the rest of the fighters would be able to pick her out and would join in the pursuit.

"Well," she thought, "it's now or never." With that, she pulled back hard on the stick and went into a sixty-degree climb. "At this speed and rate of climb I'll need about twenty seconds."

Two thousand feet.

On the TEWS radar the warning blips continued, but instead of flashing on and off, they were steady. Kenada could hear the beeping turn into a steady tone. *Somebody's got a lock*. With that thought, she punched the chaff button once. The steady tone stopped, then started beeping again.

Four thousand feet.

A second later she was in the cloud deck. Just for good measure she punched the flare button. *If one of those jets fired off a heat seeker, this ought to keep it off my trail at least until after I launch*. Kenada thought that most of the jets were more than four or five miles behind her. If they had fired an AIM-9 heat-seeking missile, it would lose its fix on the afterburners, but it would still follow her exhaust heat into the clouds. A flare on her heat trail would confuse the missiles' sensors.

Six thousand feet.

As suddenly as her external vision had vanished, it reappeared. Now she was alone above the clouds with only the lights of the moon and stars. Launch was just seconds away. A sudden flash of light from the clouds behind her reflected off of her rearview mirrors. Her instincts were correct. *That flash wasn't lightning; it must have been a missile.*

Eight thousand five hundred.

Nine.

The flashing blips on the TEWS again turned steady, and the beeping in her headphones again turned into a constant tone. Kenada looked in her mirror and could see the faint flares of several launched missiles illuminating the clouds below.

"Ten. Time to fly, birdie." Kenada squeezed the launching trigger, then touched the chaff and flare buttons twice. The sky around her suddenly turned to daylight as the Knight Hawk rocket motor ignited and started to speed away. Kim turned her head away from the brilliant light to protect what night vision she had left. With the Knight Hawk missile safely on its way to destiny, Kenada now had to resort back to the defensive mode. She inverted the Eagle, pulled hard back and dove for the deck of clouds below. Behind her she could see the flaming plumes of at least four missiles heading for the still-burning flares and the cloud of chaff she left behind.

As she entered the deck of clouds below, Kenada

switched the ECM from STANDBY back to ON. She rolled her wings level in the clouds, throttled back to mil power, then turned her Eagle to course two six five. *This will take me back to New York, and with this cloud cover nobody will find me.* She was right. Inside the veil of clouds and hidden from the eyes of radar by her ECM, Kenada caught her breath for a moment. She did a quick cockpit check. The TEWS showed that there was no radar threat tracking her.

Down under the armament control panel, the video screen displayed COUNTDOWN TO DETONATION, 1 MINUTE, 56 SECONDS. The inertial navigation system of the Knight Hawk missile had computed the time necessary to reach the point and altitude of detonation, and through the umbilical link to the Eagle's central air-data computer, transferred the data and started the countdown.

Now that the missile was launched, all Kenada needed to do was keep out from under somebody's crosshairs until after the detonation. She knew just the place to hide. She also had to prepare for her ransom of the city. Once the Knight Hawk was detonated, she would have proven she was capable of making good on her threats. Then she would make contact and restate her ransom demands. This time they would be more likely to comply.

Above the clouds, in the pursuing fighters, there was a sense of confusion. They were like hounds hot on the trail of a fox. The pilots could almost taste the kill, but just when victory was almost theirs, the fox slipped into a deep, dark hole and got away.

Of the four missiles fired at Kenada's Eagle, one heat-seeking Sidewinder missile locked onto the rocket plume of the Knight Hawk and tried to follow it. The Knight Hawk had a greater acceleration rate than the heat-seeking Sidewinder, and with its three-mile head start, it couldn't be stopped. The Sidewinder continued its futile chase for almost five miles before it flamed out and turned into a shark killer. It glided back to Earth and detonated on impact in the ocean.

The first radar-guided AIM-9L missile locked onto the chaff cloud and detonated as it passed through it. The next AIM-9L lost its lock during the detonation, but continued its flight. It crashed and exploded in a field east of Center Reach, Long Island. The fourth missile, an AIM-7 heat seeker, tracked into the explosive heat of the first missile's explosion and detonated in the same spot.

The light from the launching of the Knight Hawk had enabled many of the more than twenty pilots to get a visual fix on the Eagle. Unfortunately the flares and the two missile explosions caused enough of a visual distraction to cause them to lose sight of her, as well as to lessen a portion of their night vision. Now that the Eagle was in the clouds, and hiding behind ECM, she was gone. Radios and radars were useless. They were all in the dark, visually and electronically.

There were a few minutes of chaos above the clouds with the pursuing jets. One of the lead fighter jets, an F-15, turned on its anticollision lights so he could be seen by the other jets of his flight. Before he knew it, he had sixteen other jets lining up on his wings, using him as a point of reference. After the fighters were close enough to each other to recognize the fighters from their own units, they regrouped back into their original formations.

The three remaining F-18s from Jamaica Bay had taken enough, and were returning back to base. They had seen their lead jet perish in a ball of flames. They had lost sight of the Eagle they were chasing, and now with somebody using ECM, they had no idea where to go other than back to base. They reduced throttle and cruised back at a slow two hundred knots of airspeed, using the lights of the city as their visual references.

Chapter Thirteen

The battle staff watched the whole event unfold on a monitor that displayed a radar scope of one of the New York air-traffic controllers. They first started to view this particular airspace after the members of the battle staff were alerted by the F-4 that an unidentified aircraft was shadowing a 747 going to New York.

General Price's hunch was correct. Since the AWACS aircraft as well as all ground radar had been unable to find the Eagle in the corridor between Lexington and Norfolk, then it must have been somewhere else. Price had guessed that the Eagle was hiding in the shadow of a commercial liner.

Plane against plane, an F-4 was no match for an F-15. The F-15, being younger than the F-4, had the advantage of thirty years of technological progress. It

165

was faster, more maneuverable, accelerated more quickly, and had better avionics and weapons systems.

The members of the battle staff couldn't be chosey. They didn't care what type of fighters they sent; they had to send what was available. With luck, the skill and experience of the pilots would be able to compensate for the technological disadvantage. After all, this woman in the F-15 was not a fighter pilot.

In his mind, General Price was comparing what he knew about the two planes. He knew nothing about the skills of the pilots in the Phantom or the Eagle. He remembered what his father used to say: "A good plumber needs good tools; a poor plumber needs better tools." I hope that F-4 pilot is a very good plumber, Price thought, 'cause this Kenada woman definitely has better tools, and she knows how to use them.

From almost twenty miles away the F-4 was able to detect two aircraft where there should have been only one. When the F-4 was scrambled, the pilot was ordered to terminate the F-15 on contact if it was found. Once the F-4 pilot confirmed two aircraft instead of one, the members of the battle staff, against Price's better judgment, ordered him to launch a missile as soon as he acquired a radar lock on the F-15.

They had been able to monitor the F-4's radio frequency as well as the guard radio net and hear some of the chatter. The F-4 had kept them informed of the sequence of lock-on, missile launch, and then there was the ECM jamming. While the F-4 was engaging the Eagle, air force and navy controllers were vectoring scrambled jets to intercept it.

When the jamming was off, they could see both jets in combat, the F-15 and the F-4. Then the F-4 was gone. They also heard the 747 making its Mayday call and declaring an IFE, an in-flight emergency.

The next few minutes were extremely confusing, to

say the least. To the trained eyes of radar controllers, tracking all of the normal commercial traffic in the New York area was tough job, but to the members of the battle staff it was impossible. The convergence of close to thirty jets onto JFK all at one time was too much. Even with the IFF transponders replying to the radar with identification codes, the blips were now too close together and too fast to tell who was who.

The radio chatter was more informative. When the radio calls came in saying that two F-16s were downed by the Eagle, the members of the battle staff were shocked. Then there were more radio calls saying that an F-18 and an F-15 had been downed. Admiral Watson summed up everybody's emotions in one word: "Unbelievable!"

General Price was amazed at the turn of events and said, "Who is this woman? In less than an hour she's bagged three F-14s, two F-16s, one F-18, one F-15, and one F-4. Hell, that's more kills than most pilots get in a lifetime of flying!" Under his breath he said to himself, "Damn, I wish we had more pilots like that."

The battle staff members also had their worst fears confirmed. On the radar they all saw a tiny, unidentified blip move quickly off the screen. When one of the pursuing pilots radioed that the Eagle had launched a Knight Hawk, they knew that detonation was not far behind.

General Price picked up the hot line to the White House. He could hear the ringing on the other end; then a voice on the other end said, "This is Pethers."

Price took a breath and said, "Mr. President, I believe we have a launch from the Eagle. There's no word of a detonation. If there is one, it will occur within five minutes."

"General, what's the range of her missile? Can her missile reach us here in D.C.?"

"Yes, sir. Her range is approximately three hundred fifty miles, so that could put it anywhere between Maine and Maryland."

"Can you tell what direction the missile is headed?"

"No, sir, all we could tell was that it was traveling vertically when it disappeared from radar. That would more than likely indicate that the missile was going suborbital, and her intended target was closer to the maximum range of the missile."

There was a pause in the volley of questions from the president; then in a hurried tone, he said, "Thank you, General. We are going to seek shelter in the bunker just in case Washington is her target. I'll call you back from there." The phone went silent with a click.

The White House

Pethers and Borda made a hurried exit from the Oval Office. Pethers headed for the bunker, and Borda went to the video comm room to get Watson. The two then split up to round up all of the staff and send them down into the basement.

In the lowest basement level there was one main bunker constructed back in the early fifties at the start of the Cold War. An office area and command post were part of the bunker complex. Over the years, through the various administrations, the bunker had been equipped with the best communication systems of the times.

The bunker, large enough to house fifty people, could not hold all two hundred of the White House employees. The rest of the White House staff filed into the old train tunnel that years ago had connected the White House to the Capitol building. The musty and dimly lit tunnel had been sealed off during the Eisenhower administration, and the old electric train no longer ran.

Knight Hawk

President Pethers and the rest of his cabinet went into the bunker's command post area. The lights were on, and the three duty officers were busy following their checklists. Ironically the three were in extremely good moods. They finally had something to do to break the boredom. This could be the day they were always practicing for.

The senior duty officer snapped to attention and announced, "Mr. President, everything is ready. All communication lines are operational, and the video comm line with the battle staff has been activated."

"Thank you, Captain." The president walked into the video comm room and sat behind the desk opposite the large viewscreen. General Price's image was on the screen, but he was turned toward the monitors in the Pentagon command center, so he was unaware of the president's arrival.

As the president sat he asked, "General, is there any change to report?"

General Price, hearing the president's question, turned and said, "No, sir, Mr. President, we have not had a detonation yet. As for the Eagle, we don't know where it is at the moment. After she launched her missile she activated her ECM and disappeared. She could be anywhere within a hundred-mile radius from New York City. I'll let you know as soon as we hear of the detonation and where it is."

"Thanks, Price, I'll be here waiting." Pethers turned to look at some of the computer monitors that the bunker crew was watching.

Vice President Borda, standing beside Pethers, commented, "In light of the situation, Rick, I think we should postpone your State of the Union address."

Pethers thought about the suggestion and said, "You're probably right, Yolanda, but let's wait a few

169

minutes. What we do next depends on when and where that bomb goes off."

Pentagon

The suspense of waiting for a detonation was beginning to unnerve Price. The longer it took for it to detonate, the closer it could be getting to Washington. Price couldn't help but wonder if D.C. was the target. He began to wonder about the survivability of the Pentagon. They would be safe there in the subbasement from a close nuclear blast, but getting out from all of the rubble from the upper floors could be impossible. Price thought, How ironic it would be to survive the blast, only to starve to death or suffocate because we were buried alive.

Chapter Fourteen

Fifty miles west of New York City, two more jets were proceeding directly toward the free-for-all of fighters over JFK. They were too late for the melee and were disappointed to miss the chase above the clouds, but they would enter the scene nonetheless.

These two jets, F-16Cs, were painted with radar-absorbent paint in an ominous flat gray black paint scheme. They were equipped for combat in a special arena: the dark arena of night. These jet ninjas were F-16 Night Fighters from the Air National Guard 174th Fighter Group. They were flying out of Hancock Field near Syracuse, New York. Even at that distance, they could see the light from the exploding jets light up the clouds like flashes of lightning.

Kenada had picked them up on her radar. Oddly enough, though, on her radar screen were two IFF numbers without radar blips. She didn't worry about them. They were too far away to be a threat, especially since she had at least twenty other jets within shooting range. The two F-16s were just passing over New York City at eight thousand feet when they started to lose radio and radar functions. Within seconds all radio and radar functions were gone. Each of them knew by the quick onset of the jamming that they were flying directly into the sphere-of-influence for the Eagle's ECM. Fortunately for them, ECM had no effect on their infrared cameras and imaging equipment.

With their infrared equipment they could see the heat image of the distant missile explosions over fifty miles away. Traveling at seven hundred knots, they would be there in less than five minutes. They could just barely make out the exhaust heat trails of all the fighters pursuing the Eagle, but at this range they couldn't tell who was who.

The lead F-16 was piloted by Maj. Len "Scooter Pie" Richardson. He was nicknamed for his fondness for that snack with the same name. Richardson, a city boy from the Bronx, escaped from that borough with a scholarship from Columbia University in New York City, and then landed a pilot slot out of OTS (officer training school), for the air force.

Richardson's wingman was Capt. Lonnie Ray "Cajun" Ledet. His nickname came from his ancestry and place of birth, a back bayou southeast of New Orleans. His ticket off the Mississippi delta was a football scholarship to Louisiana State. He was good as a gridiron jock, but he knew that he wasn't professional quality, so he planned for a conventional future.

Ledet had picked up his commission through the ROTC. His wings came from undergraduate pilot training (UPT) at Columbus Air Force Base in Mississippi. Ledet disliked living in New York. It was a world apart from his life on the bayou, but he loved to fly. The only reason he was flying for Syracuse Air National Guard was because Delta had made him an offer he couldn't refuse. Ledet would do his weekly piloting duties for Delta out of JFK, and on weekends he'd fly Falcons for the Guard.

Both pilots had considerable combat experience. Between the two of them they had five kills in Operation Desert Storm. Both pilots were very comfortable with combat in the dark. Night fighting reminded Ledet of the times in his youth when he and his dad would hunt alligators at night on the back streams and bayous of the Louisiana delta. For Richardson it was like roaming the city streets with his gang as a teen.

When Richardson and Ledet were fifty miles west of the city and saw the faint glow on the eastern horizon, they thought it was the renegade Eagle being toasted. But after hearing the various radio transmission announcing the losses, they knew the fight was still on. Like moths to a candle they were drawn to the fight. They now had a multimillion-dollar flare to follow right to her.

Flying toward the fading glow in the distance, both jets were using their updated APG-68 radar systems, which had been enhanced with the Westinghouse Night Sight system. This forward-looking infrared (FLIR) system was also equipped with a helmet-mounted video display. Their radar was able to pick out the gaggle of jets fifty miles east of the city. When the ECM jamming started, their radar systems dropped off-line and left only the infrared systems operating. At this range, that wasn't enough. Their infrared cameras were able to pick up only the flash of heat from the exploding missiles, not the jets in the dogfight.

The Westinghouse system was state-of-the-art, and was developed as a result of the demands put on fighters that flew in Desert Storm. The system was designed to give fighters the ability to be effective at night and in all-weather attack scenarios. It gave the pilots a video-quality resolution, but most important, it was steered by the position of the pilot's head, and it displayed directly on the pilot's helmet visor. In essence, wherever the pilot looked, his infrared cameras looked. It almost gave the pilots the illusion that they were flying without a plane. Ultimately, this system gave the pilots better situational awareness, which meant deadlier and more effective pilots.

As for disadvantages, the system had three. First, it added almost three and a half pounds to the six pounds of weight of the pilot's helmet. The added weight under normal flight was not a problem; however, in the high-G environment of air-to-air combat, that extra weight would be extremely cumbersome. In a six-G turn, the helmet would weigh fifty-seven pounds, twenty-one pounds heavier than an unequipped helmet.

The second disadvantage of the Night Sight system was that it was forward-looking. Whenever a pilot looked more than one hundred thirty degrees off the nose, he would see only with the naked eye. He would lose the infrared and magnified, enhanced vision.

The third and probably most important disadvantage was that this was an offensive system only. When the pilot was attacked from behind he was out of luck.

The eyes of Night Sight were in two small pods that protruded from two short pylons hanging down from the fuselage and flanking both sides of the engine intake. The front of each pod was dominated by an eight-inch-diameter black glass sphere. These two spheres housed the head-steered forward-looking infrared cameras. This system, equipped with a built-in infrared search-and-track capability, was in the active search mode, trying to find the Eagle.

Flying over the cloud deck and looking through infrared eyes gave the pilots a unique view of the world. The clouds above the city were glowing from the numerous heat sources, as well as from the lights. Farther away from the city, the glow faded, of course. The less heat and light, the less of a glow.

When the jamming started, Ledet moved almost abreast of Richardson to exchange a few hand signals, then dropped back to a hundred yards behind in the trail position. Major Richardson took the lead and headed his jet toward the fading hot spots in the distant sky to the east.

Captain Ledet was scanning the skies left and right when he saw it. Four miles ahead and about two miles to their left was the heat trail from a jet. Ledet thought it had to be the Eagle. With infrared vision it looked like a glowing bubble trail from a torpedo speeding through a sea of clouds.

Ledet waited for Richardson to react to the heat trail as it passed to their left. He didn't. Now it was his turn. Ledet pushed his throttle in full burner. He accelerated in front of Richardson, rocked his wings to indicate that he was taking the lead and for Richardson to follow him. A few seconds later Ledet cranked in ninety degrees of left bank, then yanked back on the stick and went into a five-G left turn to follow Ledet. This reversed their course and put them both on the trail of the Eagle.

Since they were now almost directly above the heat trail, its glowing bubbles in the clouds were easy to follow. Major Richardson pulled abreast of Ledet and motioned for him to go below the clouds and follow from underneath. He also used his hand like a pistol, which meant use guns and shoot to kill. Ledet nodded his head, rolled inverted and dove into the clouds. Seconds later, Ledet broke through the bottom of the clouds. He righted his jet and leveled off at four thousand feet. He quickly sighted the heat trail. From below, because of all of the reflected light and heat from New York City just twenty miles ahead, the trail was not as easy to see.

What an awesome sight, the clouds above him and the lights and heat from the city in front of him. The combination of darkness and light through infrared made it look as if he were approaching a brilliant galaxy with millions of stars floating in the black void of space, instead of a city with millions of people.

Leading to the lights of the Big Apple were roads filled with the headlights from the evening rush hour. The target-tracking system of the Night Sight was in the search mode and would occasionally acquire cars and trucks on the roads below. The forward-looking infrared system presented a sharp black-and-white, magnified image of cars on the roads even at a three-mile slant range.

The pilots that used this Night Sight system loved it. They could focus their attention outside the cockpit as they maneuvered at low altitudes during night and adverse weather conditions. It also helped them to acquire targets at a longer range, thus cutting precious seconds off the time needed to find a target. In a dogfight against the weapons of a modern jet fighter, those few seconds could mean the difference between life and death.

Ledet, still in burner, was gaining on the heat source just a few miles ahead. Without radar he couldn't get an accurate speed or distance to the target aircraft, so he SWAGed (scientific wild-ass guess) three, maybe four, miles to the target aircraft. It would be just minutes to intercept whatever it was, and also just minutes to the city. Ledet could tell the heat trail was getting hotter. That meant either he was getting closer or the jet in the clouds was descending. Ledet moved to the right of the trail as he approached the source. If it was a liner, Ledet wanted to give it a wide berth just in case it dropped down from the clouds in front of him. Midairs with liners were very unforgiving.

Above the clouds Richardson had lost the trail. He looked all around but could see no signs of a heat source. He realized that either he had overflown his target or his quarry was dropping deeper into the clouds, which were masking his vision. Richardson was right on both counts.

With no sign of the target, Richardson was in a predicament. He asked himself, "Well, should I stay up here going nowhere fast, just drilling holes in the sky, or get down under and rejoin with Ledet? Who knows, he might have that Eagle in his sights right now. Ha, I can't let Cajun have all of the fun." Richardson lowered his nose and penetrated the clouds. *Well, since I stayed on the same course,* he thought, *it shouldn't be too difficult to find Ledet. I'd better throttle back just in case I did overfly.* Richardson throttled back to military power and started to slow to 450 knots.

Below the cloud deck, Ledet reached over to his armament control panel and rotated the select switch to GUNS. This was not the time to launch a missile. He wasn't sure whether he was on the heat trail of an F-15 or a commercial liner making an approach to JFK. Whatever it was, he'd be ready. The heat source was getting brighter in the clouds above and ahead. *This is going to be an easy kill. I'll just get right behind it and splash this baby when it drops out of the clouds.*

The anticipation of the kill had heightened Ledet's

senses. Here he was, a few hundred feet below the cloud deck, following the heat trail of a jet he was getting ready to shoot. His target was getting closer and lower all the time. With the infrared vision he knew he'd be looking up the tailpipes of this jet in no time. Ledet could see he was close. He throttled back to match the speed of the heat.

There it was, just ahead of him a little under a mile. The source of the heat trail was still in the clouds, but Ledet could definitely see that it was a fighter and not a commercial liner. Ledet pushed the throttle forward and felt the afterburner kick in. He could also feel his pulse rate increase, almost as if his heart were connected to the throttle. Ledet knew he had to get closer to get a clean gunshot.

Even without the help of radar, the infrared Night Sight system worked as advertised. It locked onto the jet and automatically tracked it with both cameras. One camera scanned and tracked it in a wide field of view, while the other magnified the image of the jet eleven times in a narrow field of view. The magnified image was presented as a postage stamp–sized image in the lower left corner of the video display that was projected onto Ledet's visor. The magnified image was overlaid on the FLIR's wide field of view.

Ledet had closed the distance to half a mile, and the jet ahead was at the bottom limit of the clouds. Through the infrared eyes, the exhaust gases of the jet ahead looked like the tail of a white-hot comet. The jet itself was invisible to Ledet's infrared eyes, because besides being chilled by the cold winter air, it was also obscured by the glowing gases of the exhaust.

At a quarter of a mile, a moment of indecision kept Ledet's finger from squeezing the trigger on the joystick and firing a burst of 20mm rounds. He had a clear shot.

Knight Hawk

Guns or missiles? A missile would be more accurate and quicker from this range, but the explosion and flaming debris would do massive damage to the suburbs below. If I used my gun I'd have to get closer, but it would be a cleaner kill. And the crashing Eagle would still do massive damage to the 'burbs below. Ledet could see that whatever rounds failed to hit his target would be shot into the residential suburban areas, no doubt killing a few people. To Ledet the choice was clear, guns, but at a range close enough to minimize wild rounds.

Ledet moved in for the kill. Five hundred yards. His target was flying smoothly with an unchanging course. Ledet's index finger gently caressed the joystick trigger. Three hundred yards. Ledet was getting close. Two hundred yards. He could smell the aroma of the burned JP-4 jet fuel coming into the cockpit from the jet wash of his target. He gently tightened his finger on the trigger and felt it slide into the first detente, a notch, which meant the gun camera was on and would be recording his kill.

Just as he started to squeeze his trigger, the jet in front of him banked hard to the left and turned. Ledet went into a six-G turn to follow his target, but was puzzled. As he turned he saw the tracer fire light up the sky in front of him and miss the turning jet, but something was wrong. The gun was oddly much quieter than he remembered.

Ledet pulled hard on the stick to draw a bead on his target. As the jet in front of him turned, Ledet was able to get a good view of it clear of its blurring exhaust. When he saw it had only a single engine, he realized his mistake. The jet was a single-engine jet—an F-16, not an F-15. It was Richardson.

When Richardson came down out of the clouds and couldn't see his wingman he turned to look for him.

Ledet sighed and thought, *Well, that little piece of luck saved Richardson's life. I could have wasted him bigtime.*

Ledet failed to realize that Richardson's luck was his luck. As Ledet turned his jet to intercept and rejoin, he looked over his left shoulder for the heat trail of the jet they were following. He didn't see it. What he did see chilled him to the bone. Two hundred yards behind him he could see a faint gray shadow silhouetted against the clouds. He recognized the lurking shape. It was the business end of an F-15 turning and lining up for a shot.

It suddenly became clear to Ledet what had happened. *I didn't shoot at Richardson. It was that Eagle shooting at me.* At that moment Ledet knew that in seconds he would be looking down the gun barrels of death. If he continued his turn he knew the Eagle would have him. The decision to be made in that instant was to maneuver or eject.

Instinctively Ledet did something that all fighter pilots hate to do. He shoved his stick forward hard and instantly subjected his aircraft to three negative Gs. It was like being turned upside down in a high-speed carnival ride, but this ride could be deadly. The F-16 was designed to endure negative as well as positive Gs; the human body was not. Ledet's one-hundred-eighty-pound body now weighed over five hundred pounds, and the only things that kept him from being shot through his canopy and out of his aircraft were the two shoulder straps and the belt of the ACES II ejection seat. The inertial reel of the seat sensed the onset of the negative Gs and locked Ledet to the back of the seat, but it couldn't stop the rising pressure of blood rushing to his head. It couldn't stop his neck stretching so much that his helmet banged against his canopy above him, and it couldn't stop his legs from being yanked off of the rudder pedals and slamming his shins into the bottom of the instrument panel with enough force to hurt like hell.

Ledet's instinct saved his life. As when a boxer telegraphs his next punch, pilots can tell where another aircraft is going to turn by the direction it rolls. A fighter pilot will bank first in the direction of his turn and then yank back on the stick. Ledet's move was like a boxer pulling back his right arm, pretending to throw a right punch, and then jabbing with the left instead. It worked. In the blink of an eye Ledet disappeared out of the Eagle's gun sights.

Ledet went from making the hard left six-G turn to making a negative three-G right turn. After three or four seconds he could see the signs of "redout" closing in and starting to tint his peripheral vision. From his training, he knew his body could only stand this stress for a few short seconds before he lost consciousness. Hoping he was out of danger, he pulled back on the joystick, rolled to the right and continued his right-hand turn, but now with five positive Gs. As he felt the centrifugal force jamming his body deep into his seat, he thought, I hope I never have to do that again.

Kenada was surprised by Ledet's move. She had become complacent and overconfident. She had had the advantage and she blew it. As she had descended out of the cloud deck, she was unaware that she was being pursued, but luckily for her, one of the F-16s had overflown her. Since all three of them were on the same course, the lead F-16 had come down ahead of her, and the F-16 below the clouds had followed the wrong heat trail.

When Kim had dropped out of the clouds, heading back to the city, she was pleased at the sight of two jets in front of her like sitting ducks. *What an opportunity,* she had thought. I can get two jets with one shot. So she took her time lining up a shot. To insure her kill Kenada flipped the ECM switch to STANDBY and let the radar lock onto the target. She pulled her trigger, only to see her shots miss the target. She tried to line up for a second shot on the rear F-16, but it unexpectedly sank under her nose. She had blown it.

Kenada rolled right to follow the F-16 and saw that he was quickly pulling away. She realized her predicament. If she tried to track onto the F-16 turning right, the lead F-16 would be in a position to come in on her tail. It was too late to turn left again and try to track onto the lead F-16. If she did, she'd have the same problem, another jet on her tail.

Kenada glanced at the countdown to detonation on the armament panel monitor: 01.36. She considered her choices and decided to run for shelter in the concrete canyons of New York City. She pushed the throttles into full burner and turned her nose back to the city. JFK airport was just five miles ahead. By the time the Falcons could turn to get on her tail, she would be there.

The whine over the radio had disappeared, and the radar systems came back on-line. For the hundred or so military and commercial jets in the air around JFK, the electronic chaos in the dark was over.

Richardson, halfway through a 360-degree turn, had seen the drama with his wingman and the Eagle behind him. He saw the twin burners of the Eagle stretch out and head for the city. He continued his turn to bring his Falcon back into pursuit.

When the jamming stopped, Richardson decided to inform the world where the Eagle was. He selected the guard frequency on his radio and keyed his mike button. "Attention all jets. This is Syracuse One and I have a tallyho on the Eagle. She is over JFK at a thousand feet heading west. We are in pursuit in two F-16s."

Ledet double-clicked his mike button to let Richardson know that he heard his call. Continuing in his turn, Ledet was able to pull into the trail position behind Richardson. Ledet radioed, "Syracuse One, two's in, one mile."

Richardson double-clicked his mike button.

Kenada heard Richardson's radio transmission on guard. *Here we go again.* She looked at the countdown clock: 01.19.

Flying over JFK at a thousand feet, Kenada could see three piles of flaming rubble on and near the field. The air traffic was gone. On the TEWS radar screen she could see there was a radar threat from the six-o'clock position. The warning tone on her headphones was beeping, and she knew that in a few seconds they would have a lock. *Oh, so they're going to use a Sparrow,* she thought. *Time for a little radar shade.*

Ahead of her Kenada could see the gleaming gold of the majestic lady's torch. The warning beep in her ears became a steady tone. Instinctively she looked into her rearview mirror and saw a distant plume of light coming her way. They had launched. Kenada banked hard right and dove her Eagle toward the shimmering waters under the Verrazano Narrows Bridge. Over her right shoulder she could see the missile's plume about a mile back and closing fast.

As Kenada streaked under the bridge, she punched her chaff button. Clearing the bridge, she checked the mirror on the canopy bow above her. Her maneuver worked. The missile lost its radar lock and homed in on the largest radar reflection it could find, the bridge.

A quick look to her right showed Kenada another plume heading toward her. There was no tone to warn her. "Must be a Sidewinder homing in on my exhaust." She punched the flare button. The arching turn of the missile closing in on her indicated that the heat-seeking missile was not fooled.

Kenada was now heading toward the Bayonne Terminal on the Jersey shore. As she flew she searched ahead for another heat source to distract the missile. Not seeing one, she decided to make one, but where? The answer was right under her nose, dead-ahead. She pushed her stick forward to lower her nose and squeezed her trigger. A four-second burst fired from her gun. She kicked her rudder pedals alternately to give a horizontal raking action on her target. The tracer rounds mixed in with the armor-piercing, high-explosive and incendiary rounds streaked instantly to their target, a ship. The ship was a supertanker, low in the water, laden with oil, and close to the huge fuel-oil storage tanks on the western shore of the harbor. The rounds from the Eagle easily penetrated the hull of the tanker and explosively ignited its cargo in the forward hull tank. A huge ball of fire exploded out of the ship's bow.

Kenada pointed the nose of the Eagle to the left of the black, billowing smoke rising from the ship. With another quick glance over her right shoulder, she could see the missile's rocket plume closing quickly about a half mile away. Her timing was good; she would be able to hide on the other side of the smoke and fire before the heat-seeking missile could get to her.

Thirty seconds earlier Richardson had been pleased with himself. He had radar lock on the Eagle and could almost feel the weight of the Distinguished Flying Cross being pinned on his chest. His vision of glory vanished when his AIM-7 radar-guided missile slammed into the lower deck of the Verrazano Narrows Bridge.

Knight Hawk

Still with an itchy trigger finger, Richardson now saw a chance to redeem himself and salvage the kill. He selected an AIM-9L on the armament control panel, locked on to the heat from the Eagle's engines and fired.

He watched his Sidewinder jump off the rail on his left wing tip and make a gentle turn as it tracked toward the Eagle. "A perfect launch, and in ten to fifteen seconds I'll have my kill. Now I'll just sit back and watch the show." Richardson was thinking of having a little black F-15 silhouette, the symbol of his kill, painted on his canopy rail when he got back. Then the morbid thought of painting on a few cars that he had taken out on the bridge came to mind. On second thought, he decided not to have the silhouettes painted.

"Damn it!" Richardson couldn't contain his anger anymore. He saw the tracer bullets from the Eagle's guns streak across the bay and slam into the tanker. The explosion that followed was spectacular. Richardson knew his missile would track to the greater heat source and be lost in the flames of the ship. In thirty seconds he had not only launched and lost over fifty thousand dollars worth of high-tech weaponry, but he had also compounded his expenses by destroying a ship, a few cars and a bridge, not to mention killing a few commuters.

At first Richardson felt a fleeting moment of remorse for the unnecessary damage and civilian death he caused. He remembered his preflight briefing orders. "Lethal force authorized, destroy by any means possible." This was their license to kill. Under those orders, Richardson was able to rationalize away his guilt by figuring that sometimes you have to kill a few people to save a few million.

As the two F-16s approached the flaming ship, Richardson keyed his mike. "Cajun, go left; I've got right. Watch for a turn."

Ledet steered to the left of the burning hulk and keyed his mike button twice in acknowledgment.

Just before reaching the towering smoke, Kenada banked left and pulled hard. Her plan was to put the smoke and fire between her and the missile. As soon as the smoke was in her six-o'clock position, she rolled wings level and checked in the mirrors at darkness of the smoke that blotted out the lights of Manhattan behind her. Her tactic worked; there was another large explosion in the smoke. She could see a million gallons of flaming oil shooting out in all directions. There was light upon the face of the waters. A glance at her TEWS radar screen showed that the radar threat from the two F-16s was now directly behind her on the other side of the smoke.

"Well, it's time to turn and burn and lose you two," Kenada said to herself. She turned the ECM switch back to ON, then pulled back hard on the stick. She climbed straight up and back toward the tower of smoke. Her Immulman maneuver took her into the top of the smoke cloud. "This ought to fool 'em, and give me a little more time."

Still inverted and approaching the top of her maneuver, Kenada could see the burning ship and flaming waters through the canopy above her. Just before entering the top of the column of smoke about three thousand feet above the burning ship, she spotted the two dark shapes of Falcons as they flew over the bay, one on each side of the ship. She wasn't sure, but she thought they might have seen her illuminated by the light of the flames. If she could see them, they probably could have seen her.

Kenada popped through the smoke, still inverted. For

a moment she appreciated the vision of the city in all of its splendor ahead of her. It was strange and beautiful sight, coming out of the darkness of the black smoke and suddenly regaining sight with the world upside down. In a way it was as if she were in a huge cave with stalactites glowing like an immense chandelier with gleaming layers of light over a fog-covered pool. Back in the real world, she remembered her situation and rolled back upright.

It was time to hide, but where? The countdown clock was under a minute, 00.58. *If the pilots in those Falcons are as good as they seem to be, they'll be on my tail in no time.*

A quick scan from left to right gave Kenada a spectacular view. The world was a blanket of lights. New Jersey was to her left. In the ten-o'clock position she could see the lights of the George Washington Bridge reflecting off the Hudson River. Dominating her view to the right was all of Manhattan. Looming directly ahead were the monolithic, glimmering towers of the World Trade Center. She could also see the East River winding back on the other side of Manhattan, and the dark void of Long Island Sound. She could see several of the bridges that crossed over the East River into the Bronx, Queens and Brooklyn. Off to the right she could see the lights on Long Island extending to the horizon. Kenada noticed three fires fairly close together in the distance that were still burning. That must be JFK, she thought.

Kenada dropped her nose down and aimed it toward Battery Park on the southern tip of Manhattan. Governor's Island was dead-ahead.

As Richardson and Ledet passed to the Jersey side of the tanker, they scanned ahead in the distance for the Eagle, but with no luck. Their radar was being jammed again. Richardson looked over his shoulder and saw Ledet climbing straight up. With his infrared vision he could see the glowing contrail of hot air that Ledet was following. Richardson banked left, then pitched up to follow Ledet.

Keeping the twin towers to her left, Kenada could see the Financial District and Wall Street off her left wing as she dove for the mouth of the East River. She had dropped down to fifty feet above the water. As she sped toward the lights of the Brooklyn Bridge, she had to pitch up slightly to keep from running into one of the Staten Island ferries. She was not sure she had escaped her pursuers. A glance behind her revealed nothing. As she looked forward again, she didn't even have a chance to scream. Directly ahead she saw the broadside of a helicopter, and an instant later she heard and felt a minor thud.

"Damn, that was too close. But whatever it was, it couldn't have been too bad; I'm still flying." With another glance behind her, looking for damage, she saw that she had lost the counterweight and about two inches off the top of the right vertical stabilizer. *I hope I don't need to go Mach 2 plus*, Kenada thought. *That tail will get a little shaky*. She looked ahead again. She was now close enough to the Brooklyn Bridge to see the vertical suspension cables coming down from the main cables that spanned the river and connected the towers of the bridge. She could even see the delicate truss work illuminated by the cars on the Manhattan Bridge just beyond.

It was Ledet's turn now. He had followed Kenada's trail into the smoke from the burning tanker. Coming out of the smoke, he could see her a mile or two ahead. Ledet went into full burner to close the gap on the Eagle, and was seconds away from getting a good gunshot. He had to pop up and over a helicopter that was having difficulty maintaining level flight.

Ledet resumed a firing position to track onto the Eagle and squeezed off a three-second burst. To himself he said, "Now that's more like my gun." He could not only hear the loud roar of his 20mm cannon coming to life just to his left, but he could feel the shock waves vibrating in his chest. With disappointment Ledet watched his rounds overshoot his mark. It was a long shot, but he wanted to make his kill while the Eagle was still over the water. That way, if he missed, his rounds wouldn't go strafing any buildings or people or bridges. If his aim was good, the Eagle would splash into the water instead of burning in the city. Unfortunately his aim wasn't good. The missed rounds hit the water well ahead of the Eagle and skipped off the surface like smooth stones bouncing off the calm waters of a pond.

Ledet could see that the Eagle was about to go under a bridge. He held his fire and lowered his nose to follow the Eagle's flight path. Richardson, not far behind Ledet, elected to stay above the bridge to be ready if and when the Eagle popped up.

Kenada saw the tracer fire zip above and beyond her just before she went under the bridge. "Damn, they're closer than I thought. How could they be so good? I thought I lost them. I can't see them; how can they see me?"

The countdown clock was at 00.52. "I've got to keep these guys behind me and keep them confused." She pushed her throttles past the detente and into full burner.

In her mirror Kenada caught a quick glimpse of a dark shape moving across the lighted facades of the buildings on the Jersey side of the Hudson. *That must*

*be one of the two F-16s I saw. Well, at least I know I'm
not alone out here.* The one Falcon was falling almost directly behind her a quarter of a mile back. Kim remembered that she saw two F-16s, and thought, *The other
must be flying top cover in case I pop up. I can't pitch up
now, and I've got to keep my turns low and level. I need to
stall for time.* The countdown clock was at 00.50.

Kenada kept her nose pointed up the East River and
underneath the bridges ahead. "These guys won't be
able to get a good shot as long as I'm under these
bridges. Got to slow down. I can't turn until they're
closer; otherwise they'll have me for dinner."

She pulled the throttles back to the military power
detente to keep from going supersonic. She pushed the
thumb button on the throttle quadrant forward and extended the surfboard-size speed brake just behind the
cockpit. The net effects of her actions were just what
she wanted. It slowed her down, but more important,
it made the air behind her extremely turbulent.

Just twenty feet above the water, Kenada dodged under the Brooklyn and Manhattan bridges. To make herself a harder target, she kicked the rudder pedals
randomly to yaw her F-15 left and right.

Ledet followed the Eagle with difficulty. Flying in
such close quarters at such a high speed was hard
enough, but fighting the jet wash from the Eagle's engines, the wing tip vortices, and the turbulence from
the speed brake was almost too much. Flying so low
also brought in ground effect, which added tremen-
dously to the difficulty of flying.

Cursing to himself, he said, "Hell, this puppy's shaking like a wet dog." Not only was he having trouble
staying behind the Eagle, he had to struggle to avoid
the spray of water kicked up by the Eagle's jet wash.
Ledet found it almost impossible to line up the Eagle

under his crosshairs, let alone get off a shot.

Richardson stayed five hundred feet above the bridges and quickly closed in to six hundred yards behind the Eagle.

Kenada couldn't see exactly where the Falcons were, but she knew they had to be behind her, one low and one high. Coming out from under the Manhattan Bridge, she could see in the open water ahead that the East River turned to the left and went under a bridge. *That must be the Williamsburg Bridge,* she thought. *I won't make it if I approach it from this angle and speed. Even if I make it under the pilings of the bridge, I won't be able to turn in time to clear the buildings on the shore.*

Kenada pulled back and to the right on the stick. Her Eagle pitched up and turned as if it were going to streak into Brooklyn.

Richardson and Ledet both banked right, anticipating the Eagle's turn. Richardson chuckled for a moment at the irony. He could see the Eagle lining up to go racing down the streets of Brooklyn with Ledet and himself in hot pursuit. Traveling at speeds in excess of six hundred miles per hour, he thought of his first speeding ticket for going twenty miles over the thirty-mile-an-hour speed limit. "Ha, if that fat traffic cop could see me now!" A quick glance at the airspeed displayed on the HUD showed Richardson that a speeding ticket now would cite him at exceeding the speed limit by six hundred and fifty miles an hour. "Now *that* would be a hell of a fine."

Without ever slowing her roll rate to the right, Kenada retracted her speed brake, advanced her throttles and continued her roll until she had gone 270 degrees of a roll. This low-level turning barrel-roll maneuver fooled Ledet, and also placed her into a nearly perpendicular approach for the next bridge.

Ledet pitched up and turned to follow the Eagle, but he hadn't expected her to turn a barrel roll at this altitude, and for a few seconds the Eagle was out of his sight. He quickly rolled to regain the trail, only to see that the Eagle had pulled farther ahead.

Richardson, being farther behind and above, was able to counter the Eagle's maneuver, and made a quicker recovery onto its trail. Since he was now closer to the Eagle than Ledet, Richardson dove in to get on the Eagle's tail. Ledet saw Richardson move in, so he traded positions. Richardson followed the Eagle under the Williamsburg Bridge, and Ledet flew top cap three hundred feet above.

Ledet could see over the bridge ahead that there was about a three-mile distance before the next bridge and the island ahead, plenty of space for Richardson to make the kill.

Kenada knew an attempt to cover the open water to the next bridge would be suicidal, so her only choice was to turn and burn. She quickly banked to the left and turned left, but as soon as she reached the Manhattan side of the river she banked right and went into a six-G level turn to the right. Richardson followed.

Kenada continued her turn until she was lined up with a street that cut across Manhattan. With her nose pointing west, she leveled her wings just as she cut into the Lower East Side.

With Manhattan dead-ahead, Kenada pointed her nose to the center of one of the concrete canyons of light that seemed to stretch off into infinity. "Hopefully," she thought, "this one goes all the way across."

Richardson duplicated the Eagle's turn and entered the same cement corridor. Being a Big Apple city boy from way back, Richardson recognized the street they were racing down. It was East Sixth Street. He knew this area well, and he also remembered that this particular street didn't go all the way across Manhattan. The street would come to an end at Washington Square in about two miles. Richardson knew that the Eagle would have to climb out of this canyon soon. He would be ready.

A quick glance at the airspeed indicator on the HUD showed Kenada that she was now accelerating through Mach .95. *At this speed, I'll be sonic by midtown,* she thought *"This pass will give a new meaning to the term rush-hour traffic."*

Ledet was not about to try to trade off positions with Richardson on this maneuver. He pulled back on his stick to gain altitude, and with six hundred knots of airspeed he easily rocketed up to a thousand feet. This was one chase he was going to watch from above, and with the Chrysler and the Empire State buildings to his right and the twin towers of the World Trade Center off to his left, he would be way above.

Richardson was having the ride of his life. Never in his ten years of combat flying had he ever experienced such demanding flying conditions as this. It was one thing to go one-on-one when he was chasing another jet through canyons of clouds, but when the clouds were made of concrete and steel, the stakes were different. These clouds had the kiss of death. In either situation, the desired outcome was to kill the other guy; however, now the level of difficulty was infinitely higher.

Richardson was getting a severe case of target fixation. He was going to make this kill or die trying. Still five hundred yards behind, he was beginning to question the wisdom of his decision to follow the Eagle into such close quarters. True, he was in the ideal spot where every fighter pilot wants to be, directly behind and almost close enough to spit. Unfortunately there was no way to get in a shot. Richardson's multimillion-dollar state-of-the-art fighter was experiencing severe buffeting. It was like driving a Formula One race car at top speed across a plowed field. Racing at almost supersonic speeds had thrown another twist into the difficulty of flying. Because Richardson was so close behind the Eagle, his jet was being slammed by the shock waves bouncing off the tall buildings they were passing. Each time he passed a building, he was hit by another reflected sonic wave. The buffeting was becoming so severe, he was having difficulty reading his instruments, as well as staying in the middle of the road and keeping track of the Eagle in front of him.

It was getting to the point where it was all he could do just to fly straight and level. When Richardson went between two tall buildings, the shock waves came from both sides. But what really got his attention was just passing one building. Then the shock wave would come from one side only and almost push him into another building on the other side of the street.

Richardson's instinct for survival kicked in. Seeing that it was almost impossible to get in a shot, let alone fly behind the Eagle, he decided to rise above it to avoid the turbulence and to wait for a better opportunity to shoot. A quick pull back on the joystick in his right hand pulled the nose up, and almost instantly launched him two hundred feet higher. The ride was much smoother now.

Richardson could now look for the Eagle. In his peripheral vision, he saw something flapping on his right wing tip. With a quick glance, he could tell that during his bouncing around earlier he had snagged a portion of a flag from one of the overhanging poles.

Suddenly Richardson was totally baffled. Even

though he was close behind the Eagle, he couldn't see it. He could see the twin white-hot flames shooting out the Eagles's afterburners, but not the Eagle. As he looked closer he noticed that the Eagle was being obscured by a circular cloud almost a hundred feet in diameter that appeared to be attached to the jet. What Richardson was seeing was the Eagle's supersonic shock cone creating an instantaneous cloud, formed when the high level of humidity in the air combined with the low-pressure area behind the shock wave. Since the shock wave was constantly moving with the Eagle, so did the cloud.

Confused by the newly formed cloud, Richardson failed to see the Eagle pitch up in front of him until it was too late. He was suddenly hit again with another shock wave, which caused another spasm of uncontrolled flight. To avoid hitting the Eagle, Richardson pushed his nose down, then pulled it back up as he passed underneath it. It worked. He was still alive. He could now see that the Eagle had slowed to a subsonic speed and the cloud was gone. Richardson saw the Eagle turning hard to the right. He followed.

From his vantage point, Ledet could barely follow the drama unfolding below him, since the streets were so narrow and so deeply shrouded by tall buildings. Ledet was taking care to make sure he stayed directly over Sixth Street and the two jets. If he veered to the left or right just a little, he would have lost sight of both of them. Ledet could see that in another fifteen seconds the chase would become more interesting. The Eagle was about to run out of real estate at Washington Square. There was no way for it to stay low without running into buildings. The Eagle would have to pop up.

Ledet anticipated the flight path of the Eagle and

dropped his nose to position himself for the engagement if Richardson lost the trail. As Ledet started to descend he caught a glimmer of light from the corner of his eye. He looked to his left, and couldn't believe what he saw. There, at the same altitude, coming directly at him, was a missile about three miles away. The missile was coming from over the water around Governor's Island. Just beyond the rocket's plume Ledet could also see a small group of fighters in trail formation coming right at him. "Damn, this is just great! Those guys must think I'm the Eagle."

Ledet didn't have a moment to spare. In about six seconds he'd be raining aluminum all over the Lower East Side and Greenwich Village. As he chopped his throttle to idle, he rolled inverted, punched out a few flares, and pulled back hard on his stick. The missile locked onto the greater heat source; then a bright yellow flash momentarily lit up his cockpit. Not even half a second later came the sound of the explosion, close enough for the shock wave to jostle the airplane and flame out his engine. A red warning light lit up on Ledet's dash. A quick look at the engine instruments showed that the exhaust gas temperature (EGT) was dropping rapidly. Instinctively, Ledet flipped up the autoignite switch, and almost instantly felt the thrust from his Pratt and Whitney F200 engine kick in with a surge of power.

Still diving, Ledet turned south toward the approaching three fighters. By turning into the oncoming fighters, Ledet would pass underneath them, give himself a larger separation from his attackers, and also get himself out of their targeting windows. He could see that the group, now about a mile away, was made of three F-18s. He would be passing about five hundred feet underneath them. At this range these guys should be able to see that I'm not an F-15, Ledet thought. For a moment, he forgot that his vision was assisted by his infrared. He assumed that these F-18s would disengage their attack on him once they recognized his jet. He was wrong. To the pilots of the F-18s, Ledet was the Eagle; he was a dark shadow with a glowing afterburner, flying where he shouldn't be.

Ledet keyed his mike button and yelled, "Hey, you guys in the Hornets, knock it off! Can't you see I'm not an Eagle?"

They didn't answer because they didn't hear him. Their radios were still being jammed by Kenada.

As Ledet passed underneath the approaching lead jet, he banked hard right and turned. He pointed his nose north, back into the heart of Manhattan. Over his left shoulder he watched the lead jet break hard to its right to get on his tail. The second jet turned to its left.

Just then Ledet felt a little silly when he realized that the F-18 pilots were flying with the naked eye. They didn't have the enhanced vision that he had. Of course the F-18s would continue their attack.

Ledet looked over his shoulder at the F-18s above and did a quick assessment of his situation. His number-one priority on this flight was to get the Eagle, his next was to stay alive, but now that a trio of F-18s were putting their crosshairs on his tail, it was time to rearrange his priorities. For a moment Ledet contemplated the idea of shooting back at these guys and blowing them out of the sky, but he didn't want to waste his missiles on the wrong targets. Of course, the idea of being court-martialed for shooting down the good guys was also not very appealing. Ledet made a wise decision. "Well, guys, I'd love to stay and chat, but I gotta run. Now if I can just get on the trail of the Eagle and lead them to it, maybe they'll see the error of their ways."

As Ledet looked north, he saw all of Manhattan behind him. Except for the black geometric shapes of the unlighted rooftops, the whole world outside of his canopy was covered by billions of lights.

Ledet had lost sight of Richardson and the Eagle. There were too many lights and too much heat for him to find Richardson and the Eagle's trail. They were nowhere in sight. He imagined that the two of them were racing through the abysses between the towering buildings. They're probably traveling north, he thought. "Well, if the Eagle can hide there, it's good enough for me."

Kenada saw that her avenue of escape was about to take a turn for the worse. She could see that the street she was following opened into a small park. She knew she was near the Greenwich Village area, and figured that was Washington Square Park dead-ahead.

Kenada pulled hard back and to the right on her joystick, and her Eagle responded by going into a six-G climbing turn to the right. She was now heading north. She looked ahead of her and to the right for a street that would line up with her flight path. The height of her climb peaked out at six hundred feet before she started back down again.

There it was, ahead of her, another canyon of lights just waiting for her to dive into it. Kenada continued her descent and leveled off at about one hundred and fifty feet above the street. With both of her engines in full burner, she didn't dare take her eyes off of the narrow passage ahead of her. She didn't know what avenue she was flying up, but since it was the second street to the west of the street that lined up with the Empire State Building, she guessed that it was Seventh Avenue. Kenada's airspeed indicator on the HUD showed 756 knots, almost Mach 1, the speed of sound.

Kenada had no idea where those F-16s were, but she was sure she had at least one behind her, with the other up above. Just in case they were right behind her lining up for a gunshot, she kept her flying erratic by constantly changing her altitude up and down and moving from side to side. The towering walls of buildings beside her were nothing but a blur of streaking light. Up ahead she caught a quick glimpse of the elaborate facade and marquee of Macy's department store. Before she could finish the thought of, "Times Square must be just ahead," she was already past it. Seconds later she could see the large, dark, empty void of Central Park ahead.

Richardson had learned his lesson. There was no way he was going to get caught in that shock cone behind the Eagle again. This time he would stay above and wait for the opportunity to strike.

As Kenada entered the open area of Central Park, she banked right, turning east, and then hard to the left. While she turned she looked for a street to line up with. On the tall building ahead of her she could see three tall letters: ABC. "I know this is going to be a real news flash. I hope they have their cameras rolling." Looking back just before she went behind the ABC building, Kenada thought she caught a glimpse of an F-16 turning her way.

From the corner of her eye, Kenada saw that the countdown to detonation was at 00.35.

As for cameras, ABC was out of luck. When Kenada passed by the north side of the ABC building, her sonic boom blew out half of the windows. Inside the building, people thought they were under attack, or that a car bomb had blown up in the street.

Ironically the only cameras that caught the event were those of a news crew from CBS. They were reporting on a homicide scene in Central Park, where a body was found just a hundred yards east of Tavern on the Green. Mardy Jackson, a roving reporter, was in the middle of her solo spot, describing the crime scene, when she was interrupted by the cameraman, Jake Johnson. "What the hell was that?" he asked. He took his camera off of her and zoomed at the fading flash of light in the distance. Then he started counting out loud. Fifteen seconds later they heard the loud boom of the exploding missile in the distance. Mardy turned toward the sound and Jake said, "That was three miles. I wonder if somebody's trying to blow up the Trade Center again."

While Jake was trying to see what was going on, Mardy saw something far in the distance down one of the streets. She grabbed his camera by the lens and pulled it a little to the right so he was looking straight down Seventh Avenue. "Zoom in," she said to Jake. "What do you see?"

Jake took a few seconds trying to find what Mardy saw, and when he did, he couldn't believe it. He never answered Mardy's question. By the time he finally found and focused on the two approaching jets, Mardy could already see them too.

"Those are fighters," Mardy said. "What do they think they're doing?"

Again Jake took a few seconds to answer Mardy's question. When he did say something, she never heard him. The two jets flew over both of them, and the sonic boom that hit them as the F-15 passed drowned out any noise Jake uttered. Mardy screamed. Fortunately, Jake wasn't paid for doing the talking; his job was to shoot the pictures, and as far as he was concerned, he was getting some great shots.

Richardson was disappointed to see the Eagle turn and disappear behind the ABC building. He was hoping that it would make a run for it across Central Park. It would make a perfect missile shot. "Damn, there's no way I can make that turn from this altitude. I'll go above and cut the Eagle off." Richardson pulled back and to the left on the stick to gain clearance above the building and follow the Eagle's turn. "Well, at least I'll be able to head her off and line up for a gunshot." Just as Richardson completed his turn and aligned himself on the same street with the Eagle, he dropped his nose for the kill.

Kenada was amazed that she was able to make the turn around the building and could now see open skies ahead of her. In a matter of seconds she would be a vulnerable target over the open expanse of the Hudson River.

The countdown clock was now at 00.22 seconds to detonation.

She quickly realized it was time to get back to the safety of the city streets, so she pulled hard back on the stick, chopped the throttles to idle, and popped out the speed brake.

Kenada's maneuver caught Richardson off guard. As he descended in the trough between the buildings, he expected to see the Eagle speeding ahead out over the Hudson. Instead he saw the Eagle coming at him head-on. He instinctively unloaded the Gs off the stick and pushed it forward to go underneath the approaching Eagle and avoid a midair collision. After missing the Eagle by fifty feet, he pulled back hard to avoid another deadly collision, this time with the double yellow lines in the middle of the road.

Kenada too was a bit surprised to see the F-16 dead ahead. Her first instinct was also for survival by avoidance. Fortunately for her the maneuver would also give her additional distance from her pursuer. Still pulling back on the stick, she retracted the speed brake until she was inverted and heading east back toward Central Park. She banked into a hard turn to the south down Fifth Avenue and pushed her throttles into full burner.

Richardson had recovered quickly to resume the chase, but he was not fast enough to line up for a shot before the Eagle zoomed down and disappeared behind the skyscrapers bordering the southeast corner of Central Park. He pulled back hard on his stick to align himself with the same corridor the Eagle had gone down.

Richardson made the turn with the precision of a brain surgeon, and entered onto Fifth Avenue with his wings vertical and three hundred feet above the street. As he rolled his wings level he could see the twin afterburners of the Eagle a thousand yards ahead and said to himself, "OK, baby, it's you and me, and now it's time to rock and roll."

Mardy and Jake were dumbfounded watching this aerial chase. They watched the F-15 fly over a second time and then saw the F-16 pop up from the other side of the ABC building and get back into pursuit of the Eagle.

Jake kept the camera rolling as the F-15 flew low and fast across the southern end of Central Park and disappeared into the walls of Fifth Avenue, with the F-16 following it a few seconds later.

Amazed, Jake asked, "What the hell was that all about?"

"I don't know, but keep the camera rolling," Mardy

replied. She stepped in front of the camera and started to describe what she had just seen. In the back of her mind she was wishing that the jets would come back so they could get more footage. Her wish was about to come true.

Meanwhile in lower Manhattan, Ledet was still having a party of his own. After passing under the three F-18s, he continued south to try to lose them in the skyscrapers of the Financial District.

As Ledet passed over the Manhattan side of the Brooklyn Bridge, he could see two of the three F-18s over his left shoulder. They were still turning to get on his tail. A quick glance over his right shoulder gave no hint as to where the third F-18 was. Thinking that it was time to protect his six, Ledet continued flying to the southern tip, and as soon as he came over the East River he banked right, made a high-G turn to the right and disappeared from view of the F-18s.

Ledet raced west around Battery Park and lined himself up with West Street on the Hudson side of Manhattan, just over two hundred feet up. In seconds he was passing just a few hundred yards away from the twin towers of the World Trade Center. He started to laugh, thinking how easy it was to lose F-18s, but before he had time to admire his own cunning, his train of thought was rudely derailed by a stream of passing tracers.

"Damn, don't these guys ever look at what they're shooting at?" Ledet pitched left and then right to avoid the stream. Looking back in the direction of the tracer fire, he could see the third F-18 that he hadn't seen earlier. What made matters worse was seeing the other two F-18s coming in close behind to join in the chase.

Ledet stayed low and cut in toward the center of the

island. He picked a street that was running north, dropped into it and went into full burner. Ahead and on the left side of the street he could see the Empire State Building.

Of the three F-18s, two dropped into the Fifth Avenue canyon close to half a mile behind Ledet. The third stayed high. He knew better.

Ledet was sweating bullets. His altitude was close to three hundred feet, and his airspeed was at 650 knots and accelerating. In seconds he would be going supersonic. This was the type of flying that could kill. It was extremely demanding, and with the tall buildings just a few feet from the wing tips, death was just a mistake away. At these speeds the pilot had to be extremely precise and fly way ahead of his jet. Ledet had flown low and fast over cities before, mostly Baghdad, but never this low or this fast, and never down a large street.

Ledet's world had turned into a blur, with lines of light streaking by like tracers. He didn't dare take his eyes off of the dark vertical column ahead that was the open space of the night. He knew that if he looked to the side, he might drift off the center line of the street. He wondered how far back the F-18s were. *When in doubt, dodge*, he thought. *Moving targets are harder to hit*.

A mile ahead, Ledet could see a steam cloud spanning the width of the street. Considering that it was January and most buildings were steam heated, Ledet thought nothing of it. A second later the steam cloud was gone and something shook his jet hard. It felt as if he had flown through an invisible brick wall, or as if he were a speed boat running over a submerged log in the water. "Damn, I'm hit!"

Ledet started to reach toward the ejection handle on the left side of the seat. He hesitated a moment just to make sure his jet was completely upright. Ejecting sideways into a building would be no fun at all. A quick glance at his engine instruments showed that everything was normal. He was still flying. A flash of light in his rearview mirror caught his eye. He looked to see what it was, thinking it was battle damage, but was surprised to see that the light was a ball of flame floating in the air a few blocks behind him. Ledet thought he caught sight of a shadow silhouetted against the flames in the shape of a jet.

What Ledet had seen was not a stationary cloud of steam, but the water vapor cloud trapped in the supersonic shock waves of an F-15 and F-16 closing in on him at a speed close to two thousand miles an hour. What Ledet felt was the double shock waves caused by the supersonic speed of Kenada's Eagle and Richardson's Falcon. What Ledet saw behind him was the flaming remains of one of the F-18s on his tail.

The demise of the F-18 was due to a combination of factors. The trailing F-18 was experiencing the buffeting of the reflected shock waves coming from the F-16 and F-18 that he was following. To reduce the buffeting, the pilot flew lower than the jets ahead so he could find smoother air. His visibility directly ahead had also been restricted by the cone-shaped cloud formed by the shock waves of the two jets. The killer blow was from the Eagle's shock wave. The second F-18 was a few feet off of the center line of the street, and the sudden violent shake from the wave shook the pilot's arm enough to affect the jet's flight path. That little jostling of the arm caused his right wing to dip only inches. That was the last thing that pilot knew.

Before he could recover, two feet of his right wing were clipped off by a flagpole protruding from the former B. Altman building. The slight collision induced a yaw to the right, which pulled the jet into the side of a building one block up. As the right wing was dragged across the facade of the building, the wing tanks were ripped open and the fuel was instantly ignited by the sparks from the steel and aluminum scraping against stone and concrete. The F-18 started into a faster flat spin when its radome was sheared off. The F-18 spun down and across the street like a Frisbee as it bounced off the building. It finally came to a fiery rest on the eighth floor of the building on the corner of Fifth Avenue and Thirty-eighth Street. Needless to say, in a few days, Lord & Taylor would be having a fire sale.

The F-18 flying above saw the mishap and decided that his leader needed some help, so he dropped his nose and joined in the chase. As he pointed his nose down, he recognized Rockefeller Center to the left and the tall spires of St. Patrick's Cathedral on the right.

After seeing the Hornet's shadow behind him, Ledet was feeling a little claustrophobic. A few blocks ahead he could see that the road widened. "Must be Central Park. Can't go there; I'll be a sitting duck." He decided it was time to be drastic.

Ledet pulled back hard on his stick and went into a vertical climb with his wing tip just twenty feet away from the huge glass panes of Trump Tower. While still climbing, he kicked in a little rudder, just enough to slide around the corner of the tower and keep it between himself and the two remaining F-18s.

Ledet continued his vertical barrel roll until he was three quarters of the way around Trump Tower. He was sure that at that moment he was out of sight of the Hornets.

"Time for some evasive maneuvers." Ledet punched his flare button and fired a double salvo. He immediately chopped his throttle to idle, pulled back on his stick and pointed his nose into the grayness of the clouds to the south. "Away from the city lights, these guys won't be able to see me," he thought.

Ledet kept turning and looking back at the skyscraper he flew around, and waited for the F-18s to appear. They didn't.

The two F-18s that Ledet was worrying about had troubles of their own. When Ledet had gone into his climbing, spiraling turn around Trump Tower, there was one thing that none of the pilots took into consideration: speed. Ledet was traveling at Mach 1.4, almost a thousand miles an hour. As he passed close to the large floor-to-ceiling windows of the building, his sonic shock wave shattered the panes. The rapidly dropping air pressure behind him sucked the glass shards from the broken windows out of the building into the air behind his jet.

For the F-18s, the raining glass was lethal. Glass shards pelted both jets like hail traveling at the speed of sound. The glass fragments acted as razor-sharp bullets. The one-inch-thick Lexan canopies on the F-18s were being scoured by the striking glass. Both F-18s gave up the chase. With the front of their canopies cut into, it was hard to follow something they couldn't see.

In aviation circles, it is a well-known fact that aircraft jet engines make very poor garbage disposals. When the glass shards were swallowed by the engine intakes, the fact was again proven. The shards slammed into the first stages of the engine compressor sections and shattered like diamonds into smaller pieces. The glass, along with fragments of blades from the first stages, was rammed deeper into the engine, where the shards finally destroyed the delicate and finely balanced compressor blades of the final stages. Both jets immediately lost power. Without engines, multimillion-dollar jets instantly turn into rocks with wings. Even with wings, all rocks obey the laws of gravity.

Both F-18 pilots almost instantly realized the gravity of their situation. They pointed the noses of their jets toward the dark void of Central Park, and, after reaching the zenith of their vertical climb, they each pulled the arming handles of their ejection seats and squeezed the triggers. Within seconds each had rocketed away from his cockpit, separated from his ejection seat, and was safely hanging under the nylon canopy of his deployed and inflated parachute. In the moments that followed, the supersonic F-18s became a pair of multimillion-dollar lawn darts in the grass of Central Park.

As Ledet scanned the skies, looking for the two F-18s, he was a bit surprised to see two almost simultaneous flaming explosions in the darkness of the park. He still didn't realize what had caused the explosions. It wasn't until he saw the two parachutes floating in the air that he understood that he was again alone.

Central Park

Mardy and Jake were still amazed at what was happening. They were extremely fortunate, as news crews go. They were in the right place at the right time and got some great shots. Mardy pointed to the two parachutes floating down toward the southern end of the park and said to Jake, "Zoom in on the chutes. What do you see?"

"I see two guys coming down. Looks like they're both alive."

Mardy looked at Jake, then at the descending pilots, then at the two flaming hulks of rubble in the distance. She wondered where to go first.

Jake looked at Mardy and just said, "OK, take your pick."

After a moment of thought Mardy said, "Both. I want both." She looked to see what was closer. "Jake, give me your camera and I'll go get the pilots. You go back to the truck, drive over to where the jets crashed and shoot them with the other camera. This is going to be one hell of a story."

While racing south down Fifth Avenue, both Kenada and Richardson felt the bumping shock wave of the passing jets, one F-16 and two F-18s, that were heading north. At the speeds they all were traveling, they never saw the other jets because their closure speed was too great. At close to two thousand miles an hour, something that was half a mile away would be in your face in less than a second.

To recover from the jostling of the shock wave, Kenada pitched up twenty degrees before dropping back down on the other side of Washington Square Park. The street in line with Fifth Avenue that she entered was West Broadway. She could see that she was again rapidly running out of real estate. The road ahead made a turn to the left that she wasn't about to try.

Dead ahead, rising high 1,800 feet into the air, were the twin towers of the World Trade Center. Between the two lighted towers Kenada could see a slim window of darkness.

The countdown-to-detonation clock displayed 00.03. "That should give me just enough time to make it." With that, Kenada pulled back on her stick, went into a forty-five-degree climb, then rolled until her wings were vertical. Two seconds later she was through.

Richardson was no fool. Flying between the uprights of the World Trade Center would not have been wise. After pulling back on his stick to climb up and out of

West Broadway, he banked to the right to fly around the twin towers. Just as he banked, there was a flash in the night. For an instant, the clouds above were a brilliant white, as if they were in the light of day. As quickly as the light came, it left, and with it so did the lights of New York City. For Richardson, everything went dark: the city lights, the lights in the cockpit—everything as far as the eye could see went dark.

Richardson was hit by a wave of panic and confusion. He didn't realize at first what had happened; all he knew was that he was in big trouble. Somewhere ahead of him was a pair of cloud-high towers of steel and glass and now he was blind. At first he thought that the Night Hawk infrared system had failed. It had, but that would not explain why he couldn't see the normally visible lights. Another mystery was the sudden loss of a six-G force pushing his butt deep and hard into his seat.

The flash of light was from the nuclear detonation of the Knight Hawk missile's warhead at an altitude of fifty miles. The darkness that followed was the result of the electromagnetic pulse (EMP) emitted by the detonation.

For Kenada, Richardson and all of the other aircraft in the area, the EMP had the same effect. All of their electrical systems went off-line. In both jets the main power bus circuit breaker had to be reset, but for Richardson the problem was more serious. The F-16 differed significantly from the F-15 in one crucial way: the F-15 used a mechanical and hydraulic link between the joystick and the flight controls, while the F-16 used an electrical and hydraulic link, a "fly-by-wire" system. When the EMP hit Richardson's jet, he lost all of his flight controls.

For Richardson, things were not good, and he knew

it. One moment he was staring at a skyscraper, and then with a flash of light it was gone. Everything was gone. He saw nothing. He didn't know what to think.

Richardson didn't understand why he couldn't see. During that instant when these questions were flooding his brain, another question came to mind, this one from the seat of his pants. *Where did all of those Gs go? A second ago I was heavy in the seat; now I'm not.*

Richardson instinctively pulled back harder on his control stick, only to find no response. His jet, which had faithfully obeyed his every command, was now on its own, flying without his help. Now even if he could react in time to reset his circuit breakers, it was too late.

Suddenly, in the twinkle of an eye, the world seemed to stop while he relived every second of his life plus a bit more. Richardson felt the bottom of his jet smash into something. It sounded like a Greyhound bus driving through an alley full of garbage cans. The force of the impact threw him hard into his seat and his head back into the headrest. The force pinned him into the seat, and all he could see was what was above his canopy. Above him he could see that both of his wings were pointing straight up. The only good thing about having his wings folded up was that it kept his jet from rolling. Of course, in relation to the real world, Richardson was lying on his side. To him it looked as though his jet was rapidly falling down an elevator shaft. Fifty feet above him he could see a ball of flame following him down the shaft. As he fell down the shaft in slow motion, he felt the constant bumping of the bottom of his jet. The only sound that Richardson could hear now was the metal of his bird scraping against cement as it sliced through the carpets into the supporting concrete floors. It sounded like a hundred kids dragging their fingernails across a dusty chalkboard. He recognized chairs and tables as they flew by him into the fireball above. He saw ceiling tiles and pieces of partitions being smashed to pieces. He saw his radome get ripped off the nose of his jet and disappear into the flames.

Richardson realized what had happened. The flash of light that stole away the control of his jet was the nuke, and now he was sliding through one of the floors in the World Trade Center. In a moment he knew he would be dead.

In that instant, he tensed up and remembered how in the past when he talked with pilots about other pilots that recently died in a crash, they always tried to figure out if the pilot had died tense. That meant that the dying pilot saw his death coming. Richardson had always hoped that when it was his time, he wouldn't die tense. He hoped that he wouldn't see the face of death. It was too late for that. Richardson was definitely tense.

After an eternity of jostling, smashing through walls, and the screaming sound of metal scraping against cement, there was darkness again and all was still. Except for a gentle swaying, all movement had stopped. Richardson thought this was death, and he was disappointed that he couldn't see a light to walk into. He reached up with both hands to straighten his helmet on his head. As his eyes began to focus, he could see spots of light in the distance. He could also see flickers of light dancing on the broken glass faces of the instruments on his dash. He could feel that he was hanging in his seat, and that his jet was pointed nose down. He looked over his left shoulder and with horror he saw the light. Twenty-foot tongues of fire were flickering out of the ten-by-twenty-foot hole in the side of the building above him. Water from the building's sprinkler system was flowing out of the bottom of the hole and cascading down the side of the building.

His jet had slammed through the building and out the other side. The only thing that stopped what was left of his jet from falling to the street below was several electrical cables that had been snagged by the jagged metal. The light that he saw above him was from the burning jet fuel that had gushed from his ruptured fuel tanks.

Richardson was in a new predicament. His jet had been torn in half, and the half that he was in was now hanging out the side of a building and getting ready to drop five hundred feet as soon as the fire above him melted through the lifesaving electrical cables. He thought about ejecting, but that would mean sudden death. His seat would slam him into the side of the World Trade Center like a bug on a car windshield.

After clearing the uprights of the Trade Center, Kenada turned to the left. She caught a glimpse of fire erupting from the side of one of the towers, and considering what and who was behind her, it was safe to assume that, whoever it was, they didn't make it.

In the distance to the southeast, Kenada could see a few more fires. That must be the wrecks at JFK, she thought.

Kim made a swift scan of the skies to see if there were any hostiles nearby, or any on her tail. There were none that she could see. Now that she had a moment to breathe, it was time to talk to the powers that be.

Kenada keyed the mike button but didn't hear the familiar silence over her helmet headset. She knew her radio had gone off-line.

She glanced at her utility panel by her left elbow. She could see that there were still a few white rings around some of the circuit breakers. She reset them all by pushing them back in, then made a quick scan of the instruments to see what was functioning.

The ground positioning system satellite linkup had been interrupted by the ionized upper atmosphere from the blast, but that was OK. The remaining Knight Hawk missile would still function on its own inertial navigation system. Other than that, all of her Eagle's avionics were working.

Kenada keyed the mike button again. "New York Central, Eagle . . ."

Chapter Fifteen

20:56
Pentagon

The video display screens in the command center went blank. In the blink of an eye, the most powerful financial city in the world was no more, or so it seemed. It was as if the entire state of New York had electronically fallen off the face of the earth.

The battle staff was in total shock and disbelief. The thought of New York being destroyed was unbelievable. The radar monitors that had been displaying the tracks of the airplanes and the airspace around New York City slowly faded into darkness. Telephone links with the air-traffic controllers all went dead. In fact, all telephone and radio communication with the entire New York area was gone.

Price walked over to the camera for the video comm and touched the button labeled WHITE HOUSE BUNKER.

The six-foot video screen flashed on, and the image of an army colonel appeared. He answered with a curt, "White House."

"I'm General Price; get the president."

There was a pause, after which the army colonel said, "Yes, sir." He stood and walked out of view. In the background Price could hear the colonel telling the president who was on the line.

Pethers quickly walked into view. "Price, go ahead. What's the status?"

Price took a deep breath. "Sir, we've lost communication with New York."

Pethers flopped into the chair behind him and whispered, "Oh, my God! Oh, my God, no." After a pause he asked, "Are you sure?"

Price saw the color fade from Pethers's face. "Well, sir, the only thing we can assume at this moment is that Captain Kenada has detonated one of the Knight Hawks in the area of New York City. We have lost all communications with the New York area. The only thing that could cause that would be a nuclear detonation. We haven't received any damage reports yet, so we don't know how bad it is. Depending on where it detonated, it could easily take out the whole city."

The president was visibly shaken. The thought of up to two million people vaporized by the heat of a thermonuclear detonation was mind-numbing. If the bomb had gone off near the city, Manhattan would be impossible to rebuild. The country's economy—hell, the world's economy—would be thrown out of whack for decades.

Pethers came back to the real world and said in a subdued voice, "General, do you have any idea where this, this K woman is?"

"Sir, all we can say at the moment is that Captain Kenada is within a fifty-mile radius of New York."

Knight Hawk

"Do you think she was killed by the bomb?"

"Sir, I don't know, but using the worst-case scenario, I'm assuming that she is still alive and still very dangerous." After the general spoke, there was silence on the phone line. Price could tell that the president was deep in thought again and that his waking nightmare wasn't over yet.

Pethers was trying to decide what the best course of action would be at the moment. "OK, General Price, let's assume that this K woman is alive."

"Kenada."

"Yes, Kenada. Do whatever it takes to keep her from launching the other Knight Hawk, and if we can, contain her in the New York area. If not, chase her out to sea."

Admiral Watson heard Pethers say the magic word *sea*, and he knew that was his cue. He stepped forward to bring himself into view of the camera and said to the president, "Mr. Pethers, if I may interrupt, I have a suggestion."

"What's your idea, Watson?"

Watson stepped in front of Price and said, "Sir, at this moment there is a squadron of F-14s and F-18s prepared to take off from the USS *Eisenhower*. It's about four hundred miles east of New York, and it's heading for home port at Norfolk. We can use these two squadrons to pursue and shoot down this F-15."

While Watson made his suggestion to the president, Price could see through the window that something important was happening down on the command center floor. He watched Colonel Miller move quickly to one of the controller stations, grab a headset and hold it to his ear. Then Miller started giving directions to some of the other officers in the room. Price couldn't hear what he was saying, but he saw Miller's mouth moving

217

and his finger pointing at the main screen.

When Miller finished, he looked up into the war room window directly at Price. Once Colonel Miller saw that he had eye contact with General Price, he motioned for Price to come to the command center.

Price looked back at Watson and then at the president on the monitor. Watson was deep in the middle of his plan. Price slowly backed out of camera view and walked directly to the waiting Colonel Miller. When the two were face-to-face, Price asked, "What happened?"

Miller leaned forward to speak into Price's ear. "Sir, we're picking up transmissions from Looking Glass, the navy's airborne command center in an EC-135. They are talking to Kenada now, but we're only hearing one side of the conversation, so we can only guess what she's saying."

"Have we made direct contact with Looking Glass yet?"

"No, not yet, but one of the navy controllers is trying to bring them up through one of the secure channels. If we can't get them that way we'll call them on guard."

They didn't have to wait long. Almost simultaneously there were two different radio transmissions. On the guard radio frequency came the command for all fighter aircraft to vacate the New York area and maintain a hundred-mile radius. Over a secure frequency came another radio call. "Palace, Looking Glass . . . Palace, Looking Glass."

General Price recognized the call signs. Looking Glass was Admiral Griffin, the CINCLANT—the commander in chief of Atlantic forces—and he was calling "The Palace," the puzzle palace, the call sign for the Pentagon command center.

Price picked up the table mike in front of the controller and pushed down the talk button on its base. "Go ahead, Looking Glass; this is Price at the Palace. What's going on there?"

The voice on the speaker came across clearly, but there was still a high level of background static. "Buster, we have contact with the woman in the stolen F-15. She has given us her demands. One of which is that we evacuate all fighter jets within a hundred-mile radius of New York City. She is also asking for an aerial refueling."

Anxiously Price asked, "Where is she located?"

"At the moment she says that she is circling directly over New York City."

Price was surprised. He thought, well, if she's there, then the city isn't gone. He keyed the mike again. "Looking Glass, what is the status of the city? We don't have any communication with New York."

"Palace, it appears that the only damage to the area was electrical. We're about a hundred fifty miles south of the city, and we saw the detonation. It was definitely at altitude, so I would say there was no physical damage, just electrical from the pulse."

Price could feel an air of relief come over himself. All was not lost, at least not yet.

The voice on the radio continued, "Palace, we are approaching New York and we are planning to refuel the F-15 in about fifteen minutes. That is, unless you have other directions."

Price paused for a moment, then said, "Looking Glass, proceed with refueling. Monitor this frequency; we will contact you in a few minutes with a detailed plan. Also, establish a radio relay link with us so we can hear the Eagle's radio transmissions. Once we have a plan, we may want to communicate with her."

"Looking Glass copies."

General Price turned to Colonel Miller and said,

"Monitor the channels and keep me posted if anything happens. I have an idea."

Price turned and walked back into the war room. Watson was still droning on to Pethers about his plan.

Price walked into the camera's view and said, "Excuse me, sir, but I have an update."

On the video screen Price saw President Pethers sit a little taller in his seat. "Go ahead, Price."

Price resumed the position he had been in before he had been so rudely interrupted by Watson and his elaborate plans. He looked directly into the camera and said, "We have made contact with Kenada. It appears that she did indeed detonate one of the Knight Hawks in the New York City area. Fortunately, it was at altitude, somewhere between fifty and a hundred miles up. That's high enough not to cause any damage other than electrical. The EMP, the electromagnetic pulse, is what wiped out communications."

The president sighed. "Well, that's damn good news. What's she doing now, and when the hell are you going to get her out of the air?"

"Well, sir, she's demanding that all jet fighters evacuate outside a hundred-mile radius of the city, and she also wants to be refueled. She says if we don't meet her demands she will set off the other nuke." General Price paused and waited for the president to respond. Just to let the president think that he was running the show, Price asked Pethers, "What would you like us to do, sir?" Price knew that Pethers was not a military strategist, but he was hoping that the president would either select the obvious choice or give control of the situation back to him.

Pethers finally said, "General, it appears we don't have much choice in the matter, now, does it?"

"No, sir, it doesn't."

"OK, General, I think for the moment we'll meet her demands. Clear the area and give her some gas. What else do you think we should do?"

Price was smiling inside as he thought, *Good he's giving the reins back to me. Now maybe Watson will shut up for a while.*

"Mr. President, I've had a few moments to think about this situation and here's my plan. . . ." As he spoke Price took off his jacket, loosened his tie and sat down on the table behind him.

Price turned away from the camera and saw Colonel Miller watching him through the window. As they made eye contact, Price formed a circle with the thumb and index finger of his left hand, then poked the index finger of his right hand into the circle. Price then nodded his head up and down. Miller recognized Price's hand signal. It was the sign a pilot gave to his crew chief to go on with refueling.

Price stared deep into the camera again as if he were peering directly into the president's eye and said, "Sir, I think Admiral Watson has a good plan, but since there has been a change in the situation, we should also modify the plan slightly."

"OK, General, what is it?" Pethers asked.

Admiral Watson appreciated Price's praise of his plan, but he was wary of that last bit about modifying it.

"Sir, I believe now is the time to combine the air power. Admiral Watson's plan was basically to surround New York City with navy jets and then go in after her. Now that we know Kenada can activate and launch a Knight Hawk, that part won't work. If Kenada feels she's trapped, I'm sure she'll launch the remaining Knight Hawk, and then New York will be gone for sure."

Admiral Watson's appreciation quickly waned. His suspicions were confirmed. Price had just sunk his plan in one shot. He was wondering if Price was going to use any part of his plan at all.

General Price knew Watson was perturbed, to say the least, but he didn't look at him. Instead he looked into the camera and continued, "Earlier we tried to set up a gauntlet in this corridor between Norfolk and Lexington. It didn't work because there was no prey in the trap. Now that we know where Kenada is, I think that we should try the gauntlet again. This time the corridor is between New York and Lexington. We will use a tanker as our bait for the trap, lure her over a desolate area of West Virginia and shoot her down."

As Price started to lay out his plan, he could see around the room and on the monitor that he had everybody's attention. "Since Kenada wants to be refueled and she wants to go to Lexington, we will meet her demands and use that as part of the trap. This is how we should do it.

"First, we must get control over Kenada's position. Since she needs fuel, and the Looking Glass airplane is in the area, it will be our tanker and our bait.

"Second, we need to reset the jaws of the trap. The scrambled jets that were in the gauntlet before will be used again, but the gauntlet needs to be widened.

"Third, we go in for the kill. Once Kenada's in the track and starts taking on fuel, she'll be vulnerable to attack only from the rear, and only by guns, not by missiles.

"Her radar has a forward range of about eighty miles, and will only pan the area ahead of her and sixty degrees off the nose of the jet. From the side and behind she's radar-blind. The Eagle does have radar sensors that will detect a radar lock from a missile or a jet, and the infrared sensors will detect and track a fast-moving heat source from a missile and then determine if it's a threat. As I understand it, these infrared sensors are tuned only to the high heat of missiles, not jet engines, because they're considerably cooler.

"This is where the jets from the *Eisenhower* will come into play. When the tanker and the Eagle are in position over this area of West Virginia, four Navy F-18 fighters with infrared will come in from behind for a gun kill. The rest of the navy's fighters will form the rear of the gauntlet and close off any escape if the F-18s fail."

Pethers, although not a strategist, smiled and said, "I like it, but why exactly can't you use missiles?"

General Price thought he had made his point clear, but he didn't mind explaining it again. "Good question, Mr. President. The answer is simple. She will be able to detect any type of missile we fire at her and have a few seconds of warning. Which is probably long enough to launch the last Knight Hawk. This Kenada has been able to outmaneuver AIM-7 and AIM-9 missiles several times. If you want, we could take that gamble and use missiles instead of guns. If you wish."

The president was a little embarrassed at not realizing the soundness of the general's strategy at first, but didn't let it show. "Ah OK, General, now I understand. It sounds like a good plan. Do it, and keep me posted."

"Yes, sir. Oh, Mr. President, we will have your monitors there in the bunker tied in with ours in a few minutes. That way you'll be able to watch our progress. We're in the process of linking up with the Looking Glass aircraft so we can have radio communication with Kenada. When we have that done we'll also pipe that over there."

Pethers just nodded and said, "Good."

Price turned to Admiral Watson. "You heard the man; let's get to work."

Watson was slightly disappointed that he was not calling the shots, but he had his orders, and like any good military officer, he would obey.

Price and Watson walked off camera, out of the battle staff room and into the command center.

Colonel Miller was still busy giving directions to the other officers in the room when Price and Watson walked up. Miller looked at Price and said, "Sir, we've gotten the radio relay set up between Kenada and us, but it's not a good connection. There's still a bit of static. We've heard that Looking Glass will start refueling in about five minutes."

Price was pleased that things were working out. "Good. Tell those guys in Looking Glass not to try anything. No heroics. I want Kenada to think that she's getting everything her way. Let me know when they hook up for refueling."

Price turned to the other officers and said, "There are a few things that need to be done posthaste. First, we need to have everybody on the same frequency with us: any jets that are scrambled, Looking Glass and all of the AWACS planes. We also need to refuel all of the jets that are airborne now. We need to get as many of them on tankers as possible. Those that can't will have to return to base to be refueled."

Then Price said to Watson, "OK, Watson, the second part is yours. It's time for some of your real pilots. Scramble a four-ship of FLIR-equipped F-18s from the carrier and send them directly to New York. Tell them not to use radar; they can only use infrared. The kill must be done with guns only. They are not to use radar-guided or heat-seeking missiles. When they're close enough for a gun kill, they are to shoot on sight, and I want their first bullets to hit the cockpit. Have them tune in frequency 347.25 on the UHF using Have-Quick on their radios. Once they get within fifty miles of the city, have AWACS give them intercept vectors.

"They are not to get any closer than fifty miles until AWACS gives them the go-ahead. When the Eagle is hooked up for fuel, then and only then are they to go in for the kill. That way she will be an easy target, and she'll be concentrating on refueling.

"If at all possible, make the first shots directly into the canopy. Death must be instantaneous; she can't be allowed one second of warning to launch the Knight Hawk.

"The third thing, Watson, is that after those jets are airborne, scramble everything else off that ship you can send. If your Hornets miss, I want them backed up. We can't let her get away. Got it?"

Admiral Watson was pleased with his orders from Price. Now the navy had the chance to redeem itself. After all, since the Eagle's first kills were navy jets, it was only fitting that the navy get its revenge. "I got it, Buster. Consider it done. I'll pass it on."

Admiral Watson walked over to the console where two naval officers sat, and repeated verbatim the commands from Price. The ranking officer at the console typed in the commands as Watson spoke. When he was done, he quickly scanned the message on the screen to check for errors, then hit the transmit button.

General Price said to Admiral Watson, "Find out how long it will be before the Hornets are launched. We need to know so we can plan when and where to intercept." Then Price turned back to Colonel Miller. "Get with Looking Glass and have them refuel at an airspeed of two hundred fifty knots. We need to buy some time so the F-18s from the *Eisenhower* have time to catch up. We don't want this Eagle to get past the spot where we want to drop her."

Admiral Watson approached Price and said, "We will have launch of four infrared F-18s from the *Eisenhower* in ten minutes. The remaining thirty-six fighters from the *Eisenhower* are a mix of F-14s and F-18s, with a couple A-6s. They should all be airborne in about twenty-two minutes. Those jets will be forming the eastern containment wall."

The White House

Pethers sat pensively for a few seconds. He was glad to hear that all was not lost, at least for the moment. He looked at Borda and without hesitation said, "I think it's time that I go."

"Where?"

"To the Capitol to give my address. They're waiting for me."

"Are you serious? What makes you think this is over?"

Pethers stood up, looked Borda square in the face and said, "Oh, this is far from over. In fact it's possible that in just a few minutes another Knight Hawk might be coming here."

"Well then, why not stay here where it's safe?"

"Yolanda, if that missile does come here, it won't matter. If it doesn't come down here, I can't be hiding, not while Congress is waiting. Now that there's been a detonation, I've got to tell the public. The cat's out of the bag. People will think I was a coward, and then I'd lose votes in the election. On the other hand, if I'm out there knowing that it could come, people would think I was heroic."

"Well, Rick, you're right there; people would think you're heroic. Stupid and foolish, but heroic. That's very noble for the captain to go down with his ship, but I don't think it's very smart."

"I agree with you, but it's a gamble I've just got to take. You should stay here. There's no need for both of us to go. If we do get nuked, somebody will have to be around to run the country. Besides, Yo, you always did want to be president."

Borda had no response. She thought that someday she would be the next president, but she didn't expect to get it this way. "Very funny, Rick. Get out of here."

Chapter Sixteen

21:05
USS Eisenhower

Less than sixty minutes after the call to general quarters was sounded, the floating fortress was ready for battle. Five thousand men and women had each performed their cog of a task in the gearwork of this massive war machine. The greatest of all of the activity was centered around the aircraft hangar bays and the flight deck. The maintenance and the munitions personnel were making their final preparations, loading, arming and preflighting their jets. The aircrews were all prepared for flight. Along with their Nomex long underwear, flight suit and G suit, each put on his exposure suit in the unlikely event he ended up in the bone-chilling waters of the Atlantic.

Captain Shephard had received this second message and he knew that the time had come. He stepped down the hall, down a flight of steps and into the officers mess area for the pilots' mission briefing. Other than the aircraft bays, this was the largest area where all of the pilots could assemble for the captain to brief them all at once. As Captain Shephard stepped through the hatchway, someone recognized him and yelled, "Attention!"

In three seconds the officers mess went from a noisy room with anxious officers sitting about, passing around their own speculations as to a reason for the sudden alert, to a place of rigid silence, with everybody save the captain standing stiffly at attention.

"As you were," Captain Shephard said as he walked to the podium in the front of the room. Shephard was a little surprised by how crowded the room was. Not only were all of the eighty seats filled, but there were another thirty crewmen standing along the walls. Every eye in the room was on him. The silence was deafening. Shephard could swear that everybody had stopped breathing just so they wouldn't miss a word.

"As most of you have already heard, there has been a nuclear explosion at altitude over New York City. Because of what has happened, we are at Defcon Two alpha alert. However I'm sure that most of you don't know the reason why. Let me fill you in. At 19:25 hours at Langley Air Force Base, there was an unauthorized takeoff of one of the F-15s on alert status. It is piloted by an air force officer, and this individual has threatened to detonate her remaining Knight Hawk missile over a major metropolitan area if her ransom demands are not met. Since her departure from Langley she has been engaged by numerous aircraft in combat. Up to now she has shot down three F-14s, one F-4, four F-18s, four F-16s and one F-15. She has also launched and detonated one Knight Hawk at altitude over New

York City." Shephard paused after rattling off the list of casualties and looked at the stunned faces of his pilots.

In their faces he could see disbelief, amazement, and awe all mixed with various degrees of jealousy. The combined kills of every pilot in the room were only three, but Kenada had racked up an impressive thirteen in less than ninety minutes.

Shephard read the first message aloud for the benefit of those who hadn't heard about it through the grapevine. He gave a few seconds for all of the groans to subside; then he started to read the pertinent section of the second message, which read:

USS EISENHOWER, IMMEDIATELY LAUNCH FOUR IN-FRARED-EQUIPPED F-18S TO INTERCEPT AND SHOOT STOLEN F-15. DO NOT USE RADAR OR MISSILES. KILL MUST BE DONE WITH GUNS ONLY AND AT POINT-BLANK RANGE.

AFTER TAKEOFF STEER TWO SEVEN ZERO AND CLIMB TO TEN THOUSAND FEET. LAUNCH IMMEDI-ATELY. CONTACT CRYSTAL BALL ON UHF 347.25 FOR FURTHER DIRECTIONS AFTER AIRBORNE.

ALL OTHER AVAILABLE FIGHTER AIRCRAFT WILL BE LAUNCHED WHEN READY. THE REMAINING AIRCRAFT WILL BE USED TO FORM A CONTAINMENT WALL EAST OF THE AREA OF ENGAGEMENT. ASSEMBLE AT TEN THOUSAND FEET IN SPREAD FORMATION. STEER TWO SEVEN ZERO AND CONTACT CRYSTAL BALL ON UHF 347.25 AFTER AIRBORNE."

Shephard looked around the room at the expressions on the faces of his crew. On the left side of the room he saw Cmdr. Dan Haley, Lt. Dawn Rutherford, Lt. Tom Keller, and Lt. Chip Beck. "You four are my most experienced F-18 pilots. You will be going in for the kill.

"Haley, you will do the honors, and be the lead for your group. Your job is to take the shot and splash this Eagle. You other three will be there just in case Haley misses." Gesturing to the rest of the pilots in the room, Shephard said, "The rest of you will be part of a containment barrier, and will be used by Crystal Ball to herd this Eagle where they want her. Any questions?"

The room was silent.

Captain Shephard added another layer of seriousness to his already somber face. "I have one more thing that I must say. It is imperative that this F-15 be destroyed. We cannot allow it to escape or launch its remaining missile. If something happens and Commander Haley's flight fails, you are all authorized to fire at will after you are given the launch code words 'Rolling Thunder, Rolling Thunder.'

"Commander Haley, your flight will be in a dangerous and pivotal position, especially if you or any member of your flight is in the area when the launch code words are transmitted. All aircraft inside the containment area will be a target if you or your flight fail."

Shephard again paused and this time looked at Haley, Rutherford, Beck and Keller. After they each acknowledged their predicament with a nod, Shephard continued, "OK, everybody, be careful out there; good hunting and good luck. . . . May God be with you all."

Admiral Shephard picked up the mike for the ship's intercom system and in a clear voice announced, "Attention all hands, attention all hands. Battle stations, Battle stations. Red flight, prepare to launch. Red flight, prepare to launch. This is not a drill. I repeat, this is not a drill."

The duty launch officer stepped up to the podium after the captain stepped away. He was expecting and hoping for a little action. He felt a little envious that he couldn't lead this mission. He read the tail-number assignment to all of the pilots, along with the frequencies and departure procedures. They quickly copied the pertinent information on their knee boards. The duty officer then wished them good luck.

The first four pilots grabbed their Nomex jackets, threw their arms in them, grabbed their helmets, ran out of the room and went directly to the waiting F-18s up on deck. The rest of the Red Flight pilots followed.

On the flight deck, life was miserable. It was dark, cold and damp. The chill of the wet wind was cutting right through everybody's clothes. Even with warm gloves on, all of the maintenance crews were working with cold-numbed fingers and toes. In this kind of weather the best way to stay warm was to keep moving.

The duty launch officer had tried to second-guess the scramble orders. Unfortunately he guessed wrong. Since the premier jet fighter on this ship was the Tomcat, he had two positioned in the catapults and two in line behind them. His choice would have been acceptable if the Tomcats were infrared equipped.

The four-ship of F-18s would have to wait till the catapults were cleared before they could launch. The duty launch officer was faced with a quick predicament. He had to clear the catapults ASAP. Pulling the Tomcats off would take too long, fifteen to twenty minutes, plus they'd have to move all of the Hornets too. The obvious answer was to launch the Tomcats first, then the Hornets. At least that way the Hornets would be airborne in four minutes.

Cmdr. Dan Haley was the first F-18 pilot out of the briefing room. The other members of his flight were right behind. For Haley, stepping onto the carrier flight deck was not appealing. Going from the warm, dry and cozy briefing room to the hostile weather on the flight deck gave him chills.

Haley put his head down and started to run into the wind toward his jet. Feeling the cold, wet wind bite into his face, he made a mental check just to make sure that he had his exposure suit on. He did. He knew that if he went down in this kind of weather without it he'd be dead from exposure in minutes.

Over the roar of the engines and the howl of the wind, Haley heard Rutherford's voice: "Move it, honey; you're blocking traffic."

As Haley gave a quick look back at his favorite wingman, he felt an affectionate little pinch on his behind. He smiled and said, "Hey, sailor, got any plans for tonight? I'll buy you a drink when I come back."

Rutherford smiled and yelled, "You're on," then headed for her jet.

Haley and the other pilots behind him had to carefully and quickly maneuver through the narrow passages between the waiting aircraft. What made it worse was dodging the maintenance crew chiefs dragging cords and hoses, and the munitions personnel driving bomb loaders stacked with missiles. If that wasn't bad enough, most of the jets that were preparing for launch already had their engines started. Running into a three-hundred-degree blast of hot, flaming air coming at four hundred miles per hour is not a good way to start a day.

In a way the scramble to his jet reminded Haley of his football days at the academy: zigzagging between people and things, looking for holes in the walls in front of him, and even carrying his helmet under his arm like a football. Of course this playing field was much more dangerous. The grass on this field was cold steel, and he wasn't wearing any pads. Here everybody played for keeps. On this field even running out of bounds over the carrier edge would take him out of the game permanently.

Several jets positioned in line for the catapults already had their engines started and were waiting for their pilots. Pilots from the other flights had come out and gone through the preflight checklists while they were being briefed.

Haley came to his jet and found the crew chief still talking to the pilot over an intercom line. Haley recognized Seaman First Class Bently and approached him. Bently pulled his left earphone away from his ear as Haley yelled, "This is my jet. Is it ready?"

Bently looked at Haley and pulled the intercom mouthpiece away from his face. He leaned his head close to Haley's and yelled into his ear over the roar of the running engines, "Everything's done except for the final engine run-up."

Haley, not wanting to stay out in the weather, said, "Good, I'll take over from here."

Bently nodded, put the intercom mouthpiece over his face and relayed the message to the pilot in the jet.

Haley quickly stepped to the left side of the jet and watched the canopy slowly push up. The pilot inside climbed down the entry ladder and yelled into Haley's ear, "It's a good jet. Everything is go." Then he gave the thumbs-up signal and said, "Good luck."

Haley jumped up onto the ladder and stepped into the cockpit. As he sat down, his left hand was on the canopy switch, pushing the toggle to the down position. As the canopy came down, Haley pushed the canopy lock lever forward, sealing out the weather. He was pleased to feel the hot air coming out of the vents as it warmed his legs and hands. After he strapped in and hooked himself up to the comm and oxygen lines, he started to feel comfortable again. He pressed the intercom button. "OK, Bently, I'm ready for run-up."

Haley looked to make sure Bently was clear of the intakes. He could barely see his crew chief twenty feet away. Not only was it dark, but clouds of steam from the catapult kept engulfing him. Haley thought, *Poor guy. What a scene from hell.* For a moment he felt pity; then he heard Bently's voice.

"Go ahead; all clear."

Haley put his feet on the tops of the rudder pedals where the brakes were, and pushed as hard as he could. He locked his knees and proceeded with his preflight engine checks. First he pushed the right engine throttle to mil power and watched his gauges. The right engine accelerated and he could feel the vibration of the engine. One hundred percent rpm, EGT good, fuel flow good, and then back to engine idle. He pushed the left throttle forward to check the left engine with the same results.

Haley idled his engine, then made a quick scan of all of his instruments just in case something might have been missed by the previous pilot. Everything was in order. He looked at Bently, signaled with the thumbs-up gesture, and said, "Bently, everything is A-OK, thanks."

"You got it, Ace. Go get 'em." Bently ran under the belly of his jet and unplugged the communication line to the intercom, then went back to where he was standing. He turned sharply, and even though he was soaking wet, he gave a crisp salute. Haley saluted back, then watched Bently disappear into a cloud of steam.

Haley checked his radio. He set the secondary preset frequency to 347.25 and turned to their ground control frequency. He pushed the mike button on the throttle quadrant. "Ike Control, this is Red One One Eight for check in. I'm number two in line for catapult one."

The headphones in Haley's helmet came to life. "Red One One Eight, Ike copies ready status. Estimate launch in four minutes. Stand by."

Haley double-clicked the mike button in acknowledgement. Seconds later he heard Lieutenant Rutherford making the same call.

Around him, Haley could see other pilots doing what he had just finished doing. Up ahead of him he saw the blast fence go up behind the two Tomcats on the catapults. Even inside his cockpit, shielded from the outside world, he could still feel the deep, crackling roar of the F-14s' afterburners.

Haley sat waiting in his Hornet while the next two Tomcats were marshaled into position on the catapults. He couldn't see the crewmen, only the waving, lighted wands of one of the catapult crew coaxing the jet into the final position. As the lighted wands crossed and formed an X, the Tomcat jolted to a stop. Haley thought, One down, one to go.

On the radio, Haley could hear the pilots in the jets behind him check in with him and the ground control launch officer.

The blast fence in front of him dropped, and beyond it Haley could see the white-orange afterburner flames of a pair of Tomcats heading for the clouds. Directly in front of him he could see the lighted wands of the catapult director. Both wands were waving him closer. Haley dropped his feet off the brakes and inched the throttles forward just enough to get his aircraft rolling.

The director kept waving as Haley moved closer and closer. Just before the long metal Pitot tube on the nose of Haley's jet almost impaled him in the chest, the director crossed the wands over his head and formed an X. Haley pushed the toes of his boots hard on the top of the rudder pedals to stop his jet and put both of his hands on the canopy rails. That was the signal to the catapult crew that it was safe to go under the jet and attach the nose landing gear to the catapult sled. This way, with his hands on the rails, the ground crew knew the pilot didn't have his hands on the throttles. In the past there had been unfortunate ground crew members sucked into the engine intakes when the pilot did his engine run-up.

Although he had done this a thousand times before, Haley could feel his heart begin to race. Ever since his first carrier takeoff, he used to have nightmares about getting launched off a catapult, only to crash in the water below and be run over by ninety thousand tons of floating steel. Although he had seen numerous films that had shown that happening to other pilots, he had never actually seen it happen himself.

To his right Haley could see his wingman, Rutherford, being guided onto the neighboring catapult. He gave her a nod of the head and she blew him a kiss. Under her jet he could see the crew scurrying to attach the nose landing gear to the catapult. Under his feet Haley could hear and feel the heavy metal tow bar clang against the plate steel of the carrier deck as it was locked into place on the catapult sled. With their job done, the catapult crew ran back to the side, away from the jet. Haley saw the crew under his wingman's jet finish the hookup and step off to the side for the launch. Haley looked at Rutherford and gestured with the thumbs-up, asking her if she was ready. She nodded her head and gave the same thumbs-up signal back, then double-clicked her mike. Haley keyed his mike. "Ike, Red flight One One Eight, ready for launch."

"Red flight One One Eight, launch when ready."

"OK, guys, time to rock and roll." Haley flicked his landing lights on and off. The director was still standing an inch in front of his jet with his arms raised, holding his wands in an *X*. He looked around to make sure the catapult launch crew was safe and clear. They were. The director separated both wands straight up in the air and started moving them in tight circles, the signal to run the engines up to max power. After ten seconds, when the engines stabilized at power, the director ran off to the side, still holding both wands high in the air. The crewman controlling the catapult checked the pressure in the system. Seeing that it was fully charged, he signaled the director that he was ready for the launch. The director did an abrupt about-face and took a big step forward. While keeping his left leg straight behind him, he bent his right leg, ducked his head down and pointed both wands forward.

In that moment Haley could feel himself being slammed against his seat as he was shot off the carrier into the dark nothingness of the night. What a rush, to go from standing still on a heaving deck to an airspeed of one hundred and forty knots in less than four seconds.

For an instant Haley felt himself akin to those ancient sailors who thought the world was flat, and that if they sailed too far they'd fall off. In his rearview mirror Haley could see the flat world he had just left, and nothing more. Now all he had to do was keep his nose up and make sure he was flying and not falling.

Being thrown from something into nothing was a disorienting experience for anybody. Fortunately for Haley and all pilots, there were instruments that gave them a magic window to the world.

Haley pulled his joystick back halfway between his knees and his crotch and immediately started his instrument cross-check. Looking from instrument to instrument, from gauge to gauge, his eyes would always return to his attitude indicator. In this little black instrument in the center of his dash, Haley watched the two-colored ball float, twist and turn as he moved the stick. This ball, with the top half painted light blue for the sky and the bottom half painted black for the ground, was locked by gyros so that its horizon, its dividing line between blue and black, was the same as the real world's horizon.

Haley held his pullback on the stick until he could see on the attitude indicator that he was at thirty degrees of climb. At thirty degrees nose-up he released the pressure to stabilize his climb. He then pushed his stick slightly to the left and came to a heading of 265, the course that would take him to the city.

He leveled off at ten thousand feet and throttled back to eighty percent. His airspeed indicator stopped at 410 knots. The F-18 was easily capable of going three times that speed but now he had to wait for his wingmen to catch up. Just as Haley had started to relax and become entranced by the clear panorama of the millions of stars above and the clouds below, his radio crackled to life with a familiar feminine voice. "Red One One Eight, Two's in, right side."

Over his right shoulder, Haley could see the ghost gray image of the number-two wingman's F-18 slightly behind him. Dan double-clicked his mike. He thought to himself, Another four minutes and we'll have Keller and Beck.

The next two F-18s off the *Eisenhower* had no trouble finding and joining Haley and Rutherford. In the clear, cold air above the clouds, all jets left an infrared heat trail that could be seen forty to fifty miles away.

Haley looked over his left and right shoulders to make sure his three wingmen were in position. "OK, you guys, let's dance." He raised his left fist up to eye level, then straightened his arm and pushed his fist directly in front of him. He looked over his left shoulder at his two wingmen to see if they got the signal to accelerate. They both nodded. Haley repeated the same signal with his right hand and then checked his right wingman, Rutherford. She nodded her head.

Haley raised his head straight up, and with a quick jerk pulled his head down, which meant *now*. As soon as his head came down, all four pilots in unison pushed their throttles to 100 percent. As all four jets accelerated up to 750 knots, the three wingmen kept their eyes focused on Haley's jet. They each had to continuously jostle the throttles so they wouldn't overrun the jet ahead of them or fall behind.

Well, it's time to check in, Haley thought. He keyed the mike button. "Ike Eye, Red One One Eight. Formation complete."

"Roger Red One One Eight, we have you on screen. Squawk two one one eight, turn to heading two six zero, climb to flight level one eight zero, and contact Crystal Ball on UHF 347.25."

As the voice on the radio spoke, Haley was busy writing the directions on the inside corner of his canopy with a white grease pencil. This was a practice Haley said he had picked up from one of his instructors in pilot training. Haley's mother would say that it was his childhood habit of writing on the walls that he never outgrew.

Haley returned the radio call. "Roger, Ike, Red One One Eight copies two one one eight squawk, head two six zero up to one eight zero, contact Crystal Ball on 347.25."

"Affirmative, Ike out."

Haley pulled gently back on the joystick and started a steady climb up to flight level one eight zero, eighteen thousand feet. Now that they were being handed off to the AWACS aircraft Crystal Ball, Haley needed to get his three wingmen to change frequency also. "Red flight One One Eight, freq change, 347.25."

Haley reached over to his radio. First he changed his squawk code and his radio frequency, and then he keyed his mike. "Red flight One One Eight."

Haley's wingmen responded: "Two," "Three," "Four."

Now that everybody was on the same radio net, Haley keyed the mike button again. "Crystal Ball, Red flight One One Eight."

"Go ahead, Red One One Eight."

"Crystal, we are two hundred miles east of New York, heading two six zero, climbing to flight level one eight zero, ETA New York twelve minutes."

"Red One One Eight, we have you on-screen. Maintain course, altitude and airspeed till further notice. Expect further guidance in ten minutes."

"Crystal, Red One One Eight copies."

Haley gave a little sigh of relief. They had all busted their buns to get to that spot of the sky at that moment, and now he knew that the next few minutes would be like the calm before a storm. He thought to himself, *Well, boys and girls, it's time to get ready to play ball.* He looked over his right shoulder at Rutherford to see her watching him, just as a wingman should. Haley held his fist up against the side of his helmet. His index finger was pointing up and the thumb was pointing backward. Rutherford recognized the check signal. When Haley looked back at her, she nodded her head to acknowledge his signal. He did the same over his left shoulder to his other two wingmen. When they replied, Haley wiggled the joystick quickly left and right twice to rock his wings. The three jets that had been flying so closely to Haley were now all drifting apart so they were a hundred yards away from each other. All three of Haley's wingmen recognized the signal to go into the combat spread formation so they each could perform their precombat checklist.

As briefed in the pilots' briefing on the *Eisenhower*, all four pilots armed their weapons. The primary weapon of choice for Haley would normally be his heat-seeking AIM-9L Sidewinder, followed closely by his radar-guided AIM-7 Sparrow. Both of these missiles had the ability to kill at a distance of several miles, but this mission dictated that the kill would be much, much closer, yards instead of miles. Haley didn't mind using his guns in combat when the situation demanded it, but this was going to be different.

In fact, Haley had never shot at another aircraft that was closer than five hundred yards, and now they wanted him to shoot this Eagle at a distance of less than one hundred yards. As far as he was concerned, that was hand-to-hand combat.

In the relative quiet of the moment, Haley also felt a little uneasy about this mission. From the details he was given in his briefing, this was not going to be combat; this was going to be an assassination.

Haley ignored his personal feelings and continued mechanically preparing for combat. He tried vainly to tune in several different TACAN radio beacons so he could verify his position and course to New York City. He knew that he was almost over New York, but he had no navigational or visual clues to verify his reckoning. He was puzzled. He knew the clouds would hide the lights, but he thought there would still be a glow from the city underneath. Then he remembered that the electromagnetic pulse from the detonated nuke had turned the lights of New York off.

Fortunately, Haley and his fellow pilots were using

infrared vision. In the distance ahead Haley could see bubbles of hot air rising above the relative flatness of the cooler cloud deck below them. That has to be New York City, he thought.

Chapter Seventeen

20:58

The glow above the clouds slowly dimmed, and the city of a billion lights winked into darkness. The towering skyscrapers of stone, steel, glass and light disappeared into the night. The patchwork of car-laden streets glowing with headlights and taillights was void of light and movement. The only thing that Kenada could immediately recognize as a point of visual reference was the huge burning oil slick from the flame-engulfed tanker at the Bayonne Terminal.

Kenada turned the light rheostat to dim all of the cockpit lights on the instruments so her eyes could adjust to the immediate darkness. She pointed the nose of her jet just to the right of the rising smoke column and started to circle it like a moth around a candle's flame. Flying a circle, five miles in diameter Kenada leveled off around five thousand feet, just under the clouds. She was high enough above the ground clutter to use her radar and scan the skies for other jets that might still be in pursuit.

Around the city Kenada could see some lights coming on and flickering in the distance, but the strongest lights were the still-burning flames beneath her in the New York Harbor, and the three at JFK International.

Kenada keyed the mike button but didn't hear the familiar static over her helmet headset. She knew her radio had gone off-line. When the Knight Hawk had detonated at altitude it had triggered an electromagnetic pulse that fried electrical circuits, especially those circuits with coils. The coiled wires, when hit with an EMP, became transformers that converted the EMP into an electric current. Usually the current was so strong it overpowered everything in the circuit. But Kenada knew there were safeguards incorporated into the numerous avionic systems of the F-15, as well as other military aircraft, that shielded the equipment from the damaging effects of an EMP. The last protective measure was a circuit breaker. As for Kenada's radio, the circuit breakers worked as advertised.

Kenada glanced at the utility panel by her left elbow and saw the reason for her radio's silence. There were still a few white rings around some of the circuit breakers that had popped off-line. She reset them all and made a quick scan of the instruments to see what was functioning.

The ground positioning system (GPS) satellite linkup had been interrupted by the nuclear blast, which had ionized the upper atmosphere. Kenada pressed the SELF-TEST button on the GPS display panel to make sure the equipment was functioning properly. The circuit was OK. She knew that the GPS would update once she left the area affected by the EMP. The remaining

Knight Hawk missile would still function on its own ring laser gyro inertial navigation system. Other than that, all of the Eagle's avionics were functioning properly.

Kenada keyed the mike button again. It was working now. "New York Central, Eagle." There was no answer. "New York Central, this is the Eagle." Again there was no answer.

Kenada call to New York Central fell on deaf ears. The standby backup generators for New York Central's air-traffic control facility had not yet come on-line to power up their radio nets. For the next few minutes all of the ground controllers from Boston, Massachusetts, to Trenton, New Jersey, were in the silent dark without power. So until they came back on the air, trying to talk to New York was useless.

Seconds later the static on her headset was interrupted abruptly by a deep, masculine voice. "Eagle, Looking Glass . . . Eagle, Looking Glass."

Kenada recognized the call sign of Looking Glass, and knew she was talking to the airborne command post for CINCLANT, the commander in chief of Atlantic forces. Looking Glass was an EC-135 aircraft out of Langley Air Force Base, the same base that she had stolen her Eagle from.

"This is Eagle. Go ahead, Looking Glass."

"Eagle, this is Looking Glass: what are your intentions and what are your demands?"

Kenada paused a moment to figure out just what moves were being played out, as well as to let them stew with the silence.

There were still numerous fighters in the area that posed a serious threat to the success of her plans, and Kenada knew that. With CINCLANT in the picture, that would mean that in addition to all of the air force fighters in the mid-Atlantic area, all of the U.S. Navy fighters could and more than likely would get involved.

Kenada wondered why the voice asked what her intentions were. They had to know what her original ransom demands were; otherwise they wouldn't have been scrambled. She decided this must be a stalling technique they were using while they set up a trap.

Kenada took a deep breath and keyed the mike button. "Looking Glass, this is Eagle. Identify yourself. Who am I talking to?"

A cool, very matter-of-fact and almost pompous voice responded to her question. "Captain Kenada, this is Adm. Bruce Griffin. I am commander in chief of the Atlantic forces for the navy. I have been sent to negotiate with you."

Kenada was taken aback at hearing her name being used over the radio. Now she knew that they knew who she was. Not that it made a difference. She had just never heard her name on the air; she had always answered to a call sign before. Kenada thought for a moment about her next response, then keyed the mike. "Well, Admiral Brucie, where are you?"

"I am in an EC-135 at twenty-two thousand feet heading zero two zero, approximately ninety-five miles south of New York. Where are you, and what do you want?"

Kenada detected a touch of agitation in the admiral's voice. She thought that calling the admiral Brucie would be demeaning to him and push one of his emotional buttons, and she was right. Her experience with high-ranking brass had taught her that their egos were equally as high. They were used to always getting their way, controlling the situation, and they hated to be belittled, especially by a subordinate.

Kenada knew that the admiral already knew the answers to the who, where and what, but was probably just asking to stall for time.

Kenada continued her humiliation strategy on the admiral. Her intent was to cloud his thinking with anger, which would keep him off guard and hopefully work to her advantage.

Kenada keyed the mike button again and used a snotty, indignant tone. "OK, Brucie. If you had been smart enough to listen to your intelligence source, you would have known that I'm at the Big Apple here in New York. Your intel would also have told you that I want ten thousand pounds of gold bullion loaded onto a KC-135, and that I'd meet it over Lexington."

"Captain Kenada, I'm familiar with your demands, and I understand that they have almost finished loading the gold onto a jet that you requested."

Kenada knew that the admiral was lying. There was no way in hell that they could get a KC-135 and the gold out to an airfield in the time that had passed, let alone load it. Kenada knew the admiral was stalling, so it was time to call his bluff with another bluff.

In a cool and calculated voice, Kenada said, "Admiral Brucie, you really should try to be more honest. I don't know what you take me for, but I don't like being lied to. Before you try to deny it, I want you to know that my sources haven't seen a single bar of gold leave the vault at Fort Knox, and they haven't seen anything that even resembles a KC-135 land at Lexington." Kenada was lying about her sources, but the admiral would never know.

The admiral didn't respond. There was nothing to say. He knew that he was caught in a lie. He was wondering how he was going to get out of this one.

Kenada said in a patronizing tone, "Now look here, Brucie, I know that you're just doing your job by telling me what I want to hear. I understand that. But if you want to deal with me, do as I say and don't lie to me when I ask you a question! Otherwise I squeeze this trigger and launch this puppy, and a few million people will become crispy critters . . . all because of you. And you know that I can . . . and will. Do you understand?"

With a little humility, the admiral responded, "I understand."

"Good, Brucie, I'm glad that you do, because I have a few more demands to add to my list. First, I want all fighter aircraft around New York to stay outside a hundred-mile radius of New York City. Is that clear?"

"Yes, Captain, perfectly."

"The next thing I want, admiral, is some gas, ASAP. I know that when all of these jets were scrambled some tankers were scrambled too.

"I'm about twenty minutes away from my bingo level of fuel. I'd hate to lighten my load so that I could stay up longer. Of course, I could always launch this Knight Hawk; that would lighten my load. But then if I did, it wouldn't matter how much fuel I had, would it?"

For a few moments, there was no response. Kenada expected as much. She thought, *I'll give you a minute, Brucie. I know you can't do this yourself. Besides, I'm sure you want to set up a trap.*

Kenada had learned her Air Force Academy lessons well. One of the first lessons taught in warfare was from the teachings of an old Chinese general, Tsun Tzu: "Know your enemy." Kenada knew what was going on during this silence. The admiral and the other officers in Looking Glass were busy conferring with their superiors, and that would mean the battle staff in the Pentagon.

She was right. In the EC-135 the admiral was talking to other officers on board, and he directed them to recall all of the fighters in the New York area and get them outside the one-hundred-mile radius. Other officers were directed to contact the battle staff over the radio using voice scramblers and tell them of the situation.

Kenada heard the evacuation recall command transmitted on the guard radio net to all of the jets in the area. As she circled above lower Manhattan, she was even able to pick out a small jet on the northern side of Manhattan breaking away from the city and heading north. *That must have been one of those Falcons that was on my tail earlier. I see he survived the EMP.* She was right; it was Ledet in his F-16, returning to Syracuse. Fuel was low and he was also plagued with electrical problems.

The admiral's voice finally broke the silence. "Eagle, Looking Glass."

"Go ahead, Brucie; the ball's in your court."

"Eagle, we will be over New York in twelve minutes, and rendezvous for refueling in fifteen."

"OK, Looking Glass, that's acceptable. Squawk one one one one on your IFF, drop down to ten thousand feet, fly directly to the city and I'll find you."

Admiral Griffin responded with a simple, "I copy." The admiral then clicked into the intercom with the pilot, Col. Bill Ferratto, and passed on the commands. "Ferratto, what's our heading and ETA over New York?"

"Sir, our heading is still zero two zero, and we should be over New York in about ten. Of course, that's only a guess, because all of the local TACAN and other navigation aides are out, and I sure can't see it."

"OK, maintain our heading, drop to ten thousand feet and squawk one one one one on the IFF. Looks like we're going to be passing gas to the Eagle." As the admiral spoke he could feel the nose of the plane pitch down and start the decline to ten thousand feet.

The admiral keyed the intercom again. "Ferratto, have you been monitoring my conversation with the Eagle?"

"Yes, sir."

"Good. In a few minutes we're going to be intercepted by the Eagle and I want you to reply to her radio call. Identify yourself as the pilot and follow her directions."

"Roger, sir. I'll wait for her to call."

Kenada continued scanning the skies as she circled the towering pillar of black smoke rising from the New York harbor. She powered up her radar and scanned for the tanker and other aircraft. Her radar was picking out traffic in all directions, but most were outside the hundred-mile radius or heading that way. "Well, it seems they're doing what I want. I don't see anybody trying to make a kill."

When the nose of her jet pointed south, she could see it on her radar, a big blip heading her way with 1111 right beside it. "Bingo, I've got you now." Kim keyed her mike button. "Looking Glass, Eagle."

"Go ahead, Eagle."

Kim paused for a moment. Even over the radio she could tell that this was not the admiral's voice. "Looking Glass, who are you? Where is the admiral?"

Admiral Griffin didn't wait for the pilot to respond before he cut in. "I'm here . . . Captain . . . I told the pilot to speak to you. In refueling operations it's standard procedure for the pilots to communicate with each other, and since you're giving us instructions on course and altitude, I just thought it would be better if you talked to the pilot instead of me. By the way, his name is Colonel Ferratto."

"Oh, is that you, Bill?"

"Roger that, Eagle." Colonel Ferratto, a stickler for proper radio protocol, used the radio call signs rather than Kenada's name, even though he knew who she was.

"You're right, Brucie, I do need to talk to the pilot, and the boom operator too, but I still want you on the air."

"Don't worry, Captain; I wouldn't dare leave."

"Good, Brucie. Now, Bill, I want you to turn to a heading of two three zero and drop down another three thousand feet and slow to three hundred knots."

"Roger, Eagle, Looking Glass turning two three zero and descending to seven thousand, slowing to three zero zero."

Kenada watched the blip on her radar screen change course, and looked for other blips that might be part of a trap. She maintained her heading and waited for the tanker to pass overhead. When she was sure it had passed over, she pulled hard back on the stick into a vertical climbing turn into the clouds above her. Seconds later her Eagle flew out of the top of the clouds into the moonlight like a dolphin leaping out of a frothy sea. She had no problem spotting the Boeing 707 in the moonlight. A jet that size could be seen miles away. Kenada continued pulling back on the stick until the nose of her jet tracked across the stars to the tanker now a thousand feet below her. She rolled her wings level and closed in.

The refueling boom operator was at his station, lying facedown in a little coffinlike compartment in the rear belly of the tanker, looking out the viewing port. In the moonlight he saw only a dark shadow moving across the face of the clouds, but lost sight of it against the stars. He keyed the mike button on his intercom and said, "Colonel Ferratto, this is Mitch. We've got company. I saw an F-15 a few seconds ago, but I lost it."

"Copy, Mitch; stay alert. It'll be moving in any minute now."

Kenada closed the distance and altitude difference within a minute and easily matched the tanker's speed. She stopped and held a position above and behind as well as off to the side of the tanker's tail. Before dropping down into the slot position for refueling, she made a quick visual scan of the skies around her. Kim sensed that something was not right; then she realized how awkwardly vulnerable she was, especially from behind. *Now would be the perfect time for someone to come up from behind,* she thought. *I am behind this big jet out in the open. I feel like there's a great big KICK ME sign on my back.* Quickly she reviewed her options. *My TEWS will tell me if anybody's using radar to sneak up on me, but I don't have any warning against normal vision or infrared. Well, I may not have warning but I can hide from sight.* Time was running out and so was her fuel. It was time to get the show on the road. Kim dropped into the slot and keyed her mike. "Looking Glass, Eagle. I'm here and I'm ready."

Over the intercom Admiral Griffin heard the radio call and heard the boom operator say, "OK, Major, she's in position, so hold her steady."

The pilot responded to the boomer, "You got it, Mitch." To Kenada he said, "Eagle, move into position when ready."

Kenada lightly nudged her throttle slightly forward, and her Eagle moved slowly closer. Once in position twenty feet behind the tanker and ten feet below, she turned the IFR (in-flight refueling) switch to open. She saw a light come on from the corner of her left eye, then looked over her left shoulder and visually checked that the in-flight refueling receptacle door was open and that it was illuminated. She moved in a little closer and said, "OK, boomer, fill 'er up nice and easy, and no tricks."

The boom operator, Mitch, keyed his mike button twice and nodded his head in the observation window so Kenada could see him. With the Eagle floating just fifteen feet away, Mitch used a small control joystick to maneuver the refueling boom, a long telescoping pipe with a pair of four-foot-long wings in the middle.

It's time to make life interesting, Kenada thought. "Looking Glass, Eagle."

"Go ahead, Eagle."

"Glass, I want you to descend another thousand feet."

"Eagle, are you sure you want us to do that? That will put us in the middle of the cloud deck." He asked the question so that the Pentagon and Crystal Ball would know.

"Roger, Glass, descending to six thousand feet. Do you have a problem with that?"

"Negative, Eagle. I don't if you don't. I just thought I'd let you know it's going to get a little bumpy, so hang on."

Kenada held her position as the tanker descended into the clouds. Immediately visibility dropped to almost fifty feet. As for the tanker, she could see the back half of it. The turbulence was rough and made refueling difficult. The first time she was bounced off the bottom of the refueling boom, and the operator had to quickly retract it away from the refueling receptacle in the Eagle to keep it from being damaged. The constant disconnecting because of the turbulence would turn the simple five-minute refueling operation into a twenty-minute roller-coaster ride. For Kenada the inconvenience and time delay were worth it. At least now she would have the peace of mind of knowing that nobody was going to sneak up from behind.

Admiral Griffin knew that going into the clouds would put a new twist on the plan. He keyed the intercom button to talk to the pilot. "Ferratto, have the crew chief start handing out parachutes to the crew. We need to be prepared just in case something goes wrong."

"Consider it done, Admiral," Ferratto answered.

In the cockpit Ferratto looked at the young pimple-faced crew chief sitting in the jump seat and said, "Sergeant Warren, start grabbing chutes and hand them out to everybody." After a quick nod of his head, Warren unbuckled himself from his seat and went about his new duty.

Pentagon

General Price and Admiral Watson had also been monitoring the radio conversations between Looking Glass and Eagle. Now that the refueling operation had commenced, it was time to spring the trap and send in the jets for the kill.

AWACS Crystal Ball

On board the AWACS aircraft, numerous military air-traffic controllers were getting ready to spring the trap.

As Lady Luck would have it, Col. Jeff Fugami was the commanding officer of operations on the AWACS aircraft. When it came to directing and posturing aircraft for combat, there was none better. Fugami was well qualified for this position. During Operation Desert Storm, he was responsible for controlling and directing all of the fighter air traffic over Baghdad. He practically lived aboard the AWACS aircraft. Rumor had it that even when he took naps on board the AWACS during those eighteen-hour days, he slept with his earphones on so he could hear what was going on in his sleep. Not only had he been one of the strategists who helped organize and orchestrate the air war over Iraq during Operation Desert Storm, but he was also a good friend of General Price. The two, Fugami and Price, had never met face-to-face, but they had spent a great deal of time together electronically. In a way, it was just like old times, Fugami and Price working together. Price would launch them into the air, and Fugami would make sure they were all in the right positions at the right times.

Fugami was not a cook, but he liked calling this strategy his three-layer cake. He would have groups of fighters at three different levels. The bottom layer would fly in at a thousand feet, the next layer would be around five thousand feet and the top layer at fifteen thousand, flying top cap. Fugami had baked this cake several times before, at Grenada, Panama and numerous times in the skies over Baghdad. This particular strategy worked well against small numbers of enemy aircraft. "Like shooting fish in a barrel," he used to say.

Captain Austin, one of the controllers who was eavesdropping on the conversation between Eagle and Looking Glass, heard the direction to refuel at a lower altitude. He said to himself, "This is not good." He turned and said, "Colonel Fugami, did you copy that they're refueling in the clouds?"

"What's their altitude?"

As he spoke Austin pointed to the Eagle and the tanker on his radar scope in front of him. "They're cruising at six thousand feet and doing about three hundred knots."

"Where are those navy F-18s with the infrared?"

Captain Austin pointed to a tight grouping of radar blips several inches away from the Eagle's blip. "They're here, about two hundred eighty miles behind them to the east."

Colonel Fugami stared intently and quietly at the scope as if it were a chess board and it was his turn to move. "How long will it take the F-18s to intercept the Eagle?"

Captain Austin did some quick punching on his pocket calculator, then said, "Sir, if they continue at their current speed of seven hundred fifty knots, they should catch up to them in about twenty to twenty-five minutes. Of course, if the Eagle and the tanker are deep in the clouds, they might not be able to find them for another forty of fifty minutes."

"Damn. This changes things considerably." Colonel Fugami reached for the frequency-select dial on the radio panel he was connected to, hit the preset button for the Pentagon and said, "Palace, Crystal Ball . . . Palace, Crystal Ball."

In the Pentagon, Colonel Miller answered the call. "Go ahead, Glass; this is Palace."

General Price and Admiral Watson both heard the call from Looking Glass and walked over.

"Palace, this is Specter with a change of conditions. The Eagle has dropped into the clouds to refuel, and that will probably mean that there will be a delay of engagement until after refueling of the Eagle is completed."

General Price recognized the nickname *Specter* and knew that Fugami was on the job. He said to Miller, "Tell Specter that Buster says to stand by."

Colonel Miller keyed his mike button and said, "Crystal Ball, Palace, Buster requests Specter to stand by."

"Crystal Ball, copy," came out of the speaker, fol-

lowed by silence. In the AWACS aircraft Colonel Fugami realized who he was working with in the
Pentagon. A warm feeling of familiarity came over him
and he thought, Just like old times.

While he was waiting for the Pentagon to rethink and
respond to this new situation, Colonel Fugami looked
at the radar scope to see if he could guess their next
move.

In the Pentagon, Price asked Watson, "If they're in
the clouds, can your F-18s go in after them, and if they
can, how long will it take?"

Watson thought for a moment before answering. "I
don't know, Buster. It's a toss-up. That system on the
18s is made primarily for night-fighting against slow-
moving ground targets. I don't know if they could find
a fast-moving airborne target in the clouds. If they can,
it might take thirty or forty minutes."

"That's too long. We've got to intercept her while
she's most vulnerable, while she's refueling. Now that
she's in the clouds, she probably thinks she's safe from
attack."

Watson looked at Price and said, "Well, rather than
wait to find them, why don't we just get the 18s into a
close position while she's refueling and then let a couple Sidewinders go into the clouds and find them? We
might lose the tanker, but we might also get lucky and
get the Eagle."

"I don't like it. That's too much of a long shot, and
it'll be certain death for the crew on the tanker."

Lieutenant Colonel D'Auria, who had been paying attention to their conversation, interrupted and said, "Excuse me, Admiral, General, but I think I have a possible
solution for you."

General Price looked at D'Auria and said, "Go ahead,
Don."

Knight Hawk

D'Auria pulled a laser pen out of his pocket and pointed it at the radar scope from Crystal Ball that was displayed on the main screen on the wall ahead of them. He moved the bright red dot onto one of the radar blips to the west of the tanker and the Eagle and said, "I think if we want to go with the original plan of a gun kill, here's our answer." D'Auria paused for a moment. "This aircraft is one of the two infrared-equipped F-16s that had tracked the Eagle back to New York while it was still in the clouds. It's about a hundred miles ahead of the Eagle and the tanker and has just finished refueling from a KC-10 tanker over Pennsylvania. If we have it change its course, we could have this jet go into the clouds for the kill while she's still refueling."

At first Watson didn't like the idea because it let the air force have the glory shot, but when he considered the fate of thousands, if not millions, he agreed. "Sounds good. Let's do it."

"I agree," Price said, "and I also think that we should bring the F-18s in as close backup, with two above the clouds and two below, just in case."

Watson agreed too. He could see the logic of Price's strategy and was also happy that his Hornets were still part of the action.

Price turned to D'Auria and ordered, "Make it happen."

"Crystal Ball, Specter, Palace."

Colonel Fugami in the AWACS answered, "Go ahead, Palace; this is Specter."

"Specter, locate and identify on your scope the F-16 squawking one one three eight. It's approximately one hundred miles southwest of the Eagle and the tanker."

Seconds later, without a verbal response from Specter, the blip and the numbers 1138 started flashing.

Price said, "Good, we're looking at the same jet."

"Specter, confirm that is the F-16 that is IR-equipped."

"Palace, Buster, confirmed."

General Price leaned toward the microphone and keyed the button. "Specter, this is Buster. Vector the F-16 squawking one one three eight, to intercept and shoot down the Eagle ASAP. The F-16 is to assume the mission of the lead F-18 coming off the *Eisenhower*. The *Eisenhower* F-18s will back up the F-16, two at five thousand feet and two at eight."

Colonel Fugami was surprised by the change of plans, and thought, *Good idea, Buster. Interesting move.* Aloud he responded, "Buster, Specter, I copy change. Expect intercept in six minutes."

General Price keyed the mike button again and said, "Specter, Buster, emphasize that this must be a gun-shot to the canopy from point-blank range. No radar and no missiles."

"Buster, Specter copies."

Fugami thought, Well, this is just like old times, changing plans on the fly. Fugami started directing his controllers about the change in plans.

One of the AWACS controllers keyed his mike button and said, "Syracuse One, Crystal Ball."

"Go ahead, Crystal Ball, this is Syracuse."

"Syracuse, say armament."

Capt. Lonnie Ray "Cajun" Ledet felt a little excited about being called by Crystal Ball. To himself he thought, *Could this be? . . . Do they want me to continue in the fight? Am I going to get another shot at this Eagle?* Ledet looked at the rounds-remaining window on his weapons panel and said, "Crystal Ball, this is Syracuse One with one AIM-9, two AIM-7s, and five seven zero rounds of twenty mike mike combat mix. My TACAN is inop, but FLIR and INS are operational."

Ledet paused and waited for a response from Crystal Ball. He wanted desperately to have another shot at this Eagle. That was why he opted for in-flight refueling rather than returning to base and ending his flight. He owed it to himself so he could avenge his fellow pilot, Richardson. Besides that, he needed to redeem himself for putting a Sidewinder missile into that oil tanker in the New York harbor.

On the AWACS, Colonel Fugami looked over the shoulders of his controllers and listened intently to the status report from the F-16 using the call sign *Syracuse*. To get a better understanding of how he was going to use this pilot and his jet, he needed to ask a few more questions. Colonel Fugami touched one of his controllers and said, "Let me talk to him." Fugami keyed his mike button. "Syracuse One, this is Specter."

Ledet was surprised that he was talking to the head man on Crystal Ball. "Go ahead, Specter." He had heard of Specter during Desert Storm and even received commands from Crystal Ball, but he never rated enough importance to be talking with the big kahuna.

"Syracuse, are you one of the F-16s that pursued the F-15 into New York City using infrared?"

Ledet's first thought was, Uh oh, I bet I'm about to catch hell for blowing up that bridge. He answered sheepishly, "Uh, Specter, that's affirmative." Ledet waited for the big hammer to come down on him. He just knew that he was going to be sent back to base for a court-martial.

"Syracuse, what type of FLIR system do you have and what are your capabilities?"

"Specter, I have the Night Sight FLIR system with helmet-mounted display, and it's state-of-the-art. The system is also tied in with radar for tracking and visual enhancement."

"Syracuse, how good are you at following heat trails in the clouds?"

With a little bit of pride Ledet answered, "Specter, I'm the best."

"OK, Syracuse, I've got a job for you. First go EMIS, and then break formation with that tanker and steer zero eight five and maintain twenty thousand feet."

Ledet turned to the new heading and flipped his radar switch to STANDBY. Since he was given the command to go EMIS, which meant minimizing electronic emissions, he just double-clicked his mike button.

Colonel Fugami heard the clicks and saw Ledet change his course on the radar scope. Now was the time to give him the rest of the commands. "OK, Syracuse, here's your mission. In three minutes you will be able to see a heat trail in the clouds coming at you from eleven-o'clock low. This trail will be from a KC-135 and the F-15 that is refueling. Your job is to go into the clouds behind them, fly up the heat trail and use a gunshot into the canopy at point-blank range. Remember, this is guns only, no radar and no missiles. We don't want her to see you or know that you're coming. We don't want to provoke her to launch her other Knight Hawk."

Ledet felt relieved that the hammer never came down. He understood that not only was he being given another chance for a kill, but that everybody was depending on him. He keyed his mike button and said, "Specter, Syracuse copies."

Fugami could see over the main scope that his three-layer cake was coming together. Far to the east on the scope, close to two hundred miles away, he could see the fighters from the *Eisenhower* coming in to form the eastern wall of the gauntlet circle. Ahead of those jets he saw a tight group of four jets. He pointed at the four blips on the scope and asked one of the controllers, "Who are they?"

"Those are F-18s from the *Eisenhower*, coming in to back up Syracuse. They're at their assigned altitudes of five and eight thousand feet, and about fifty miles behind the Eagle and Looking Glass."

"Good, when Syracuse gets into the clouds I want the four F-18s to move in and trail two miles behind the Eagle and tanker. They will have about three to four minutes to get into position once Syracuse starts his turn."

The controller looked up at Fugami, nodded and said, "Yes, that should be in about two or three minutes."

More to himself than the controllers Fugami muttered, "Well, I sure hope that Syracuse can do what he says."

The controller heard Fugami's comment and said, "If you want, I can also guide this Syracuse and give him directions and distances to help him close in."

"Do that. It won't hurt, but it could sure help him."

While they watched the scope they heard a radio call. "Specter, Syracuse. Tallyho on the trail." Seconds later they saw the radar blip for Ledet's F-16 pass over the radar blips for Kenada's Eagle and the tanker.

From twenty thousand feet, and using infrared, Ledet easily followed the tanker's and the Eagle's heat trails in the clouds below. As the heat trails passed under the nose of his jet he rolled his F-16 upside down, chopped his throttle to idle, and pulled back on the stick. He felt a slight pain in his ears as he dropped quickly in altitude. To equalize the pressure he pinched his nostrils closed through his oxygen mask and gently exhaled through his nose. Ledet watched the clouds below rushing toward him. He pulled back on the stick just hard enough to be above the clouds when he leveled off.

Ledet lined up with the heat trail of the two aircraft to make sure that he was on the right heading. As he increased his throttle he heard on his radio, "Syracuse, Looking Glass is three miles, same heading, three ten knots, at eight thousand five."

Ledet double-clicked his mike button in response. As he advanced his throttle toward mil power, he did a little mental math. *Let's see, if I do three seventy for three minutes, I'll be there, so I'll hold this speed for two and a half minutes, then slow to three fifteen.* Ledet hit his timer on the cockpit clock and adjusted his throttle so his airspeed leveled off at three hundred seventy knots. As he lowered his nose into the glowing heat trail in the clouds, he said to himself, "OK, Lonnie Ray, time to clip some feathers."

In the AWACS, Colonel Fugami intently watched the scope just to make sure that Syracuse was on the right trail. "OK, looks good," he said. He leaned his head close to the ear of the controller talking to Looking Glass and said, "Call Looking Glass and tell them to hold their course speed and altitude steady. They can expect company in three to five minutes."

"Yes, sir." The controller carried out his orders.

Colonel Fugami reached for the frequency-select switch on his belt radio pack and turned to the Pentagon frequency. He keyed the mike button. "Palace, Specter."

"Specter, Palace. Go ahead; this is Buster."

"Buster, Syracuse, a Falcon is in pursuit. ETA in three to five minutes. The circle is closing."

On his headset Fugami heard Price respond, "Buster copies."

Pentagon

General Price took his hand off the mike button and looked at the circular pattern of radar blips on the main screen. "Well, gentlemen, we'll know one way or another in just a few minutes. Excuse me for a moment. I'm going to pass this on to the White House."

Price walked over to the telecomm area and stood in front of the camera. He saw Vice President Borda's image on the monitor and said, "Mrs. Borda, I just wanted to give you an update." Without turning around, Price gestured toward the situation map on the main screen. "As you can see by this screen behind me, our containment wall is now complete and the trap is about to be sprung. I expect it will all be over in another three to five minutes."

Borda smiled. "Good, I'll relay that information to the president. He's just started giving his address."

Chapter Eighteen

Hangar Seven, Eglin Air Force Base, Florida

After a hasty five-minute drive from the simulator building, Meridith Henson's red Z28 pulled up the entry control point for hanger seven. Henson rolled down her window and placed her and Captain Datz's line badges into the little bank teller–type drawer that extended out from under the bulletproof glass window of the guard booth. The drawer closed and withdrew back into the guard booth. Twenty seconds later the drawer extended and the outer gate of the double fence surrounding hangar seven opened. A deep male voice came out of a speaker and coldly said, "Thank you; proceed."

Henson couldn't tell who was behind the tinted window, but she waved anyway and said, "Thank you," as she retrieved the badges. She eased through the outer gate and up to the inner gate, which opened as the outer gate closed. Before the gate had come to full open, Henson was already easing forward. She pulled into the back parking lot of the hangar in the spot closest to the door. Before she had turned the car off, Captain Datz was already out of the car and behind it, waiting for the back hatch to open up.

While Datz pulled her helmet out of the back, Meridith was beside her, lifting out the case containing the hard drives from the simulator.

As Captain Datz walked toward the back door of the hangar, she couldn't help but notice the almost full moon high in the southeastern Florida sky. Her feelings were mixed. She wondered why Colonel Lee spoke with such a sense of urgency on such a calm, beautiful night. Whatever it was, it didn't matter. Datz loved to fly, and tonight the weather was perfect.

Henson stopped behind her at the door and said, "If you would be so kind . . ." Then she waited.

Datz opened the door and politely said, "After you."

The back door opened directly into an office area, and the two of them walked in. Datz and Henson both saw Col. Terry Lee on the other side of the room, having an intense conversation on the phone.

Colonel Lee noticed the duo enter the back door and nodded at them. With his left hand he directed them to a table and some chairs. He said into the phone, "OK, I've got everything and she's just walked in. . . . Yes, they're both here. . . . Fifteen to twenty minutes . . . Yes, sir . . . OK . . . Bye."

Datz and Henson had just sat down when Colonel Milsten hung up the phone and walked over. "You've got fifteen minutes to be airborne, fifty-five minutes to be at forty thousand feet over West Virginia."

A bit shocked and irritated, Datz replied, "What? That's impossible."

The colonel cocked his head, peered over his glasses

at Datz and asked sarcastically, "Impossible?"

"Yes, impossible. It'll take me that long just to do the preflight, and then after that I have to load the mission profile, whatever the hell it is, into the battle computer, and that's another twenty to thirty minutes."

The colonel looked at the captain and calmly asked, "Are those all of your objections?"

Datz thought for a moment, then said, "Well . . . yes."

Colonel Lee smiled. "Good. The maintenance crew has already done the preflight. Come with me; I'll brief you on our way to the jet. Let's go. Miss Henson, I'm glad you're here. We can use your assistance programming in the mission profile. Reggie Smith is out there working on that now."

The three of them stood, and Datz and Henson followed Lee close behind. Colonel Lee opened the door for the two of them and let them walk through first. They walked into the hallway that led to the hangar.

Before Colonel Lee could begin his briefing, Captain Datz stopped in front of the door that was labeled WOMEN. As she handed her helmet case to him, she said, "Excuse me, Colonel, but I need to—"

"Now?"

"Yes, Colonel, now. I've been sitting in ejection seats for almost two hours, and I don't think I can wait another hour or more. Besides, you wouldn't want me to short out the biocircuits in this suit, now, would you?"

Before the colonel could answer the question, Datz ducked into the ladies' room and headed for a stall.

Colonel Milsten was momentarily speechless. He looked at the helmet case in his hands and then at the door closing behind Datz. Colonel Lee's sense of urgency overruled his sense of etiquette. The colonel had a briefing to give, and he was going to give it, wherever.

Without thinking, he pushed open the door to the ladies' room and walked in.

Meridith was a little surprised by the colonel's behavior and felt a little awkward. Since she didn't have to go to the bathroom, she spoke to the closing door behind the colonel. "Ah, Colonel, if you'll excuse me I think I'll give Reggie a hand."

In the ladies' bathroom, Datz, too, was surprised when she heard the colonel's voice on the other side of the stall door. She made sure the door was locked behind her, and then unzipped her flight suit from her neck down to her crotch and dropped it, along with her underpants, down to her ankles. A little embarrassed to be caught on the toilet with her pants down, Datz said, "Colonel, do you mind? I'd like a little privacy."

"Sorry, Captain, we don't have time for that luxury. If you are not where you are supposed to be in forty-some minutes, millions of people could die."

Datz, resigned to the fact that the colonel wasn't leaving, proceeded with her immediate business at hand and said, "OK, Colonel, give it to me."

Now Colonel Lee was starting to feel uneasy. He had never had to brief anyone who wasn't wearing briefs, and he never had to compete over the noise of water. "Well, Captain, an hour or so ago someone stole an alert bird from Langley Air Force Base. It was an F-15 loaded with two Knight Hawk missiles. She has already launched and detonated one of her missiles over New York."

"My God! No. When?" While Datz listened she pulled up her flight suit and zipped it.

"About ten minutes ago. There wasn't any damage, though; the detonation was at altitude. Just the EMP. The pulse from the detonation shut down all electricity for a hundred miles around New York. The Pentagon thinks that must have been a warning shot just to prove that she could do it."

"She?"

"Yes, I believe the woman's name is Captain Canada, or something like that."

Datz opened the stall door suddenly and stared face-to-face at Colonel Lee. "Kenada, Captain Kim Kenada."

Colonel Lee was again surprised. "Yes, that's the name. How'd you know?"

"She was one of my last students when I was a flight instructor out at Williams. She was a good pilot, in fact good enough to stay on as an instructor pilot."

"Hell, good is an understatement. From what I've heard so far, she's a double ace. In less than two hours she's downed twelve jets. Enough of this small talk; you've got a job to do." Colonel Lee handed the helmet case back to Datz and then held the door open for her.

"Well, Colonel, what is it that they want me to do? Do they want me to go out there and shoot her down? God knows I'm not a combat pilot, and New York is a long way from here."

The two of them had reached the end of the hall, and Colonel Lee put his hand on the knob. Before he pulled the door open, he turned and looked Datz square in the eyes only inches from her face. "Captain, I know that you're not a combat pilot, and you and your jet are not going to do combat. The general has seen you wax other pilots in the simulator, and he's been very impressed with the way you handle the F-22. Fortunately for us we're not depending on you to shoot down an airplane."

Milsten paused for a moment and peered into her eyes with a deeper intensity. "We are, however, Captain

Datz, depending on your airplane to shoot down a missile. That is, if the need arises."

"What?"

"You heard me. If this Captain K woman launches that second Knight Hawk, your jet is supposed to be in the neighborhood to shoot down the missile before it can detonate. You and your jet will be a stopgap measure just in case the primary plan doesn't work." Colonel Lee broke off the eye contact, turned and opened the door to the hangar for Datz and then followed her through.

Datz walked straight toward the F-22A. Colonel Lee stopped a few feet into the hangar. He was awed by the beautiful sight. He had never been in hangar seven before, and he had never been this close to the F-22A. It was like walking into NASA's clean room, or a huge hospital-white sterile operating room twice the size of a basketball court. The patient was surrounded by doctors—that is, doctors of aeronautical engineering. The hangar floor looked like a wall-to-wall pool of milk, and the F-22A was perched in the center of the windowless hangar, with its image reflected off of the shiny white acrylic floor.

The F-22A was surrounded by the Lockheed tech reps and maintenance crew. Underneath the nose of the F-22A, Lee could see five pairs of legs. He recognized the shortest pair of legs clad in blue jeans as belonging to Meridith Henson, and he guessed that Reggie Smith must be in the pair of white pants beside her. The hum of generators echoing in the hangar was loud but not deafening.

Colonel Lee snapped out of his trance when he saw Captain Datz climb into the cockpit with her helmet on. She waved at him to come closer, and as he did she motioned for him to walk around the front of the jet to the other side.

Colonel Lee felt a little out of place being in his blue uniform while everybody else, except for Henson and Datz, was in clean white overalls. Since everybody there went about their business and ignored him, he forgot about it too. He had a job to do, and that was to get this jet on its way.

Lee walked around the nose of the F-22A stepping over a few power cords and computer comm lines. He could see Reggie Smith and Meridith Henson half-hidden under an open panel just aft of the radome and before the cockpit. Over their shoulders he could see the twenty-by-thirty-inch active matrix computer touch screen that they were busy using to program the parameters of the mission into the F-22A computer system. On half of the screen they were using, he could see a map of the eastern United States going from Florida to West Virginia. On the map he could see that they had already loaded the flight plan, complete with headings, altitudes, speeds, checkpoints and radio frequencies.

In the cockpit, Datz motioned for Milsten to come closer. When he did she pointed to a nearby worktable on wheels. Lee walked to the table. It was covered with tools and computers and a few helmets. He looked back at Datz and saw her tap her helmet and then point at the helmets on the table. He picked one up and put it on. Hanging from the left side of the helmet from a yardlong cord was something that looked like a computer notepad. Holding the notepad in his left hand, Lee looked at its face and then pushed the button that said POWER. The screen on the notepad prompted Lee with the question, CHANNEL ? Lee looked back at Datz and saw that she was holding up three fingers. He touched the number three, and then heard Datz over the headphones in the helmet: "Colonel, can you hear me?"

Colonel Lee looked up at Datz and responded by nodding his head. He looked for a mike button to push so he could speak back, but he couldn't find one on the notepad.

Datz realized what Lee was looking for, since he didn't respond verbally. She said, "Colonel, don't bother looking for a button; just go ahead and speak. It's voice activated."

"Nice, very nice. I'd go deaf trying to yell over the noise in this place." The snug fit of the helmet cut most of the ambient noise in the hangar, and the radio headset in the helmet made talking easy.

Datz finished hooking up her helmet and flight suit and said, "OK, Colonel, why don't you go over to the computer screen with Smith and Henson and give me just a minute so I can boot up the battle computer and do the self-test on my suit and helmet systems? Then you can give me a quick brief so I can get outta here." Datz pointed to the two under the open panel door.

Colonel Lee walked up behind Henson and Smith and tapped Smith on the shoulder. Once he got his attention he asked, "Are you finished loading the mission yet?"

Smith saw the colonel's lips move, but he didn't hear him. Smith picked up the notepad hanging from the colonel's helmet and saw that he was on channel three. He spoke to his coworkers. "Meri, I'm going to three to talk to the colonel."

Meridith just nodded and said, "Go ahead. I still need a few more minutes to finish loading the tactical programs into the battle computer."

While Lee and Smith chatted, Captain Datz finished setting the voice-recognition protocol with Peg and the battle computer. When the battle computer recognized Diane's voice, it responded, "Hello, Hoots, welcome back. I am ready."

Datz said, "Peg, run helmet and suit systems self-test."

Within the minute Peg responded, "Hoots, all systems are operational. Ready for engine start."

"Peg, project mission profile map."

Almost instantly Captain Datz could see the same map projected on her visor that Smith and Henson were looking at, and the computer responded, "Hoots, this flight plan has been filed with base operations."

"Peg, thank you." Datz put her right index finger on the touch pad on her right thigh and slid a flashing cursor to each checkpoint on the map. As the cursor touched each point along the flight path, pertinent information appeared to the right, such as altitudes, compass headings, airspeeds, winds aloft and radio frequencies. Datz made a quick study of the mission information and then touched her mike button. "Colonel Milsten, are you ready?"

"Yes, I am, Captain," Milsten replied, "but how can I brief you if you can't see what I'm pointing at?"

"Colonel, go ahead and touch the screen with your finger; don't worry, I'll see it."

Milsten proceeded with his briefing while Captain Datz listened, and so did Peg.

When Milsten finished, Captain Datz said, "OK, Colonel, I've got it. Now clear the area." Datz then switched from channel three back to one, the channel that everybody in the hangar was monitoring, and then broadcast, "OK, everybody, clear the area for engine start, and would somebody be so kind as to open the door for this lady?"

The level of activity area quickened as everybody prepared to launch. Henson and Smith closed the computer access panel, and together they pushed the worktable away and up against the hangar wall.

Without another word from anyone, the hangar doors started to open. The crew chief, clad in white coveralls and radio-equipped helmets, stood thirty feet in front off to the left of the F-22A, and raised both arms straight up. As he spoke he raised the index finger of his right hand and twirled it in tight circles. "OK, Diane, engine areas are clear; start number one."

Datz did a quick scan of the cockpit switches to make sure they were all properly positioned. Rather then manually starting the engine, Datz spoke first to the crew chief—"Starting number one"—and then to the computer—"Peg, perform engine start checklist and start number one."

Seconds later the computer answered, "Hoots, engine start checklist complete; starting number one."

Datz waited for the engine to wind up to idle speed.

"Number one running normal; ready to start number two."

The crew chief in front of the aircraft squatted down to look underneath for any fuel leaks. Seeing none he stood up, raised his right thumb, signaling that it was OK, and then moved to the right of the nose. He raised his left hand with his index finger pointing up and said, "OK, Diane, number-two engine area is clear; start number two."

Datz, seeing the signal, replied, "OK, starting number two. Peg, Start number two."

The response was almost immediate. "Hoots, engine start checklist complete; starting number two."

Datz again watched all of the engine instruments while the engine rpm increased up to idle speed. She could also see the crew chief giving her another thumbs-up signal.

"Hoots, number two running normal. Pretaxi checklist is complete. Landing gear pins and weapon pins need to be pulled."

Datz keyed her mike button again and said, "Engines at idle; go ahead and pull the pins."

The crew chief looked to his right at another tech rep maintenance technician. He raised his right hand, with his right index finger pointing left, his left hand making a fist around the right index finger. He slid his index finger in and out of his left hand several times. This was the signal for them to go in and pull the pins.

Two tech reps ran under the F-22A; one went from gear to gear pulling the pins that were attached to the yardlong red streamers, while the other tech rep did the same to the pins in the weapons systems. With the pins in hand both of the tech reps scurried back to the side of the hangar.

The crew chief, seeing they were out of the way, stepped off to the side of the aircraft. "OK, Diane, you're clear to roll."

"I copy, Dave, thanks," Datz responded. To herself she thought, Now to get the gates open. "Peg, prepare to taxi." Datz then watched as Peg changed the radio to the ground-control frequency. Datz keyed the mike button and said, "Eglin Ground, Pegasus One, request taxi from hangar seven."

"Roger, Pegasus One, this is Eglin Ground; you are clear to taxi, active runway is one one right, and winds are one three zero at ten. Contact tower at 215.5."

Datz, like a true test pilot, decided to test all of the F-22A's systems. *All right, Peg, let's see you do your stuff.* Datz said, "Peg, respond to radio instructions and then taxi."

"Hoots, I copy. Eglin Ground, Pegasus copies eleven right is active, winds are one three zero at ten. Going to tower frequency 215.5."

Without Datz moving a muscle, Peg increased the throttle and the F-22A started to roll out of the hangar. Peg spoke again. "Hoots, taxiing to eleven right."

As they started to roll, Dave, the crew chief, stiffened to attention and snapped his arm up into a salute. Datz returned the salute, and then she made a gesture Dave didn't quite understand. She put her fingertips to her oxygen mask and then held her hand flat and palm-up in front of her face, with her fingers pointing at him. It took him a moment to realize that she was blowing him a kiss. Just for grins, he blew one back and said, "Good luck, Diane."

"Thanks, Dave. Hopefully I won't need it. See you."

Coming out of the hangar, Datz could see that the closed security fence blocking the exit to the taxiway was now opening. She felt the brakes engage to slow down the F-22A. As the gates opened wide enough to pass through, the throttles advanced slightly and the F-22A proceeded.

Captain Datz was beginning to feel uneasy, and she thought to herself, *Peg, I hope we're ready for this. Hell, I hope I'm ready for this.*

Datz thought about her mission and what she might have to do, and then she thought about what a great airplane she was in. She remembered that after hearing the cliché about eggs and baskets, Mark Twain once wrote, "Put all of your eggs in one basket and then watch that basket." There was never more applicable advice and guiding influence for the construction of the F-22A and its technical wizardry. The brains of the military and industry had loaded this aircraft with state-of-the-art everything. The boron graphite and titanium aircraft was designed around a pair of Pratt and Whitney F-119–100 engines each capable of pushing out thirty-five thousand pounds of thrust. The F-22A's top speed of Mach 2.8, which was 1,850 plus miles per hour at sea level, was second only to another Lockheed aircraft, the SR-71, the Mach 3-plus infamous blackbird.

Besides being fast and maneuverable even at high angles of attack, the F-22A was extremely lethal. The aircraft carried four missiles internally: two radar-guided AIM-120 AMRAAMs (advance medium-range air-to-air missiles) and two heat-seeking AIM-9Xs. It was also armed with twenty laser-guided hypervelocity missiles, and a 20mm six-barreled Gatling cannon.

Even the pilot's personal equipment was a marvel of technology. Under the flight suit Diane was wired with a net of body sensors that monitored her blood pressure, pulse, breathing rate, body temperature and even her level of perspiration.

The helmet was also revolutionary in design. Besides having warning probes to indicate the direction of threats, there were sensors in the helmet that monitored the level of brain activity of the pilot. In the event the pilot was dead or unconscious, the BC system would activate and perform the needed evasive maneuvers, or engage the boomerang sequence. The helmet visor was more than just a piece of Lexan; it was a holographic screen tied into the jet's computers. Although it was clear, the visor was a virtual-reality screen for the pilot. Depending on what the pilot wanted displayed, he could see with radar, low-level light, infrared or all three, as well as with the naked eye.

The helmet was the key interface between the pilot and the Pegasus computer. The helmet was also equipped with laser eye-movement detectors coupled with servos, which were the guiding heart of the eye-targeting mode (ETM) computer system. The eye-targeting mode system allowed the pilot to steer the aircraft as well as fire weapons just by looking in the desired direction. The laser detectors followed the movement of the eyes and input the information to the targeting and flight computers.

To complete the basket full of eggs, the flame-resistant Nomex flightsuit was also a marvel of technology. The pilot's flightsuit not only provided a full body pneumatic G-suit system, but also a thermal detection and heating/cooling system that was monitored and controlled by the onboard computers.

Captain Datz was still admiring her winged steed as it taxied and steered itself to the active end of runway eleven. The onboard computer system had been programmed with every airfield location and layout in North America, and Peg knew exactly where it was, thanks to ground positioning satellite (GPS) systems, and the ring laser gyro inertial navigation systems. The radar and infrared eyes of this aircraft also guided the F-22A precisely down the center of the taxiway to the end of the runway.

On the bottom of Datz's helmet visor came the message for frequency change to the tower frequency, and then she saw the electric request Peg made directly to the air-traffic control computer. Datz also heard Peg make a verbal request to the tower: "Eglin tower, Pegasus Zero One requests eleven right for immediate max performance takeoff."

After a short pause Datz heard the response: "Pegasus Zero One, Eglin tower. You are clear for immediate departure on eleven right to flight level four two zero. Max performance takeoff is approved. Contact Looking Glass immediately after departure."

Captain Datz could feel the excitement build up in

her as the F-22A pulled onto the numbers at the end of
the runway and pointed its nose down the darkness between the runway lights. This would be her first max
performance takeoff in the F-22A. That privilege had
been reserved for the other test pilots who were more
experienced. Had the other pilots been as knowledge-
able of the onboard computer systems as Datz was,
somebody else would be having this thrill.

Datz felt the rudder pedals push forward as Peg
locked the brakes and ran the engines up to full throttle.
She felt the control stick on the right armrest of her
seat cycle through as it checked the flight controls. In
her mirrors she could see the ailerons, rudders and el-
evators obey the commands of the stick. Datz watched
the engine instruments climb up as the roaring cre-
scendo of the engines increased. Just as the engines
reached their peak settings, Peg spoke. "Hoots, preflight
complete; starting takeoff roll." As the same words
flashed on the bottom of Datz's helmet visor, the brakes
released and Datz could feel herself being thrown back
into her seat from the seventy-eight thousand pounds
of thrust shooting out behind her.

The runway lights started blurring past, and the accelerating airspeed was registering on the bottom half
of her visor. In less than fifteen seconds, the F-22A had
leaped off the ground and was accelerating through one
hundred fifty knots. The nose of the F-22A pointed upward at a forty-five-degree angle and turned toward a
northerly heading. Among all of the information projected on the inside of her helmet visor, there was a
thin, flat ribbon of gold extending upward toward the
stars. This was the programmed mission profile flight
path that Peg was following. To herself Datz said, "OK,
Toto, let's follow the yellow brick road."

A few miles ahead and above Datz could see the

golden flight path level off and continue northward. Below and all around, she could see air traffic of all sorts, most of it commercial. It was a busy sky, and at the speeds she was traveling, traffic could be a problem if she were at their altitude. Fortunately for Datz and her winged steed, traffic was not a concern; nobody would be flying at her altitude, forty-two thousand feet.

An advantage for flying so high would be speed. Even while climbing, the afterburners on the pair of Pratt and Whitneys behind her had pushed her speed well past Mach 1, the speed of sound. On the bottom of her visor she could see her airspeed was stable at 950 knots. The disadvantage of afterburner speed was high fuel consumption, and because she had been in burner for so long, she would have to refuel to top off her tanks.

As Peg started to level off the F-22A at forty-two thousand feet, Datz said, "Peg, map mode one."

Instantly and without verbal reply from Peg, the map mode was added to Datz's vision. It was as if a giant map had been laid over the world underneath her. In addition to all of the air traffic and symbols displayed on her visor, there were now simple geographic boundaries. Datz could now see an electronically drawn Florida/Georgia state border pass underneath her. Further north, close to the horizon, she could see the state borders of the Carolinas and Tennessee. Names appeared by all of the major cities around her. Even the major highways and rivers were labeled and highlighted.

Datz cycled through all of the different modes of vision—low light, infrared, and radar—to make sure they were all operating, as well as to see which gave her the best vision. She selected radar and low light in the multivision mode of the sensors. The radar mode would give her the greatest range in her vision, and the low-level light would help sharpen the image.

"Peg, give me magnification of fifty, left eye."

"Hoots, magnifying fifty, left." As the computer spoke, the image in Datz's left eye changed. All around, miles away, Datz could see glowing bubbles around flying aircraft. Each bubble was labeled with altitude, airspeed and the air-traffic controllers' assigned radar identification code. When she looked at these bubbles through her left eye, she could easily tell the type of aircraft even at twenty miles.

"Peg, I'm ready to contact Crystal Ball for further directions. Tune in and monitor Crystal Ball frequency." Datz didn't want to be a silent partner on this ride. The command to monitor would mean that Peg would listen to the conversation and that Datz would make the radio calls. Datz thought it wouldn't be appropriate to let the computer do all of the work and have all the fun too.

Now that she was airborne and well on her way, Datz knew it was time to check in. "Crystal Ball, Pegasus Zero One. Crystal Ball, Pegasus Zero One."

Two seconds later her headphones crackled with a response: "Go ahead Pegasus; this is Crystal Ball."

"Roger, Crystal, I'm airborne from Eglin, level at flight level forty-two, entering south Georgia now; request vectors to a tanker for a top-off."

"Pegasus, maintain course and speed; contact tanker call sign, 'Mobile Twenty,' frequency three five five ten. ETA to intercept is ten. Mobile Twenty is squawking three five two zero. Your new squawk is two two zero one on IFF. Expedite refuel; you have twenty minutes to be on station. Crystal Ball out."

Datz responded, "Pegasus copies." *Boy, talk about drinking from a fire hose.* Using her fingertip as a pen, she copied the instructions on her right thigh touch pad. Then she said, "Peg, did you copy all of the information from Crystal Ball?"

"Hoots, yes."

"Peg, good. Continue monitoring Crystal Ball. Change frequency to Mobile Twenty and change to new squawk, two two zero one."

"OK."

"Peg, do you have Mobile Twenty on radar?"

"Hoots, yes."

"Peg, what is cruise altitude and ETA to tanker?"

"Hoots, cruise altitude is forty-two thousand, and rendezvous with tanker in twelve minutes, at flight level three six zero."

"Peg, plot intercept course and proceed direct to Mobile Twenty."

"OK."

As Peg's computer responded to the commands, Datz noticed a slight change on the yellow flight path projected onto her visor. With the magnified vision in her left eye, Datz could see a tiny red ball off in the distance with the numbers 3520 floating in the air beside it. *Well, there it is. Time for a pit stop.*

"Mobile Twenty, Pegasus Zero One."

"Go ahead, Pegasus."

"Roger, Mobile, request refuel; maintain your course and speed. ETA to you is seven minutes."

"Pegasus, I copy. We'll be waiting. Lights are on and you will be number one in line."

"Mobile, thanks, but lights are not needed."

"Are you sure, Pegasus? It's mighty dark back there."

"Affirmative, Mobile, no lights; my receptacle is lit and I'm using low light."

"OK, Pegasus, no lights."

Datz was thinking, *This should be interesting. I've never done an aerial refuel, but I know that this computer can; well, at least it's programmed to do it.* As she thought about it, she said, "OK, Peg, Intercept Mobile Twenty and perform refuel."

As the nose of the F-22A dropped down a few degrees and the throttle was pulled back, Peg verbally responded, "OK."

Datz thought, *You got it, Peg; now let's see what you can do.* She watched the glowing red sphere in the distance grow in size as they approached. On the bottom part of her helmet visor Datz could see that she had descended to thirty-two thousand feet, and the airspeed had dropped to 750 knots. Four thousand feet above, she could see the tanker passing from right to left overhead, and she knew what Peg was about to do. Without warning Peg rolled the F-22A to the right into a seven-G turn. When the plane was on an opposite course to the tanker, it rolled wings-level again, followed by an immediate climb into an Immulman maneuver, half of a loop starting from the bottom. At the top of the loop Datz could see that she was upside down to the world and directly behind the tanker. As the F-22A rolled wings-level in the upright position, she was impressed to see that she was only a few hundred yards behind the tanker and closing. She thought, *Nice move, Peg; I couldn't have done better myself. Now let's see how well you can suck gas.*

The F-22A slid into position ten feet directly underneath and behind the tanker and then matched its speed and movements.

The message STATION KEEPING ENGAGED appeared on Diane's visor. Datz heard a change in the sound of the wind behind her; when she turned she could see that the in-flight refueling receptacle door had opened and was illuminated by its own internal light.

Just twelve feet above her Datz could see the face of

the boom operator give a double take to the lit receptacle. Obviously, in the dark, without its lights, he didn't see the F-22A come into position.

The boom operator in a KC-135 tanker worked in an awkward position in the tail of the fuselage. His job was to guide and extend the refueling boom into an aircraft's refueling receptacle while both planes flew in extremely close formation, and then let the boom do the rest. The operator was lying down on his stomach in a telephone booth–size compartment with his head toward the tail of the plane. His right hand controlled a little joystick that flew the refueling boom into position, while his left hand controlled a lever that extended and retracted the boom. When the tip of the refueling boom mated with the receptacle in the aircraft, the boom automatically pumped fuel at a thousand gallons per minute, with the help of gravity and boost pumps.

The boom operator in Mobile Twenty had a skilled hand that deftly probed the boom into position. Datz heard the receptacle lock onto the boom tip with a metallic clang. She felt the pitch of the F-22A change ever so slightly as Peg compensated for the sudden added fuel weight. Within minutes, the fuel gauges registered the full capacity of the tanks, and the receptacle unlocked. Datz felt her jet fall away from the tanker, bank hard right and then go into a shallow climb to return to the original course. Before Datz could key the mike button, Peg took the words right out of her mouth and sent a radio transmission: "Mobile Twenty, Pegasus Zero One. Thank you. Good-bye."

Peg's radio transmission received a double–mike button click in response. As an afterthought the pilot added "Good luck, Pegasus."

Peg again responded with a quick "Thank you."

Datz was a little surprised that Peg initiated the radio

call by itself, but was even more surprised by the polite thank-you. She wondered if that was part of the original program or if that was learned behavior. She made a mental note to check that tomorrow.

Since the refueling task was over and no other command had been given, Peg remained in the automatic mode and returned to the original flight plan program, and then informed Datz, "Hoots, resuming original flight plan. ETA to programmed position is five minutes."

"Peg, OK, resume flight plan. Tune radio to Crystal Ball frequency and I will be talking to them."

"OK."

"Crystal Ball, Pegasus Zero One."

"Go ahead, Pegasus."

"Roger, Crystal, I'm passing through thirty-eight to forty-two en route to assigned position. ETA in five minutes."

"Pegasus, Crystal, disregard assigned position and proceed directly to Pittsburgh VOR and do standard orbit twenty miles on one eight zero radial. Be in position in thirty minutes. Go EMIS and await orders."

"Crystal, Pegasus copies direct to Pitt VOR for one eight zero radial standard orbit at twenty and EMIS."

The controller for Crystal Ball confirmed Datz's radio call with a double-click of the mike button.

"Peg, did you understand transmission from Crystal Ball?"

"Hoots, yes, I did."

"Good, Peg. Plot a course to Pittsburgh VOR and proceed directly. Compute airspeed to arrive in thirty minutes."

"Hoots, OK." As the computer responded to the new orders, it turned the F-22A in a northeasterly direction and then pushed the throttles to supercruise-mode power setting. The F-22A's supercruise mode allowed the aircraft to reach supersonic speeds without having to use afterburners. The F-22A accelerated to speed and stabilized at Mach 1.2.

On Datz's visor numerous numbers were displayed underneath; the airspeed of Mach 1.2 was listed. The ground speed was over a thousand miles per hour. Ground speed in relation to airspeed increased as the altitude increased. In other words, the same airspeed at twenty thousand feet was actually faster than the same airspeed at sea level, because the higher-altitude air was less dense, which meant less air resistance.

Halfway to Pittsburgh Datz could see the southwestern edge of the storm system that was drizzling on the East Coast, as well as the states in the Ohio river basin area. The map mode was still being projected onto Datz's visor, so she easily knew her exact location. The state lines and city locations were still clearly visible even though they were cloud covered. Datz could tell that she was over Kentucky and about to cross into southwestern West Virginia. At her speed she'd be over Charlotte in minutes.

Datz was about to go into the EMIS mode, where all electronic emissions were minimized, when she saw something that piqued her curiosity. All around her Datz could see the bubbles the radar used to mark aircraft, but there was something that was unusual. To her right in the south she could see rows of grouped bubbles, and far to her left, in the north, she could see more rows of bubbles in groups. From the positions of the bubbles in relation to each other and the fact that they all seemed to be traveling in the same direction, Datz knew that they must be fighters flying in formation. Directly ahead, close to three hundred miles away, Datz could see one bubble coming toward her.

Pat O'Connell

Datz said to herself, "Oh, I see what's going on here. They're setting up an ambush."

She was a little surprised when Peg asked, "Hoots, explain ambush, please."

Before Datz responded to Peg she was wondering how much this computer was understanding. *Why is Peg asking this question? Is Peg learning from this situation?* Datz knew that Peg was the most advanced computer made when it came to artificial intelligence and the use of fuzzy logic. *Could it be?*

Without answering any of the questions jumping into her head, Datz responded, "Peg, an ambush is a trap where the victim is surprised."

"Hoots, I understand ambush. Explain, please, where is the trap?"

"OK, Peg, do you see this group of fighters?" As Datz asked the question she slid a finger up the touch pad and then used her fingertip cursor to circle the rows of bubbles to the north.

"Hoots, yes, I do. That grouping is composed of fifty-two fighters; thirty-four of them are F-15s and eighteen are F-16s. They vary in altitude from two thousand feet to thirty thousand feet. The grouping extends a distance of forty-five miles—"

Datz, not wanting to hear all of the information that Peg had gathered, cut Peg off. "Peg, that's very good. Now do you see this grouping?" Datz turned the aircraft slightly to the east, looked at the fighters to the south of her and said, "Peg, do you see these aircraft?" Again Datz circled the groups just as before.

"Hoots, yes, I do. That group is composed of—"

"Peg, I don't need to know everything about that group. Now, Peg, resume course to Pitt VOR."

"Hoots, resuming course. Continue explaining trap, please."

Knight Hawk

Using the eye-targeting mode, Datz looked at the distant bubble directly ahead and said, "Peg, do you see this target?"

"Hoots, yes, I do. It is a group of two aircraft flying in close formation. The IFF response code from the leading aircraft indicates that it is an EC-135 tanker. That would indicate with a high probability that the other aircraft is Eagle Zero One, the F-15 that is the target aircraft."

"Very good, Peg; that is a valid assumption. Now I will explain the trap. The two groups of fighters you have observed make up the trap, and the F-15 behind the tanker is the victim. When the target F-15 gets closer, those fighters will surround it and keep it from escaping by shooting it down. Peg, do you understand the trap now?"

"Hoots, yes, I understand, but what will stop the F-15 from firing the Knight Hawk missile, and where is the surprise?"

"Peg, I don't know where the surprise is yet, but if we watch closely and follow directions from Crystal Ball, I'm sure we will find out soon enough. As for firing the Knight Hawk, I hope she doesn't fire it, but if she does, well, Peg, that's what we are here for."

"Hoots, I understand. Thank you."

Datz responded with a polite, "Peg, you are welcome. Oh, Peg, go EMIS now."

Datz was amazed by this short conversation. It was like talking to a kid. This was the first time the computer system had carried on a conversation that was almost human. She felt as if she had just had a conversation with an inquisitive young child. In some ways she had.

"Hoots, OK, initiating EMIS."

Instantly Datz's vision changed. With the aircraft in

EMIS, the radar was put in a standby mode, which meant no radar enhancement to the multivision mode projected onto the helmet visor. The computer automatically initiated infrared and low-level light enhancement to replace the missing radar input. Datz could still see clearly, but her range of vision had been cut down to about thirty miles.

The F-22A fighter was developed to be a stealth fighter aircraft. Technology learned from the first stealth fighter, the black, bat-shaped F-117, was instrumental for the F-22A's construction. The F-22A was just as invisible to radar as the F-117, but it was a hell of a lot faster and deadlier. Going EMIS kept the F-22A invisible to electronic detection. The emissions from using radar or radio could betray its presence.

Datz knew that this reduced-vision capability was the trade-off for going EMIS, but nonetheless she didn't like it. Datz was spoiled by having her vision enhanced by radar, and she wanted it back. Thinking that there was no harm in asking, she said, "Peg, is there any way you can improve on the range of vision and still be in EMIS?"

"Hoots, yes, there is. Shall I do it?"

"Peg, yes, please."

"Hoots, one moment." Ten seconds later the image projected onto Datz's visor returned to almost the same as before.

"Peg, this is amazing. How did you get this image without radar?"

"Hoots, you did not specify that I could not use radar; you said that I must maintain EMIS. Shall I not use radar?"

"Peg, I'm sorry, I don't understand. How are you getting this information?"

"Hoots, EMIS requires that I don't use radar; however, there are other sources of radar emissions that I can use."

"Peg, explain."

"Hoots, there are numerous ground and airborne radars using different frequencies. My phase array radar system is able to receive numerous frequencies simultaneously and match the reflections with its source. The reflected signal is then processed into the radar computer, and through triangulation I can determine the various positions of the different aircraft."

"Peg, is this ability part of your original program?"

"Hoots, no, it is not."

"Peg, then how can you do this?"

"Hoots, you asked if there was a way to improve on the range of vision and still be in EMIS. I reviewed the different sources of information available to me and found the answer to your question was yes, but to accomplish your request I had to modify normal program parameters."

"Well, Peg, again I am impressed. Good job."

"Hoots, thank you."

In the relative silence of the moment, Datz was being flooded with mixed emotions. She thought to herself, *What an interesting situation. On one hand I'm feeling nervous and excited because the lives of millions are at stake, and on the other hand I'm happy and excited because my computer program, my Peg, is progressing better than I ever expected. I feel like a proud mother watching her baby learning to walk.*

"Peg, let me know when we are five minutes away from Pitt VOR."

"OK, Hoots."

To herself Datz thought, *Well, Peg, now we sit and wait. I hate waiting.*

The pilot diagnostic program nestled deep within

Peg's program detected the notable difference in Datz's heart rate and blood pressure. Because of this it was prompted to ask, "Hoots, are you all right?"

Surprised by the question that broke the silence, Datz said, "What?"

"Hoots, how are you feeling?"

Still puzzled, Datz replied, "Peg, I'm fine. Why do you ask?"

"Hoots, I have detected that your heart rate is accelerated to ninety-five beats per minute, and your blood pressure is currently one forty over ninety-two. These symptoms indicate an unhealthy condition. Are you all right?"

"Peg, I am all right. I'm just nervous and excited. When people are nervous and excited, their blood pressure and heart rate increase."

"Hoots, does being nervous or excited cause problems?"

"Peg, sometimes being nervous can cause a person's stomach to produce extra acid, which causes ulcers."

"Hoots, can I help you overcome your nervousness?"

Datz said, "No, I'll be fine." What she really wanted was a Tums about the size of a hockey puck.

Peg added this information into her memory and continued on with her assigned task.

Chapter Nineteen

21:08
Pentagon

General Price excused himself from his conference with Vice President Borda. He said good-bye, stood up and walked out of view of the telecomm camera. He was confident that he knew what was about to happen. General Price walked back over to where Colonel Miller and Admiral Watson were standing and watching the situation map. "Any change?"

Colonel Miller answered, "Nothing yet, maybe another two minutes."

A woman's voice from behind the general said, "I don't think it's a good idea."

Watson and Miller didn't hear the soft voice, but Price did. He turned around and saw Dr. Laut behind him. "Doctor, what are you talking about?"

Dr. Laut pointed to the telecomm area and said,

"Mrs. Borda said that the president is giving his address. I don't think that's a good idea. In fact, at this moment, I think that he and we are in extreme danger."

General Price looked at this woman in wonder. "Doctor, in a few minutes this whole thing will be over. Why do you say that he's in danger?"

Laut looked at the situation map and said, "I hope this plan works, but if it doesn't, how long would it take for a Knight Hawk to get here?"

Price wiggled his lower jaw left, then right, and then said, "Oh, I'd say about ten or eleven minutes. Why do you ask?"

"General, at this moment, what is the most important target in this country? Where could that bomb do the most damage?"

Before Price could answer the question, Laut spoke again. "It has to be the Capitol building, because at this moment everybody who's anybody is there. All of the political and military heads of the country are there, except for the generals who are here. If the bomb went off there now or in the next few minutes, our country would be out of business for months, politically and militarily. The great American war machine would be headless.

"Do you remember listening to one of the first contacts Kenada had with Admiral Griffin? She said that he was lying about the movement of gold because she had sources. *Sources* implies that she is not alone. Who would stand to gain if all of the political and military heads were cut off?

"We've been going on several assumptions here that may not be valid. We assumed she wants the ransom that she's asked for. Surely she must know that we won't give it to her. And even if we did, there's no way she could actually know that she could reach a place of safety before we shot her down.

"We assumed that she probably wouldn't launch the second missile because she was going to Cuba so they could have it and steal its secrets, so they could make their own.

"The bottom line here is that I think she knows that we are not going to let her get away with that Knight Hawk. And in her mind, the only way that bomb is going to be any good to her is if she uses it."

Admiral Watson and Colonel Miller had overheard everything that Dr. Laut had said, and Watson spoke up. "Doctor, you have some good points, but I think you're worrying over nothing—"

"Excuse me, Admiral," Laut interrupted, "but do you think that it's just a coincidence that this woman decided to steal a jet on the same day the president gives his State of the Union address? Hopefully I am worrying about nothing, and in a minute it'll all be over. If we're lucky, Kenada and the Knight Hawk will be nothing but a smoking hole and a new source of bad press for the military."

Watson squirmed over the logic of Laut's question and said, "Well . . . no."

General Price listened to the doctor's logic and said, "Watson, hopefully you're right, but to play it safe we can give ourselves some added protection just in case we've underestimated this woman again." Price turned to Colonel Miller and said, "John, scramble more jets from Andrews and Langley and have them form a barrier between us and Kenada just in case she breaks out of the containment area. Also, scramble another alert F-15 from Langley with a Knight Hawk. If Washington is her target and she launches from her current position, the Knight Hawk will have to go suborbital to reach us. We can destroy the missile while it's at the apex of its trajectory by using another Knight Hawk."

Pat O'Connell

Without hesitation Colonel Miller nodded his head to Price and then activated the alarm to scramble the alert Eagles at Langley, as well as all of the other available fighters.

Crystal Ball

In the E-3 AWACS aircraft, Colonel Fugami keyed his intercom button and said to his controllers, "OK, Syracuse is in the slot and almost ready to shoot. The circle of fighters is complete; now it's time to close the noose. Bring all of the fighters in and form the barrier circle at ten miles from the Eagle."

The three controllers were directing different portions of the gauntlet circle. One controller directed the northern grouping, another controller directed the southern grouping, and the third controller directed the navy fighters coming in from the east. As the controllers passed on their directions to their respective fighters, the change taking place showed up almost immediately on the scope.

Looking Glass

In the KC-135 tanker, Admiral Griffin had just received the radio transmission that an infrared-equipped F-16 was stalking up the heat trail of the Eagle for the kill. To himself he thought, Maybe we can make this a little easier. He keyed the mike button and said, "Eagle, Looking Glass. Our boomer is having a little difficulty keeping you hooked up for refueling; are you sure you don't want to refuel at a lower altitude below the clouds? We can come down to where the weather is less turbulent."

Captain Kenada, sitting in the cockpit of her Eagle,

couldn't have agreed more with Griffin. For the past few minutes she had worked up a sweat white-knuckling her control stick, trying to fly steady in the turbulent air. There were several times the bumpy air had bounced the refueling boom out of the receptacle. Kenada knew why Admiral Griffin made the request. She thought, *Well, Brucie, it ain't gonna happen. You must have somebody behind me just waiting to move in for the kill.* Kenada looked at her fuel gauge and could see that she was close to being three-quarters full. *At this rate I should have full tanks in another four to five minutes.*

Kenada keyed her mike button and said, "Nice try, Brucie, but we stay in the clouds. I appreciate your concern, but do as you're directed. This is not open for discussion." Kenada knew that the man was right, but flying at any level outside the protective cover of the clouds would make her easy prey.

All was going well with the plan. Kenada knew that she was going to be escorted to Fort Knox, or at least partway there. Somewhere along the way, they would try to shoot her down, and from the sound of the admiral's request, it would be soon.

As for white knuckles, Kenada wasn't alone. Captain Ledet in his F-16 had his own. Using the Westinghouse forward-looking infrared system, he was able to fly directly into and follow the heat trail from the two jets, the Eagle and the tanker. To himself he thought, *This must be what a shark feels like when it's following the blood trail of its next meal. When I get out of here I'm gonna have to thank the whiz kids who made this baby.* The infrared images displayed on the helmet visor were the only way Ledet could track his prey. Ledet's infrared vision made the warm exhaust from the jet engines glow brightly against the cold clouds, which appeared black. All Ledet had to do was stay in the light. That was easier than it sounded. The turbulence of the clouds was bad enough, but to follow the heat trail he had to fly in the middle of the jet exhaust, which was shaking his jet every which way but loose.

He glanced at his cockpit timer and saw 01:58, and he thought, OK, just forty more seconds and then slow down. Over his headphones he heard a radio transmission that had to be from Crystal Ball: "Syracuse, one mile."

As his timer showed 02:40, Ledet slowly brought his throttle back and reset his timer. He watched his airspeed drop down to 330 knots as he heard another radio call: "Syracuse, .25 miles."

He knew he was getting closer; the heat trail in the clouds was getting brighter and the ride was a hell of a lot rougher. As Ledet continued driving his jet into the light, he tried doing some more mental math. *Let's see now, I've got twenty knots of overtake speed, and I'm doing a third of a mile a minute, and the Eagle's only a quarter of a mile. Then that would mean about forty-five seconds.*

Lt. Cmdr. Dan Haley and Lt. Dawn Rutherford now had their F-18s in position. They were two miles behind the tanker and the Eagle flying at eight thousand feet. Haley's other two wingmen, Keller and Beck, were in the same position, flying the same course and speed, except they were below the clouds at four thousand feet.

All four of them were flying in a combat-spread formation with their lights off. Each of them could easily see the heat trail in the clouds from the tanker, the

F-15 and now the F-16. Unfortunately, they couldn't tell them apart.

For the moment their job was to wait. They were the backup for the F-16 in the clouds that was given the mission to kill.

Haley was relieved but disappointed. He would have liked to be the one going for the kill, but he did not relish the idea of sneaking up on somebody from behind and shooting his 20mm cannon into an unsuspecting pilot's canopy. There was no sport in just being an assassin taking potshots at a brain bucket. Haley also didn't envy the F-16 pilot for trying to fly up the heat trail. Haley was good with his FLIR, but not that good.

Haley looked at Rutherford's jet five hundred yards to his right. The heat trails in the clouds from the three jets were between them. He looked all around at the moonlit clouds and thought, *What a perfect night for a dogfight. Go ahead, Falcon driver, screw up. I'm ready.*

Rutherford was not as eager for a fight as Haley was. She was not afraid. She had gone head-to-head against F-15s on the range at least two dozen times and fared well in more than half. What bothered her the most was the fact that they were backup. They were in the middle, surrounded by over a hundred fighters with their missiles pointed their way. She knew that if the Falcon failed to splash the Eagle and they, the four F-18 pilots, didn't shoot it down immediately, there would be trouble. They would be dodging missiles as if their lives depended on it; and they would. She asked herself, *What were those missile-launch code words? Rolling. Rolling what? Oh, yes, Thunder, Rolling Thunder, that's it.*

At four thousand feet, Keller and Beck were scissoring back and forth as they followed the heat trails below the clouds. The scissoring maneuver allowed them to keep up a high speed, just in case it was needed.

At forty-two thousand feet on a moonlit night, the view was spectacular. The visibility was clear, with thousands of stars visible to the naked eye. With low-level-light-enhanced vision, Capt. Diane Datz was enjoying the view. As much as she wanted to gaze at the stars above, she forced herself to ignore the splendor and pay close attention to the scene playing out six miles below her. Through some of the breaks in the clouds she could catch a glimpse of the tanker and the Eagle refueling. Since her vision was a also enhanced by low-level light as well as by infrared, she could even see their heat trails. All around her in the distance she could see groups of fighters approaching at high speeds and at different altitudes. She thought, Any time now, things are going to hit the fan.

Datz's concentration was interrupted by a radio call: "Pegasus Zero One, Crystal Ball."

"Go ahead, Crystal Ball."

"Pegasus, Looking Glass and Eagle Zero One are entering your area from your eleven-o'clock low position. They are at six thousand five hundred feet, traveling at three hundred ten knots. You are clear to use weapons against any missiles launched from Eagle Zero One."

"Crystal Ball, Pegasus Zero One copies."

Datz was still feeling the nervousness in the pit of her stomach. She was being torn apart by her emotions. Part of her wanted the Eagle to launch the Knight Hawk so she could get the chance to prove how good she and her systems were. Part of her was sad because she had personally known Kenada as a student and friend. Datz also felt fear, fear of failure. If the Knight Hawk was launched and they failed to shoot it down, millions would die. While considering the consequences she thought, *Damn, that's a lot of pressure. I hope we don't choke. Of course if we did, who would know?*

Datz was brought away from her worries by her jet's computer voice. "Hoots, has the ambush started?"

"Peg, do you see all of the approaching fighter aircraft coming toward the target F-15 and the tanker it's refueling from?" As she spoke she used her finger on the computer touchpad on her thigh to point to some of the approaching fighters and to draw a circle around the tanker and F-15.

"Hoots, no, I don't."

Datz, fearing that the onboard computer was malfunctioning, asked, "What? You can't see them? Why not?"

"Hoots, at the moment I can see only eighty-three fighters approaching. There are fifty-seven fighters that are currently behind me and out of my sensor view. That is why I can't see all of the approaching fighters as you asked. I can only see the ones in front of me that are within one hundred twenty degrees off of the longitudinal axis."

Datz thought, *Oh, great, now I've got a smart-ass for a computer. I must remember to be more precise with my words.* "All right, Peg, do you detect numerous aircraft approaching at high rates of speed toward the F-15 and EC-135 below us?"

"Hoots, yes, I do."

"Peg, identify all other aircraft you detect that are within a five-mile radius from the target F-15."

"Hoots, there are only six aircraft within five miles." As Peg spoke it bracketed each aircraft in a flashing white square. "The EC-135 that is refueling the F-15, the F-16 that is approximately four hundred meters and closing behind the F-15, and the four F-18s that are 4.5 miles behind the F-15."

"Peg, this is the way that this ambush is supposed to work. The F-16 that is closest to the F-15 is going to approach the F-15 from behind and shoot it while it is refueling. The four F-18s farther behind are there as backup in case the F-16 fails. All of the other fighter aircraft you detect are here to prevent the F-15 from escaping if the F-16 and F-18s fail. Our mission here is to destroy the Knight Hawk missile in the event it is launched by the F-15. To do that we must always be in close proximity."

"Hoots, you are correct. Your definition of our mission matches my mission program parameters, but you still have not answered my question."

"Peg, what was your question?"

"Hoots, my question is a yes or no question. It does not require an essay. Has the ambush started?"

"Peg, yes, it has."

"Hoots, thank you."

Datz was slightly surprised by Peg's comment. She thought, *What is going on with this computer? . . . Yes or no reply . . . My definition is correct. Am I being tested here? Who's in charge here? I wonder what would have happened if my definition didn't match Peg's program? Would she obey me if it didn't? I'll have to find out the next time we're in the simulator.*

"Peg, let's position ourselves five miles behind the Eagle but maintain our altitude. We want to be in the optimum position to fire at a missile if she fires one."

As soon as Datz finished giving her command, the F-22A gently turned to put itself in position. There was a conflict in Datz's command, so Peg said, "Hoots, optimum position at this altitude is 3.6 miles. Do you still want us five miles behind?"

Knight Hawk

"Peg, no, make the distance 3.6 miles. What is our weapons status?"

"Hoots, hypers are armed and ready for launch. Laser is powered, and targeting radar is in standby until missile launch is detected. AIM-120 missiles and guns are in standby."

"Peg, that's good, thank you." No sooner did Datz say that then she thought, *That was silly; why am I being polite to a computer?*

While the thought of politeness was still fresh in Datz's mind, Peg replied with a very polite, "Hoots, you're welcome."

OK, Peg, now we wait.

The strain of the chase was wearing on Ledet. The ever increasing turbulence, combined with breathing the exhaust fumes from the jet he was following, was making him nauseous. He recognized the smell of burning kerosene and knew it was JP4 jet fuel. Finally the fumes were so bad he switched his oxygen regulator to 100 percent oxygen. The exhaust fumes were still coming into the cockpit through the bleed air off the engine, but at least he didn't have to breathe the fumes.

As he came closer and closer to his prey, the Eagle, the turbulence became rougher and rougher. The glowing heat trail from the hot engine exhaust was getting smaller, brighter and much more violent. Several times the turbulence bounced him out of the heat trail, but Ledet was able to find it again quickly. Finally, he couldn't stay in it anymore. The fumes were strong enough to make his eyes sting. He lowered his nose slightly so he could fly just below the trail. It helped. The air was smoother and cleaner.

Ledet knew he was close. He gauged the size of the trail and thought, The heat trail is now about ten feet across, so I must be about a hundred feet behind. As he quickly double-checked to make sure that his guns were armed and ready to fire, he ever so softly rubbed his index finger on the joystick trigger. He pulled his throttle back slightly and watched his airspeed slow to 315 knots. He thought, *Better slow down, Cajun. I don't want to do any rear-ending. It would play hell with my insurance.*

Finally, a few seconds later, Ledet could barely see the back end of a jet engine glowing though the fog of the clouds. It's about time, he thought, now to get into position. Ledet pulled back on the stick and was quickly bounced up by the turbulent exhaust. He was above the heat trail and he was putting the boresighted crosshairs just above the glowing rear of the engine. *Come on, just a little bit closer.* He started to put a little more pressure on the trigger but hesitated. He thought, Something's wrong. When he was close enough to see clearly through the fog of the clouds he realized his mistake. "Damn." It was an engine in front of him all right, but it was the outboard engine on the left wing of the tanker. To his right Ledet could clearly see the outline of an F-15.

Ledet eased back slightly on his throttle and slipped back into the dark cover of the clouds. He was relieved that the pilot of the F-15 didn't see him. He thought, It's a good thing she was too busy refueling.

Captain Kenada was busy. She was concentrating hard on holding her Eagle steady while she topped off her fuel tanks. Just a few more minutes, she thought, and I'll be done.

Ledet tapped his right rudder slightly and slowly glided over behind the Eagle. "Now this is more like it." Ledet could now see the glowing exhaust of two engines close together. He advanced the throttles slightly to

bring himself closer. *Closer, closer, where's that canopy?*
Ledet was inching in and he was nervously fingering
the trigger. As soon as he could see a canopy in the
center of his targeting pipper he was going to fire. *Come
on, come on, closer, a little bit more, closer . . . closer.*

Slowly things came into view: first it was the Eagle's
towering twin rudders straddling the glowing engines.
Then he could see the body and wings. Finally, there in
the dead-center of the targeting pipper, Ledet could see
the canopy, the back of the ACES II ejection, and most
important, the sides of Kenada's helmet. To the left of
the canopy he could see that the refueling boom was
still engaged and pumping gas. Ledet was having difficulty holding the pipper on the canopy. The turbulence from the clouds, and the exhaust from the
engines, made smooth, level flight difficult, to say the
least.

Come on, come on, hold still, just a little bit more. Several times Ledet was ready to squeeze the trigger when
his aim was spoiled by the jostling air.

In the tanker, the boom operator, Mitch, had an
open radio channel to Kenada so he could give her directions. Mitch hadn't been told to expect company.
When he saw a ghostlike image of a jet lurking in the
dark behind the Eagle he inadvertently uttered, "What
the . . . ?"

Kenada heard the boom operator utter something,
and she could see that he was looking at something
behind her. Kenada looked into her rearview mirrors
on the canopy bow, and chills ran up her back. It was
too late; she knew she was dead if she didn't do something immediately.

Before Kenada had a chance to react to the vision of
an F-16 behind her, Lonnie Ray "Cajun" Ledet's index
finger squeezed the trigger firmly back into the joystick,

and he said "Die, sucker." For three seconds Ledet held his finger in place. For three seconds his six-barreled 20mm Gatling cannon roared to life. Instead of pulverizing Kenada in her cockpit, the bullets were two feet above and six feet to the left of the intended target. Thirty of the 20mm rounds blew apart the lower portion of the refueling boom.

Three people saw the tracers rip through the dark of the clouds: Ledet, Kenada and Mitch the boom operator. The same three yelled "Noooo!" all at the same time, but they each said it for different reasons. The boom operator said it because he was too close to the action. Kenada said it because she knew that she was the target. Ledet said it because he not only missed, but he made a deadly error, and he had just realized his mistake. He had failed to consider that his gun was about four feet to the left of the centerline of the jet, and the camera he was looking through was also below and two feet to the right of the centerline. Both of these mistakes combined caused him to miss his target by six feet. In normal air-to-air combat this wouldn't have been a problem, because targets were never this close; however, in this case, at point-blank, it was.

When the bottom of the boom was cut off, fuel spilled out into the airstream at fifty gallons a second. The fuel was ignited by the tracers that passed through the fuel, turning it into a hellacious stream of fire. Before Ledet could react to the fire and fuel that raced at him at over three hundred knots, he was in it. The fire and the fuel rammed directly into his engine intake, sucked back into the compressor section of his engine, and close to thirty gallons of flaming fuel went into the bleed-air ductwork that vented directly into the cockpit. Liquid fire shot out of the air vents in the dash and all around the insides of the cockpit. Ledet screamed as he could feel the burning heat splash all over him and soak through his Nomex flight suit to his skin. There was nothing left for him to do except to get out. He instinctively grabbed the two arming handles on the seat by his knees. He pulled them up hard and then squeezed the triggers. A second and a half later Ledet was catapulted into the cold, wet darkness of the clouds. Fortunately for him, the wind extinguished the flames.

Kenada was much more fortunate. The instant she realized she was the target she shoved her joystick forward to dive away. She saw the tracers rip by her jet and the tanker. She dropped into the clouds below and instantly lost sight of the tanker with the flaming boom and the F-16 behind her. "I don't know how you found me, but I'm outta here." Kim pointed her nose to the ground and rolled and turned so she would be heading southeast when she came out of the bottom of the clouds. She thought, *Now's no time to be flying blind.* Kim reached over to her radar panel and turned her radar from standby to on.

Mitch, the boom operator, watched in disbelief as the sequence of events unfolded. Within a few seconds he saw the Falcon appear and fire its gun, which hit the refueling boom. He saw the boom turn into a flame thrower, ejecting hundreds of gallons of fuel into the air at the F-16. In horror he could even see the flames jump into cockpit and watched the pilot still on fire eject into the darkness and disappear. When Mitch finally got his wits together enough to speak, he could see that the Eagle was gone and that he was alone there with his boom spraying flaming fuel at a pilotless airplane behind them. The next words out of Mitch's mouth were, "Ferratto, get us outta here now."

Mitch's warning was not quick enough. As he spoke fuel continued to pour into the air. Hundreds of gallons went into the Falcon's intake. The way that all jet engines worked was simple; fuel and air mixed, ignited and shot out the exhaust. More fuel meant more thrust, which meant more speed. When the additional fuel was rammed into the Falcon's engine intake, it accelerated.

Mitch's next and last word was a screaming "Nooooo!" as he watched the pilotless F-16 accelerate. It rammed directly into his viewing port, crushing him in the metal of his coffinlike compartment.

Colonel Ferratto reacted to Mitch's last warning. As he pulled hard back on the control yoke, making the EC-135 start to climb rapidly upward, he felt the sudden impact of the Falcon slamming into the tail of his tanker. As the tanker climbed the F-16 fell away.

The force of the impact caused the fuselage of the Falcon to bend, and its fuselage fuel tanks ruptured open. The hydrozene fuel tank that fueled the emergency generator also split its side open. JP4 jet fuel, along with the hydrozene fuel, mixed with explosive results.

Three seconds after the F-16 hit and bounced off the bottom of the tanker, it detonated and was consumed in flames. Shrapnel from the exploding F-16 peppered the already damaged tail of the tanker, causing another deadly problem. Pieces of hot metal ripped through the rear belly of the tanker into its aft fuselage fuel tanks and ignited the fuel. The exploding fuel blew the bottom half of the tanker's tail section off.

Admiral Griffin was standing just forward of the aft section when he heard Mitch's "Noooo!" which was followed by the sound of crunching metal as the F-16 crashed into the tail of the tanker. He was knocked into the ceiling of the fuselage and bounced to its deck. There was a rapid decompression, and he could see many of the other crew members who were behind him

being sucked toward the rear of the tanker. He heard
and felt the shock of an explosion outside of the tanker
and then felt another, much more violent explosion.
Admiral Griffin saw a hugh ball of flame eat away the
back of the tanker. One second there were a dozen men,
and a bank of computers and communication gear. The
next second it was an open hole that was big enough to
drive a Cadillac through. Fire clinging to the rim of the
hole made it seem even bigger. To Griffin, it looked like
a doorway to hell.

Griffin tried to hang on, but the depressurizing air
sucked him toward the black mouth of a hole with fiery
teeth. He grabbed the leg of a seat and held on for dear
life. It didn't take much cognitive reasoning for Griffin
to realize that he was in big trouble. The difficult thing
was trying to figure what to about it. Seconds later he
decided it was time to get outta Dodge. His only problem now was the fact that he wasn't wearing a chute.
When the parachutes were being handed out, he had
put his on a seat rather than on his back, and now his
seat was gone.

Griffin started to go forward toward the cockpit,
where he could get another parachute, only to see a
wall of flames blocking his path. Unable to think of an
alternative, Griffin, without thinking, closed his eyes
and prayed, "Oh, God, please don't let me die now."

When the admiral opened his eyes his prayers were
answered. By the light of the fire Griffin could see the
unconscious face of the young crew chief who had
handed out parachutes. He had a chute; he was wearing
it. For a second Griffin thought about stripping the
chute from the young sergeant to save himself. Two
things made him change his mind: first, it wouldn't be
a Christian thing to do, and second, from the looks of
the plane around him he doubted that he had the time.

Instead, Griffin picked him up, threw him over his right shoulder and then ran toward the fiery hole of hell gnawing on the ass of his plane. He could feel the heat of the flames burning the exposed skin of his hands and face. He closed his eyes, sheilded his face with his arm and threw himself and the crew chief into the fires of the open hole.

In an instant everything changed. Griffin thought, How could hell be so cold? The two of them went from a flaming inferno to a freezing windstorm in only a second, from intense bright heat to frigid, dark cold.

Within seconds gravity accelerated the falling bodies to terminal velocity. They scuttled through the air and felt the bite of hundred-mile-an-hour wind. The tiny ice crystals in the cloud felt like a sand blaster.

Faster they fell, and Griffin held as tight as he desperately could to the unconscious sergeant. The wind was causing them to spin, and the centrifugal force pulled the sergeant from his grip. "Oh, God, No!" he yelled. Griffin knew death was near. Ice crystals were coating on his clothes and skin. He couldn't see anything in the blackness of the cloud, and he couldn't hear anything except the wind. The crew chief and the lifesaving parachute were gone.

Just as Admiral Griffin was losing all hope, he fell out of the bottom of the cloud deck. With the lights of the city below him he could see. With the light came relief. There at the same level was the crew chief falling forty feet away. Griffin rolled over on his belly and assumed a skydiver's free-falling position. Using his arms and legs like the flight control surfaces of an airplane, he steered himself over to the sergeant. As soon as he made contact, Griffin locked his legs around the crew chief's waist and locked his left arm around his neck. Griffin made sure he had a good hold and then pulled the rip cord D ring. The shock from the chute opening almost made him lose his grip. Admiral Griffin was grateful. It was too dark to see the full nylon canopy of the chute above him, but he knew it was open. Admiral Griffin closed his eyes again and prayed. This time all he said was, "Thank you, Jesus. Thank you."

Under the clouds Keller and Beck were still scissoring their F-18s back and forth, waiting for something to happen. Without warning, Kenada's Eagle dropped out of the bottom of the clouds in front of them. A near miss. Kenada didn't see them in the darkness under the clouds. She never would have known that they were there had she not seen their afterburners kick in when they came after her.

When Kenada saw them turning toward her, she said, "I can't stay here either." She pushed her throttle into full burner and put her nose in the clouds above. Keller and Beck followed.

Above the clouds Haley and Rutherford in their F-18s could easily see that something big had just happened. Whatever it was, they didn't need infrared vision to see it. Haley keyed his mike button and radioed to his wingman, "Twink, did you see that? Looks like we can go home now."

Haley radioed back, "I hope so, but something's not right. Why is there still so much light?"

Haley and Rutherford quickly got their answer. They heard Beck on the radio: "Twink, Comet, the Eagle's loose and coming up at ya."

At the speed of light, Beck's radio transmission reached the AWACS aircraft a hundred miles away. These were not the words that Colonel Fugami wanted to hear. He immediately hit the transmit button and said the launch code words, "Gauntlet, Crystal Ball, Rolling Thunder, Rolling Thunder . . . Gauntlet, Crystal Ball, Rolling Thunder, Rolling Thunder."

There were one hundred forty fighters that formed the gauntlet. There were air force F-15 Eagles, F-16 Falcons, and there were navy F-18 Hornets and F-14 Tomcats. Each of these fighters carried at least six missiles; most of them were carrying eight. Without hesitation each of the aircraft in the gauntlet fired two missiles, either heat-seeking AIM-9L Sidewinders, or the radar-guided AIM-7 and AIM-120 Sparrows or the radar-guided Phoenix missiles.

The three controllers sitting in front of Fugami heard a chorus of "Fox One" and "Fox Two" over the radio.

They all knew, the controllers and Fugami, that at that moment hundreds of heat-seeking and radar-guided missiles were being fired at whatever aircraft were in the center of the circle.

Two of the controllers looked back at Colonel Fugami as if to say, Now what? Fugami, still staring at the scope, prayed, "Dear God, help us."

Beck, Keller, Haley and Rutherford all heard the Rolling Thunder code words, and all four of them knew they were in big trouble. Each of their lives would depend on what they did in the next few seconds.

Kenada didn't hear the radio transmissions saying Rolling Thunder, Fox One or Fox Two, but she knew she was in big trouble nonetheless. Her TEWS scope, tactical early warning system, had lit up all around its face, and she could hear the radar lock tones. When she jumped out of the clouds into the clear air above she could see them. All around her Kim could see the fiery plumes of missiles coming at her from five to ten miles away. Besides the missiles Kim also saw Haley's and Rutherford's F-18s. She came out of the clouds right between the two of them.

Haley saw the fast-approaching danger of the incoming missiles. His TEWS scope was all lit up, and from the sound of the tones in his ears, he knew at least one radar-guided air-to-air missile had his tail number on it. He keyed his mike button and said, "Hey, guys, hit your flares and chaff; we've got incoming."

Haley remembered the old cliché, "He who fights and runs away will live to fight another day." Well, this was definitely a time when discretion was the better part of valor. Haley hit his mike button again. "OK, guys, break, break, break. Get outta here."

Just as Haley and Rutherford were turning to run for cover, they saw the Eagle shoot out of the clouds between them. Haley saw the F-15 and got an immediate case of target fixation. He thought, *Hell, if I'm gonna die, at least I can take that damn Eagle with me. Besides, that's just as good a way out of here as any.* Haley continued pulling hard back on his stick. He was going to get on that Eagle's tail if it was the last thing he ever did.

Rutherford saw the Eagle and saw Haley start to go for the chase. Without hesitation she turned to follow her leader.

Colonel Ferratto heard the radio transmissions. He heard "Rolling Thunder" but he didn't know what it meant. He heard "Fox One" and "Fox Two," and he knew what that meant. It meant air-to-air heat-seeking and radar-guided missiles were coming toward him. He didn't care. He had bigger problems. He was in the clouds, on fire, with a third of his plane gone, and just barely flying.

Ferratto was desperately trying to keep his crippled bird aloft. With several thousand pounds of fuel and metal gone from the aft of the tanker, it became nose-heavy. Ferratto struggled with the yoke and succeeded in bringing the crippled tanker to the clear air above the clouds. He ordered the flight engineer to start dumping fuel out of the nose and main fuselage fuel tanks.

Considering that there were close to a hundred heat-seeking missiles converging toward all of the aircraft in the center of the gauntlet's circle, the dumping of thousands of gallons of raw fuel into the air was not a good idea. Unfortunately it was the only way Ferratto could keep his plane flying. The fuel that was dumped overboard into the airstream quickly caught on fire and turned into a tongue of fire that could be seen for a hundred miles.

Kenada was heading southeast, away from the tanker and the F-18s. With her radar on she could see a couple dozen aircraft forming a wall headed right at her. In the night sky she could see a wave of fifty or more rocket plumes. To herself she said, "Damn. This is not good." Kenada knew that in addition to the threat in front of her, there were at least four F-18s on her tail.

Kenada thought, It's time to turn a liability into an asset. She rolled over and pulled hard back on her stick. She was performing a split-S maneuver that would vertically turn her around and have her heading back toward the tanker she had just left. Haley and Rutherford saw the Eagle turn and continued to follow.

Keller and Beck were also hot on Kenada's trail. Keller was ahead of Beck and was able to get a radar lock onto the Eagle, even though he was still in the clouds. He blindly fired his AIM-120 and yelled "Fox Two" over the radio.

Before the Eagle reached the peak of its loop, Keller and Beck shot out of the clouds also right in behind Haley and Rutherford, who had turned to climb up after Kenada. Keller had a sick feeling when he saw where his missile was going. Keller yelled in the radio, "Twink, break right!"

Keller's warning was too late. His missile slammed into the tail of Rutherford's jet and put it into a flat spin. Keller and Beck broke left and right to avoid running into the flying debris.

As they flew by the tumbling F-18 rolling through the sky in flames, Keller thought he saw an ejection seat rocket out of the wreckage; at least that was what he hoped he saw. Now there were three.

Haley, Beck and Keller each followed the Eagle's maneuver, which was just what Kenada had hoped for. Kenada had succeeded in putting three jets between her and the flock of approaching missiles.

Keller and Beck should have been watching where they were going, or at least what was coming toward them. While Keller and Beck were belly-up to the stars doing their split-S to chase the Eagle, their exposed undersides were being painted by the radars of about twenty missiles. Beck and Keller never felt a thing. Two pairs of radar-guided AIM-120s fired from the rim of the advancing jets found them. Like moths to a flame, the forty or so missiles were attracted to that part of the sky. Even after the two F-18s had been blown apart and were still hanging in the sky on fire, they still attracted missiles. The flaming wreckage and debris still presented a large radar reflection, as well as an intense heat source.

Kenada saw the crippled and flaming tanker rise just above the tops of the cloud deck. In her rearview mirror she saw the flash of the two F-18s exploding, followed by a staccato sequence of numerous explosions. Her TEWS scope was still lit up from behind, so she knew she wasn't safe yet. She needed another shield to break the radar lock.

For Kenada, the flaming tanker was a godsend. She flew high over it and then rolled her Eagle upside down so she could pull back on the stick and loop over it and then dive in front of it. She knew the fire and heat from the burning tanker would draw all of the heat-seeking missiles like sharks in a feeding frenzy to a bleeding, harpooned whale in the sea. With any luck all of the radar-guided missiles would lose their lock and go for the tanker.

Haley saw numerous explosions ahead of him at the flaming tanker. He could see plumes of more missiles still racing toward the flying tanker wreckage and decided that overflying the tanker to chase the Eagle was not a wise option, but he did it anyway. Haley rolled inverted as he overflew the tanker, and just to play it safe he punched his chaff button.

Haley had no idea about the fate of his three wingmen. He had chosen to pursue the Eagle and tried to get on its tail for a missile lock. As he started his downward pull over and in front of the tanker, he saw, heard and felt at least six explosions. Pieces of shrapnel streaked through the night sky in front of and all around him like fireworks. Several pieces bounced off of the wings of his jet. One golfball-size piece got his attention when it smashed through his canopy just behind his head and landed on his lap.

Haley continued to pull back on his stick and dove into the clouds, pursuing the F-15.

Knight Hawk

Kenada had doubled back toward her original southeast course.

Capt. Diane Datz in the F-22A was watching from her perch at forty-two thousand feet, where she waited to shoot down any launched Knight Hawk missile. Her jet was flying in the auto mode and staying in the best position in relation to the Eagle. With the aid of her jet's combovision, using infrared and low-level-light vision, she could easily see and follow the events occurring below. Unfortunately, without using the radar mode in the combovision, she was unable to see clearly what had happened in the clouds while the Eagle was refueling. When the first flash of light lit up the clouds, Datz said, "The heck with EMIS, Peg, add radar to combovision and magnify."

Instantly the clouds disappeared from view and Datz had a clear view of the drama unfolding. In amazement she watched as the F-15 dropped away from the tanker, and the F-16 rammed the back end of the tanker and exploded. She saw the Eagle drop down and then immediately climb back up with the two F-18s in pursuit. She saw the other two F-18s also join in the chase. She even gasped when she saw one of the F-18s take a missile in the tailpipe and blow apart.

Datz thought, These guys need some help. She said, "Peg, target the F-15 and launch four hypers."

The computer answered, "Hoots, I cannot comply; our prime directive for this mission is to destroy the Knight Hawk missile if it is launched. We were directed not to engage the Eagle."

"Peg, disregard directives. Target the Eagle and launch hypers."

"Hoots, I cannot disregard directives."

Datz was furious about being disobeyed by a computer. She thought, *How dare you. If I didn't need you right now, I'd unplug you.*

When Datz heard the Rolling Thunder code words, she saw well over a hundred missiles start to form a huge, smoking spiderweb in the sky, with the tanker and the five remaining fighters in the center of the web. Datz thought, Well, I don't think they're going to get out of that one. Still mad, she said, "Boy, and what a waste of missiles. If it wasn't for that damn directive, we could've taken out the Eagle with a couple of hypers and she never would've had a clue we were on her."

Peg did not reply.

Datz thought about taking the computer off-line and firing the hypers manually, but at this range it would be impossible for her to accurately track such a small, fast target without the radar-laser interface in the computer.

Datz saw the Eagle heading straight for a wall of missiles and fighters coming right at the Eagle, with the three Hornets right behind. She knew that it was only a matter of seconds and everything would be over. She was surprised by the Eagle's double-back maneuver, especially after two of the F-18s were blown apart by the missiles, and said out loud, "My God, would you look at that; she used them as a shield."

Datz was distracted when she heard her computer say, "Hoots, who is 'My God,' and what is it that you want God to look at?"

As Datz watched the chase continue, she pondered Peg's question and said, "Peg, I'll explain later about God, but for right now we need to keep an eye on that Eagle."

No sooner did Datz finish her statement than Peg complied. A capital letter *I* appeared in the cursor box that framed the F-15. Datz asked, "Peg, what's that in the targeting box?"

"Hoots, it is the letter *I*, as you requested.

Datz made a mental note to do something about programming figures of speech into Peg's memory. She then said, "Peg, disregard the 'I' comment and remove the letter *I* from the cursor."

The letter *I* disappeared.

When the F-15 and the F-18 flew over the burning tanker, she saw several explosions and thought, Well, it's over this time. She was surprised when she saw that the Eagle and the Hornet had doubled back to the southeast again by going over, then under the tanker.

Seeing the chase continue, she said, "Peg, look at that; the F-15 and the F-18 are making another run at those fighters. I bet she's going to use that same double-back maneuver to try to get that one F-18 blown away like the other F-18s."

Kenada had succeeded in eluding the first wave of missiles from the east, and now she could see on her radar that she was heading straight for the wall of navy fighters. She could see that the fighters were stacked in three layers, with the bulk of the fighters spread out at her level. Kenada recognized the formation from all of the pilot debriefing sessions at Desert Storm. *Well, this looks like Colonel Fugami's handiwork. If that's the case, what would Eddie Rickenbacker do?*

From her academy days, Kenada remembered an old quote from Vince Lombardi or some other aggressive soul: "The best defense is a good offense." Kenada thought, It's time to get offensive and make a doorway through. Then another quote came to mind: "Knock and the door will be opened." *Well, boys, I'm knocking.* She reached over to her weapons select panel and touched MISSILES. Without waiting for a lock-on tone, she launched all four of her AIM-120 missiles at the fighters coming at her at the same level. She hit the mike button, transmitted on the guard frequency and yelled, "Fox Two, Fox Two, Fox Two, Fox Two!" *Well; that ought to get their attention and make a hole in their lineup.* Just to make sure the hole was big enough, she put a thirty-degree spread between the four missiles. Her idea worked. The missiles selected their own targets, and the fighters who heard the tones and saw the fire streaking toward them turned all over the sky to stay alive. The formidable wave of aviation power was broken in two, with a gaping hole in the middle. In the vernacular of Lombardi, Kenada saw daylight in the middle and advanced her throttle to full burner to go through the hole.

Kenada reached for the weapons select panel and turned the switch to MISSILE #2. It seemed that all was lost and the plan was a bust. Since it looked like she might not get out of this one, she decided it was time to launch the Knight Hawk and then fight her way out.

Without hesitation Kenada flipped the cover over the guarded switch and squeezed the firing trigger on the joystick grip. Nothing happened. Kenada looked at the display screen for a clue to why the missile failed to fire. She had her answer. The screen displayed the message, TARGET OUT OF RANGE.

Kenada's mind raced. There had to be a way to use it as a weapon against all of the fighters. Kenada knew she didn't have the time to reprogram the coordinates, so she said, "Well, if Muhammad won't go to the mountain, then it's time to take the mountain to Muhammad." Suddenly Kenada had a moment of brilliance. "I know; I'll get these guys to follow me to Washington. After I fly over D.C., I'll launch the Knight Hawk and have it detonate behind me. That way I'll get my target and all of the fighters behind me. I'll kill a hundred birds with one stone."

High above the foray of fighters, Capt. Diane Datz saw the Eagle launch her missiles. Instinctively she said, "Peg, laser lock and fire double hypers." With her right index finger on the touch pad, she slid a cursor over the image of each missile and marked it for targeting. She said, "I don't know if any of those are the Knight Hawk, so let's take them all out."

Immediately on Peg's getting the command, the nose of the F-22A dropped down thirty degrees to get the optimum launch angle, and eight hypervelocity laser-guided missiles launched from the pod, each with its own explosive pop and swishing noise. Datz watched the missiles alter their courses to follow the reflected laser light her F-22A was shining on the missiles. Datz was pleased that Peg obeyed.

Datz watched and said to herself, "It's going to be close."

The fighters in the wall were jinking in all directions to get out of harm's way.

The first pilot to see the missiles coming at him was Cmdr. Leo "Doc" Sullivan in the lead jet of a two-ship of F-14s. Doc keyed his mike button and warned the rest of his flight, "Looper, Lucky, break low now. We've got snot lockers at twelve-o'clock level, two miles. *Snot locker* was the term for a missile that was headed right for the nose of the target aircraft.

Doc's backseater, his radar intercept officer, Lt. Ann "Nurse Rio" Alvord, didn't need to be told twice. While Doc was slamming his stick and throwing their jet away from the incoming, Rio was busy punching the chaff buttons and trying to keep an eye on the threat.

Pat O'Connell

While their F-14 was diving for the deck, Rio was watching the AIM-120 get dangerously closer. She keyed the intercom and said "Break right, Doc, now, or we're not gonna make it!"

"Hold on, Rio, just a few more seconds."

"Do it now, Doc. Now!" Rio had a better view of the missile coming at them than Doc did, and she could see that they were about to be toast.

Kenada's missiles were weaving back and forth as each missile tracked its own target. The F-22A's radar tracked the movements of Kenada's missiles, and the computer directed the aiming of the lasers to guide the hypers to their targets.

Rio reached down and grabbed the arming handles of her ejection seat, and then waited for the missile impact. To the amazement of both Doc and Rio, the missile detonated just seconds before it would have meant their doom.

With a little relief in his voice, Doc said, "What the . . . Rio, I don't know what you did, but whatever it was, it worked."

"Doc, it wasn't me."

"Well, if you didn't, who did?" Without thinking Doc transmitted, "This is Doc. Whoever took care of that missile, thanks. We owe you."

Datz heard Doc's radio call and couldn't resist. She answered, "Doc, do you believe in guardian angels?"

Rio responded in a more somber tone, "Doc, check four-o'clock low. I think that's Lucky and Looper."

Kenada was two miles behind her missiles when she saw all four of them detonate, one right after the other. She was puzzled by the streaks of light from above just before the explosions. One of the explosions was larger than the others and was followed by a staccato of smaller secondary explosions. She could see the shadows of broken wings against the fireball and knew that was a definite kill. The other three were just huge balls of light. Kills or no kills, it didn't matter to Kenada; she just wanted to disrupt the line of fighters long enough for her to fly through. The missiles did what she wanted to do. She said, "There's my door; now to go through it."

As she entered the void in the line, she could see a fighter coming head-to-head with her. Her targeting computer showed that she was in the window to fire. Instinctively she pulled the trigger, and tracer fire cut into the night and ripped into the F-14 Tomcat, making it a ball of flame. Lucky was no longer lucky.

Haley in his F-18 was a mile behind Kenada, and now lined up for a launch. He had selected an AIM-7; he got the radar lock-on tone and fired.

Kenada heard the lock-on tone and saw her TEWS light up with the threat coming from behind. She punched her chaff and flare button and then flew past the still-burning wreckage from her victim. Seconds later, the radar-guided missile fired by Haley was fooled by Kenada's maneuver and detonated in the tumbling pieces, scattering them even more.

Kenada thought, *That was too close.* On her radar she could see clear skies ahead. Clouds but no fighters. Her airspeed indicator on the heads-up display showed her airspeed was accelerating past 1,525 knots. Her TEWS scope lit up, showing threats from behind. Kenada thought, I need more speed. Kim dropped her nose twenty degrees, plunged down into the clouds and disappeared. She came out under the clouds and continued down till she was three hundred feet above the ground. She knew the clouds would keep all of the fighters above from being able to launch heat-seeking missiles, and the close proximity to the ground would confuse some of the radars with ground clutter.

Haley jinked left and then right around the fighter debris to try to stay on Kenada's tail. His radar had tracked the Eagle going into a dive, but now it was gone, no longer on the scope. Even if Haley could still track the Eagle, there was no way he could keep up with the Eagle in full burner.

Colonel Fugami was furious and frantic. The wall of navy fighters from the *Eisenhower* had been breached. Judging from the fact that most of the fighters were still heading toward the center of the containment circle where the tanker once was, Fugami knew that most of them had lost the Eagle. Fugami and his three controllers were amazed. The cake Fugami baked had flopped. Fugami yelled at his controllers, "Get everybody in this navy group heading one three two at max speed. Direct them to her location."

The controllers carried out Fugami's orders, and on the scope he could see the fighters turn. Thirty-some navy jets were now turned and following the Eagle. As he watched he realized just what Kenada was doing, and out loud he said, "She's heading east. She's going for Washington."

Colonel Fugami looked at the scope to see what was available. He pointed at a small group of blips just fifty miles north of Norfolk and said to one of the controllers, "What are these?"

The controller replied, "They're four F-15s out of Langley."

Fugami pointed at a spot on the scope near Frederick, Maryland, and said, "Get them to this spot. We've got to head off the Eagle and do it here."

* * *

Knight Hawk

Leading the pack after Kenada was a two-ship formation of F-14 Tomcats. From their vantage at fifteen thousand feet, they had never lost track of the Eagle as it penetrated through their wall. They had turned and were diving in pursuit with their wings swept back and engines in full burner before Fugami and Crystal Ball controllers could give directions. The two Tomcats were tracking the Eagle on their scopes and were trying to line up for missile shots. The radar intercept officer in the lead Tomcat got his lock-on tones and squeezed the trigger; ten seconds later he squeezed it again. Two Phoenix missiles jumped off the rails out from under each wing and raced ahead. In less than a minute the fiery tails of the Phoenix missiles disappeared in the clouds below.

Captain Datz had guessed wrong, and her computer reminded her, "Hoots, you lost your bet; the Eagle did not double back. It appears that the Eagle is escaping."

"Peg, you are correct. Follow—" Datz didn't have a chance to finish her sentence when she felt herself being thrust back into her seat, along with a rapid nose-down push over.

"Peg, what are you doing?"

"Hoots, the Eagle has accelerated and I am pursuing to the maintain the optimum position."

"Peg, position us for hyper missile shots, and when ready, fire."

"Hoots, I am maneuvering; however I cannot fire hypers."

Datz was starting to get a little perturbed about being told no by a machine. After all, who was in charge here, the pilot or a computer program? She thought about asking that question but decided not to; she was afraid of what Peg's answer might be. Instead she asked, "Peg, why won't you fire? Is it that programmed directive about not engaging the F-15 in combat?"

"Hoots, I cannot fire the hypers because the Eagle has descended below clouds that are too dense for the targeting lasers to penetrate."

Datz felt slightly better because the reason Peg refused was not disobedience. "Peg, OK, disregard hypers and launch AIM-120s."

She was even more frustrated when she heard Peg reply, "Hoots, I cannot comply."

Datz assumed, there's that damn program directive in there again. "Peg, override the program directive and launch AIM-120s."

"Hoots, I cannot comply."

"Peg, why won't you override the program directive?"

"Hoots, I can override the program directive."

"Peg, then do it."

"Hoots, it is done."

"Peg, now target the Eagle and launch AIM-120s."

"Hoots, I cannot comply."

Datz thought, Great, now what? She was really getting bothered by being disobeyed by a machine. She controlled her frustration and anger, and with difficulty asked slowly, "Peg, why can't you launch the AIM-120s?"

"Hoots, there are too many aircraft in between us and the Eagle. They are interfering with my ability to get a radar lock."

"Peg, we've got to get ahead of them. Stay at this altitude and accelerate to Mach 2.5. Same heading as the Eagle. I've got an idea."

Datz felt the F-22A level off at eighteen thousand feet and accelerate. Peg spoke up and asked, "Hoots, what is your idea?"

*   *   *

Knight Hawk

Kenada still wanted more speed; fifteen hundred knots per hour was not enough. She needed another couple hundred knots if she wanted to get enough separation from the jets behind her and to get out of the range of their missiles.

She could hear the tone telling her that missiles were coming at her using radar. Over her left shoulder she could see two streaks of fire coming out of the clouds. She estimated their distance at about three miles. She thought, *Well, I'll kill two birds with two stones. I'll get rid of those missiles and also give myself more speed.* Kenada pitched her aircraft up in a forty-degree rate of climb and turned so that the missiles would be coming at her from the six-o'clock direction. She rolled the Eagle inverted and continued the climb up to three thousand feet. Rather than punch the chaff button again to fool the missiles, Kenada dropped her hand off the throttles and broke the seals off the guarded pylon switches, pushed the guard covers up and pushed each switch to JETTISON. The now empty pylons, one under each wing, blew away from the wings and floated upward. She rolled right-side up, and with her nose pointed down descended at the same rate of speed as the jettisoned pylons. This would keep the falling pylons directly in between her and the missiles.

The ploy worked. The falling pylons provided enough of a mass and radar reflection to draw the missiles. When Kenada saw the two explosions behind her, she turned back to her original course, straight for Washington. With the pylons gone there was no extra drag hanging down in the wind. Kenada got the extra speed she needed, another two hundred knots. She looked at her airspeed on her HUD and saw 1708 KIAS (knots indicated airspeed) and looked over her shoulder. When she saw no missiles heading her way, she said to herself, "Good, I must be out of their range. Now for D.C."

The sudden lock-on tone blaring in her ears told her that she had spoken too soon. She held her course and continued to accelerate.

In the lead F-14, the radar intercept officer had gotten a solid lock on the Eagle and picked off two more missiles. The Eagle was just inside the ten-mile range of the Phoenix missile. He knew that one missile would do the trick, but decided to fire two, just in case. The flight of F-14s watched the two missiles disappear into the clouds below and ahead, first one, and then three seconds later the other.

Kenada could still hear the tone but couldn't see anything yet. She didn't know where the missiles were, so she dropped down as low as she could. As she looked around and checked her mirrors she thought, Come on, where are you? Finally Kenada could see a rocket plume, then another, come out of the clouds. Judging from the dimness of the light she guessed that they were about four or five miles behind. Still too far back to use chaff.

The first formation of F-14s came out of the bottom of the clouds, and the lead pilot spoke to his RIO over the intercom: "Spike, I've got a visual and radar tallyho on the Eagle. Looks like the missiles are on track three to four behind. We'll have a kill in about twenty seconds."

Before the lead pilot finished counting his eggs before they had hatched, the flames from the rocket motors of the two Phoenix missiles went out and he lost sight of them.

Kenada too was showing great concern over the two flaming lights that were starting to get brighter in her mirrors. She glanced ahead at the radar screen scanning the way ahead, and punched her chaff button. Kenada's concern was heightened even more when she looked back and couldn't see the flames anymore. She rolled left and then jinked hard to try to break the radar lock. Kenada was immediately relieved when she saw two distant explosions and heard the lock-on tone stop.

The lead pilot saw the explosions and saw on his radar that the Eagle was flying and nowhere near the detonations. He keyed his intercom and asked, "Spike, what the hell happened? Those missiles missed by a mile."

After a moment Spike said, "Damn! She outran our missiles. It was a long shot, and I didn't figure her speed in when I fired."

"How can that be a long shot when it's still in range?"

Spike was bothered by the fact that he had just wasted two missiles at forty thousand dollars each and said, "Easy, if I had done the math before I fired I would have known that our missiles would have to go through about sixteen miles of air to get to the target."

Well, I'll stay on her tail and you tell me when we're in range."

The RIO checked his scope and then said, "The Eagle is about five miles out of our range, and the way it's hauling ass we're going to need another five hundred knots to catch up."

As he watched his quarry quickly escape the reach of his weapons, the lead pilot had only one thing to say: "Damn."

Chapter Twenty

There was a new level of concern in the military command center. All of the battle staff members, as well as the secretary of defense, Jeff Howard, and the secretary of the air force, Alex McKenna, were intently watching the radar blips dance across the map. What bothered them all was the single flashing blip that was leaving the circle of fighters and heading toward Washington. They all knew what that meant.

McKenna asked Price, "Where is she going?"

Price turned to her and just said, "Looking at her current direction, I'd say she's coming here. We are her target."

Admiral Watson said, "I don't think we are her target. In fact, I don't think she intends to use the missile. If we were her target, she would have launched it a long time ago. We've been in range of her Knight Hawk for the past twenty minutes. I think she's bluffing. I think she still wants the gold. Maybe we can still negotiate."

Price didn't agree with Watson's opinion and said, "Well, what makes you think she doesn't want to just kamikaze it to us?"

Dr. Laut heard the discussion and decided to voice her opinion, "Excuse me, General. I am not a military strategist, but if I were her, I would hand-deliver it rather than launch it, but for a different reason. She's not suicidal. If I'm right, I think that she's going to use the Knight Hawk as a defensive weapon." Dr. Laut picked up the laser pointer on the desk, pointed at the dots of lights on the main display and said, "You see now that she is heading this way; all of those fighters are behind her. I would say that she is going to overfly Washington, shove that bomb down our throats and then have the bomb detonate safely behind her. That way she'll blow up D.C. and probably most if not all of the fighters behind her."

Admiral Watson spoke up again. "Even if she is coming here, I don't think she'll make it. Look at all of the jets coming after her. All they've got to do is just get a lock and launch a missile and she's toast."

Price looked at Watson and commented, "I don't know if you've noticed, but the distance between her and the other fighters is growing. I'd have to say that she's leaving those navy jets in the dust."

Howard, in his excitement, said, "Hey, if that's the case, we've got to get the president off the Hill."

Price said, "I've already tried doing that through Borda, and she said that there's no way to get him to leave. Besides, he's already started his address."

"Well, what can we do?" McKenna asked.

"We? We can do nothing . . . except pray. Right now

it's up to a handful of F-15s from Langley and a half dozen F-16s from Andrews.

"Crystal Ball has vectored these jets to intercept the Eagle northwest of here, close to Harper's Ferry. If they don't succeed then it'll all be over in about ten minutes."

The White House

Vice President Borda watched the situation map intently from the relative safety of the basement bunker in the White House. Just to make sure she understood, she asked the army colonel beside her, "What is happening here?" Borda pointed at the flashing spot of light on the scope and asked, "Is this the F-15?"

The colonel responded, "Yes, it is, and it looks like they won't be able to stop her from coming here."

"Is there anything we can do?"

"Well, we can't do anything except get ready and wait for her to arrive, that is if she does come here. We've already activated the Hawk missile battery. If she comes within a five-mile radius of us she'll be in our range. We control the missile from down here. This is the radar system monitor. We will fire if we see the radar blip without the proper IFF code beside it."

"How effective is it?"

"The system is very successful. Our only real problem with it is that it is such a small decision window."

"Decision window, what's that?"

"Decision window is the time period that you can launch and still hit the target. In this situation, where a jet is coming in at high speed and low altitude, the decision window to shoot is only three or four seconds long. If you don't shoot during that time period, the jet will be out of range and the missile will miss."

Borda looked at the young army sergeant manning

the console and asked, "Have you ever fired one of these missiles at a target?"

"No, ma'am, but I have had all of the training courses for it, and I've even manned a missile battery at Aviano Air Base in Italy during the beginning of the Bosnian crisis."

Borda looked at the missile-launch console with doubts. She turned to the colonel and said, "That's nice, but I sure hope we don't have to use it."

The colonel could have and should have responded by simply agreeing, but instead he chose to express his confidence. In an almost condescending tone, he spoke with a slightly southern drawl and said, "Don't worry, ma'am, we've planned for everything to take care of this woman and her jet."

Vice President Borda caught the inflection in the colonel's voice and was offended. He was talking as a man to a woman, not showing the respect for her position as the vice president or vice commander in chief. Borda calmly looked at the colonel and said, "Colonel, are you familiar with the cliché that starts, 'The best-laid plans of mice and men . . . '? Have you noticed it doesn't say anything about women?"

Crystal Ball

The pilot of the AWACS aircraft turned the Boeing 707 to a heading of one four zero. The course correction was needed to keep the escaping F-15 in radar range.

Colonel Fugami was feeling a frantic panic beginning to gnaw at him, but externally he appeared calm. The three-layer cake he had baked had flopped. Now he was desperately trying to piece together a last-ditch defense. By watching the radar scopes, he could see that Captain

Kenada had broken through the wall of fighters and was rapidly accelerating away from the bulk of the fighters and heading toward Washington.

Looking at the scope, Fugami noticed there was one aircraft that was matching the speed of the F-15. "What is that aircraft?"

The controller moved the cursor over the radar blip and clicked the IDENT button on the mouse. Instantly five short lines of text appeared beside the blip. The controller turned to Fugami and said, "That's that F-22A that was brought in to shoot the Knight Hawk. It's at twenty thousand feet and doing about eighteen hundred knots."

"What kind of weapons does it have?"

"I don't know; let me find out."

"Yes, do that."

The controller keyed his radio mike button and said, "Pegasus Zero One, Crystal Ball."

"Go ahead, Crystal."

"Pegasus, state your armament."

"Crystal Ball, I have two AIM-120s, two AIM-9Ls, and forty hypers." Diane felt a little chuckle and wondered how long they would wait to ask about her hypers.

There were a few moments of silence; then another voice cut in over Datz's earphones, "Pegasus, this is Specter of Crystal Ball; what are hypers?"

Datz replied, "hypervelocity laser-guided missiles."

Fugami thought for a moment, and then he remembered reading about some experiments being performed using hypers. He said, "Pegasus, do you think you could down an F-15 using your hypers?"

Datz keyed the mike and said "Affirmative, Crystal."

"Have you used your hypers against any moving targets?"

"Crystal Ball, I don't know if you knew this or not,

but just two and a half minutes ago I used eight hypers to take out three AIM-120s launched from Eagle One."

Fugami was surprised and saw similar expressions on the faces of the three controllers. He keyed the mike and said, "Negative, Pegasus, we didn't know that. Pegasus, do you have Eagle Zero One on your radar?"

Datz replied, "Affirmative, Crystal. I have it in sight and I'm closing."

Fugami looked closer at the scope and studied the situation. About fifty miles ahead of Kenada at her twelve o'clock were six F-16s flying at five thousand feet, and at her two o'clock were four F-15s about sixty miles out at twenty thousand. He turned to one controller and said, "Have the 16s form a wall ahead of Kenada and see if they can keep her away from D.C." Fugami turned to another controller and said, "Have the F-15s do a pinch maneuver here if she gets through the 16s."

Both controllers nodded their heads and started vectoring their respective jets.

Fugami keyed his mike button and said, "Pegasus, do you see approaching fighters?"

Peg understood Fugami's question and immediately went into the targeting mode to highlight the aircraft. Datz could easily see glowing red bubbles in the sky surrounding each group of fighters. Datz answered, "Crystal, affirmative, I have a tallyho on six Falcons twelve-o'clock low, and at two o'clock, four Eagles."

"Roger, Pegasus, you are to maintain current altitude, course and speed. The approaching Falcons and Eagles are going to engage Kenada. If she gets through these aircraft, I want you to join in the chase. Try to shoot her down before she has the opportunity to launch her Knight Hawk."

Datz thought, *This is great; that should override that*

program directive that Meridith and Colonel Lee put in.
Before she replied to Crystal, Datz said, "Peg, did you
hear our new directive from Crystal Ball?"

"Hoots, I did."

Datz said to Peg, "Good." She keyed her mike button
and then said, "Crystal, I copy. After Eagle Zero One
clears Falcons and Eagles, Shoot Eagle Zero One."

"Pegasus, that's affirmative."

Datz could tell from the speed and altitudes that the
Falcons were not going to stop Kenada. They were too
late in getting down to her altitude and then trying to
turn onto her tail.

The F-16 pilots had a radar track on Kenada's Eagle,
but grossly underestimated her speed. In the dark, they
never saw her when she passed underneath, but they
knew where she went. When they turned to chase her
from behind, she was already long gone.

Datz could see that the four F-15s were using a
smarter attack. Two of the F-15s stayed high and circled in above, and once they were behind Kenada,
dropped down to her altitude. The other two Eagles
dropped to Kenada's altitude and started turning in to
her for a head-on gunshot.

F-15s were one of only two types aircraft in the air
force inventory that were capable of successfully shooting a head-to-head shot at another aircraft. Kenada
knew this, and when she saw the two aircraft on her
radar, she wasted no time getting radar lock, and then
fired her guns. It was time to shoot first and ask questions later. Kenada stepped on her rudder pedals to
spread her bullets around while the two approaching
fighters were turning toward her.

Kenada's ten-second burst was effective. One Eagle
took a double hit in the left engine and the cockpit. The
pilot never felt a thing as the 20mm round pierced his

Knight Hawk

canopy and then smashed through his upper chest, his seat and the forward bulkhead of the fuselage fuel tank. The other Eagle driver was much luckier, but still not fortunate; he took a hit in one engine and a wing fuel tank.

Datz saw Kenada's Eagle get past the four F-15s. She was about to give Peg a verbal command to go in for the kill, but before she could, Peg had already lowered the nose in a steep dive and advanced the throttles. Datz thought, *Way to go, Peg. Let's go get 'em.*

Kenada's TEWS scope indicated that another radar missile was homing in on her from behind. She thought, I knew that was too easy.

The other two Eagles traded off their altitude for more speed and put themselves behind Kenada. As soon they were in position, the lead Eagle fired off an AIM-120 at Kenada.

Kenada picked up the threat on her TEWS. She wanted to turn on her ECM, but she knew if she did it would interfere with the Knight Hawk's navigational computer. She thought, *Well, if I can't use it for ECM, then what good is it? Let's see if it'll make a good decoy.* Kenada pitched her nose up ten degrees and then did a quick aileron roll. When she was inverted she jettisoned her ECM pod and punched her chaff button twice.

After her roll, Kenada put her Eagle down in the weeds. She saw the Potomac below her and decided to take advantage of the lower terrain.

The AIM-120 homed in on the radar reflection from the cloud of aluminum flakes of chaff. The proximity fuse in the missile closed when it passed close to the ECM pod, and the missile detonated.

The pilot of the lead Eagle, Maj. Rick Platt, was excited when he saw the missile's detonation. His joy was short lived. Seconds later Platt's radar had picked out Kenada's jet, still racing ahead.

Kenada's TEWS let her know that she was not in the clear yet. There was an occasional beep of a lock-on tone in her headset, which told her the terrain was helping. Kenada could see that the river ahead was turning more sharply than she could, and out of instinct she pulled back on her stick to fly over the trees. A few seconds later she overflew the eight lanes of the Capital Beltway just ten miles north of the city. Once over it she saw the river again, and dove back down into the valley around it.

Kenada's little pop-up was all that Platt needed. As soon as he had a lock-on tone from his missile, he let it fly.

Kenada knew she was in trouble again, her TEWS was glowing and the tone in her ears was steady.

Ahead was the Key Bridge, spanning the Potomac from Georgetown to Rosslyn. Kim saw the opportunity and took advantage of it. She said to herself, Well, as long as it works, I'll keep doing it. It worked; the missile locked onto the bridge and took out two lanes of traffic.

Both Platt and his wingman saw the missile slam into the bridge. When Kenada's Eagle cleared the bridge, they both had radar lock, and they both launched another missile.

One missile was gone, but by the tone in her ear and the light on her TEWS, Kenada knew that she was not in the clear. *There must be at least one more behind me. I need another shield . . . aha, and there it is.* Directly ahead of her were the marble white walls of the Parthenon-styled Kennedy Center, and behind it the towering stones of the Washington Monument, all 555 feet of it. She pulled back hard on her stick, and her Eagle cleared the roof of the Kennedy Center by fifty feet. Once over the top she pushed her stick forward to keep her nose low and her altitude lower. In the rearview mirror she could see a flare of light and thought, This is going to be close. She steered her Eagle to the white monolith ahead and passed to the right of it with her wings vertical. Kim had succeeded in putting the Washington Monument between her and the missiles that were targeting her.

No sooner had Kim said to herself, "Ha, that'll work" than she saw the flashes from two explosions on the other side of the monument.

Kenada did not have the proper vantage to appreciate all of the damage that the missiles caused. The two F-15s and the F-22A following Kenada saw it all, and in amazement watched the monument lean and then start to collapse into itself. They had passed it before it completely toppled down.

Kim used the monument as a shield, even after it was hit. She dropped her eagle down to fifty feet and flew up the Mall between the Smithsonian Institute toward the Capitol building.

The White House

Back in the basement bunker, Sergeant Roberts suddenly saw an unlabeled blip on his radar scope. The army colonel yelled into the sergeant's ear, "Fire, fire!"

The sergeant hit the launch button, and a second later one Hawk missile melted the tar on the White House roof as it started its short journey toward the fighters overhead. No sooner had Roberts hit the launch button than he saw two, then three, more aircraft on the scope. Roberts thought, I sure hope we're shooting at the right one.

*   *   *

As Kenada approached the east end of the Mall, she pitched her Eagle to climb up and over the north side of the Capitol building. With her Eagle in a forty-degree nose-high climb, she hit the pickle button to launch the Knight Hawk. Kim felt the missile ejector push the Knight Hawk down and away from the Eagle. To protect herself from its rocket plume, she immediately rolled right and made a hard level turn. The two F-15s following behind her were still trying to get another lock, but couldn't. They were still unaware that Datz, in the F-22A, was behind them.

Datz held the F-22A on target and made sure the lasers locked onto the first Eagle, and she thought, *But which one? Well, when in doubt, take them all out.* Then she said, "Peg, target mode," as she slid her fingertip on the touch pad, which moved the cursor toward the jets in front of her.

Suddenly there was a flare of fire shooting off the side of the first Eagle. "Peg, that's got to be the Knight Hawk. Peg, target the missile and fire hypers."

The F-22A pitched up violently to follow the missile. Peg had to maneuver the aircraft so that it could bring the hypers in line to fire.

Great minds thought alike. Platt's wingman in the trailing F-15 also saw the Knight Hawk launch, broke off his chase of Kenada's Eagle and started to turn toward the launched missile. He thought he would try to line up for a missile shot on the Knight Hawk, if he could.

Datz saw him pull up and thought, Damn, I hope he doesn't get in the way. She then said, "Peg, fire when you get in the window."

"Hoots, I copy."

Knight Hawk

Datz felt electrical shocks in the back of her head warning her of an incoming missile.

Peg spoke up again, "Hoots, we have radar lock coming from our six."

"Peg, that's OK, fire chaff but maintain laser lock on the Knight Hawk."

"Hoots, there is an inbound missile impact in seven seconds."

"Peg, hold it; maintain lock." Datz looked at her accelerometer and noticed that she was pulling nine Gs and still not turning fast enough to bring the hypers into line to fire. Her peripheral vision was gone, and she was getting tighter and smaller tunnel vision. Her vision was starting to totally black out. Datz remembered that somewhere nested in Peg's program were safeties that kept the computer from doing maneuvers that would damage the aircraft or overstress the pilot. This program safety was the mechanical version of the human instinct for self-preservation.

The G suit was helping Diane stay conscious in the nine-G pull, but she was losing it fast. She felt like a rag doll, a very heavy rag doll. She couldn't even hold her head up. Under the nine-G force, the eighteen pounds of head and helmet resting on her neck were now a hundred and sixty. To save D.C., Diane knew what she had to do. Under the strain of the Gs, Diane grunted out, "Peg, pull harder; override all safeties. Shoot the Knight Hawk."

Without a response from her computer, Diane felt the immediate onset of more Gs. She lost her vision and then lost consciousness.

The Knight Hawk continued its climb. The Knight Hawk's onboard navigational computer plotted its trajectory to the detonation coordinates. The missile climbed straight up, and then started arcing back toward the heart of Washington. When the Knight Hawk reached an altitude of three thousand feet, its rocket motor cut off and its navigation computer guided the gliding missile toward the detonation point.

The F-15 pilot trying to line up on the Knight Hawk was out of luck. He popped out his speed brake and throttled back to idle, but his Eagle was traveling too fast to turn in for a shot on the missile.

Peg was flying the F-22A now, and it wasn't going to miss. The computer pulled the aircraft, exerting 12 Gs. To get a higher angle of attack and rate of turn, Peg vectored the jet exhaust nozzles.

Peg fired a volley of eight hypers at the Knight Hawk, which was now directly overhead and starting its downward glide toward its detonation point, eight hundred feet from the Washington Monument. Kenada had chosen this particular point because a detonation there would destroy the Capitol building, the White House and the Pentagon, not to mention every other building within two miles.

When the F-22A pitched up to track the Knight Hawk, it presented a large radar target for the Hawk missile.

The TEWS on the F-22A continued sounding the lock-on tone, and Peg continued launching chaff packages. The urge to perform evasive maneuvers was almost overpowering to Peg. Hoots's last words— "Override all safeties; shoot the Knight Hawk"—kept echoing through the circuits and chips of Peg's electric brain.

The Hawk found its mark. It struck the F-22A directly between the two tail rudders, ten feet from the end of the jet. The explosive force ripped apart the entire tail section, as well as destroying both engines. Shrapnel from the explosion ruptured the wing and fuselage fuel tanks, putting the whole back half of the F-22A in flames.

Five of the eight hypers found their mark also. The titanium tips of the hypers ripped into different parts of the missile. One grazed the guidance head, while another pierced through the beryllium reflector shield and the outer shell of plastic explosives surrounding the plutonium core of the nuclear device. The body of the Knight Hawk was ripped in half and spilled the warhead. One of the hypers bisected the partially spent solid-propellant rocket motor. The remaining propellent exploded and caused a chain reaction explosion in the warhead detonators. Because the detonators did not explode simultaneously, the plastic explosive shell detonated unevenly. The essential pressure wave needed to compress the plutonium and cause the fusion reaction never occurred. The Knight Hawk's demise was explosive but conventional—not nuclear.

The combination of the two explosions was massive, and centered directly over the Mall. The shock waves from the explosion broke windows as far as a mile away. The glass windows of the Capitol building, which was almost directly underneath, didn't survive at all. The loud explosions, the roaring jets overhead, and the breaking glass triggered a congressional stampede. Needless to say, the president's State of the Union address was over.

The pilot of the climbing F-15 was amazed. Just as he cursed himself for not being able to get the Knight Hawk, he saw the simultaneous explosions. In that instant he did not fully understand what had happened. He saw the fiery trails of the hypers' rockets draw lines across the sky to the exploding Knight Hawk. From the corner of his eye he also saw the exploding tail of the F-22A. For a moment he wondered how that got there, and then he turned his jet to rejoin his wingman and get back in the chase of Kenada.

In flames, the F-22A tumbled downward toward the Mall. Datz was still unconscious in the cockpit. The logic circuits in Peg's brain analyzed the predicament. When Peg realized that the F-22A could no longer fly, it activated the ejection sequence, and Captain Datz was rocketed out of the cockpit. The gyro-steered vernier rockets of the ACES II seat turned Datz upright and propelled her limp body higher into the air. The seat separated from Datz and her chute opened.

Datz regained consciousness just in time to see the flaming hulk of her magnificent F-22A smash through the roof of a large, squarish sandstone building on the Mall. Through the open areas where huge panes of glass had been seconds before, she could see wings of airplanes, and, she knew it was the Air and Space Museum.

After Kenada launched the Knight Hawk, she pushed her throttle into full burner and pushed her nose down to get as close to the ground as possible. She had flown her Eagle out of the lower flatland that nestled the capital and headed east. She was going to use the low ridge that surrounded D.C. as protection from the blast. Her TEWS kept lighting up, and there were occasional beeps. She knew that she was not alone. A quick glance at the missile launch monitor showed the countdown-to-detonation: clock: 00.03 . . . 00.02 . . . 00.01 . . . 00.00.

Kenada kept her head down and closed one eye so she wouldn't be partially blinded by the flash from the nuclear explosion. Her TEWS was still lit, and now the tone was steady. She hit her chaff and flare buttons and turned hard right to break the lock. Kenada knew her maneuver had succeeded in decoying the missile when she saw the flash of light well behind her.

Kenada yelled, "Damn." When she looked at the countdown clock, she saw that it was now counting up: 00.05 . . . 00.06 . . . 00.07. Something had happened. The Knight Hawk didn't detonate. She was disappointed, but there was another problem that concerned her more: the F-15 behind her.

At two hundred feet above the ground and racing in the dark at close to a thousand knots, Kenada saw the lights below as a blur, but she knew exactly where she was. She had just overflown the Capital Beltway, and from the layout of the massive intersection below, she knew that she was heading east and following Route 50. Up ahead she could see the lights of Annapolis. In her rearview mirror she could see another steady glare of light, a missile flume. There was no tone or light on the TEWS, and Kenada knew it was a Sidewinder closing in for the kill.

Kenada punched the flare button on the throttle quadrant and then banked right and turned. The heat-seeking went for the flare and detonated.

Major Platt saw his missile go for Kenada's flare and yelled, "You stupid missile." He thought, *This game is not over yet, Kenada. I've still got two more missiles and a full can of rocks.*

Platt's concentration was rudely interrupted by a voice. He immediately recognized the voice of "Bitching Betty" saying, "Warning, warning, your fuel levels are low. Your fuel levels are low."

Great, now I just wish I had a full tank of gas. Platt was nervously glancing at his fuel gauge; he knew that at his current rate of consumption he had less than five minutes of fuel left. He also knew that if he didn't do something soon, she would outrun him. Even though they were flying the same jets, Kenada didn't have the two pylons hanging down off the wings, creating extra drag.

Kenada kept changing her altitude and course, but generally steered toward the east. She knew this constant movement, left and right, up and down, would make it difficult to get a good lock. Kenada had another idea. As she flew she quickly punched a programmed course into the flight computer. She finished programming in time to see the Severn River pass underneath. She even recognized the buildings of the Naval Academy and its own little harbor. Searching ahead in the darkness, she finally saw what she was looking for: the towering twin suspension bridges that spanned the four and a half miles across the Chesapeake Bay.

Two miles from the bridges, Kenada stopped jostling the control stick and held it steady. She heard the telltale tone of a missile lock. In her mirror she saw the flash of light from the missile.

Platt in his Eagle was ecstatic; suddenly everything was perfect for a radar missile shot. To himself he said, "I've got you this time." Over his radio he yelled, "Fox Two." As soon as he fired, he saw Kenada's Eagle change course and steer straight for the bridges.

Kenada had changed her course to draw the fire of another missile. She estimated the distance of the missile from her and its time to impact, and she knew she could make it to the bridge. She was becoming an old hand at this barnstorming under bridges, but this time she knew that it would be different.

Platt saw where Kenada was going, and he knew what she was planning to do. He realized that she was drawing another missile into a bridge, and would escape it by going underneath.

Knight Hawk

Kenada's plan worked, and another radar-guided missile fell prey to the old bridge trick, much to the dismay of a few eastern shore commuters. Today was not a good day for commuters and bridges.

Seeing his missile detonate on the bridge, Platt said, "Damn it." He yanked his stick hard right so he could catch her coming out the other side. He could see that since she had committed herself to going under the bridge, she had to continue under both. Platt pointed his jet to the side where the Eagle was to emerge, and before he even got a ready tone from his Sidewinder, he fired. He said, "Come on, baby, this better be good."

Just as Platt had predicted, the Eagle came out from underneath the bridge and turned hard to the left as it started climbing. The Sidewinder missile caught the heat from Kenada's engines and homed in. Three seconds later the Sidewinder missile detonated deep in the afterburner section of the Eagle's left engine. The explosion broke the backbone of the Eagle and blew the left rudder and elevator off. The back half of the Eagle was now nothing but flames and twisted metal.

Platt watched with pride as he saw the Eagle turn into a ball of flames. It arced high in the sky and then tumbled down and crashed into a marshy field on the eastern shore of the bay. He keyed his mike button and said, "Crystal Ball, this is Wrangler Two Seven. . . . Splash Eagle Zero One."

Chapter Twenty-one

21:55
Chesapeake Bay, Near Annapolis

Captain Platt and his wingman in their F-15s made a high, circling pass over the burning wreckage of Kenada's Eagle, like vultures over a dead carcass in the field.

Platt felt good gloating over his kill; he was now a hero. He thought, I hope the colonel won't be hard on me for trashing those two jets at Langley. A quick glance at his fuel gauge brought Platt back to the real world. He needed a place to land quickly or he'd be crashing another jet.

Platt said to his wingman, "Let's go to BWI and get some gas."

His wingman agreed and turned toward Baltimore/ Washington International Airport. It was the closest airport with a runway that was long enough. Fortu-

Knight Hawk

nately it was only five miles away.

Platt turned his Eagle and started toward it. Not even halfway across the bay, one engine flamed out and started winding down. Platt knew BWI was not a player. There was a short airport runway underneath him just where the bridges came onto the eastern shore, and Platt considered what other choices there were and thought, It's not long enough, but it will have to do.

His wingman continued to BWI, but Platt turned back, lined up and did his final approach, and throttled back to go as slowly as he could without falling out of the sky.

As Platt came over the numbers of the runway, he didn't have to worry about chopping his engines; his empty wing tanks did it for him. His rear wheels touched hard on the end of the runway, and Platt held his nose up using aerodynamic braking. Halfway down the short runway Platt let his nose wheel come down. When it squealed on the cement he stood on his brakes as hard as he could. Just to make sure that he stopped before running off the other end, Platt dropped his tail hook to get some extra braking power. The sparks from the brass shoe on the bottom of the hook lit up a rooster tail of fire behind his jet, until it came to a stop on the far end of the runway.

Platt climbed out of his jet a happy man.

The Capitol Mall, Washington D.C.

Cap. Diane Datz had been ejected from her F-22A aircraft and landed in the grassy are between the Capitol Reflecting Pool and the East Building of the National Gallery of Art. Fully conscious now, she was aware of the devastation around her. The center section of the Air and Space Museum was in flames. The 555-

foot-tall Washington Monument at the end of the Mall, which was the tallest freestanding stone structure in the world, was now a twenty-foot-tall pile of rubble.

Datz could hear screams of terror from the hundreds of frightened people who were running out of the Capitol building. In a way they reminded her of ants running out of an anthill that had just been stepped on.

Behind her Datz heard a car alarm sounding. She turned and saw that her still-smoking ejection seat had landed on a red BMW parked on Pennsylvania Avenue. Still stiff in the back from the ejection, she walked over to it and pulled the stack of hard drives out of the protective receptacle in the seat. She walked back to where she had landed and finished bundling up her parachute.

Datz started to walk toward the Air and Space Museum when she heard a gruff voice from behind: "Police. Stop or I'll shoot."

Datz turned toward the voice and saw three policemen standing behind her with their service revolvers pointed at her. She raised her hands in surrender and they charged her, knocked her to the ground, rolled her facedown in the grass and then cuffed her.

"Hey, you guys are making a big mistake. I'm Cap. Diane Datz. I'm one of the good guys."

The officers set her on her feet and said, "Maybe you are, maybe you're not, but for right now you're coming with us."

Datz couldn't believe what was happening to her. "Look, you idiots, before you go dragging me off, get on your damn radios and have your dispatch call the military command center in the Pentagon. They'll verify who I am."

Suddenly a deep voice came from behind. "They won't have to do that. I can." Diane turned and saw a park policeman mounted high in his saddle atop an auburn Arabian horse.

He looked at the three officers holding Datz and said, "You can uncuff her and let her go. You three also owe her a big apology. Instead of arresting her, you should be thanking her for saving your lives."

One of the officers said, "Oh, yeah? What the hell for?"

The mounted officer didn't answer the cop who asked the question. Instead he casually rested his hand on his holstered 9mm Glock pistol and said, "I think you should uncuff her and apologize."

Diane watched the few tense moments of the standoff and wondered who was going to shoot first.

The mounted officer calmly said, "Do I need to remind you that you are on National Park property and in my jurisdiction, not yours?"

The three D.C. cops yielded and began to uncuff Datz.

The mounted park policeman climbed down off of his horse, and as soon as Datz was uncuffed, he held out his hand to shake hers. He looked her in the eyes and said, "That was some great flying you did, and your shooting was unbelievable. I didn't think there was anybody alive that was good enough to shoot down a missile. That was truly amazing. I'm especially glad to see that you're still alive. After that other missile blew off the back half of your jet, I thought you were a goner."

Datz, no longer angry at being manhandled, began to blush a little from such high praise. She then said, "Thank you, but I had help. Speaking of missiles, we need to find that missile that I shot down and cordon off the area. Even though it's been blown apart, it has nuclear material in it that's giving off dangerous radiation."

Pat O'Connell

In the military command center, they all felt the earth shake from the falling of the Washington Monument, even though it was almost a mile away and on the other side of the Potomac.

Admiral Watson said, "What the hell was that? Was that the Knight Hawk?"

McKenna and Howard had heard the explosions, and they knew that it was over. That had to have been the Knight Hawk.

General Price shook his head, frowned and said to them, "I don't know what that was, but I know it wasn't nuclear."

Colonel Miller heard it first; then he told General Price, "General, I just overheard a conversation between Wrangler Two Seven—that's one of the F-15s chasing Kenada—and Crystal Ball. That wasn't the Knight Hawk we felt; the Knight Hawk's been destroyed, and two of the F15s are chasing Kenada, heading east."

The feeling of relief came over everybody in the MCC.

Howard sighed. "That's the best news I've heard all day."

Colonel Miller tuned in the frequency that the two F-15s were using and put it on the loudspeakers. Everybody in the room was watching the map. The blips on the situation map were quickly moving east. While they watched, one of the blips disappeared. Everyone wanted to ask, Was it her?

Finally a voice came over the loudspeaker with the message that everybody was waiting to hear. "Crystal Ball, this is Wrangler Two Seven. . . . Splash Eagle Zero One."

The response on the radio back to Platt almost went

352

unnoticed because of the cheering. "Wrangler Two Seven, Crystal Ball . . . Good job. Thank you."

General Price recognized the voice on the radio. It was Colonel Fugami in the AWACS aircraft. Price picked up the table mike and keyed the transmit button. "Specter, Buster."

"Go ahead, Buster."

"My kudos to you and your crew. We are going to stand down from our alert, and I want you to give everybody involved up there my thanks. Who was it who downed the Knight Hawk?"

"Buster, that would be Capt. Diane Datz, a test pilot in an F-22A from Eglin, call sign Pegasus Zero One."

"Well, Specter, give her our special thanks."

There was a pause to Price's reply, and then Specter spoke. "Ah, Buster, no can do. She is off the air and not on the screen. My controller says she took a SAM hit over D.C."

"Specter, sorry to hear that. Give our thanks to everybody. See you next time. Buster out."

Fugami responded, "Next time."

Colonel Fugami looked at his controllers, hit his intercom button and said, "The Joint Chiefs of Staff want me to pass on to their thanks for a job well done. I also thank you. I want you all to pass on the thanks to the jets that you were controlling and then tell them to go home. If any of them need refueling to get back, make tankers available to them."

In the Pentagon's military control center, the secretary of defense, Jeff Howard, gave the order to stand down from the alert and return to normal status. Howard looked at McKenna and said, "That was a horrible ordeal. I'm glad it's over."

McKenna looked at Howard, and with a little bit of

a frown on her face said, "Boy, Jeff, you really are new at this, aren't you? Horrible ordeal is an understatement. We've had a renegade pilot steal a multimillion-dollar jet from an area with the highest security. She nukes New York City, and God only knows what kind of damage is there. We've got a couple dozen fighters scattered all over the eastern half of the U.S. I have no idea how many people are dead, and to top it off, one of our national treasures, the Washington Monument, has become a rock quarry.

"Just wait till the media and Congress get hold of this. There are going to be lots of questions and hell to pay. Heads will roll . . . even ours. Hell, when they're done with us, we'll be lucky if we don't go to jail."

Howard knew that McKenna's words were true. Realizing that they were at the dawn of a media storm of hurricane proportions, he just looked at her and said, "Alex, thanks. You've always had a way of brightening up my day."

Howard walked over to where General Price and Admiral Watson were standing and said, "I want you two to put together an investigation team right away and find out what happened here tonight. I want to know everything. I want to know how this could have happened and who's responsible. I want to know who were the players and what were our losses. Have it ready by noon tomorrow."

Price and Watson both responded, "Yes, sir" as Howard walked away.

In the basement bunker of the White House, everyone thought that the world was over and D.C. had just been nuked. Even underground they heard the explosions and felt the ground shake. Colonel Webster turned to Borda and said, "Well, looks like we're going to be down here a while, at least until the radiation levels drop."

Borda looked at him oddly and said, "Colonel, I heard the explosions, and I know that was not a nuke. If it was, how come we still have electricity and a video link with the Pentagon? Besides, look at the outside TV monitors."

The colonel, a little embarrassed by his quick and erroneous conclusion, meekly said, "Oh, yeah, you're right. Maybe the loud explosion was our missile getting the jet."

Borda pointed to the joystick that controlled the outside cameras and said, "Pan all over the grounds."

Webster pointed the cameras over the grounds, and everything seemed normal. He said, "Nothing. There must be something—we heard and felt it."

Borda said, "Pan the skyline; maybe we'll see some smoke."

As the camera angle changed from looking downward to a level view, they could see what had made the earth move. They peered through the dust still hanging in the air and saw the rubble of the Washington Monument. They were all speechless.

Chapter Twenty-two

23:00
Sandy Point State Park

On the Eastern shore of the Chesapeake Bay, Kenada's Eagle was still burning an hour after the crash. Above the smoldering wreckage, helicopters' searchlights scoured the surrounding marshland for more debris. Fire trucks were nearby, but they couldn't get close enough to put out the fire because of the marsh. The firemen had the hoses stretched out, but still couldn't get close enough.

Watching it all from a deserted beach on the opposite shore was a woman, and under her arm was a flight helmet. It was Kenada.

What Major Platt and the world didn't know was that as she had passed under the bridge, she had engaged the autopilot with the programmed course and then ejected. She had hoped that her ejection would be undetected by the other fighters, and it was.

Kenada was able to swim the four hundred yards to shore. She walked the quarter-mile stretch of beach to the Sandy Point State Park Beach House. A wet boot through the glass pane in the door made it easy to unlock. Shivering from her swim in the cold water, Kenada looked for dry clothes. She found a park ranger's uniform and coat in the closet. She took a quick, hot shower to warm up and put on the dry clothes.

From the front picture window, Kenada could still see the flames from her crashed Eagle burning away. In the dark she picked up the phone on the desk and dialed a number. When a man answered the phone on the other end, she told him where she was and that she needed a ride. The voice on the other end said he'd be there in about two and a half hours.

While she talked, Kenada looked through the desk drawers and found a set of keys with a float on the ring. She looked across the parking lot at the marina and saw the twenty-foot Boston Whaler at the dock that belonged to the keys. She thought for a second and then said, "Ahneese, no, pick me up at the parking lot for the Baltimore Aquarium in the inner harbor. I'll be there in about an hour and a half. I'll be coming up in a park police Boston Whaler."

The marina was deserted, and the whaler was easy to start and drive away. Kenada was starting to feel a little less tense. She had failed at her mission, but at least she had tried, and now it looked as if she was going to get away.

After ninety minutes of hard driving in the cold night air, Kenada drove the whaler past Fort McHenry. The inner harbor was dead-ahead.

Kenada pulled the whaler up to the dock by the marina, cut the engines and then tied it off. She climbed out of the boat and onto the deserted dock. She walked toward the aquarium parking lot and recognized Ahneese's car. The headlights flashed twice.

Kenada came out of the shadows, walked over to the car and opened the door. She stepped in and sat down. Before she could get her right leg in, she looked at Ahneese and stopped. He was holding a silenced Beretta semiautomatic pistol pointed at her head. Before she could say a word or ask why, a 9mm round was fired into her forehead. Kenada's lifeless body fell out of the car onto the ground. The door closed and the car drove away.

The driver Maj. Ahneese Ahkmed, pulled out of the park and headed for Washington. He picked up his car phone and punched in an overseas number. He said in Arabic, "This is Ahkmed; the Eagle has failed, and the angel has fallen. She will tell no one."

The Middle Eastern army general said good-bye and hung up the phone. He rose from his desk and knocked on the office door behind him, entered and then relayed the message to the man behind the desk.

Infuriated by Kenada's failure, the man threw a half-empty coffee mug against the wall, and muttered curse words to himself. The man behind the desk asked the general, "Any word on the other two?"

The general replied, "No, sir, not yet."

The man behind the desk, Saddam Hussein, said, "Leave me. Go tell the others the attack must wait." He stood up and peered in the mirror behind him and said, "Mr. President, just you wait."

LADY OF ICE AND FIRE
COLIN ALEXANDER

Colin Alexander writes "a lean and solid thriller!"
—*Publishers Weekly*

With international detente fast becoming the status quo, a whole new field of spying opens up: industrial espionage. And even though tensions are easing between the East and the West, the same Cold war rules and stakes still apply: world domination at any cost, both in dollars and deaths. Well aware of the new predators, George Jeffers fears that his biotech studies may be sought after by foreign agents. Then his partner disappears with the results of their experiments, and the eminent scientist finds himself the target in a game of deadly intrigue. Jeffers then races against time to prevent the unleashing of a secret that could shake the world to its very foundations.

__4072-7 $5.50 US/$6.50 CAN